PRAISE FOR *NEW YORK TIMES* BESTSELLING AUTHOR CATHERINE COULTER

"Bawdy fare, Coulter-style . . . romance, humor, and spicy sex talk."
—*Kirkus Reviews*

"A hot-blooded romp."
—*People*

"Coulter is excellent at portraying the romantic tension between her heroes and heroines, and she manages to write explicitly but beautifully about sex as well as love."
—*Milwaukee Journal Sentinel*

"Unexpected plot twists, witty dialogue, and an engaging cast of characters."
—*Publishers Weekly*

"Catherine Coulter delivers . . . straightforward, fast-paced romance."
—*Minneapolis Star Tribune*

"Sexy."
—*Booklist*

"Coulter's characters quickly come alive and draw the reader into the story. You root for the good guys and hiss for the bad guys. When you have to put the book down for a while, you can hardly wait to get back and see what's going on."
—*The Sunday Oklahoman*

"Charm, wit, and intrigue. . . . sure to keep readers turning the pages."
—*Naples Daily News*

Titles by Catherine Coulter

The Bride Series

THE SHERBROOKE BRIDE
THE HELLION BRIDE
THE HEIRESS BRIDE
THE SCOTTISH BRIDE
PENDRAGON
MAD JACK
THE COURTSHIP

The Legacy Trilogy

THE WYNDHAM LEGACY
THE NIGHTINGALE LEGACY
THE VALENTINE LEGACY

The Baron Novels

THE WILD BARON
THE OFFER
THE DECEPTION

The Viking Novels

LORD OF HAWKFELL ISLAND
LORD OF RAVEN'S PEAK
LORD OF FALCON RIDGE
SEASON OF THE SUN

The Song Novels

WARRIOR'S SONG
FIRE SONG
EARTH SONG
SECRET SONG
ROSEHAVEN
THE PENWYTH CURSE

The Magic Trilogy

MIDSUMMER MAGIC
CALYPSO MAGIC
MOONSPUN MAGIC

The Star Series

EVENING STAR
MIDNIGHT STAR
WILD STAR
JADE STAR

Other Regency Historical Romances

THE COUNTESS
THE REBEL BRIDE
THE HEIR
THE DUKE
LORD HARRY

Devil's Duology

DEVIL'S EMBRACE
DEVIL'S DAUGHTER

Contemporary Romantic Thrillers

FALSE PRETENSES
IMPULSE
BEYOND EDEN

FBI Suspense Thrillers

THE COVE
THE MAZE
THE TARGET
THE EDGE
RIPTIDE
HEMLOCK BAY
ELEVENTH HOUR

The Deception

Previously published as
An Intimate Deception

SIGNET
Published by New American Library, a division of
Penguin Group (USA) Inc., 375 Hudson Street,
New York, New York 10014, USA
Penguin Group (Canada), 90 Eglinton Avenue East, Suite 700, Toronto,
Ontario M4P 2Y3, Canada (a division of Pearson Penguin Canada Inc.)
Penguin Books Ltd., 80 Strand, London WC2R 0RL, England
Penguin Ireland, 25 St. Stephen's Green, Dublin 2,
Ireland (a division of Penguin Books Ltd.)
Penguin Group (Australia), 250 Camberwell Road, Camberwell, Victoria 3124,
Australia (a division of Pearson Australia Group Pty. Ltd.)
Penguin Books India Pvt. Ltd., 11 Community Centre, Panchsheel Park,
New Delhi - 110 017, India
Penguin Group (NZ), cnr Airborne and Rosedale Roads, Albany,
Auckland 1310, New Zealand (a division of Pearson New Zealand Ltd.)
Penguin Books (South Africa) (Pty.) Ltd., 24 Sturdee Avenue,
Rosebank, Johannesburg 2196, South Africa

Penguin Books Ltd., Registered Offices:
80 Strand, London WC2R 0RL, England

Published by Signet, an imprint of New American Library, a division of Penguin Group (USA) Inc. Originally published in a somewhat different version by Signet under the title *An Intimate Deception*. Previously published in a Topaz edition.

First Printing (Revised Edition), October 1998
10 9

Printed in the United States of America

To Catherine Lyons-Labate.
She loves chocolate and gardenias.
She loves to laugh, she's unconditionally cheerful.
Best of all—she laughs at my jokes.

Chapter 1

London
December 2, 1814

He was hot and impatient, wanting nothing more than to bury himself in her and forget for a while at least that there were monsters out there that could bring a man to despair. He was heaving with the effort as he managed, finally, to balance himself over her. "I'm sorry," he said, his voice as raw and naked as his soul, "I'm sorry," and he knew in that moment that he simply couldn't be of any use to her at all. He wondered if indeed he was being any use to himself in those moments he exploded deep inside her, losing all sense of self, all sense of who and what he was, or of belonging to anyone or anything. He was scattered and drifting, and he relished the brief oblivion. But after the shattering pleasure receded, he was again incredibly alone. And once again he remembered there was evil out there in the night.

He slowly moved away from her, feeling himself come back into painful focus, seeing the shadows the fire cast on the walls opposite her bed, following them to the deeper shadows that filled the corners of the bedchamber, bathing everything in gray emptiness. No, the emptiness was inside him, and he was the one who yet lived.

He turned to her. She was lying on her back, her legs still spread, one graceful hand lying fisted on her white belly. He lightly closed his hand over hers, lifting it. "I'm sorry," he said again. "I will do better."

She wasn't going to tell him it didn't matter to her if he treated her like a vessel of convenience, because it did matter. She'd known him for two years, not a very long time to know a man as complex and proud and ferociously sexual as Richard Clarendon, but enough for a woman who was as arrogant in her own way as he was, and well used to gratification, to say, "You're never a careless or selfish lover. You might as well tell me what's wrong."

He lightly kissed her knuckles, then laid her hand back onto her belly. He smoothed her fingers, splaying them on her white flesh. "You're beautiful," he said, his voice as absent as his mind was from her.

"Yes, I know, but that doesn't matter. You're beautiful as well. Now, what's wrong, Richard?"

He rose slowly, walked to the fire that was no longer raging but soft and glowing, and stretched himself. His large body was bathed in golden light. She admired his mind as well as she admired his body—both were quick and graceful and powerful.

"You're tired," she said, breaking into his silence.

"Yes, very tired." He was more than that. He was also a fool. He had hoped that being with her would somehow renew him, make him savor life and its living once more, but it hadn't. He felt even more tired than he had an hour before. "Yes," he said. "Very tired. I'm sorry," he said yet again.

She rose and walked to him, pressing herself against

his side. "It's that girl, isn't it? The one who married Phillip Mercerault? The one who turned you down? Your man's spirit still wants her?"

That made him smile. Things would be much simpler if Sabrina was responsible for the pain that had burrowed so deeply in him that he doubted if it would ever retreat. "Man's spirit? How is a man's spirit different from a woman's spirit?"

"They are very different. Your spirit nurtures your belief in yourself. If a woman rejects you, it's your own worth that is wounded, not your heart. A woman's spirit is a desert to be filled with a man's attention. Hers is easily wounded, for men don't excel in giving full attention, it isn't their way. So both men and women suffer from pain; only their pain is very different from each other's."

"To debate that would be an impossible task. No, this has nothing to do with Sabrina. She and Phillip did as they should. She's pregnant, and Phillip is happier than I've ever seen him."

She nodded, realizing that he was telling her the truth. "Then what is it? Is your mother ill?"

"No, she's perfectly fit."

"You miss your father?"

"Yes, of course. He was the very best of men. I will miss him until I die myself." He paused, then looked down into that quite lovely face. "You won't cease, will you, Morgana?"

"No." Her hand was on his arm. There was nothing seductive about it, but still his body reacted. She saw the renewed heat in him, the force and energy of him turning to her, and she quickly backed away. "Before you leap upon me again, tell me."

"A woman shouldn't plague a man. Oh, hell, it's all about murder, Morgana, the needless murder of someone who shouldn't have gotten himself killed, someone who was very close to me."

"Did you kill the murderer?" She said it so matter-of-factly that he started. The duke rammed his long fingers through his black hair, sending it to stand on end. "No, I don't know what particular man killed him. I'd like to dispatch that man to hell where he belongs, but it's what's behind him that drives me to fury and despair. I begin to wonder if any of us are safe anymore." He turned back to the fire, his head down, and she knew he wouldn't say anything more. He was in pain. She would help him. He paid her to be at his beck and call, but this was one time when she would have quite willingly taken him into her arms for absolutely nothing at all.

"I'm sorry," she said, and pressed herself against him. He was hard against her belly. She kissed his shoulder, laid her face against his chest. "Come, let me help you forget, at least for a little while."

He didn't take her back to her bed. He lifted her, driving upward deeply into her. He wondered if he was hurting her, but then he touched her and she made that soft sound deep in her throat, and he knew she was close to her climax. He didn't let her down this time, but when he left her forty-five minutes later, she knew that he still felt as cold as stone.

Chapter 2

Romilly-sur-Seine, France
February 10, 1815

It was late. Evangeline set her brush beside the silver-handled comb on the dressing table, too tired to braid her hair. She heard her maid, Margueritte, laughing softly and humming even as she smoothed the wrinkles from the blue velvet gown that Evangeline had worn that evening.

She stared at herself in the mirror. She was too pale, and there was no laughter in her eyes or on her lips. She was tired, so very tired, and it was deep, all the way to her soul.

She knew a horrible wrenching inside. She knew what it was as well. She wanted to go home, to England.

She hated France.

But she couldn't tell her father, it would hurt him deeply. And she loved him more than she loved anyone on the face of this earth. When they'd heard that Napoleon had been defeated and Louis would be returned by the English to the French throne, he'd been so pleased that he'd grabbed her up to dance with her.

They'd returned six months before to Romilly-sur-Seine, not to their ancestral home but rather to a smallish manor house that lay but two miles from the château. A wealthy merchant lived in their home now, with his fat wife and six offspring.

Her father hadn't cared. He was pleased to be home, to speak his own language again, to laugh at the things a Frenchman was supposed to laugh at. He'd never really understood the English humor. She imagined that he'd simply never wanted to take all that was English into himself, and so he hadn't. He spoke English beautifully, but his thoughts were always in French. She wondered what her mother, a very English lady, had thought about that, for surely she knew that her husband would never move his thoughts and dreams toward her.

He'd lived for twenty-five years in Kent, married to the daughter of a local baron, who'd lived with them since he'd lost all his own money gambling. She'd liked her English grandfather. She doubted now that as an adult she would care for him at all, but a child had no such qualifying notions. He'd died before she'd gained an adult's mind, and thus he would be forever a romantic figure in her thoughts.

She was the mirror image of her father. She spoke French beautifully, like a native actually, but she simply wasn't French. How to tell her father that she was miserable, that she would die before she married a Frenchman like the Comte de Pouilly, Henri Moreau, a rich, handsome young nobleman who left her cold and rigid, no smile in her mind, much less on her mouth?

The evening had been long and trying, largely because Henri, for no good reason she could think of, had determined with appalling certainty that Evangeline would make him the ideal wife. The good Lord knew she had discouraged him, but his hide was thicker than the bark of an oak tree. He wanted her. Every chance he got, he tried to trap her against a wall or against a tree, or push her into the bushes to try to kiss her. He'd managed it once. She'd bitten his tongue.

There was a light knock on her bedchamber door. She smiled automatically, rising, for she knew it was her father. He always came to her every night before she went to bed. It was one of her favorite times.

She called out in French, because she knew that's what he wanted to hear from her, *"Entrez."*

Her father, Guillaume de Beauchamps, the most handsome man she'd ever seen in her life, strode through the bedroom door like a warrior he really wasn't. What he was, she thought, still smiling as he came toward her, his hands outstretched, was a philosopher. Women flocked to him. Even when he spoke to them of the metaphysical underpinnings of Descartes, they usually just smiled at him and moved closer.

"Papa," she said, and walked into his arms. Nature had given him the face and the body of a warrior. He was magnificent. Few people knew that his heart didn't beat properly, that she worried about him constantly now, for he was fifty five on his last birthday, and the English doctor had told her that there was nothing to be done, that he must rest and remain calm. He had said it was a good thing her father was a philosopher; that would keep him seated and thinking. The only problem was that her father became dreadfully excited when he read Montaigne.

"Tu est fatigué, ma fille?"

"Oui, Papa, un peu." And she thought to herself,

yes, she was tired, but she more than just a little tired. All of her was tired, and dispirited.

She turned to her maid. *"Margueritte, c'est assez. Laissez-nous maintenant."* And again, as she always did when she spoke French, she thought in English. "Leave us now, that's enough."

Margueritte's plump fingers batted a final wrinkle before she gave Monsieur de Beauchamps a lustful look, hummed her good nights, and closed the door after her.

They grinned at each other, listening to Margueritte's humming as she walked down the narrow corridor to the third floor.

"Ah, Papa, *assieds-toi."* She eyed him closely as he sat on the other chair in her bedchamber. She took a deep breath and said in English, "You had so many of the ladies after you this evening."

He sighed, seeming not to notice her shift, and replied in French, "Even if they are with their husbands, they feel compelled to flirt with me. It's very distressing. I simply don't understand, Evangeline. I do nothing untoward to bring them to me."

She laughed, unable not to. "Oh, bother, Papa. I have never seen you distressed in my life. You adore the attention. And you know very well that all you have to do to bring the ladies to your side is to simply look straight ahead with no expression at all on your face. You could probably be drooling, and they would still come to you.

"Now, tell me. Did you speak only about your philosophers when the dozen ladies told you how very handsome you are?"

He said with great severity, "Naturally. I spoke tonight of Rousseau. A dunderhead, but his ideas give one some pause, in a manner of speaking. Not much, really, but he is French. Thus one must pay him some attention, occasionally."

She couldn't stop laughing. Her father merely looked at her, his handsome head slightly tilted to the side, a mannerism they shared. When she finally wiped her eyes, she said, "You are the best papa in the whole world. I love you. Please don't ever change."

"Your mother, bless her sweet heart, was the only one who tried to change me."

Evangeline, still chuckling, said, "My mother simply tried to pry something out of her husband other than ramblings of a metaphysical nature. Now, I am given to understand that it is a wife's duty to gather her husband's attention to herself and not let him ramble off too often seeking answers to unanswerable questions."

"You mock me, my girl, but since you are so very dear to me, I will forgive you." He sat back in the chair, set his hands on his knees, and continued after a moment. "You did not enjoy yourself this evening, *ma fille.* You were surrounded by all the young people, all the young gentlemen admired you greatly, and you danced every dance. I only managed to snag one with you. And my dear Henri was gratifyingly attentive."

"There is nothing gratifying about Henri. He is more persistent than a hungry gull, and more stubborn than our goat, Dorcas, in Kent, and his hands are sometimes damp. If he would just realize that there are other things in this vast world besides his horses, trying to feel my bottom, the income from his rents, and the prospect of adding me to his possessions, perhaps I could remain in his company for more than five minutes without wanting to smack him."

"You said a lot there, Evangeline, but naturally all

I heard is that he is trying to seduce you. Your bottom? Oh, dear, I suppose I will have to speak to the boy."

"He is no boy. He is twenty-six."

"*Oui*, but that is very young for a man. It has always been evident that boys take longer to ripen than girls. It is unfortunate, but it is evidently God's plan. Henri is perhaps a bit foolish, but he will mature as he gains years. Henri is high in his family's favor. He now manages the family estate whilst his uncle spends all his time with King Louis in Paris. This will mature Henri, that is what his uncle told me.

"And, my dear child, you are nearly twenty years old. It's long past time for you to take a husband. You have been ripe enough for two years now. Yes, a husband is just what you need. I've been too selfish."

"No, I've been the selfish one. Why would I wish to marry, Papa, when I have you?"

"You have never been in love," he said, a magnificent frown furrowing his brow and making his beautiful gray eyes glitter with humor. "You would never think to say such a stupid thing if you had."

She was dead serious now, leaning toward him, her hair falling over her shoulder. "I cannot see that marriage is such a wonderful thing. All the ladies who swoon over you, what of their husbands? What of love with them? It seems to me that marriage is simply a way for a lady to go from her father's house to her husband's house; the only difference is that with her husband she's expected—indeed, it's demanded of her that she produce children and obey her husband's every whim. I don't think so, Papa."

Monsieur de Beauchamps just shook his head. She was stubborn, his daughter, just like her dear mother, Claudia, who'd dug in her English heels more times than he could begin to remember. That brought a thought. Could it be that Evangeline was even more stubborn than her lovely mother had been? Could it be that she was as stubborn as her great-aunt Marthe? He must take a firm hand; he didn't like it, but it was his duty. He had to sound unutterably serious. "My child, you must be set onto the proper road in your thinking. Love isn't necessary for a successful marriage."

"You weren't in love with Mama?"

"Oh, yes, but as I said, it isn't necessary. A similarity of thought, of values, of philosophies, that is what is necessary. A certain respect for each other. Nothing more."

"I never heard Mama agree with you on anything, yet I heard the two of you laughing many times when you were alone in your bedchamber. I used to listen with my ear pressed against the door when I was young. Bessie, one of the maids, caught me, and told me never, ever to do that again. And then she blushed fiery red." Evangeline laughed at her father's own rise in color. "It's all right, Papa. As you said, I'm nearly twenty years old, old enough to know a bit about what happens between a husband and wife. But as I said, as far as I know, neither of you ever agreed on anything, even down to what you had for dinner. Mama hated sauces, and you hated to see a piece of meat naked.

"Mutual respect? I don't want a marriage like that, Papa. Besides, Henri is so very un-Eng—" She stopped cold.

"Ah," said her father.

She gave him a smile that was on the sheepish side. She fanned her hands in front of her. "The truth is, many times words fail me when I speak of Henri."

"Perhaps you would wish to say that poor Henri is

so very un-English?" Monsieur de Beauchamps regarded his daughter from beautiful deep gray eyes. He felt a surge of concern. He knew with perfect clarity in that moment that his daughter would never find contentment in his country. But she would try to pretend, for him. No, he was wrong. He was tired. She would come around. Hadn't he finally given in and assumed contentment for England? He'd spent more years there than she had lived.

"Papa, I'm sorry, truly, but I would rather depart this earth a withered spinster than marry Henri Moreau. Then there are Etienne Dedardes and Andre Lafay—they're oily, Papa, yes, that's exactly what they are. Their eyes don't meet yours when they're speaking to you. Oh, I don't know, they're nice, I suppose, but they're just not to my liking. And their politics, surely they shouldn't speak of the king as they do." Then she gave a sublimely Gallic shrug, most unlike, he thought with a fleeting smile, her English mother.

"There has been so much change, Evangeline. Louis has not behaved as he ought since his return to France. As much as I deplore it, I understand that many Frenchmen feel betrayed by his stupidity, his excesses, his lack of understanding of the situation here."

"I don't see that the common folk can lay claim to the high road. They themselves are so cursed petty toward each other. And they have the gall to mock the English, who saved them. I must tell you it makes me quite angry." She shut her mouth, rubbing her palm over her forehead. "I'm sorry, Papa. I'm tired, that's it. My tongue doesn't always obey my brain when I'm tired. I'm a witch. Forgive me."

Monsieur de Beauchamps rose and walked to his daughter. He lifted her out of her chair. He looked into her brown eyes, Claudia's eyes, full and wide and so deep, a philosopher could find the meaning of some truths in them. He patted her shoulder and kissed her lightly, in his ritual manner, on both cheeks.

"You are beautiful, Evangeline. You are more beautiful on the inside than you are on the outside."

"I'm a pea hen and you know it. Compared to you, I'm not even a pea."

He merely smiled, lightly rubbing his knuckles over her chin. "You are also too used to the stolid English. They are, I suppose, a comforting race, if one doesn't mind being perpetually fatigued by their heavy meals and boring conversation."

"So what you love about me is merely my French half? Surely, Mama never bored anyone."

"No, she never did. I love even your fingernails, *ma fille.* As for your dear mother, I'm convinced that her soul was French. She admired me, you know. Ah, but I digress. Perhaps an old man should accept the fact that you are, despite his wishes, more English than French. Do you wish to return to England, Evangeline? I am not a blind man, you know, and I realize that since your return you have not been happy."

She hugged him tightly, her cheek against his, for she was very tall for a woman. "Papa, my place is here with you. I'll grow accustomed. But I won't marry Henri Moreau."

Suddenly there was loud banging on the heavy doors downstairs, and the sounds of boots kicking against wood. There was a scream. It was Margueritte. Then there was Joseph's voice, loud and frightened. Another scream, the sound of someone being struck hard, and a man's loud voice.

"Don't move," Monsieur de Beauchamps said to her. He was at the bedchamber door, flinging it open.

She heard the sound of heavy men's boots thudding on the wooden floor of the corridor. It sounded like a small army.

He suddenly backed away, and Evangeline rushed forward to stand beside him. Two heavily cloaked men appeared in the doorway. Both of them held guns.

One of them, his face pitted and dark with beard stubble, stepped forward, his eyes on Evangeline. He said nothing, looked at her, not just her face but her breasts, her belly. She felt such fear she thought she'd vomit.

He said to the other man, "Look at her. It is as we were told. Houchard will be very pleased."

The other man, fat, his face pale and bloated, stared at her. Guillaume de Beauchamps yelled as he managed to wrest away his gun and rammed it into his big belly. "You won't touch her, you puking little pig."

A gun slammed down on his head. Evangeline rushed to her father, trying to catch him as he fell unconscious to the floor. She ended up half on top of him. The man with the pitted face raised the gun again. She covered her father's head with her body.

The other man was clutching his fat belly. He gasped with the pain. "No, don't hit him again. He won't be any use to us dead."

"The bastard hurt you."

"I'll live."

"The old man will pay." He turned to Evangeline. Houchard had taught him the value of fear and shock, particularly when it was deep in the night. He looked at her breasts, then said, "Take off that nightgown now. Hurry or I'll do it for you."

Chapter 3

Chesleigh Castle
Near Dover, England

The bloody rain had finally stopped. The late afternoon sun was still bright. Seagulls whirled and dived overhead, then wheeled back to the ocean not a hundred yards away. The smell of the sea was strong in the breeze. It had turned out to be a beautiful day.

Richard Chesleigh St. John Clarendon, eighth Duke of Portsmouth, turned his matched bays onto the gravel drive of his ancestral home, Chesleigh Castle, an old pile of gray stone that had held reign over this section of the southern English coast for the past four hundred and twenty-two years. He pulled his horses up in front of the wide stone portico. A gull flew close to the head of his lead horse, Jonah, and he laughed aloud at the look of utter outrage in that magnificent animal's eyes.

"It's all right, boy," he called out, and jumped down from his curricle to the gravel drive. His head stable lad, McComber, was standing there looking at the bays as if they were his own. He rubbed his gnarled hands together, then took the horses' reins. "Been good boys, have ye?" he said, stroking first Jonah and then Benjamin, feeding them bits of apple as he told them of their bloodlines, all unspoiled for at least five hundred years. The duke rolled his eyes.

"Rub them down well, McComber. They've worked hard today. I wonder why the gulls are so aggressive all of a sudden?"

"I hear tell it be a storm that's coming," McComber said.

"We just had a storm. We have a storm every week, sometimes twice a week."

"Well, it do be winter and England, yer grace. Put the two together, and ye don't have much reason for perkiness. Aye, I know. Meybe it be some smugglers and the gulls don't like the smell of 'em."

"We haven't had smugglers in fifty years," the duke said. "You sound like you're coming down with something, McComber. Take better care of yourself. I'll wager you caught it from Juniper, who'd better be tucked snug into his bed as we speak."

"I'd niver get close enuf to that little bug to catch nuthin'."

His tiger, Juniper, and McComber hated each other. He'd never discovered why. It was apparently a deep, strong hatred of longstanding, a tenacious hatred and abiding, a hatred one couldn't help but admire.

"I don't care if you're sickening from Cook's blood pudding, have a care."

"Aye, yer grace," McComber said. "But 'tis true, I'll niver ketch a whimpering thing from that little bleeder, never ye mind wot 'e says aboot me mother." Then he began talking a mile a minute to the bays as he led them to the magnificent stables to the north that the duke's father had enlarged some thirty years before.

The sun was getting low in the west. The wind was rising. It was getting colder. The duke sniffed the salty air, breathed in deeply, then looked again at that wonderful sun which hadn't shown itself for three days.

He looked up to see Juniper, who should have been in bed, running hard toward him, his crimson livery coat flapping in the breeze. "Your grace! I'm here. Oh, dear, I particularly asked Bassick to tell me when you neared. He likes McComber better, and thus he didn't give me warning and so I'm late, and all of a flutter. Oh, dear, he's taken the bays, hasn't he? He's taken my boys."

"Yes. And he won't knobble them or harm them in any way at all. Go back to bed, Juniper. Trust me to take care of the horses. You will remain in bed until you no longer are hacking your tongue out of your mouth."

Juniper gulped, coughed, gulped again. "It's just a touch of something bilious, your grace," he said, looking toward the stables, seeing the bays prancing happily behind that blackguard McComber.

"I don't want to have to bury you just yet, Juniper. Out of my sight."

Juniper continued to look up hopefully at the duke, a very large, handsome young man who, in all the years Juniper had known him, had never been ill from anything other than drinking too much brandy. It was nothing for the duke to ride in an open curricle, the rain battering down on him, the sea winds tearing through his thick hair. For Juniper, had he done something so ill-advised, he would be shortly six feet under the ground with a stone on his head and a daisy planted on top of his belly. The air was still damp from the interminable rain, the breeze off the Channel damp and chill. He shuddered. "Go," the duke said again.

"Aye, your grace," Juniper said. "Oh, your grace, I forget to give you this. It was brought just an hour ago by one of those men who works for your friend Lord Pettigrew." He handed the duke a thin envelope with turned and twisted edges.

The duke didn't wait. This had to be it, he thought. It just had to be over now. He tore open the paper and read:

> *We thought we had him, but he escaped our net. Sorry, Richard. Keep faith. We'll get the murdering bastard yet.* DH

The day turned suddenly and completely black. He looked up and saw only bleak clouds that were filling the sky, turning it a nasty ochre color. He crushed the paper in his hand. They'd all been so certain, knowing that they'd catch the miserable traitor who'd brutally garroted Robbie Faraday in an alley near Westminster in early December.

He wanted to smash his fist into something. He turned to see Juniper staring at him in fascinated horror.

"Go away, Juniper. Now."

Juniper ran back up the wide, deep front steps, wondering what horrific news was in the letter he'd happened to snag from the messenger while Bassick was in the pantry chastising one of the footmen.

Well, the young duke had many things on his mind these days, though Juniper couldn't say what any of them were. Maybe it was a woman. Now, he knew, everyone knew, that the duke was a randy young man, so randy that he was already a legend in this part of

England. And that brought Polly, the in-between maid, to mind. Maybe he could cozen her into bringing him some of Mrs. Dart's hot quail-egg soup. Maybe he could even talk her into spooning some into his mouth. Maybe after he ate, he could convince her that he wasn't too sick to slick his fingers through that pretty hair of hers.

The bleak look faded from the duke's face. He frowned at Juniper for a moment, his dark eyes narrowed. He yelled as Juniper's foot hit the top step, "You won't tumble Polly, and that's the end to it, Juniper. I don't want her ill. Go away and stop your dreaming."

Just then the great oak front doors were flung open by his ancient butler with a flowing mane of white hair that any man of any age would admire to the point of black jealousy. The duke remembered that when he was a little boy, he had believed God must look like Bassick. His father had grinned down at him and said, no, not God. He looks like Moses.

"Send Murdock out here, Bassick."

Scarce an instant passed before a tall redheaded footman, impressive in his crimson and gold livery, appeared at the duke's side.

"Escort Juniper to his bed and tuck him in. If he doesn't stay put, tie him to his bed. Tell Cook to prepare him some nourishing soup. Tell Polly not to trust a thing he says. Tell her simply to stay away from him." Murdock gave Juniper a commiserating look and led him away.

"His grace shouldn't know these things," he heard Juniper say low to Murdock.

"Aye, that's the truth of it, but he does. He once knew I'd taken off my shirt to show Betsy the scar on my right shoulder." Murdock sighed deeply. "She loved that scar."

"Then why did she marry the butcher's son in Eastbourne?"

No answer for that question, the duke thought, and smiled, but it was quickly gone. He eyed the crumpled letter in his hand. Damnation. They'd been so close. He'd been awaiting word for two days that they'd finally won. His mood was blacker now than it had been but an instant before. "Juniper, Bassick will have Mrs. Needle see to you. You do whatever she tells you to do. That's an order."

He heard his tiger groan and saw Murdock give him a pat on the back.

Bassick said in his slow, stately way, "Mrs. Needle alarms him, your grace. Understandable, I suppose. She has the aura of a witch, with her gray, twisted hair, her pink scalp showing. She even has a pot that sits on a hob in her fireplace. If it were just a bit larger, it could pass for a witch's cauldron. The concoctions she prepares tend to be on the odorous side. And she talks to herself. It's unnerving to the more uneducated of those around us, your grace."

"It won't destroy his manhood," the duke said, "and believe me, that's all Juniper ever thinks about. As for Mrs. Needle, my mother has always maintained that she is responsible for more people coming back to health than God even wanted to live."

Bassick cleared his ancient throat. "I am given to understand that Mrs. Needle now praises the restorative powers of spicy French mustard, mulled wine, and a small pinch of fresh seaweed. I'm not certain if this is imbibed or applied to the offending part of the body."

"Hopefully neither of us will ever have to find out."

Bassick said an amen to that even as he looked briefly toward the second floor of the north wing of the castle. He fancied he could smell the noxious odors that emanated from her herbal laboratory. The duke turned and strode up the deeply indented stone steps. He didn't wait for Bassick to catch up with him to relieve him of his greatcoat and gloves, but continued in without a backward glance, his Hessians landing loudly on the marble entrance floor. He wanted privacy. He wanted to brood, then begin to plan again. This time he would involve himself in the actual strategy. If there was bait needed, he would be it. Drew Halsey had had his chance to catch Robbie's murderer, and he'd failed.

"Your grace! Wait a moment, please. I forgot to tell you something important."

The duke's black brows snapped together. He called back without turning around, "It can wait, Bassick. I'm in a devil of a mood, truth be told. A black cloud is hanging just over my head. It will rain buckets on me any minute.

"Leave me be. Just keep everyone away for a while."

"But, your grace, it's something you really should know."

The duke recognized Bassick's hovering tone. If he weakened now, he wouldn't be free of him until midnight, if then. "Let me alone," he yelled. "I'll call you when I wish to hear your important news. If you hired two new parlor maids, it's all right. Swell our rolls. Let us employ every able-bodied person in the county." He turned slightly and waved a dismissing hand toward the old man, who had been at Chesleigh Castle since before the duke was born. "Keep everyone out of the library. If you really care about me, that's what you can do to make me bloody happy."

"But, your grace—"

The duke felt a sudden stab of apprehension. "Is Lord Edmund all right?"

"Certainly, your grace. His lordship spent his afternoon on his pony. He is now enjoying his dinner with Ellen, in the nursery."

"Excellent. Then say no more. If Mrs. Dent is beating the scullery maid, tend to it yourself."

The duke turned on his heel, his tan greatcoat swirling about his ankles, and strode the length of the entrance hall, past the medieval tapestries that hung like thick curtains over the ancient stone walls. He left Bassick with his mouth unbecomingly open, half-formed words still on his tongue, a look of perturbation in those rheumy blue eyes of his.

Enough was enough, the duke thought. He'd not only spent two hours with a friend of his father's, Baron Wisslex, who was dying bravely, with his son hanging about, just waiting for his turn at the title, but then he'd come home to hear the damnable news from Drew Halsey, Lord Pettigrew. He pulled up short, feeling a stab of pain in his foot.

He had a rock inside his boot, of all things. He sat down on a heavy Tudor chair set beneath the portrait of a bewigged ancestor, a great-great-uncle of the last century, and pulled off his Hessian. He flicked out the small pebble, rubbed the sole of his foot, then rose again, not bothering to pull his boot back on. He ignored the footman who was standing not ten feet from him, magically appearing from one instant to the next to see if there was anything required.

He tucked the boot under his arm and opened the library door.

The Chesleigh library was the present duke's favorite room. It was a dark chamber, somber and rich, its shadows deep and full, and it smelled always of lemon wax and old books. He looked briefly at the walls with all the inset bookshelves that soared up to twenty-five feet, the long, narrow windows covered with rich maroon velvet curtains, hung there by his father not two years before. There was a good-sized fire built up in the cavernous grate, and a single branch of candles had been lit against the coming night. Bassick, as was his way, had known he would be home soon, and had the room prepared for his comfort.

It was a masculine, very comforting room to the duke, and he felt himself begin to relax, felt the black rage, the sense of helplessness that he felt to the depths of him, begin to recede. He stripped off his gloves and greatcoat and tossed them over the back of a dark blue brocade chair, then sat down and tugged on his boot. Since this was a chore that he rarely performed by himself, he found himself cursing at his own ineptness.

A low, musical laugh came out of the gloom. He jerked around to see a woman standing at the side of the fireplace in the shadows, swathed from head to foot in a dark cloak.

"A nobleman and his boots," she said, shaking her head. "I wonder how poor mortal men manage. I suppose I could offer to help you." Her voice was amused.

However, she didn't move.

Chapter 4

The duke rose swiftly to his feet, his boot, thankfully, snug where it belonged. He nearly stumbled over his feet in his haste and surprise.

"I could have killed you," he said. "Hiding in here was a stupid thing to do."

"Oh? How would you have dispatched me? Perhaps you would have hurled your boot at me?"

"If I'd had a gun with me, you could be lying on the carpet with a bullet in your gullet. Sometimes I do have a gun with me. Today I don't. However, I do have my hands, and they would, doubtless, fit nicely around your neck."

"Oh, I don't think you'd kill me. Your very nice butler wouldn't allow murder to be committed beneath his nose."

"Don't wager your dinner on that."

"He's fascinating. If he wore a white robe, he would look like a biblical prophet."

"He isn't a prophet. However, he is supposed to guard the portals to my kingdom. Now, who the devil are you? How did you get in here?"

She didn't answer, just stood there like a specter in a black cloak. Anger began to replace surprise. He'd wanted to be alone, and now this female had forced her way into his house and into his library.

Actually, he was beginning to feel ripe for murder. Then he understood. "Bassick's head will roll for this. Damnation, the servants' entrance is in the north wing. If you want to keep your position here at Chesleigh, you will use it in the future, not come into this part of the castle. Tell Bassick that I don't need to interview you. Go away. Now. I want to be alone."

"You said a great deal there and I did hear all of it, but still, I don't quite understand. Could you please speak again? Only this time perhaps you could just reduce all your thoughts to one that is the most pertinent?" The woman had the gall to sound both amused and offended. But there was more amusement, all of it at his expense. His fingers itched to lace themselves about her neck.

He drew himself up even taller, his head cocked a certain way, his shoulders drawn back—the medieval seignior at his most intimidating—something he'd seen his grandfather do, something his father did better than any other human being, and said, all black hauteur, "I am tired of this, my girl. You will remove yourself now. I have no wish to be bothered, no matter what a wench offers. Send my butler in. The fellow has a lot to answer for."

"This is the first time I've been called a wench. Are you normally so very rude, your grace? Or is it just that it's Wednesday, and this mid-week day offends you? Or perhaps it's the weather? I myself was delighted when the rain stopped. I was beginning to grow mold."

"Shut up, damn you."

She shut up, contenting herself with staring at him and praying she hadn't misjudged him.

A discordant note finally tolled in his mind. He'd been locked inside his own black soul. Damnation, the female wasn't a serving girl, here in his library for the lord and master to interview. She was well spoken. And wasn't there just a hint of a French accent popping up every once in a while? But it didn't matter. She was here and she shouldn't be here. She was in his private lair, the last place she should be. He was smoldering with impotent anger, and now, with her here, he saw a fresh goat standing right in front of him, ripe for sacrifice, so to speak, and so he let out his anger.

He advanced on her. She didn't move, didn't even shrink back an inch. Of course, if she had, she just might have tipped herself into the fireplace.

"You call me rude?" He was close to her shadowed face now. "Rude? You have the audacity to call me *rude?* How would you like me, wench, to take a birch rod to your buttocks?"

"I think, your grace," she said slowly, stepping away, sideways, pulling the strings at the throat of her cloak, "that you have perhaps mistaken the matter. Truly, I'm not a wench." She turned to face him fully, the light of the candle branch on the mantelpiece behind her, and drew back the hood of her cape. The duke drew up short. He felt as if someone had poked him hard in the belly with a very big fist. This wasn't a serving girl. This certainly wasn't a wench of any stripe.

He wasn't quite certain what he had expected, but the young lady who faced him, her chin high, fit no image he would have conjured up. He stared at her white skin, her high cheekbones, flushed from the heat of the fireplace, and her proud, straight nose. Her hair was neither brown nor blond, but somewhere in between, a strong, opulent color, and like the rest of her, it looked to be rich and full and soft as a lamb's fleece. She had it drawn into an ugly knot at the back of her neck. There were loose tendrils cupping her face. Very nice tendrils. She was beautiful. Not as beautiful as some women he'd seen, admired, and bedded. No, her face wouldn't launch even a hundred ships, but, oddly, she was more than just the sum of her parts. What was she, then? That face of hers held mysteries and a richness of expression and shadows that begged to be explored and plundered. Her eyes were brown, on the dark side, which sounded plain and not at all interesting, only it wasn't at all true of her eyes. Again, there was this richness, this hidden cache of secrets. They slanted slightly upward, an almond shape that struck a familiar chord in his mind.

This was absurd. He was staring at her as would a starving man at a feast. He'd had a feast just four days before in London. Surely Morgana was more than enough for any man, even if he'd starved for a year. Then, despite himself, he looked at her face again, watching as her wide mouth slowly curved into a smile. She showed lovely, straight white teeth.

"I hope you will soon be finished with your examination, your grace. I'm beginning to feel like a slave on the block. Shall I keep smiling?"

"Yes, you've got a charming smile. You're wondering if I'm going to decide to buy you?"

He'd gotten her on that one. He saw those fascinating eyes of her widen ever so slightly. But she wasn't a coward. Nor did she seem the least bit afraid of him. She said, with just the slightest hesitation, "I was actually wondering if perhaps you subscribed to the belief of your ducal ancestors, that every woman who came onto your acres was at your beck and call."

"Of course," he said.

"Of course what?"

"Naturally I subscribe to such a notion. Perhaps it's outdated, but I have to ask myself why a woman would force her way into my private domain if she didn't want me to see her as a bed partner." He realized that he wasn't being at all a gentleman, closer to being a bastard actually, not that the two were necessarily unrelated. But if his scrutiny and roughness of manner upset her, she gave no sign. She didn't move, merely stood there, looking at him and, dammit, he wondered what she was thinking as she looked at him.

As she continued to be silent, he said slowly, trying to be less intimidating, "I think that it's time for you to tell me exactly who you are, and what it is you are doing in my library."

Those eyes of hers, their shape—why was it so familiar to him?

She found that she was examining him almost as closely as he had her. He had changed not one whit from her girl's image of him; he still seemed as large and overpowering now as he had six years before. His dark features were more finely honed now, his face was lean and hard, but just as perfect. No, there were differences. His eyes had seen a lot more than that young man six years before. That young man had known only pleasure, had experienced only the willfulness and wildness of youth. But this man, he'd experienced a lot as he'd gained in years. He'd learned and suffered, and it showed in his eyes, on his face.

"Aren't you going to answer me?"

"Yes, I suppose that I must."

When he'd strode into the room, one boot tucked under his arm, Evangeline had wondered how she was going to get through this. He was in a foul mood—

that was readily apparent—but she hadn't particularly minded. What bothered her was that he didn't have a clue who she was. That hurt, even though it would be a miracle if he had known who she was. Finally, she said, "Don't you recognize me?"

He'd already stared at her too long. He merely shrugged. "Why are you angry? Are you perhaps a discarded mistress? It couldn't have been too long ago because you're very young. Yes, if I dismissed you, then I suppose you wouldn't be pleased at my forgetting you."

She said, her voice as cold as a block of ice, "I was never your damned mistress."

"No? I hope not, because that would lead me to believe that you'd borne my child and were here to collect. That would be upsetting, surely you'd be willing to admit that."

She stood stock still, words lying in shambles about her tongue. She just stood there, staring at him stupidly. "I didn't have your child."

"Well, I'm relieved. I don't believe a gentleman should have bastards scattered around the county. It doesn't speak well of him or of his family. So, we didn't bed together, then. Who are you?"

"When last I saw you, your grace, if you had taken me to your bed, then you would have been guilty of molesting a child."

He was still looking at her in that odd way. Now he cocked his head to one side. She was impertinent. She was, it seemed to him, testing him in some way. That was surely odd. He would outdo her; at least he would try. He flicked a nonexistent bit of lint from the arm of his jacket. "Since that is something that turns my belly, I'm pleased it wasn't the case. Just how old are you? Still silent? Ah, a woman and her age. You never seem to begin too young with your coy protests. You could show me. I have the reputation of judging a woman's age nearly to the very year and month of her birth by studying her breasts, her belly, her legs. Aren't you overly warm in that thick cloak?"

He watched her swallow. He'd just bet her mouth was really dry now. No one could best him, in particular this unknown girl standing here in his library.

She realized then that he was a gentleman of the first order. She opened her mouth, only to see him slash his hand in front of him and say, "Enough games. Who the devil are you?"

"Yes," she said. "I'm warm."

"Then let me help you off with that cloak. You are safe. I've never been drawn to rape, ma'am. Whatever virtue you still possess is quite safe with me."

"I can't imagine you would ever have need to resort to such a thing. Also, just think of what it would do to your name."

"Is that some sort of backhanded compliment? No, don't answer that." He watched her untie the strings of her heavy wool cloak and slip it from her shoulders.

"Before you decide to examine my person, your grace, let me tell you that it could be considered a very rude thing to accord such treatment to your cousin."

"Cousin? The devil. You say you're my cousin? Now, that's an impossibility."

"You're right. I'm not precisely your cousin. Actually, I'm your cousin-in-law. Marissa was my first cousin, my father's niece."

He stared at her dumbfounded. It made her feel better that finally she'd managed to halt him in his tracks. That certainly must be some feat. Then he searched her face for the likeness to Marissa.

She cocked a figurative gun at him and slowly pulled the trigger. "You do remember Marissa, don't you?"

"Don't be impertinent," he said absently, his eyes roving over her face. "Yes," he said at last, "it's the shape of your eyes, just a bit slanted, that resemble Marissa." It was what had looked familiar to him. Marissa's cousin. "Your name, Mademoiselle?"

"De la Valette, your grace."

"My wife's family was Beauchamps."

"Yes, it is my father's name as well. De la Valette is my husband's name."

"You're married? That's bloody ridiculous. You don't look married."

"Why is that? You wondered if you'd bedded me. Surely that is all that being married means."

"Well, not quite all. Not at all. Where is this wonderful husband of yours? Hiding in the pantry? Over there behind my desk?"

"No."

"Surely you see my dilemma. I'm quite unused to finding ladies alone in my library, ready to accost me on the minute I walk through the doors. But there's a husband somewhere? Is he behind the wainscotting?"

Suddenly it was much too much. "May I sit down, please? It's been a very long day."

"While you're resting, why don't I look behind that wing chair over there for this absent husband of yours?"

She didn't say anything, just eased herself down on a very large leather chair near the fireplace. The flames had died down. They were a warm glow now. She smoothed the outmoded dovegray gown about her, a gown that had been expensive four years before. It was a gown that screamed that she was a lady fallen upon hard times. Houchard had laughed, pleased with himself, when she'd first worn it for him. He'd told her that his mistress had selected it for her. He'd told her that the duke, a man of vast experience, despite his limited number of years on this earth, would know exactly what she was.

The duke said finally, "All right, then. No husband. I see that the gentleman has left you high and dry. Now, I'm surrounded by faithful retainers, Madame. Would you be so kind as to tell me how you managed to be in my library without my being informed of your presence?"

"I arrived but a few moments before you, your grace. Your butler was kind enough not to make me wait in the entrance hall. I was very cold, you see, and he did not wish me to be uncomfortable."

"So that's what Bassick wanted to tell me. I can just hear him now: 'Your grace, I've a pretty young piece bundled up in your library, waiting to see to your pleasure.' Yes, that would have been Bassick's style, but of course he would never intend that I—never mind that. I trust you're now sufficiently comfortable. Would you like some tea? Brandy? Something to eat, perhaps off my best china plates?"

He was elusive, swift as quicksilver, not at all like a soft, gentle rain falling through her fingers, but more like a typhoon roaring over her, flattening her, but at the same time drawing her admiration. He was charming, undoubtedly ruthless, his sexual word play utterly inappropriate to a lady's ears. What was he thinking, really? "No, your grace."

He sat down on a settee opposite her. He stretched out his long legs, the cloak falling to the floor on either side of them. His boots were big and shiny black. He folded his hands over his belly. "So, when will this husband of yours make an appearance?"

"He isn't here. I don't know exactly where he is. He's dead, you see. I'm a widow."

He sat back, even more at his ease. "Aren't you very young to be left in that saddened state, Madame?"

"No more than you, your grace. You were made a widower quite young yourself." The words slipped smoothly from her mouth, and to her own ears, she sounded perfectly at her ease.

"I was married older than you, and I was made a widower older than you," he said after a moment. "Now I am twenty-eight. I daresay you haven't yet gained your twentieth birthday."

"I am just turned twenty last week." She lowered her eyes, but it didn't help. She hated this even more than she'd thought she would. "I was married when I was only seventeen. You were only twenty-two when you married Marissa, were you not? And Marissa had just gained her eighteenth year."

"You are well informed."

"I have an excellent memory. I was at your wedding, your grace."

"I see. So, I did remember you, a bit. Do you have children?"

She shook her head. "Have you many more questions for me? I'm getting thirsty."

"Yes, certainly I have, but for the moment, let me reminisce. I married Marissa six and a half years ago. You would have been thirteen years old."

"Yes. After the wedding I never saw either of you again."

"So your husband is dead. Is your father in England?"

Safe ground, she thought, and although she hated giving the words any credence, just speaking them aloud gave them more that she imagined. It felt very strange, even terrifying, that she managed to say without hesitation, "No, he died just a short time ago. My mama, who was English, died three years ago. After Napoleon fell and the Bourbon king was returned to the throne, Papa and I returned to France. My papa was in poor health. But his passing was easy, thank God." Actually, her papa was currently residing in Paris, in a room that was comfortable enough, for she'd seen it before she'd left to come to England. He had one servant to see to his comfort and a woman to cook for him. She'd insisted that he have all the books he wanted. Houchard had agreed, the damnable bastard. And why shouldn't he agree? She was doing what he demanded of her. And there was a physician; she'd said she wouldn't budge unless there was a physician available to him. She'd begged him to be calm, told him again and again that she would be all right. But, she'd thought, how could her father remain calm when she was here in England against her will? What if something happened to him?

"I'm very sorry. The loss of parents is difficult. My own father died last year. I loved him dearly. I'm sorry."

"Thank you," she said, and lowered her eyes so he wouldn't see the lie in them. She had a sudden memory of his father, a beautiful man with charming manners, tall and straight as a post, darker even than his son. "I'm sorry about your father. I remember him. He was very kind to me."

He nodded, then sat back and eyed her, wishing she wasn't so pale, that her father hadn't died, for he knew what a difficult thing that was. "Yes, that makes sense." He balanced his elbows on the padded arms and tapped his fingertips thoughtfully together. "Marissa's father, as well as your own, was an émigré. Marissa's father also hated Napoleon, as did, I assume, your father. He wouldn't ever go back until Napoleon was out of power. Actually, Marissa's father still resides in London, quite content with his adopted country. Does your uncle know that you're here?"

"No. He didn't even know that Papa and I had returned to France. We have no further ties to his family, or to yours."

"Did your husband die in England, Madame? Was he also an émigré?"

She knew he would ask. She knew because Houchard had known he would, and had asked her question after question until she was clear and smooth in her answers. Still, she felt a stab of nausea low in her stomach. The lies would stack up, higher and higher until she wouldn't be able to see beyond them. "He did, your grace. Like my father, he was also an émigré. I just realized that I'm now thirsty, your grace. May I have a cup of tea, before I leave?"

He rose and walked to the wall, and pulled the bell cord. Without saying anything more, he left her sitting alone in the library.

Now, this was certainly strange, she thought, rising to warm her hands in front of the fire. Where had he gone?

Chapter 5

Ten minutes later, he reappeared, carrying a large tray himself. No servant accompanied him.

"Am I so disreputable a visitor that you don't wish your servants even to see me? Are you afraid that they'll gossip about you, alone with a young woman who shouldn't be here in the first place?"

He grinned at her. It was devastating. In that instant she knew that he wasn't just a very wickedly handsome man; he was also a man of infinite charm, if he chose to be charming, and he appeared to wish it now. All that charm was in that grin of his. Even for a strong woman that grin could be a killing blow.

"How did you know? Ah, perhaps you've already heard my servants talking. Yes, I'm quite in the habit of entertaining young ladies in my den of iniquity." He set the tray down, then expertly poured both of them a cup of tea. "No fluid retort to that? I don't blame you. That was quite a detour into idiocy, Madame. Now, do try one of Cook's lemon tarts. I don't want to unleash you just yet on my people. Actually, I don't want them to see you until I know what I'm going to be doing for you. I cannot imagine that you just came to Chesleigh Castle on an afternoon lark.

"Yes, do try one of the lemon tarts. You're on the thin side, even though your endowments look quite sufficient, at least from my perspective. Now that you've got your mouth full, do tell me about your husband. Was he an émigré? Did you meet him here in England?"

"Yes, I did," she said around a lemon tart that tasted so crisp and sharp, it nearly made her eyes water. It was the best lemon tart she'd ever eaten in her life. She immediately reached for another. To her surprise, his hand covered her. "No, you don't want to fill yourself on just one thing. Here, try the apple patty. Cook has a way with the pastry that makes your belly sing."

She ate the apple patty in two bites. She reached for another, then drew her own hand back. It required all her resolution not to grab for that single small slice of what looked to be raisins and pears, all stuffed inside a round pastry.

"You're smart to desist. I admire anyone with such willpower. A friend of mine, Phillip Mercerault, is also the proud and possessive employer of an excellent cook. We've talked about a competition between the two kitchens but haven't done it yet. Like Phillip, I'm very careful when I'm here, as was my father before me." He paused a moment, then gave her that devastating grin again. "My father always told me that ladies didn't particularly take to gentlemen with fat on their bellies."

"You don't have any."

"Thank you for noticing."

"But I really can't be certain. You're still wearing your cloak."

That was well done of her. He rose and untied his

cloak, tossing it over the back of the settee. He stood there a moment, letting her look at him.

"I suppose you are still without fat."

"Naturally, I was a dutiful son. I always attended my father." He sat back down, folding his hands over his belly. "Now, about your husband."

"I met him here, since we lived in Kent. We married here."

"What was his full name?"

"André de la Valette. His father was the Comte de la Valette. The line is now dead. It is a pity." Say no more, Houchard had told her. Let him wonder. It will amuse him to wonder. He is a man easily bored.

"I see. Now, I suppose I must ask you why you are here."

She sat forward in her chair. "As you know, your grace, I have never seen my cousin Edmund. Mama was quite ill throughout those years, and I could not leave her. Also, I believe, there was some sort of falling out with your family, and such visits, had they been possible, were discouraged."

She saw a sudden flash of anger in the duke's eyes. "I don't suppose that your father or your esteemed uncle told you the reason for the estrangement? Oh, yes, most assuredly there is one, of many years standing."

She shook her head. "I should like to know, your grace, for I was very fond of Marissa and missed her. I always wanted to meet her son."

The duke laughed. It wasn't a nice laugh, but an angry one, that held not a whit of humor. Then he shrugged and drank some of his tea. "Perhaps someday you will know. If you father did not tell you, it is not my place to do so. As for your cousin and my son, he is the very best of lads, five years old now."

She heard the softening of his voice, saw the pride in his dark eyes. He loved his son. She waited. He set down his empty teacup. "Now, no more thrashing the bushes, Madame. I don't imagine you came here to see the view from my windows, although it is spectacular when the blasted rain doesn't turn everything gray. Tell me what I can do to assist you."

She looked at him full face and said baldly, "I have no money. After my father's death the French took everything left, not that there was very much. They claimed that my father and I weren't really loyal to the country of our birth, and thus with his death I would get nothing from his estate."

"Why did you not write to me and tell me of this?"

"There was not time. Besides, you might have simply ignored a letter. You cannot ignore me, at least now that I'm here, you can't."

He said nothing, just looked at her.

"I had nowhere else to go. I have given this a lot of thought, your grace. I don't wish to be a poor relation, clutching at your sleeve. I don't wish to be dependent. In short, your grace, I would like to remain here at Chesleigh Castle and become Edmund's nanny." There, it had all spilled out of her mouth, much more quickly than was wise, but she couldn't bear the suspense any longer. She added, "Please, your grace. I'm not a frivolous ninny. I'm educated, my father saw to that. He was a brilliant philosopher. I know the classics. I love children."

"That relieves my mind greatly."

Suddenly she looked very alone and vulnerable. "I spent my last francs on a packet from Calais to Dover. One of the blacksmiths was coming this way. He gave me a ride in his cart."

He didn't know where the blasted words came from, but they did come out of his mouth. "Was it raining?"

"It stopped shortly after we left Dover."

"Did you know I was in residence here?"

She shook her head. She drank a sip of tea. "I didn't know. I prayed you would be." Of course she'd known he was here, but she couldn't tell him that.

"Did your father turn you against me?"

"No, not at all. I believe he approved of you. Not only was there a rift between your family and my uncle's family, my father also didn't speak to his brother. I don't know the reasons for either rift. I wish I did know." If it was true. She didn't know anything. She'd heard servants' gossip some years before, something about her uncle being in love with her mother, but she hadn't said anything to either of them. After her mother had died, it seemed cruel to ask her father. Naturally, it could be something else entirely.

Before she'd been bundled out of Paris, it hadn't occurred to her to speak of such unimportant things to her father.

"If I hadn't been here, then what would you have done?"

She managed a crooked grin. "I suppose I would have had to build a willow lodge at the edge of the Grampston forest and wait you out."

"It's the dead of winter. It rains all the time. You would have caught an inflammation of the lung."

"But you were here." She drew a very deep breath and plunged forward. "Will you let me meet Edmund? If we suit, will you let me remain here as his nanny?"

"I had no clue of your existence yesterday, and now here you are, sitting in my library, offering yourself up as a nanny. It is unexpected, Madame."

"I know, and I'm sorry for it. I had no choice. I

didn't want to become Monsieur Dumornay's mistress. That was my only other option."

"Who is this Dumornay?"

"He was one of my papa's supposed friends. I'm certain his wife had no idea that he would have gladly set me up in a house and supported me. She is a very nice woman. He is a lecherous idiot."

"Most men of his stripe are idiots. Now, did you bring a maid?"

She shook her head and looked down at a particularly round and seductive scone. It looked to have raisins in it. It looked delicious. She said, "There was no money to pay for one. I left Margueritte in France."

"I see." He had become the formal nobleman. He was looking at the narrow arcs of flame that leapt upward from the smoldering embers in the fireplace. He looked about ready to nap.

If she'd had a rock, she would have thrown it at him. She jumped to her feet, grabbing her cloak. He had no interest in her at all. He didn't care if she died on the side of the road. He didn't care if she caught an inflammation of the lung.

She was interrupting his solitude, the bastard. She wanted nothing more than to march out of his damned library, out of his damned castle and never look back.

But she couldn't.

She drew a deep breath, took a hold of herself. "I'm hungry. Surely before you dismiss me I may eat something? Perhaps in the kitchen with this goddess cook of yours?"

"Eat the scone you've been eyeing." He rose slowly to face her. She found herself staring at his snowy white cravat. Evangeline was tall, taller than just about any woman she'd ever met. She been called a maypole by Tommy Barkly when she was twelve years old and he'd been thirteen. As she raised her eyes to the duke's face, she felt suddenly quite short. It was the strangest feeling. He was giving her this brooding look that she couldn't begin to decipher.

And he remained silent, merely looking down at her. It was over. She'd failed.

She was angry. He was cold. He wasn't a gentleman. She drew up, stiffer than the fireplace poker. "Very well, I'm not all that hungry. I don't want that scone. I'm leaving."

He said mildly, even as he snagged her arm in one of his big hands, "No, it's all right. I'll feed you, although I don't think you'll still be all that hungry if you satisfy your gluttony with that scone. Ah, yes, now I understand. It's meat and substantial vegetables you want. Very well."

He paused again, then added, "I can't believe you, a young lady, traveled all the way from France here, with no escort."

"What would I have used to pay an escort? One of my boots?"

"If I had been the escort, I would have demanded both boots and a chance to put my hands on you."

He couldn't believe he'd insulted her like that, but what was said was said. He watched her brown eyes change color, literally change from a rich dark brown to a lighter whiskey color. It was fascinating.

She said, very low, "I'm a widow, your grace, not a trollop."

"Dammit, I know that." Still, he didn't apologize, saying instead, "First thing, I will have Mrs. Raleigh, my housekeeper, show you to a room. At the very least, you will meet Edmund in the morning. Do you have any luggage?"

He hadn't made up his mind. Well, had she been in his boots, she wouldn't have either. It was his son, his heir, and he loved the boy. He would be very careful whom he allowed near Edmund. "I have one valise. Bassick has it." Then, because she couldn't bear it, she said, "I didn't come to plead for you to assist me. I came to offer myself as a nanny. Honest work, that's all I'm asking for, your grace. I won't steal the silver. I'm responsible, I swear it. You'll not be disappointed in me."

Her voice was defensive. She didn't look much like a nanny. At least she didn't look like his own Mrs. Tucker, who'd spanked him, hugged him against her massive bosom, sung to him, rapped his knuckles when he was rude, and loved him until she'd died ten years before.

He thought about sitting here all evening in solitude, anger smoldering in him, and helplessness, because the bastard who'd killed Robbie Faraday was still loose, doubtless laughing at them because he'd escaped whole-hide. No, even brandy didn't sound all that appealing now.

He couldn't very well have dinner served to her in her bedchamber. That wouldn't be well done of him. There was no hope for it. Actually, he didn't mind at all.

"I know," he said finally, not really remembering what she'd said, only that it had been pitiful. He turned back to her. He dashed his fingers through his thick hair, standing it on end. "Damnation."

"Goodness. I didn't realize what I was about to say would upset you so much, your grace."

There was wit in her, when she wasn't terrified that he would kick her out. No, that wasn't precisely true. She'd used that tongue of hers to try to outdo him from the moment he'd stomped into his library. He said, "The proprieties, Madame. My mother is in London. There is no one here to be your chaperone, to protect your good name."

She smiled at that. "Oh, that's not important. I'm a widow, your grace, not some young girl, pure and innocent of mind and person, with hopes of finding a rich husband. I'm also a relative, of sorts. No one would believe you would have your wicked way with me, surely."

"You must be remarkably ignorant of my reputation, Madame."

"Oh, no, I know many wicked stories about you. Again, I'm a widow, a mature woman, a woman who surely couldn't be of any interest to anyone, a woman beyond the need for such observances."

"Not only are you appallingly ignorant, you are also obtuse."

"I'm a cousin. Relatives are a different matter entirely."

She couldn't know his reputation or she wouldn't be so flippant about the matter. But the fact remained that she was destitute. Where would she go? No, there was no choice. She had to remain here. He would try to prevent anyone knowing why she was here. The fact that she was related to him by marriage only made it worse. She didn't realize that a simple unknown employee would be perfectly safe because, frankly, that simple unknown employee would have no reputation to protect. He would leave her in ignorance.

"Doubtless you are right, Madame. You also forgot to mention your advanced years."

"No, I told you I was a mature woman. Maturity means advanced years."

"I've always hated the word. So does my beautiful mother."

Not a full minute passed before Mrs. Raleigh came to the library, her lustrous purple bombazine skirts rustling with every light fairy step she took. She was very small, beautiful white hair piled atop her head, framing an unaged face. She wore a thick key ring about her narrow waist. It was highly polished key ring, one that the duke's mother had given her some years before.

"Mrs. Raleigh," the duke said, smiling down at her. On a good day when she was wearing slippers with heels, she came to his shoulder. This day he could easily fit her under his arm. "This is Madame de la Valette, my cousin. Actually, she was her ladyship's cousin. She's come to pay us a visit, to meet Lord Edmund. Perhaps, if I can convince her to remain, she will become Lord Edmund's nanny. Unfortunately, all but one of Madame's valises were lost in a Channel storm. Her traveling companion became very ill and insisted on returning to France. Thus we have her to ourselves for a time."

Evangeline wanted to applaud his tale. It was generous and fluent and well done of him. "Mrs. Raleigh," she said, and nodded to the small woman with the large key ring. Mrs. Raleigh gave her a graceful curtsy. "Ah, you're another tall one, just like his grace's mama. We are glad you are here, Madame. Such a treat this will be for Lord Edmund. If you will come with me to your bedchamber. Do you wish to dine at six o'clock, your grace?"

"Yes, Mrs. Raleigh. Do tell Mrs. Dent that she has a new convert, one who will doubtless eat every dish that's placed in front of her, one who will likely kill the butcher if he displeases her."

"Mrs. Dent will be pleased. I will also tell her that Madame is too slight and needs to gain flesh. It will become a mission for her."

"Why not show Madame to the duchess's bedchamber? Perhaps it will comfort her to be in her cousin's room."

Mrs. Raleigh said to her, "We keep the bedchamber spanking clean, but no one has stayed in it since her grace left us over two years ago. Oh, dear, such a sad time. I hope it will please and comfort you, Madame."

"It is bound to do something," she said, nodded to the duke, and followed the very youthful Mrs. Raleigh from the library.

The duke heard Mrs. Raleigh say in her high musical voice, "How terrible for you, Madame, to lose not only your luggage but your maid as well. Just look at all the buttons on that gown. It's a miracle you managed to get them all fastened yourself. I will send Dorrie to assist you. If you find her helpful, she can assist you for your stay here at Chesleigh Castle."

Just an hour ago he'd been alone. Now he had a cousin staying with him. A young cousin who, if he wasn't mistaken, and he wasn't ever mistaken when it came to anything doing with a female, had beautiful breasts.

Life was unaccountable. He leaned down to pick up the crumbled letter from Drew Halsey. He locked it in the top drawer of his desk.

He walked to the fireplace and gazed down thoughtfully into the glowing embers. He remembered now the thirteen-year-old girl, tall for her age, taller than her older cousin Marissa, who'd reached her full growth. He vaguely recalled thinking her oddly mature for her years, her thin shoulders proudly set, and her dark brown eyes wide and serious when they rested upon his face. Seven years later, her eyes held an appeal that as her kinsman he couldn't dismiss.

"What," he said to the huge silent room, "have I gotten myself into now?"

Chapter 6

"Your grace."

The duke came to a halt at the foot of the massive, wide staircase. "Oh, Bassick, don't concern yourself. It isn't your fault that I refused to listen to you. Thank you for seeing to the comfort of my cousin."

Bassick stepped closer and lowered his voice to a whisper. "It was no bother, your grace. She seems a very nice young lady. She will be remaining with us for a while?"

"Therein lies a question. I will tell you when the matter is decided."

"Oh, yes, your grace. I finally pried out of Juniper that a note from Lord Pettigrew had arrived for you. Was it bad news, your grace?"

"Yes, the worst. The traitor remains unmasked. Drew doesn't want me to involve myself, but I am now. Robbie won't go unavenged. I vowed it to his wife. Damnation, he left two twin boys, not much older than Lord Edmund." He stood there, nearly shaking with impotent rage. Finally, he got hold of himself. "Sorry, Bassick. Now, I understand that Madame de la Valette arrived in the blacksmith's gig."

Bassick nodded. "She didn't see me do it, but I paid the smithy. He expected it, the good Lord knew that, but she didn't. A young lady traveling alone, it fairly curled my toes. And she's obviously a lady. One can look at her for the barest instant and know that."

"Yes," the duke said. "My toes curled as well at how she got here. But she's safe now, here with us."

He nodded to Bassick and began to climb the stairs. He turned abruptly, laughing. "As you rightly surmised, she arrived with no funds. Actually, there's no reason not to tell you, since she tells me that she would like to become Lord Edmund's nanny. Nothing's decided yet. What do you think?"

"It makes my hair white to think of it, your grace."

"Your hair is already white, Bassick."

"I will contrive to think of another utterance that is more appropriate to the situation, your grace. I can only say now that I hope she is firm of spirit. Actually, I hope that she has a will of iron."

"We will find out." The duke grunted and headed upstairs, his destination his son's nursery.

When the duke reached the landing, he turned into the east-wing corridor. He knew servants were about, but he couldn't hear anything. He walked slowly past the scores of portraits that covered the walls of the interminable corridor. Corridor, that was a jest. It was a good ten feet wide, that corridor. What a rabbit warren of a house, he thought as he walked the fifty more feet to the nursery suite. As his hand turned the knob, he paused, listening to his son's laughter. It never mattered what kind of a mood he was in. When he heard Edmund laugh, he smiled.

He was barely through the door when Edmund dashed a straight line to him and leaped. The duke, used to this, caught him handily, holding him high in front of him, then bringing him down and hugging the sturdy little body against his chest.

Edmund reared back in his father's arms. "Papa, Ellen has set my table just like Bassick does yours. I am now about to begin my third course. It's a fish course." He twisted in the duke's arms. "Isn't that right, Ellen? Didn't you say I was to pretend you were serving me baked sea bass?"

"That's right, Lord Edmund. It's Mrs. Dent's recipe and quite delicious."

"Ellen is my butler," Lord Edmund said.

The duke noticed that Edmund's normally rather shy nurse, Ellen, all of nineteen years old, daughter of a local seamstress, was wearing a black coat, probably one loaned to her by Bassick, the sleeves rolled up. She'd fashioned a napkin around her neck to resemble a cravat.

"Does he use the correct silverware yet, Ellen?"

"He is all that is brilliant, your grace."

"Papa, what's wrong?"

"I'm debating whether or not to become ill. You, brilliant, Edmund? That's a thought that has never crossed my mind."

"Oh, he is, your grace," Ellen said, then quickly stepped three steps back. He intimidated her, he knew it, although he did his best not to. She'd done well until just now. The duke smiled at her, even as he hugged his son again. "If you believe it to be true, Ellen, then I won't argue."

The duke felt memories flow over him and into him each time he came into the Chesleigh nursery. It was the most important room of the castle, not the great entry hall downstairs. No, here in the Chesleigh nursery, every single generation of Chesleigh boys and girls had spent their formative years. When Edmund had begun his lessons the year before, the duke had had the large room repainted and papered in the colors and patterns Edmund himself had picked out of the pattern books. Each occupant of the nursery had left his and her own stamp. The duke's mark was the beautifully carved bookshelf in the far corner, his initials proudly etched onto the underside of the top shelf. He'd worked nearly a year on that bookshelf, staining it until he'd finally achieved the particular fluid shade of brown he'd wanted. His father and mother had praised him endlessly.

He strode across the long, carpeted expanse toward his son's dining table, which Ellen had pushed into a place of honor in front of the fireplace. He set his son down and watched him walk to his chair at the head of the table, standing still until Ellen could pull it out for him. He looked serious and somewhat abstracted. The duke wondered if his son was trying to ape him. Actually, he realized that it was exactly what his own father had done, and probably his father before him. He saw Bassick's fine hand in this. When Edmund selected the proper fork, he looked up at his father, his dark eyes shining with excitement.

The duke grinned at Ellen. "It is rather brilliant. You're absolutely right, Ellen."

His five-year-old son began to carefully cut a pastry that Cook had shaped like a slice of fish. He then took a bite, chewed slowly, and nodded thoughtfully. "It's excellent, my good man. Please give my compliments to Cook."

He had even achieved the duke's own tone. It was frightening and comforting at the same time. My good man? Where the devil had his son heard that? Continuity, the duke thought, it was yet another example of continuity. Ellen abandoned her pose long enough to hug Edmund. He imagined she loved his son more than had Edmund's own mother. No, he wouldn't think about Marissa. It gained naught to do so.

"While you dispatch your sea bass, let me tell you that Bassick informed me that you rode Pansy this afternoon."

Lord Edmund offered his father a glass of pretend wine, then took a pretend sip of his own from a very nice wine goblet. "Yes, sir, Grimms and I explored the beach after we brought Pansy back to the stable. We built a castle with turrets and a moat. Grimms said we would consider the tide to be William the Conqueror and his soldiers. We watched the castle disappear from where we were standing on the cliff path. Nothing was left when William was done with it."

The duke squatted down to his son's eye level. The tide doesn't have a man's brain, Edmund. It destroys, nothing more. Were you or I to attack the castle, we wouldn't want to destroy it. We'd want to capture it. We'd want to rebuild it and have our people work it and grow fat and prosperous. Now, I have a surprise for you. We have a guest."

"Is it Phillip?"

"No, it isn't Phillip Mercerault. He's at Dinwitty Manor with his new wife. Her name's Sabrina, and you'll like her. She could lead a cavalry charge."

"I didn't think ladies could be soldiers."

"I didn't mean it that way. I just meant that she's brave and she's got guts. You know Phillip, a lady would have to know strategies to deal well with him."

"Is it Drew?"

"No, it isn't Drew. Now, before we spend the next three hours guessing, let me tell you that it's a lady and you've never met her. She is your mama's cousin.

Her name is—" He broke off, feeling like a fool. He had no idea what her first name was. "You will call her Madame de la Valette. Perhaps if you're really nice, she will tell you her first name."

"She sounds foreign, Papa."

"She's only half foreign. She's really quite English. You'll see. Now, I must change for dinner. I will bring her along tomorrow morning to meet you. Ellen, do have him presentable for his cousin."

"Yes, your grace."

"I don't have a choice, Papa?"

"No, Edmund, you don't."

Edmund looked resigned. "She'll want to pat me on the head and try to look interested in me. Worse, she'll want to kiss me and whisper sweet things to me."

"If you're worthy of interest, then she will be interested. If you're not worthy of interest, then she will doubtless be polite, nothing more. Now, don't be impertinent."

"Is she as pretty as Ellen or Grandmama?"

Ellen gasped at this. "Perhaps," the duke said. "You will have to decide for yourself."

"Well, I know she can't be as pretty as Rohan's mother. She's the most beautiful lady in all the world."

That was probably true, the duke thought, thinking of Charlotte Carrington, Rohan Carrington's mother, who was, indeed, a goddess, a glorious creature, a Venus in English clothing. He'd heard Charlotte had given Sabrina eye lessons so she could flirt with her husband. "Go to your fourth course, Edmund."

He gave his son a pat on the shoulder, nodded to Ellen, and left the nursery.

* * *

Truth be told, Evangeline hadn't been the least bit hungry, not after stuffing Cook's delicious pastries into her mouth, but the food she'd managed to nibble on had been beyond anything she'd ever eaten in her life. "It was delicious, your grace. Your cook is a genius with veal. Actually, I begin to believe she's a genius with everything." Evangeline sat back in her chair with a sated sigh and wiped her fingers on a napkin.

"Thank you. Bassick, please convey Madame's compliments to Cook. Would you care for a bit of sherry?" He heard nearly the same words coming out of his son's small mouth. He smiled down the table at her.

Evangeline gulped. That smile, she thought. It should be outlawed. No man should be allowed to smile at a hapless woman like that. She carefully watched Bassick pour sherry into a delicate crystal goblet.

The duke dismissed Bassick. "I won't need you any more tonight, Bassick. I know you and Mrs. Raleigh play whist on Wednesday nights. You must keep our male dignity intact. I expect you to win."

"I shall try, your grace. However, Mrs. Raleigh is a fierce opponent."

After Bassick had herded the two footmen out of the dining room, the duke leaned back in his high-backed, intricately carved chair that looked fit for royalty, and looked down the table at his cousin-in-law. "There's too much distance here," he said. "I hadn't realized it before. I'll have Bassick take the leaves out of the table. That should bring it down to no more than ten feet in length." He lifted his goblet toward her. "Welcome to Chesleigh, Madame. May I be so impertinent as to drink to your health?"

"It is kind of you, your grace," she said, clicked her

glass toward him, and took a very small sip. It was exquisite sherry, deep and rich, curling a warm path to her belly. "This is a very impressive room. I believe this table, fully extended, seats at least forty people?"

"About that, yes. Bassick likes to leave it in all its splendor. At least he moved the three epergnes so that we could see each other. Oh, yes, it occurred to me earlier when I was with my son that I don't know your name."

"De la Valette."

"No, your given name."

"It is Evangeline, your grace."

"A lovely name, that." She'd behaved just as she should during dinner, what with Bassick and the footmen hovering, speaking of mundane things that neither cared a farthing about. He matched her, never leaving any lurching pauses in the conversation, a coolly friendly host, not overly interested in either his dinner or in his guest.

"My mother selected it, she told me. She was older when she birthed me, and thus when I came, she thought I was a miracle. She said that Evangeline was her name of thanks for me." She broke off, realizing that what she'd just said, she'd never told another person in her life. She just stared at him.

"When I was born, so my father told me later, my mother looked at me and said, 'Saints be praised. Finally I have the heir.' She'd had three miscarriages before she carried me."

"You were a miracle too."

"When you meet my mother, you will have to ask her that."

"I doubt that will happen," she said, then sucked in her breath. She'd spilled a bit of Cook's excellent gravy on the sleeve of her gown, her only gown fit for evening wear. She quickly dabbed it with water and patted it dry. She had no other gown. It was high-waisted dark gray muslin, with no ruffles or lace or underskirts. At least it was one of hers, not one that Houchard or his damned mistress has selected. She looked down the table at him, the glow of soft candlelight making his black hair gleam, admiring his formal black evening wear and his stark white linen. Her child's memories of seven years ago, frozen in time, hadn't done the real man justice. He was magnificent, and of course he was well aware of that.

That made her smile. She looked to be exactly what she wanted him to believe. So they were both exactly right for what they wished to present to the world.

"You are smiling at your glass of sherry."

"Oh, no, that smile had nothing to do with any libation."

"What did it have to do with?"

"I will tell you the truth, your grace. I was thinking that the two of us very nicely suit exactly what we are."

"I am a gentleman and you are a lady. I see nothing in that to make you smile. It wouldn't make me smile. What would make me smile is a beautiful woman walking through that door wearing only sheer veils to tease me."

"I doubt a gentleman would say that. He would think it but hardly say it. Isn't that true? Veils?"

"Let me say that my mother would probably prefer that I only think of such things. That way she wouldn't have to act all flustered. Although now that I think about it, I seem to remember my parents laughing when they didn't realize I was close by."

"Laughter is an excellent thing. My father and mother laughed as well, and at the strangest times."

"I know exactly what you mean. I remember seeing my father kiss my mother. He had her pressed against a wall, and he was kissing her thoroughly. It's something I've never forgotten. Naturally, I didn't understand at the time." He paused a moment, then said low, "My father's death has been difficult for her."

"And for you as well."

"Yes. All my friends wanted to visit me simply because my father was the best of parents. He took to all my friends, treated them just as he should, made them want to be brave and solid and honorable." A lump was in his throat. He hated it, but he couldn't prevent it. He also couldn't prevent speaking of his father, a man he believed to be the best father in all the world. He thought of Edmund and what he had missed by losing his grandfather. He shook his head. "Do you find your bedchamber satisfactory?"

"Very. I remember that Marissa had excellent taste. The bedchamber combines her favorite colors, light blue and cream."

"I don't know about Marissa's taste. I have never set foot in her bedchamber."

Chapter 7

He'd never visited his wife's bedchamber?

She started to open her mouth, to ask him, quite frankly, if he'd never visited his wife's bedchamber, then how could he produce a son.

He knew exactly what was in her mind at that moment. Her thoughts were writ clearly on her expressive face. She had no guile. She would have to learn if she was ever to enter Society.

"I bedded my wife. I just never bedded her in her own bed. Actually, Marissa never touched the rest of the castle. She didn't care to stay here. She much preferred London. Indeed, she was only here when she was pregnant with Edmund." He picked up a fork and lightly began tapping it against the white tablecloth. "She hated the sea, the dampness. She looked forward to birthing Edmund here so she could return to London. She's buried in the Chesleigh family plot in the churchyard in Chesleigh village. You can visit her grave if you wish."

His voice, when he'd spoken of his father, had been filled with passion. With Marissa his voice was expressionless. She said, "Do you spend much time here at Chesleigh, your grace?"

"I try to spend a quarter of the year here. Besides the London town house, where my mother currently resides, there are three other houses in England. I am responsible for the Chesleigh properties. I spend time at all of them."

Spoken like a duke, she thought, a man who knew his responsibilities and accepted them. Well, she would remain at Chesleigh. Houchard had been adamant about that, at least until she received further instructions.

"Truth be told," he continued after a moment, "like Marissa and my mother, I prefer London. I have many friends there. There are countless attractions."

She said, "If you will allow me to remain as Edmund's nanny, it perhaps will relieve you to know that, unlike you, I much prefer the country and the sea. I have always detested large cities. I find them dirty and noisy. If you allow me to remain, your grace, you can be certain that I will be quite content right here at Chesleigh. It is written of in all the guidebooks as one of the most noble and stately residences in all of England. Not Blenheim, to be sure, but nonetheless."

"Blenheim is a tasteless heap of stone, of no particular style and no antiquity. Its gardens are paltry, its forests scraggly. It has no pride of ancestry in its walls, no sense of permanence. Warwick Castle, now, is quite another matter. One can feel centuries of human misery and triumph within its walls. Unfortunately, my ancestors had not the famous Warwicks' wherewithal." The duke arched a black eyebrow. "I'm not a useless fribble, Madame. Don't give me that surprised look. Sometimes my attention turns to politics."

Her heart nearly stopped. What the devil did he mean by politics? Oh, God, she had to know. Houchard had said that the duke didn't deign to care about politics. "What do you mean, your grace? Do you sit in the House of Lords? Do you propose new laws?"

"No, not exactly. Not at all, really. It's not important. Actually, what I should have said is that I try to do precisely what pleases me at any given moment. Much of what pleases me is not fit conversation for a lady's ears."

He'd left something out. She wondered what it was. She said, "That didn't stop you this afternoon, or just thirty minutes ago either."

What else was one to do? He laughed. "Touché, Madame. Perhaps you would like to go to the drawing room? I imagine that Bassick would serve us some tea shortly."

"But we just finished dining."

"Bassick believes that tea is the foundation of happiness, health, and well-being. If we adjourn to the drawing room, the tea tray will be brought within an hour."

The duke settled her in a lovely pale blue silk-covered chair near the fireplace. He himself remained standing, his back against the mantel, his arms crossed over his chest.

"Have you thought about me remaining here, your grace?"

"You arrived only four hours ago, Madame."

She looked down at her hands and said truthfully, "I'm afraid, your grace."

"I shan't boot you off the premises."

"No, but perhaps you would simply allow me to remain, doing nothing, having no importance at all. I wouldn't like that. In fact, I couldn't have it."

"Why the devil do you sound so nervous?"

"Because you haven't yet told me if I may remain as Edmund's nanny."

"You are a young woman, Madame. I would think that you would prefer to join Society. I am your kinsman. It is my duty to see that you are established, that you don't want for anything. I know that my mother would be delighted to introduce you into the *beau monde.* With your French blood, and your undeniably lovely face and figure, I predict your instant success. I'm not at all tight-fisted, Madame, and will provide you sufficient dowry to support a suitable second alliance."

It had never occurred to her that he would be so wretchedly generous. She had to stay at Chesleigh at all cost. She finally said, "Even though I'm half French, I'm actually English to my very bones. I don't like the French."

"Those are my sentiments as well, particularly Napoleon. Now, what do you say?"

"I don't want to go to London."

"I beg your pardon?"

"I have no wish whatsoever to leave Chesleigh. I've told you. I love this house, the sea. I want to stay with Edmund. Even though I haven't met him, I'm sure that we will suit."

Suddenly he looked bored with her, and cynical. He looked as if he would say something, but contented himself with just shrugging his shoulders.

She jumped to her feet, accidentally tipping the chair and sending it onto its back on the beautiful Axminster carpet. "Oh, dear," she said, picked up the chair and righted it.

"I gather you are perturbed about something?"

"I don't understand your skepticism, your grace. I

have told you what it is I wish, yet you pretend to disbelieve me."

"Were you widowed so recently that good taste forbids gaiety? If that is your reason for wishing isolation, then I will accept it."

"I was widowed over a year ago, your grace. My father died shortly after my husband. I have fulfilled my social obligations. Now I just wish for peace and rest."

He said, his voice becoming distant, "You must have been very attached to your husband."

"No—yes, I mean, certainly I was attached to him. André was a great man."

"And a poor one, evidently."

"I am left penniless because I did not bear him an heir. That is the way of the world, everywhere, even here in England. His younger brother is now master. I never got along well with his younger brother. After André died, I returned to my father."

"Did the young fool try to seduce you?"

Again, his cynicism burned the air between them. "Well, yes, I suppose he did. I couldn't abide him. I left. His breath smelled always of garlic."

"I see," the duke said, and examined his thumbnail. It was a bit jagged. "Exactly who was your husband, Madame?"

"The eldest son of the Comte de la Valette, André Neigeon, by name."

"I can't very well continue calling you Madame or cousin. May I call you Evangeline?" She nodded and thought that her name sounded like smooth honey when he said it. It also sounded seductive and provocative. It was odd about this man. Other than being the most beautiful man she'd ever seen in her life, his was a brooding, complex nature that she doubted anyone understood. Perhaps his father had.

"Certainly, your grace."

"You may call me Richard."

She nodded, but she didn't want to be close enough to him so that his first name came naturally to her. She wanted to keep him apart from her, separate. She should have been relieved that he had so quickly accepted her, but instead she felt so ashamed she wanted to slink away and hide.

"If you truly wish to remain at Chesleigh in the company of my son, I suppose it would be ill-natured and unreasonable of me to disallow it. You will not, of course, be treated like a nanny. Indeed, I will expect you to be mistress at Chesleigh when I am not here."

From an unknown to the mistress of his house in his absence. She just stared at him, words vague in her mind and dead on her tongue. She began to pace, her strides long, bounded only by her skirts. She whirled to face him. "That is ridiculous. You don't know me. I'm nobody at all. Never would I agree to such a thing. I would be your employee, just like your other hundred or so employees."

"How did you know their number? Were you counting faces all afternoon?"

"No, but this place, it's immense. Every time I've looked up, there's been a different footman or maid standing not three feet from me."

"The fact remains that you were my wife's first cousin. You have no family left except your uncle, who doesn't even know you're in England. Thus, I'm now the head of your family, or, if you wish, you have become part of my family. I am now responsible for you. I cannot in good conscience place you in an airless room in the attic."

"I didn't mean it to sound like that. But it is impossible. Forgive me."

He withdrew from her as effectively as if he'd walked from the room and left her alone. He looked indifferent. He said, "Having my lovely cousin in residence at Chesleigh cannot but make every gentleman of my acquaintance red with jealousy. Besides, it is what my mother would insist upon. If you don't choose it, it is unfortunate, but it is what will happen.

"Once you have settled in, I will bring my mother here to meet you. The propriety of your living here, without proper chaperone, cousin or not, is another matter upon which my mother is well versed. We can't have your reputation sullied by being here with me. Perhaps my mother should come to Chesleigh now, though her health suffers from the sea air."

"I've been married. There's nothing for you to sully. I see that you are quite bored with me, with this entire conversation. I will excuse myself."

"Am I bored? I don't think so. So there's nothing for me to sully? Given that you are half French, I find that opinion extraordinarily naive. Where, Madame, is your touted French common sense? Surely you plan to wed again some time in the future. Let me assure you that the gentleman of your choice will be much concerned."

"I have no intention of ever marrying again. Also, the thought of your poor mother being dragged here just because of some nonsensical rule is ridiculous. The fact is that I'm nothing more than a poor relation. No one cares about my reputation or lack of one."

He wasn't even looking at her, merely frowning at his face in the shine of his boots. "Very well," he said. "In a month or so, after Edmund has driven you distracted, and you find yourself on the point of throttling him, you will pay a visit to London. You don't have to marry any man there, I promise you."

"I won't ever want to leave Chesleigh."

"We shall see," he said. He drew his watch from his waistcoat pocket and consulted it. "It's late. Perhaps your nonsensical opinions result from fatigue."

"Just because I have no liking for your kind of life, your grace, you believe me stupid. Oh, dear. I've insulted you, haven't I? I am sorry for it. Will you still let me remain as Edmund's nanny?"

"Do you know," he said after a moment, "I don't believe I've ever met a woman like you before? You run smoothly along a certain road, then suddenly take a turn that leads to another road that goes in the opposite direction. You're something of a puzzle. I have always been quite good at solving puzzles. Why don't you say good night? No, don't say any more. I'm giving you the chance to escape the drawing room without further offending your host."

He took a step toward her, then paused. His long fingers stroked his chin. "Before you retire, let me inquire exactly what you believe my kind of life to be."

She looked up at him full face. "I believe you to be a man of the world, a man who can have most anything he wishes with but a snap of his fingers, a man, in short, who, because of his wealth, rank, and personal attributes, can indulge himself in any pursuit he fancies."

"In conclusion, not a very estimable man."

She said without hesitation, "I will always believe you an estimable man, your grace. I think you have a good deal of kindness. Indeed, how could I ever believe otherwise?" She turned and walked to the drawing room door. She paused, her hand on the doorknob, and said over her shoulder, "After all, have you not allowed a poor cousin-in-law to invade your stronghold?"

"Yet another different glimpse of you," he said quietly. "I trust you won't regret coming here."

"I cannot regret it, your grace," she said, and quickly left the room.

Her choice of words perplexed him. He went to his library. He decided an hour later, before he went to his bed, that he would postpone his return to London, at least for a week, until he was certain that she and Edmund rubbed along well together.

Chapter 8

It was raining hard; the building was old gray stone, an open gutter flowing in front of it. Inside, she could hear the echo of her boots on the stone floors. She'd never known such fear in her life. One of the two men shoved her through a door into a small, narrow room. There was only one high window in that room behind a young man who appeared so thin as to be gaunt. He looked like a monk in his cell. He was sitting behind a very old, scarred desk that held no papers, nothing, on its surface. The young man rose slowly, never looking away from her, his eyes never leaving her face. He was wearing a black, musty-looking wool coat and trousers.

He walked up to her and took her chin in his long, thin fingers, lifting her face. She tried to jerk away, but one of the men twisted her arm behind her, saying low in her ear, "You hold yourself still, Mademoiselle, or I'll break this pretty wing."

The fingers on her chin tightened, then suddenly released her. He motioned to a chair. "Sit down."

She sat. There was no choice. She wanted to ask where her father was, but the words were buried too deep in her throat. Why had they brought her and her father here? To Paris? She was so afraid, the words were stuck in her throat. The man said, "My name is Houchard. I need you. You will do exactly as I tell you, or I will kill your father."

Where were the words to scream at him, to demand why he was doing this, whatever this was?

"I'm relieved that you're well enough looking. The duke only likes beautiful women. If you must, you will bed him."

She leapt from the stingy chair and screamed, "What are you talking about? What duke? I know no duke. What have you done with my father?"

"Oh, you know the duke. Soon you will know him even better. You're half English. I find it amusing that you will aid me in my cause. You bloody English, you are always so certain that you and only you are right. I wonder if I should bed you first to see that you'll know how to properly seduce the duke, if, naturally, the need arises." He turned to one of the men. "Did you strip her? Examine her?"

The man shook his head. "The little chick was too frightened and her father too incensed. I didn't want to have to kill him. Do you want me to strip her now?" Houchard looked at her, slowly shaking his head.

He threw back his head and laughed and laughed. Then, with no warning, he started singing in Latin, in a deep monotone, as would a priest intoning a benediction to the people.

The two men standing behind her began to sing as well, their voices high as young boys', pure and light, their Latin beautiful and smooth and resonating in that monks' cell of a room.

Evangeline jerked awake, her heart pounding, sweat

heavy on her face, breathing so hard she thought she'd choke.

A dream.

It had been nothing but a dream. But most of it had happened. She wondered why she'd dreamed that Houchard and his henchmen had sung in Latin? She hadn't understood what they were singing, and perhaps that was the point. She had no idea what would happen now.

A dream.

God, it had been so very real. She shook away the last remnants and pushed back the covers. She could deal with this. If she didn't, her father would die. She'd won the major concession, thank God. The duke, for the moment, had accepted her, had welcomed her as a member of the Chesleigh household. She would be Lord Edmund's nanny, if Edmund accepted her. Houchard's drama was set irrevocably into motion, and there was nothing she could do to prevent his characters, herself included, from playing out their roles.

The morning sun was shining brilliantly through her bedchamber windows. There was no fire lit, and indeed there was no need for one. It was so warm one would believe it was summer. This had happened several times during her growing-up years in England. There would be torrential rains, freezing weather, snowstorms, then several days so vivid and bright, so warm, that one dreamed of summer, lush and hot and so very green. She looked out at the naked-branched elm trees. Well, not really summer.

Then, naturally, winter would return with a vengeance. There was so much she had to do, the most important thing to make friends with the duke's son. If he took an instant dislike to her, she was ruined.

She remembered saying this to Houchard. He'd merely shaken his finger at her, saying, "If that happens, my dear, I suggest you prepare yourself for your father's funeral. The problem will be, of course, that you will never find his body." She'd believed him then. She still believed him.

She was dressed and ready to leave her bedchamber when she heard the sound of slow, heavy steps dragging closer and closer to her bedchamber door.

She knew a spurt of terror. The two men who'd taken her and her father from their home, their image, their voices, were deep and strong in her mind. The smooth, younger one had been called Biron. She couldn't remember the other man's face, just his voice. He'd been a little ferret of a man who looked as if he hadn't ever said a kind word to anyone in his entire life. At least they hadn't harmed their servants, Margueritte and Joseph, merely left them staring out through the drawing room windows toward the carriages, their faces drawn and pale in the candlelight, wondering what was happening. They'd thrown her in one coach, her father in another. At dawn they'd arrived in Paris. And they'd shoved her into that narrow room that held Houchard.

So quickly, her life had changed so very quickly, and irrevocably. No, no, she was being foolish. She was in England, in her bedchamber at Chesleigh. No men were waiting outside her door to drag her anywhere. She quickly pinched her cheeks to bring color to her face. She patted the severe chignon at the nape of her neck and called out in beautiful, clear French, "*Entrez!*"

She heard someone mutter something, then shouted out, this time in English, "Enter!"

The muttering continued. Frowning, Evangeline opened the bedchamber door.

An old woman shuffled into the room, small feet peeping beneath a beautifully woven dark blue gown, fitted at her meager waist in the style of the last century. Her face was the texture of fine parchment paper, her back hunched forward with age. Her sparse white hair was pulled into a skinny bun, revealing patches of pink scalp. She didn't come higher than Evangeline's chin. She looked ready to fall over at any moment; indeed the look of fragility was frightening until she raised her eyes to Evangeline's face. She had beautiful eyes, bright with awareness and intelligence, as blue as a summer sky, a young girl's eyes.

Was she a mad great aunt the duke kept hidden away in the attic? She had a hand ready just in case the old lady decided to crumble where she was standing. She said, "My name is Evangeline. Who are you?"

The old lady didn't say anything for the longest time, just stared up at Evangeline, her head tilted to the left, like an inquisitive sparrow.

"May I do something for you, ma'am? If you're lost, I'm afraid I can't help you. I only arrived at Chesleigh yesterday afternoon."

"Och, I know where I am, and I know who ye be, my little lass. Ye be her dead grace's cousin, all grown up now." She had the softest voice, lilting in a faint Scottish accent. It was like singing.

"I'm not such a little lass," Evangeline said, smiling. "My father calls me his grand big girl, and so I am. Would you like to sit down, ma'am? I could ring for tea if you would like some."

"Oh, no, I don't drink that vile brew. Nay, I only drink the distilled ochre bark from the pine nut tree.

Aye, ye're a grand big girl all right, a perfect height ye are. Now, ye think I'm going to croak it here, right on this carpet, don't ye, lass?"

"I sincerely hope that you won't. Please, sit down. Tell me who you are and what I may do for you."

"I'm Mrs. Needle." She stopped cold, expecting, naturally, that Evangeline knew exactly who she was.

"Hello, Mrs. Needle. I'm very glad to meet you." What was she to do?

"Ye're not as pretty as she was—her dead grace—but ye've more character than that sly little peahen, who hadn't hardly enough character to fill a thimble, and ye've got the heat in yer eyes. Smart eyes ye've got, not a little lassie's eyes, not her dead grace's eyes. She had tempest eyes, all quivery with temper when she was thwarted. Jest a young little thing she was: spoiled, petulant, and demanding one minute, the little charmer the next, aye, a winsome child, fooled my boy but good, but that didn't last long. A pity she tried to cheat my boy, thwarted him she did, all because she was terrified she'd die birthing another babe. Then she died anyway.

"Aye, and jest look at that chin of yers, all strong and no nonsense, that chin. Ye'll give as good as ye get. What do ye think of that, my little lassie?"

Evangeline said after all that, without hesitation, "What do you mean, I've got heat in my eyes?"

The old lady laughed, a dry, choking laugh that made Evangeline think her fine old bones would crumble with the strength of it. "Och, little lassie, ye won't know until ye have his hands on ye. Once that happens, ye'll niver be the same again. Ye'll be lost and found, both at the same time, jest as it's supposed to be, but hasn't yet been for my boy."

"Mrs. Needle!"

It was Mrs. Raleigh, standing in the open doorway, her hands on her hips, looking as if she'd faint and spit at the same time. Her gown today was a pale lavender with darker lavender lace at the wrists and neck. Her hair was a billowing rich white piled atop her head. Her ring of keys looked even shinier today than yesterday.

"Mrs. Needle, whatever are you doing here? This is his grace's cousin, Madame de la Valette. It's very early. Surely you should be resting in your room."

But Evangeline didn't want the old lady to go anywhere. She wanted to know more about this heat in her eyes business, but she was afraid it was over now.

"Oh, it's ye, Clorinda. Always sticking yer nose in between the cracks where it don't belong. I need more time with the little lassie here. She'll be jest perfect, don't ye think? I've waited and waited and so I told her grace, and she shook her head. Doubted she did, but now she's come jest as I knew she would."

"Mrs. Needle, Madame needs to come have her breakfast. Perhaps she can visit you later."

"Actually, now is a very good time for me, Mrs. Raleigh. I'm not at all hungry, and we were just—"

"No, little lassie, ye go with Clorrie here. She frets, ye ken? All will be well, ye'll see. I know ye're afraid, but it will be all right. I promise ye. I've already seen it all. Aye, I can see ye and my boy laughing. It's good."

Evangeline stared at her, mesmerized. This mad old lady knew she was afraid? How, for God's sake? How did she know things would be all right? She and her boy were laughing? It was nonsense, an old lady's madness. Nothing would ever be all right. The only thing she could look forward to was saving her father, if Houchard allowed her to save him.

All else was betrayal. She turned reluctantly to Mrs.

Raleigh. "Yes, very well. May I take you back to your rooms, Mrs. Needle?"

The old lady laughed one of her creaking laughs and waved a small veined hand. "Och, no, lassie. I'll make me own way back to the North Tower. Ye don't worry aboot things, no, don't."

"Now, Mrs. Needle," Mrs. Raleigh said, seeing Evangeline's pale face, "you don't want to make Madame uncomfortable. She doesn't understand you just yet. Give her a while."

"Time grows short," Mrs. Needle said. "I had to come now. Mind to yer own affairs, Clorrie. Now ye may take my little lassie here down to her breakfast."

The old lady shuffled out of the bedchamber. She turned, studied Evangeline for a very long time, then said finally, "Ye'll come to the North Tower, Madame. I'll wager yer only memories of yer cousin are from yer child's mind. But ye've come home, just as I hoped ye would. We'll talk, lassie. Aye, there's much we have to speak about, but we must do it soon. So little time left."

"I'll come," Evangeline said. She didn't move, just stared after the old lady as she made her way slowly and painfully down the long corridor. She felt gooseflesh rise in her arms.

Mrs. Raleigh sighed and lightly patted Evangeline's hand. "Mrs. Needle was the old duke's nurse. She's been here forever; some say she came with the Conqueror. The present duke allows her to do anything that pleases her. Actually, there's no harm to her. If you do go to the North Tower, be warned. Mrs. Needle is considered a witch, a healing witch. You'll be able to smell her concoctions before you are even allowed into her inner sanctum.

"You're pale, Madame. Did she say something to

overset you? Of course she did. She's always mysterious, prides herself on leaving folks' brains all scrambled. She quite enjoys it. Come now, you'll forget once you have one of Cook's raspberry scones in your mouth."

Evangeline said, "She must be very old indeed."

"That's the truth of it," Mrs. Raleigh said, walking beside her. "His grace will not hear of removing her from Chesleigh. Of course, no one has ever suggested it, even when the wind is blowing from the wrong direction and one of her potions pervades the entire castle. Once everyone's eyes watered for two days. I remember quite clearly the burned cinnamon. Dreadful. His grace just laughed. His grace indulges her every whim.

"I must say, though, that her herbal laboratory is magnificent. Everyone brings her clippings and sprigs of this and that. It's interesting. Normally she stays in the North Tower. But she came to see you. Perhaps she'd just heard about you and was curious. I doubt she'll bother you again."

Evangeline shivered. She knew she'd see Mrs. Needle again. In fact, she'd go to the North Tower to search her out herself.

"It's very early, Madame. I was surprised to find you awake and dressed." Mrs. Raleigh eyed the same gray muslin gown she'd been wearing the day before. "Such a pity about your luggage. We will see what the duke wishes to do about that."

"I assure you the duke won't do a thing, Mrs. Raleigh."

"Well, he already has Dorrie attending you."

Evangeline thought a moment. "Yes, you're right about that. He moves quickly."

"His grace decides something, and it's done before

the stable cat, Lambert, can catch another mouse. Did you find her satisfactory last evening?"

"Dorrie is very nice."

"You didn't ring for her this morning. That is why I came myself, to see that you were all right. The poor girl was worried that she'd displeased you."

Evangeline thought of her own dear Margueritte, always humming, always laughing, always chattering even if no one was there, always looking at Evangeline's father with lustful eyes. "Dorrie will suit me just fine, Mrs. Raleigh. I promise to let her assist me this evening."

Evangeline imagined that she was the first nanny to be assigned a maid, but she didn't say anything more. Mrs. Raleigh, doubtless all the staff, believed her position with Edmund to be nothing more than a sham, something to salve her pride since she was indeed a poor relation. Poor or not, she was related to the duke, and thus she would have a maid.

"His grace is already in the breakfast parlor. He always rises early. He has told Bassick that he won't be leaving for London today." She rubbed her lovely, narrow hands together. "Now we shall have him here for at least another week, so Mr. Bassick believes, and I've never known him to be wrong before, and that pleases everyone, Madame. All of us thank you for keeping him here."

She was keeping him here? No, surely not. Surely he had other reasons for remaining unless, of course, he wanted to be certain that she wouldn't strangle Lord Edmund in his bed. It would have been easier if he'd simply settled her in and removed himself back to London. But things didn't tend to unfold in a nice orderly manner. Then, suddenly, with no warning she was back in Paris, in that narrow room. And, he was there as well, staring at her closely as he said, "Do you know how to bed a man?"

She stared at him, shriveling on the inside, white as her lace on the outside.

"You are nearly twenty years old, not a young chit with stars in her eyes and the sense of a goat. Have you ever bedded a man?"

She shook her head. She watched, just as a rabbit would watch a snake slithering toward it, as he walked to her, stood there, smiling down at her. Then he reached out his hands and cupped her breasts. "Very nice," he said, low. "He will love your breasts. You, naturally, will do whatever you must to succeed." She jerked away, but he hadn't released her. It hurt and she gasped.

"Oh, God," she said, and stumbled.

Chapter 9

"What, Madame? Goodness, are you all right?" Mrs. Raleigh grabbed her arm and held her firmly.

Evangeline shook her head, but Houchard was still clear in her mind, damn him. He was always there, sometimes so clear she just knew she could reach out and touch him, and he would speak to her, his voice clear and hard in her ear, or he would touch her, stroke her with as much feeling as he would stroke the arm of a chair.

She managed a pathetic smile. "I'm sorry, Mrs. Raleigh. I was just thinking about something else, something that happened to me in France. Forgive my inattention. Who is that gentleman with the huge white wig?" She pointed at a large portrait, its frame heavy with gold, painted early in the last century.

"Oh, that was the Fourth Duke of Portsmouth, Everett Arysdale Chesleigh. I've heard that he was a wild one, that duke. Too handsome, if you ask me, and all the girls swooned around him. At least most of his bastards are dead now."

Evangeline wasn't thinking about the fourth Duke of Portsmouth. She was thinking about this one, a man who was too handsome for his own good as well, and for any woman's peace of mind. She'd been very aware of him every moment, not just because she was terrified that she wouldn't succeed in convincing him to allow her to remain, but also because he looked at her the way several other men had looked at her, most notably the Comte de Pouilly. Only with the duke she wasn't at all offended. It made her feel warm in places she'd never before even been aware of. It made her feel slightly off balance, but that was something that during the past week had been her constant companion, so it wasn't all that noteworthy. But the warmth, that was something strange, something she couldn't explain. She just knew she liked it.

She'd played a role with him. She'd parried his questions with her rehearsed answers, always wondering what he was thinking, how he was reacting when she said something that was the least bit out of the ordinary.

His moods changed so quickly, from an arrogant hauteur that was such a deep part of him, to the indifferent politeness when he'd withdrawn, deep into his own thoughts. Well, there was nothing for it.

She had to succeed. She had no choice, none at all.

Mrs. Raleigh's graceful, birdlike movements, her soothing chatter, continued as she led Evangeline down the long, carpeted corridor in the west wing to the wide, curved staircase that rose in ancient dignity to the upper floors. She followed Mrs. Raleigh across the vast Italianate entrance hall, with its massive chandelier hanging from a silver chain at least the thickness of her upper arm, past the library and the formal dining room. They entered a small octagonal room that was flooded with the bright morning light from the low, wide windows. There was no heavy furniture, no dark wainscotting, just this light, airy space, the walls painted a pale yellow. Several of the windows were open, a gentle, warm breeze billowing out the gossamer light draperies.

She stopped in the middle of the room. "How very lovely."

"I thank you. Doubtless my mother would also thank you. She ordered the room done this way some twenty years ago."

Startled, Evangeline looked at the duke, who was seated at one end of the small table, just lowering a newspaper. He wore a buff jacket and light brown knit riding breeches, exquisitely tailored from what she could see of them. His dark hair was tousled, his complexion healthy and tanned. He'd already been outside, probably riding along the cliffs.

He was without a doubt the most exquisite man she'd ever seen in her life. But then again, she hadn't seem all that many gentlemen. Perhaps those in London would put him to shame, although she tended to doubt it.

She realized she was staring at him and quickly looked down at the toes of her slippers.

"Is something wrong, Madame?"

Yes, she wanted to tell him. You're what's wrong. It's painful for me to look at you. I held you in my child's memories. I'd hoped you would look differently now, but you don't. I've lost my mind.

She said coolly, getting a hold on herself, "No, nothing, your grace. Just a moment of visual distress." She thought he laughed. She remembered suddenly how she had envied Marissa all those years ago, lucky Marissa who had secured his hand. But Marissa hadn't been so very lucky. Dead when she was but twenty, in an accident, she'd heard.

She gave him a wicked look, a look that was quite natural for her to give to him, a look that seemed to have been waiting inside her, for him to come so she could give it to him. And she knew he liked that look, all that wickedness that promised everything, yet only promised. She shrugged, seeing no hope for it. He was giving her a bland, very knowing smile, as if he knew what she was thinking. Well, he was right. Why not tell him? Her wicked smile grew sharper when she said, "Actually, I was thinking that you look splendid."

He sat back in his chair, his arms crossed over his chest. "A dose of French candor. I thank you for the compliment. If I were a lady, I could preen and demand that you become specific in your compliments, but alas, I'm a gentleman and thus I must take the general compliment and content myself with it. But I do wish I knew what the specifics were in this case." The wicked smile faded. "Have I embarrassed you? Yes, I believe that could be called a discreet flush starting on your neck. Come and sit down. Mrs. Dent has prepared a breakfast that will have us feeling fat as geldings."

She refused to look at him again as she slipped into the chair on his right. She knew he was no doubt quite used to being shamelessly flattered, to being endlessly admired, undoubtedly to being compared to a god.

No, he wasn't a god. She remembered Houchard's graphic descriptions of the duke's likes and dislikes, particularly when it came to women, and wanted to sink through the floor.

No, none of that would come to pass. The duke would never see her as anything more than a fully dressed penniless widow here to take care of his son, if only his son would cooperate and adore her at first sight. He mustn't ever see her as a woman who admired him more than was proper. Bassick, smiling at her, poured her rich black coffee, then, after nodding to the duke, left the morning room.

She was English, she'd always said about herself. She wished she could smash the French part of her out of existence. The funny thing was that even as a child, she'd never liked the heavy English breakfasts, but she'd been thinking about him, about this damnable situation, about what Houchard had told her, and piled her plate high with kidneys, scrambled eggs, kippers, and bacon. Slowly, not wanting to draw attention, she shoved the plate away and reached for a slice of toast. She began spreading it with thick butter.

"You didn't sleep well."

Evangeline nearly choked on her mouthful of toast. She forced herself to chew slowly. When she swallowed, she took a sip of coffee, then gave him a cool smile. "You're wrong, your grace. How could one not be perfectly content in such a beautiful room and a comfortable bed?"

"I suspect that anyone wouldn't sleep particularly well in a new place. Did you hear strange noises? The castle rattles and moans. When there's a storm off the Channel, you sometimes think you'll be buried beneath a pile of stone. You'll become used to it."

"Yes, I can see that would be possible. You're right, for a moment there I'd forgotten the moans and the chains rattling."

He didn't smile, merely toyed with his fork. "Do you always come awake ready to fence with words?"

"No, not usually. Very well, if you're going to pry. I didn't sleep well because I was scared you'd find fault with me today and boot me out. I don't want to starve in a ditch, your grace."

"Oh, I haven't changed my mind. Stop your worrying, if that is indeed the truth you're telling me."

"I had an early morning visit from Mrs. Needle."

He speared up a piece of thin-sliced ham, his fork pausing halfway to his mouth. "Mrs. Needle came to see you? How very odd. She scarcely ever leaves the North Tower anymore. What did she want?"

"Simply to meet me, Marissa's cousin. She said some strange things, but she was kind to me."

"She's a witch."

"That's what Mrs. Raleigh told me, but not a bad witch. She heals people."

"She tries. She quacked my tiger, Juniper, last evening. I haven't heard otherwise, so I will assume he's still breathing and twitching. You've only eaten a slice of toast. Mrs. Dent will be upset if she doesn't have you waddling by spring. Come, try the kidneys, they're quite delicious."

She looked at the kidneys on her plate and actually shuddered.

"You're tall, Madame, and at the moment far too thin, except for your—" He was looking at her breasts, fully and completely at her breasts. At least he hadn't said it aloud. That showed some restraint. He was outrageous, but of course she knew that already.

Very well, she thought, wondering just how far he would go. She said, "Except for what, your grace?"

"I was watching you spread butter on your toast. I couldn't help but notice your fingers, Madame. They're stubby. I'm sorry to have to be so frank about this, but you did ask. Yes, you're cursed with stubby fingers. Could it be your French blood that's done you in?"

She wanted very badly to jump out of her chair, grab it up, and throw it at him. "Stubby fingers? Why, that's ridiculous. You know very well that you were looking at my—no, I won't say that. It wouldn't be proper. It would probably make you laugh and make me want to sink behind the wainscotting except there isn't any wainscotting in here, so I must remain seated here, with you looking at me and laughing your head off."

He didn't laugh, but she knew he wanted to.

She looked down at her long white fingers. "That was really well done, but naturally you know it. Now, do you think that Mrs. Needle could provide me with a potion to elongate these poor short fingers of mine?"

"I will look at them more closely and tell you. It isn't too grave a physical flaw. I'm a tolerant man. All know that and appreciate it. You do as well, now."

She opened her mouth, but nothing came out.

He leaned forward, his elbows on the table. "Do you enjoy crossing verbal swords, Madame?"

"Oh, yes," she said. "As do you. You were probably born telling jests and poking fun. You're quite good at it. In another year or so, though, I will be better than you, and then we shall see who just sits there, staring at his toes, without a thing to say."

"All that? Ah, I must remember to call you Evangeline. It's just that Madame sounds so very dignified, like an abbess, even."

"I've never been all that religious."

He gave a start, stared at her, then laughed. "I suggest you look up abbess in the dictionary. There's a remarkably large one in my library." Then he frowned. "Perhaps that particular meaning isn't there. It's rather a specialized meaning, one that isn't exactly suited for innocent young minds like yours. Forget it.

Now, I will endeavor to call you Evangeline. Were you ever called something shorter?"

"My mother called me Eve."

"Interesting. I cannot help but think about the biblical Eve. Look what she did to poor Adam. She even got him evicted from Paradise because of her wicked ways, which probably began with a wicked smile. As I recall, she never wore a stitch of clothing, even after the eviction. She loved the way he looked at her, loved to watch his eyes cross, which I don't doubt they did."

"I know nothing about that. That is, I know, but your mind is wandering into paths that should be completely untrodden."

He gave her a grin. "I've never found a path I didn't want to tread." He paused, then said in a philosophical voice, "I've often wondered where paradise is located. I can't believe it was anywhere close to the English coast. Surely there would be no moans or rattling old castle walls in paradise, no storms to chill the naked flesh, just warmth and beauty. No, that's ridiculous. Of course there would be moans. I wonder what your poor husband would say about your lack of knowledge about paradise."

Her husband. Her poor late, lamented husband. She dropped the toast from her fingers onto the tablecloth. She couldn't think of anything to say.

Bless him, he completely misunderstood. "I'm sorry, Evangeline. I didn't mean to recall memories to wound you."

Her voice was hard as a stone. "I already told you that my husband, André, was a great man, a sensitive man. I adored him. I worshiped him. He taught me everything I needed to know about this paradise of yours."

"I don't recall yesterday that he had quite achieved

such a pinnacle of perfection. No, I'm sorry. Let's leave dear André to his eternal peace." She was pale. He'd done it again. "Now, Evangeline, if you've eaten enough to fill one leg, I'll take you to meet Edmund. He was hoping our visitor was Phillip Mercerault, a friend of mine who always brings him presents and takes him up with him on his horse, or Rohan Carrington, another longtime friend of mine who has constant winners in the cat races held at the McCulty racetrack near Eastbourne. He tells Edmund endless tales of the cat contestants and the various training methods. Rohan is the owner of the renowned champion Gilly.

"Poor Phillip, he's always wanted a racing kitten to train. Perhaps now that he's married, the Harker brothers—the premier trainers in the area—will deem him worthy to have one. The cat races run from April to October. Have you ever before been to a cat race?"

"No, but I've heard of them. Have you ever had a racing cat?"

He shook his head. "Perhaps someday. Like my friend Phillip, the Harker brothers haven't yet deemed me worthy. I am too flighty, they'd say, and a racing cat must have a firm, steady hand and an owner who is always there for him. Now, let's go see my son."

Chapter 10

Lord Edmund was having his face and hands washed by a smiling Ellen, who was alternately kissing him and scrubbing him. He hadn't yet reached the age, the duke knew, when he would react with appalled outrage at such blatant displays of affection, particularly from a female.

When Edmund saw his father, he yelled, dashed to him, and as was his habit, leaped upward, to be caught and hugged and tossed into the air, all accompanied with gales of laughter that warmed the duke to his bones.

"Well, my boy, you've nearly got all the egg off your mouth. Good morning, Ellen. Has he eaten all his breakfast?"

"He's done very well, your grace," Ellen said, staying back where she was, as was her wont, and quickly curtsied in his general direction.

"Where's my cousin, Papa? Did she bring me a present? You won't let her pet me, will you?" He broke off as he stretched his head over his father's shoulder. He said in a loud, worried whisper, "Is that the lady who's come to visit me?"

The duke said, laughter lurking in his voice, "Does

she have hair the color of honey? Brown eyes nearly the color of mud? Is she nearly as tall as I am?"

"Yes, Papa. She's big. I'm not sure about the mud in her eyes, though."

"I wanted to come alone first, to prepare you, but she must have followed me here." The duke held Edmund loosely and turned to face her.

"Evangeline, this is my son, Edmund. Edmund, say hello to your cousin."

Edmund studied her closely. "I don't think your eyes look exactly like mud. Let me down, Papa, so that I may make a proper bow."

The duke's eyebrows shot up even as he lowered his son to the floor. Edmund gave her a grand bow, showing a perfect leg, so his grandmother would say, and said, "Welcome, Cousin Evalin. Ellen said Mrs. Raleigh told her that you're half foreign. From France, she said."

"Yes," she said, "I'm half foreign," and came down on her knees next to him.

"Welcome to my home. This is Chesleigh."

"I know, and thank you."

"That was creditably done, Edmund. I am pleased." The duke turned to Ellen. "You did well."

Ellen, who could never look at the duke without a flush on her face, said, "Lord Edmund insisted that we practice, your grace. His honor depended upon it, he said."

"And so it does. Edmund, why don't you call your cousin Eve? It's much easier than all the other renditions of her half foreign name. Is that all right with you, Madame?"

"Certainly. I was your mama's first cousin, Edmund. I've always wanted to meet you, her son."

Edmund placed his fingertips on her palm. "Do you

look much like my mama? I don't remember her very well."

"Not really. Your mama was a beautiful lady, like an angel, all soft and white with gold hair and eyes the color of a summer sky. Except for your dark coloring, you have somewhat the look of her." She quickly saw that this did not find favor with Lord Edmund, and added, "But you know, Edmund, I think you will be a great, handsome man like your father. You have his dark hair and a wicked twinkle in your eyes. And a good laugh, Edmund. That's very important, being able to laugh well. Having heard your papa shout out with laughter, I know you'll grow into it very well indeed."

"That's what I want," Edmund said. "Was Mama short? I have no wish to be short when I grow up."

"Yes, but don't forget she was a lady, a fairy princess. Fairy princesses are always small and light and ever so graceful and beautiful. As for you, you're the son of a prince, and they're never small or light. Yes, you'll be just like your papa. You have no reason to worry. Look at your feet, Edmund. You have huge feet. Your body will have to grow just to keep up. And you have long fingers, not the least bit stubby. Ah, yes, I see a giant of a man in the making. You might perhaps even surpass your papa. He's not all that tall, after all, not all that splendid, not all that impressive, actually."

The duke said to no one in particular, "I always thought that it was dogs who had to grow into their paws."

"That too," Evangeline said, not turning to him.

"I'm a prince, am I?"

"A metaphor, your grace," she said over her shoulder to the duke, "nothing more. Merely an example Edmund could understand."

"I rather liked being a prince among men. I'm really not impressive? Didn't you tell me just an hour ago that I was splendid?"

"I don't remember."

"I'll really be taller than Papa?"

"There is no doubt at all in my mind."

Edmund beamed at that. "It's all right that you're here, then, and not Phillip or Rohan. Do you know any stories about Gilly, the racing cat champion?"

"Not as yet, but you can be certain that I will discover stories about Gilly."

"Did you perhaps bring me a present?"

"What a greedy little beggar you are, Edmund," the duke said. "You will make your cousin think that I deprive you."

"Well, I did bring you a present, Edmund. I hope you will like it." Evangeline withdrew a small wrapped box from the pocket of her gown and held it out.

She'd thought of Edmund. It pleased the duke. He watched his son rip away the paper and push open the lid of the box. Edmund crowed with pleasure as he drew out a carved wooden pistol, so finely constructed with wires and weights that the hammer cocked and the trigger could be pulled. However had she afforded it? Had she spent her last groats on a toy for his son? It was an expensive piece.

Edmund couldn't believe his good fortune. He hugged the gun close, then held it away from him, stroking it, admiring it. "Oh, my goodness. Even the barrel is hollow, Papa. Now I can duel, now I can make Ellen take away the green beans." He clasped the pistol in one small hand and aimed it at Ellen. "Don't worry about the green beans yet, Ellen, I'm just practicing. After you don't bring me green beans anymore, will you pretend you're a bandit so I can practice shooting you?"

Ellen drew up very tall and straight. "Certainly, Lord Edmund, I am yours to kill."

Excellent, Evangeline thought, she'd brought out the killing instincts of a little boy.

"Papa, will you teach me how to aim properly?"

"Only if you promise not to torment Ellen."

"I promise," he said, but he wasn't looking at Ellen. He was staring at Evangeline with naked adoration. "Thank you, Eve. Phillip never gave me a gun. Rohan didn't either. Phillip doesn't like guns."

And Evangeline knew that Houchard had succeeded beyond his wildest dreams. Like this Phillip friend of the duke's, she would have never given a small child such a gift, but Houchard had said the boy would be mad for it, and so he was.

The three of them, Edmund skipping between Evangeline and his father, waving his wooden gun about, walked downstairs. The duke said, "Should we take your cousin riding with us, Edmund? We can show her perhaps one or two of the paths we take to go to our hiding places. It's a beautiful day. Umberto, our Italian gardener," the duke added to Evangeline, "says that there will be two days of summer weather, so hot that we'll be sweating like stoats."

She just stood there, her mouth open, shaking her head. "I'm sorry. I can't. I don't own a riding habit." She looked down at her muslin skirts. "I can't ride in this. I'm sorry." And, he thought, she seemed ready to burst into tears. He said easily, "How I wish that occasionally—just every once in a while—I was presented with a problem to test my mettle. Ah, not this time. Just a small problem that I've already addressed.

Perhaps you'll even consider me yet a prince among men. Evangeline, go to your bedchamber. I'll send Mrs. Raleigh to you."

"But why? There's nothing for it. This gown won't change itself into a riding habit."

"You have known me for nearly twenty-four hours, Evangeline. Have I given you any reason at all to distrust me?"

"No. But on the other hand, you're a gentleman, and gentlemen have odd notions about ladies' clothing and—"

He lightly touched a finger to her mouth.

"Go," he said, and she went.

"Trust Papa," Edmund said, but he was looking at his gun, not at her. She wondered if he even knew what they were talking about.

Thirty minutes later, Evangeline made her way down the wide, ornately carved staircase clad in an elegant royal blue riding habit, a plumed riding hat set jauntily over her plaited and pinned hair. She'd stared like an idiot when she'd opened the door to her bedchamber, and there'd been Mrs. Raleigh, holding the beautiful habit in her arms, smiling at her, telling her that it had belonged, naturally, to Marissa. "Indeed, her grace only wore it once, as I remember. It's from her favorite *modiste* in London, Madame Fallier."

"Oh, goodness. Surely I can't wear my cousin's riding habit. Besides, it wouldn't fit. I am much larger than my cousin. No, Mrs. Raleigh, I simply cannot wear my cousin's riding habit."

Mrs. Raleigh just shook her head. "Surely you don't think this was her only riding habit? It is merely the newest one, ordered just months before her death. His grace ordered it altered for you, Madame, early this morning. Unfortunately, I had only enough time to let down the hem. Since her grace's death, we do not have a seamstress on staff."

"Three inches," Evangeline said when she met the duke and Edmund, who was showing Bassick all the finer points of his gun. "Mrs. Raleigh let the hem down three inches. Look, it nearly covers my ankles."

"I see that it does. Ankles would surely overset me. This addition greatly relieves my mind."

She laid her hand on his arm. "It is very kind of you. Why, you even foresaw that I wouldn't have a riding habit and you ordered it up. You are too kind, your grace."

"I can see that more alterations are in order." He was staring at her breasts. She hunched forward, and he laughed. "No, don't do that. I suppose Mrs. Raleigh has some ideas on enlarging the jacket at least another five inches?"

"She said that she would have to add material from the skirt. The waist is too tight as well."

"I hope the skirt has enough extra material to—ah—cover your other parts."

Bassick frowned at the duke and cleared his throat.

"You acted very quickly," she said.

"Yes, I tend to act quickly when meticulous deliberation isn't required."

She knew he was jesting with her. But she didn't understand what the jest was, and so she just nodded.

"So that went sailing right over your head, did it? I'm shocked, utterly stunned really, that you don't understand my impertinent reference, Evangeline. The sainted André, surely he knew about easing into things, about moving forward to the next step only after being completely certain when it was appropriate to move forward?"

She stared him down. "He was very deliberate."

"Ah," he said, lifting his fingers to straighten the dyed blue feather on her riding hat. "I wonder, would you tell me what he was deliberate about?"

She couldn't think of a single thing. Then she thought of her father's meticulous housekeeping accounts and said, "André never paid the butcher until he remembered eating every haunch of beef that came from the shop. And that required that Cook keep all her menus, with proper notations. Now, that certainly demonstrates a high level of meticulous deliberation, don't you agree?"

He stared at her, fascinated. "A haunch of beef?"

She gave him a triumphant look and called out, "Edmund? Are you ready to go? Would you show me all your special paths?"

Edmund, who had stuffed his gun into the belt of his trousers, walked out the front doors just in front of Evangeline, Bassick standing behind them as he said in a low voice to the duke, "Your grace, she is a young lady."

"I know," the duke said, and frowned after his son, who was gesticulating toward one of the Chesleigh peacocks. "Yes, I know. It's strange." He shook his head.

Bassick frowned at his master, watching him follow the young lady in question and his excited son. However had she known to bring Lord Edmund a gun? It was his experience that ladies couldn't even bear to look at one of the ugly things. She was an unusual young lady, he was certain of that. He wondered what was in his master's mind.

Bassick heard the duke call out, "Do the riding boots fit?"

"No," She said, turning to face him. "They pinch. All of me is bigger than Marissa." She stopped and lifted the skirt of the riding habit to show her own short walking boots. "It really doesn't matter; mine are fine. But I do thank you for lending me the habit, truly."

"I'm not lending you anything. The riding habit is yours, as are all of Marissa's other gowns."

"You are kind, but I will not take my poor cousin's clothes."

"Why not? The cost of her wardrobe would support a small village for a year. The clothes are merely hanging in her armoire, currently of use to no one. My mother taught me to despise waste. So, you are assisting me to be virtuous.

"Besides, having you well dressed will make my neighbors think more highly of me."

"Papa, I just shot Rex!"

"Not a clean shot," the duke called out. "He's still staggering around. The peacock," he added to Evangeline.

"Oh, dear, I didn't want him to do that," she said. "That poor bird."

"What did you expect him to do with a toy gun?"

She looked distressed. He lightly touched his fingers to her chin. "Don't worry. It's a wonderful present. I will have a father-to-son talk with him later, but I can't imagine what I will tell him. From what I remember, children are bloodthirsty savages, at least all the boys I knew. We dispatched each other with swords, knives, rocks, tree branches, boulders, you name it. Actually, I wouldn't mind it a bit if Rex would go to his fowl rewards. The blighter never shuts up, except perhaps now, since Edmund shot him."

Rex squawked and Edmund shot him again.

The duke called out, "Edmund, tuck your gun back into your belt and ask McComber to saddle Pansy for you."

The Chesleigh stables stood in splendid isolation near the north wing of the castle. Just outside in the yard, the scent of freshly cut hay mixed with the salty smell of the sea. There was a slight rise just off to the right of the stables, and Evangeline walked there, then stood still, staring out over the water, some three hundred yards beyond the rugged promontory upon which the castle was built. The water was deep blue, calm save for the frothy white caps of the waves breaking on the beach. For the moment she felt almost carefree, as if nothing could touch her here. But it was a lie, of course. It was an odd thing, to live a lie.

"You can't see France, even on the clearest of days. If you like, we can take my yacht to the Isle of Wight. I own a small estate near Ventnor. Edmund loves it there. There's a protected cove where he swims, and a small sailboat I bought him last summer."

"I enjoy sailing," she said. "I've never sailed in the sea. It is different, is it not?"

"Oh, yes. You'll see. It's far more exciting. Do you swim well?"

She nodded, turning to follow him back to the stable yard. Why, she wondered, had he spoken about visiting the Isle of Wight, and what had he really meant about deliberations?

Chapter 11

"McComber," the duke called to a tall, gaunt man dressed in homespuns and wearing the most beautiful leather boots Evangeline had ever seen. He was as gnarled and weathered as an old witching oak tree, and looked as strong as Hercules.

"Good day, yer grace. Emperor's snorting his head off, heard ye, he did. He wants a good gallop, and ye can wager yer best carriage he'll try to hurl ye off. I thought Biscuit could do the young lady. Tommy's saddling Lord Edmund's pony."

Edmund, hearing his name, stuck his head out the open stable door. "I'm showing Tommy my gun, Papa," he shouted, then disappeared inside again. They heard popping sounds.

"I don't know how well you ride," the duke said to her. "Biscuit is a sweet old girl who's never caused anybody a moment's worry in all her twelve years. She loves McComber's apple pieces. Give her just two slices, and she'll swim the Channel with you and three pieces of luggage tied to her back. Give her an entire apple, and she'll seduce every stallion in the area."

"Aye," McComber said, "that's true enough. She's a good girl, my Biscuit, a plodder, but that's just fine if that's what ye need. Biscuit is the only mare her former grace would ride." McComber shrugged his massive shoulders, giving her a look that clearly said, *You're probably not much at all on a horse, so give over. Ride the sweet old girl.*

A great black stallion, with a white stripe down his nose, came prancing out of the stable, held by a nervous-looking stable lad. He was at least seventeen hands high, utterly magnificent, and knew it. He sent a look at the duke and reared back his head, snorting loudly. It sounded like a challenge to Evangeline. The duke laughed and strode to his horse.

"He's incredible."

"Aye," McComber said, his eyes on the man who was now being butted backward by Emperor's mighty head. "The stallion is a pretty boy as well. He's full of vinegar, he is. His grace would kill for that animal. His father brought him four years ago, a gift to his son."

"The duke's father, he was a good man, a good father?"

If McComber thought this an odd, too personal question, he didn't let on. He scratched the side of his head. "Aye, his old grace was big and strong, loved life and his family more than any man I've ever heard of. He shouldn't have died when he did. A stupid accident it was. He tried to stop two friends dueling, and he was the only one to get killed."

"That's horrible. What happened?"

"My master"—he nodded toward the duke—"he went to see both men after it happened. Odd thing was that they both left England only three days later. Left their families here and picked up and left. Never heard of them again. I heard him tell her grace, his mother, that he'd rather have shot both of them and left the bastards in a ditch to bleed to death, but he knew he couldn't get away with it. So his grace just made sure they lost everything that was important to them. Ah, there's sweet old Biscuit."

Good God, to have your father killed so stupidly. She wondered what she would have done. She looked up to see a lovely, gentle old black mare, all flowing mane and black and white withers, swaybacked, sweet-eyed, blowing softly.

The thought of those two horses side by side, one of them snorting and rearing, the other plodding and swishing her tail, made Evangeline laugh. "Oh, no, McComber, not dear Biscuit. That would be a travesty. Have you another horse with perhaps enough spirit and heart to keep pace with Emperor?"

The duke, who'd just been nearly knocked into a bush by his exuberant stallion, called out, "McComber, get her Dorcas. We'll test her mettle."

Dorcas proved to be a velvety bay mare whose brown eyes held wickedness. She was much smaller than Emperor, but she had strong legs, a deep chest, and a proud head. Evangeline drew a deep breath. It was possible she was being a bit impetuous. She hadn't ridden since she and her father had returned to France. She looked up briefly at the clear summer sky, so blue it could have been August. She felt a trickle of perspiration at the small of her back. She gave a brief prayer and sent it winging upward. If her prayer wasn't answered, well then, it was a beautiful day to take a toss. At least she wouldn't have to worry about breaking her arm on a slick of ice.

The duke strolled over, Emperor walking behind him, his reins loose, chewing on an apple slice from McComber. The duke cupped his hands and tossed her into the saddle. Dorcas wasn't seventeen hands, but she was high enough off the ground for Evangeline to think again that it had been a very long time indeed since she'd ridden. She stared down at the gravel drive that was surely an inordinate distance away. Even before, she hadn't been a horsewoman of extraordinary ability. This should prove interesting. She just hoped it wouldn't also prove a broken neck. Evangeline held Dorcas's reins firmly, knowing that Dorcas would lay her low if she gave her the smallest chance.

Pansy was a Shetland pony, all shaggy and gold, and Edmund would outgrow him in a year. At least Edmund wasn't trying to shoot him. The duke led the small cavalcade down the lime-bordered drive toward the homewood that lay to the north of the castle. He skirted the forest and headed east, paralleling the coast, and pointed out the various tenant farms as they passed the neat patchwork fenced fields.

"Papa, let's go down to the beach. I want to show cousin Eve my boat. Eve, do you want to see my boat? Say you do, please?"

"Oh, yes," she said. "Please, your grace." She was thinking that she had to become very familiar with the cove and all the terrain between there and the castle. She didn't know when Houchard would have someone come to her, but she knew it would be soon. Thinking of Houchard, of her father, she jerked on Dorcas's reins. The mare snorted and snapped up her head. She reared, then slammed back down to the hard ground, nearly knocking Evangeline's teeth loose in her head. It took her a few moments to bring her horse back under control.

"Evangeline, pay attention!"

"Just a wayward thought, your grace," she said, leaning over to pat Dorcas's neck.

If she remembered the directions Houchard had given her, the cave was in this cove, at the southern end, just before the out-jutting finger of land. "Let's go, Edmund," she called out and wheeled Dorcas around to face the cliff.

The incline to the beach was slight because it cut back and forth across the cliff, easing very slowly downward, the path well trodden and very wide. The path appeared to be ancient. She wondered if some long-ago druid had walked down this way to the beach below. Evangeline turned in her saddle and looked back at the castle, judging its distance. It was a half mile, no more. The terrain wasn't hazardous. She wouldn't kill herself getting back and forth in any case.

Chesleigh's private stretch of beach was, Evangeline knew, blessed with a curved inlet surrounded by scrubby bushes and trees and hundred-foot, steep cliffs. It was indeed a very private spot, Evangeline soon saw, well hidden from the path above.

Traitors needed to be hidden, she thought, and wanted, quite simply, to fold up into herself and die. But she couldn't yield to conscience. If she did, it would mean her father's life. No one, nothing was more important than her father. And Houchard knew it.

Before Evangeline had a chance to swing off Dorcas's back, the duke clasped her waist and lifted her down. He didn't release her immediately, just stood there, staring down at her, his hands still at her waist, tightening just a bit, his fingers splaying to cover more of her, and then he said, "You're a big girl. I will enjoy waltzing with you. I won't get a crick in my neck."

"Then it's a good thing you're a big boy," she said.

He threw back his head and laughed, sending gulls careening into the sky overhead.

"Papa, what did Eve say to make you laugh? Can I shoot some of the gulls? There are dozens of them. Just a few won't matter, will it?"

"Shoot away, Edmund. You have more than enough bullets. As for your cousin Eve's humor, she put me in my place. Come along, Eve, let's show you Edmund's boat."

A half dozen gray-and-white bellied sandpipers scurried across the coarse beach sand as fast as they could run, as the duke and Evangeline walked toward a small sloop anchored at the end of a long wooden dock. Then Edmund ran in front of them, dashing onto the narrow dock. He was waving his gun in the air, shouting like a pirate after booty.

"Edmund, be careful," the duke shouted. He said to her, "The boy has no fear. He fell out of a tree six months ago right into a briar bush and came away laughing. It's natural, I suppose," he added, more to himself than to her. He turned to see that Evangeline had paused and was staring back at the cove and the surrounding steep cliffs. She appeared to be completely absorbed. He lightly touched his hand to her arm. "It's beautiful, is it not?"

No, she wanted to yell at him, it was terrifying, and she had no choice, no choice at all. He had welcomed her to his home, given his son into her care, provided her clothing, and she would betray him.

Evangeline looked down at the sand clumping on her boots. She wanted to howl. But she couldn't. She'd also been too obvious, studying her surroundings as if it were an assignment, which it was. She said quickly, "Yes, certainly. Smell the air, it's so very invigorating. I love the sound of the waves. They're endless, those sounds. We could all be gone, and still the sound would be there; it wouldn't matter that there was no one to hear it."

"Are you perhaps a changeling?"

"I don't believe so. My father always said that I was the picture of my mother when she was young. Now I'm more the picture of him."

"You misunderstand me. Your uncle and your cousin Marissa, both hated the sea. Marissa would never walk down here, said the salt air was too cold, and gave her gooseflesh. The noise from the waves made her head ache. As for the nasty salt spray, it made her hair stiffen into tight little screws."

"Actually, your grace, my uncle was afraid of the sea, for he nearly drowned when he was a boy. Perhaps he passed his fear on to Marissa. I wonder, though. Why did she consent to live here? It's not as if you don't have other houses."

It was impertinent, she knew, but it had come out of her mouth. She waited. He didn't change expression, just shaded his eyes with his hands to look at Edmund rocking himself in his small sloop.

"My father and mother believed it was romantic here at Chesleigh, just perfect for two young people newly wed. They returned to London, leaving us here." He laughed, but it wasn't a pleasant laugh. "This romance my father spoke of, I never imagined such a lunatic thing possible. Two people cooing at each other, whispering nonsense, looking into each other's eyes, spending hour upon hour in bed." He laughed again, and this time it was even deeper, uglier. "Well, the last certainly, but that has nothing to do with the finer emotions. After marriage to your cousin, I can still not imagine such a thing. The only time your cousin ever whispered to me was when she told me she never wanted me to touch her again." He sighed, slicing his fingers through his thick hair. "Forgive me. Leave be, Evangeline. Marissa was very young. She shouldn't have died. She would have loved her son. She would be living in London."

"I was told only that she died in an accident."

"Yes," he said. "Ah, you really want to know, don't you? Very well. Marissa was terrified she would die in childbirth. She didn't, but her terror only grew. When she became pregnant again, she went to this woman in Portsmouth to rid herself of the child. Her life bled away. She was dead before she was even back to the castle. A damnable waste. I didn't know until I found and read her journal after her death that she was so very afraid. I wouldn't have ever touched her again, had I but known."

"I'm sorry," Evangeline said.

"Yes, I know." He strode away from her to the dock, where Edmund was preparing to unloop the sloop's rope from the ring on the dock.

He called out, "Edmund, if you fall into the water and I have to come in after you, I'll turn you over to Bunyon. He'll pin your ears back, my boy, if my Hessians get soaked with salt water."

Edmund couldn't get the rope unlooped. He tried three times. Then he shot it.

Evangeline waited until father and son were talking together before she turned her attention back to the beach. But she pictured her cousin's face as she remembered her from all those years before. Poor Marissa. Poor girl. The duke was right. It was tragic.

She looked back toward the path, so wide and easy, trod upon by hundreds of boots and horse hooves over the years, over the centuries. Even Edmund's Shetland pony hadn't hesitated to go down the path. The three horses stood in the sand, nickering to each other, eyeing the stream of gulls that dipped and wheeled over their heads, just out of reach. She scanned the cliff face for a sign of the cave Houchard had told her about. Nothing. She thought she saw a shadowy indentation and walked toward it. No, it was just a sharp bend in the rocks. Where was the bloody cave?

She slewed about at a shout of laughter. The duke held Edmund high above his head, threatening, she imagined, to toss him into the water. Then he lowered Edmund and tucked him under one arm, like a small, wriggling package.

"I think he's half fish," the duke said as he set Edmund back on his feet.

"You mean, Papa, like Eve's half foreign?"

"Yes, that's exactly right." His eyes roamed over her, pausing at her breasts. He opened his mouth, then shut it. He said finally to his son, "Have patience, Edmund. We'll leave your cousin in a ditch somewhere and come back for a swim. If, of course, it stays hot a while longer. Do you think Eve would like to join us?"

"My gun would float," Edmund said.

"True."

"But we don't wear any clothes," Edmund said. "Girls always wear clothes."

"He is very young," the duke said to her.

Houchard had described him very well, but this man, he was so very alive, so outrageous, so utterly wicked. Such a short time she'd been here at Chesleigh, with him, and she felt that wickedness twining around her, burrowing deep inside her, and she liked it very much. She said, "I am very likely a stronger swimmer than your papa, Edmund. Perhaps if it continues this warm, why then, you and I will swim together and we'll leave your papa in a ditch. But you know, even though it's so very warm today, it's still February, the dead of winter. The water must be frigid."

"What's frigid?"

"It means," the duke said, "that a girl's parts would become too chilled to react. She wouldn't drown, she'd just freeze. She wouldn't be any fun at all."

She said, "I haven't the faintest notion what you just said, but it was probably perfectly wicked."

"Here you are, an old married woman, and you don't know anything about freezing up."

"I'm not old."

"You're older than I am," Edmund said. "And Papa says I'm quite the young gentleman now."

She looked from father to son. It was time to give up. She threw up her hands, laughed, and said, "I retire from the field, defeated."

"Good," said the duke. "It isn't healthy for a lady to ever win a battle. Remember that, Edmund. Although it's true that sometimes a gentleman must pretend that a lady wins. Remember that as well."

"I will, Papa, but I don't know what it means."

"You'll learn soon enough. I doubt the lessons involving the ladies ever stop until you croak it."

"You are a cynic, your grace."

"I have become a realist, Madame."

They said nothing more. Evangeline was vastly relieved when the horses climbed back up the cliff path with no hesitation.

Chapter 12

Dorrie, a slight, gentle-looking girl of eighteen, Evangeline's new maid, said as she fingered a pale yellow silk dress, "I remember this gown. Her grace wore it on Christmas morning. Goodness, it must have been five years ago, when I was just a young girl, newly here in service. She gave me my Christmas present herself—a sewing box. Mrs. Raleigh told her that I wanted to become a seamstress. So very lovely she was. Such a pity that she was taken so soon."

"You sewed for her?"

"Not then. She told me to do mending for the servants. I promise I'll be careful, Madame. I've learned a lot in the past five years. I'll make it more fashionable if you wish. You are tall. The ruffles wouldn't look well. You need simplicity in the styling."

"I agree with you, Dorrie. Remove all ruffles and anything else that moves you to remove it. As you can see, her grace and I were of a very different size. I am the maypole of the family." Or, as the duke had said, she was a big girl. And he'd held her waist between his two big hands.

Dorrie examined the seams, the hem, then said briskly, "When I'm finished, all the gowns will look as if they were made especially for you, Madame. And they won't look old-fashioned. His grace's mother sends me magazines with all the latest fashions. I read them constantly. You will look a dream, Madame."

Evangeline left her, wondering if Houchard, who seemed to know everything about the duke's family, had known that the duke would insist that she take his dead wife's gowns. Houchard probably assumed that the duke would more or less use the gowns as payment after he allowed her to seduce him.

She knew that Edmund was taking his nap. The duke was with his steward in the estate room. The castle was quiet, at least as quiet as it ever was with nearly fifty souls moving about in it. She went to the North Tower. It was late in the afternoon. She saw only a lone footman in this part of the castle. She smelled the tower room before she was even close to it. It was a sweet yet tart odor, like rosemary mixed with cinnamon. She intended to find out what Mrs. Needle had meant when she'd told her she had heat in her eyes.

The odor grew stronger as she climbed the winding wooden steps. She rapped lightly on the old oak door and heard Mrs. Needle's lilting singsong voice telling her to come in.

The old woman was standing in the middle of a circular room with windows cut deep on all sides, at least ten of them, thick wooden beams between them. It was an incredible room, divided into sections by thick silk screens. Tables curved against the walls, obviously built especially for this climber, especially for Mrs. Needle. On the tables were dozens of labeled jars in neat rows, three jars deep. There was a fire in the fireplace, a hob with a pot seated on it, sending out the cinnamon smell along with comforting warmth.

Even on a warm day like today, the fire felt good in this open room.

"Och, ye've come sooner than even I guessed ye would. Sit over here, little lassie, and I'll give ye a nice cup of herbal tea."

Evangeline nodded, and followed the slight old woman into the sitting area that faced the immense fireplace. A sleeping area was set in an alcove. The rest of the huge space was devoted to Mrs. Needle's herbal laboratory. While she prepared the tea, Evangeline walked to one of the tables and examined the labeled jars. DRIED ROSEMARY, she read. CRUSHED GINGER BERRY. ROSE PETALS. IRINGO ROOT. JAMARIC SEEDS. And so many others, names she'd never heard of. There were several small braziers, small pots set atop them. From one came the strong odor of roses. She breathed in deeply.

"This is a wonderful room, Mrs. Needle," she said, coming back into the sitting area.

"Aye," Mrs. Needle said as she pointed an arthritic finger toward a worn crimson brocade settee. Evangeline sat down. "His grace's father, Duke William, had it arranged just for me. He was a good lad, the former duke, strong and pure, loved his boy more than anything."

"I have heard that. His grace—the boy—appears to have cared mightily for his father as well."

"Aye, that's true enough. His grace was such a wild lad, always into some sort of trouble, hurling himself into adventures to make a parent shriek, but not Duke William. He just laughed and told his boy not to kill anyone, not to impregnate any girls, and not to cause pain. He would have given his life for his son. It was a sad day when Duke William died. His grace changed on that day. For the longest time he seemed sober as a monk; his eyes became cold and hard, all the laughter sucked out of him. Even now he doesn't try anymore to turn his mother's hair white. He's become staid." Mrs. Needle smiled, showing only two remaining teeth, both of them very white. "Aye, her grace still has hair as dark as a sinner's dreams, just a few threads of gray."

"I understand his grace married my cousin because his father wanted him to settle down."

"Mayhap there was something to that. I think Duke William was very fond of young Marissa. He wanted her for a daughter and knew if he didn't push his grace to the altar, some other gentleman would snap her up. And, as I said, his grace would have done anything for his father, anything at all, including marrying a girl he didn't love. Don't mistake me, lassie, the duke wanted her, and marriage was the only way he would ever have her in his bed."

Evangeline was appalled. She sat forward, shaking her head. "Oh, no. The duke married my cousin because he loved her. I was told that by the people I loved and trusted."

"Och, love, what a fanciful thought that is for a lad so young as his grace was when he met Marissa. He wanted her, little lassie, he wanted her in his bed and he didn't want to let her out of his bed, and all knew it. He made no bones about it. He was young and wild and randier than a goat. Lust is the guiding principle, the only motive for a young man, nothing more, ever. His grace was no different. He saw her and he wanted her. His father was pleased. His son's lust played into his plans perfectly."

She poured Evangeline's green herbal tea, which looked nauseating, into a lovely Wedgwood cup, then sat down opposite her. Evangeline took a very small sip. It was surprisingly delicious, like tart apples mixed with something sweet. Mrs. Needle drank her own tea, slurping it between her teeth, and continued. "It all seemed to go so well until young Marissa discovered she was pregnant. Then she changed. She was afraid she'd die birthing Edmund, but she didn't. But she remained changed."

"Marissa's mother died in childbirth. She was doubtless terrified of dying in the same way."

"I thought that was true until I spoke to her. She trusted me, you see, to save her. She spent time here, questioning me endlessly. Her labor wasn't arduous. I gave her laudanum to lessen the pain. Lord Edmund was born in just over six hours. She was just fine two days later. I even gave her herbs to dry her milk since she didn't want to nurse Edmund."

"Marissa was fortunate you were here."

"Aye, that fool of a doctor that his grace brought from London, he didn't want to give her anything. He believed that women should suffer, it was their lot, God's will. Bosh, I said, and gave her laudanum when he stepped out of the bedchamber. She was bleeding too much after the birth, and the fellow simply shook his head and said he hoped it stopped, for he had not an idea of what to do. I took care of her. She healed quickly, as I said, after just two days. But it still didn't seem to matter.

"I don't wish to speak more of Marissa. Forgive me for being blunt, but at my age every moment is a gift granted by God. I don't like to waste a single one of them. I know that ye don't want to be here. Ye're fighting yerself every minute about it. I wonder why. Perhaps ye'd tell me why ye came, came against yer will."

Evangeline froze. "You're a witch," she said.

"Och, mayhap it is so, but there's this feeling I get from ye. Ye're afraid. But the strangest thing—ye belong here. That's odd, now, isn't it?"

"You know why I'm here, Mrs. Needle. My husband died and left me with no money. I'm dependent on his grace's good will. I will be Lord Edmund's nanny. There's nothing at all odd about it. I'm most certainly not afraid of anything, at least anything that has to do with Chesleigh."

"Ye're a terrible liar, little lassie. Just terrible. Her grace spoke to me of ye several times. It was fond of ye she was. She wished she could see ye, see how ye were growing up, but her father and the former duke weren't speaking to each other, and thus yer father had to side with hers. Wicked it was."

"Do you know the reason for the falling out between the two families? I also missed my cousin, and Lord Edmund."

Mrs. Needle sipped her tea, then set the cup on a small, very old table at her side.

"Her father didn't sever the connection. Far be it from Old Rolfe to close off the till when his pockets were to let."

"I don't understand what you mean, ma'am. Marissa's father was an honorable gentleman, and a man of some means."

"Rolfe was a gambler, little lassie. He spent three fortunes. I believe he's now spending a fourth fortune, one that he managed to steal by marrying his son to an heiress. Poor girl, with Old Rolfe as a papa-in-law."

"My father never told me that," Evangeline said. "Surely you are mistaken."

"Believe what ye want to believe. Old Rolfe never paid a single sovereign of the girl's dowry to Duke William, not even a sou." The old woman laughed.

"Oh, goodness. That bespeaks a fine gall, Mrs. Needle."

"Aye, a very fine gall. He's still doing so, as far as I know. I listen, but there's no more to hear since Marissa died. Now, as for ye, little lassie, why don't ye tell me what is troubling ye?"

Evangeline was silent as a post.

"Ye're impetuous, just as she was, but ye've known a very different life. Yer English mother was the saving of ye, child. She gave ye balance, curbed yer willful ways. Ye're proud, but not so proud that ye'd lose sight of what is right. Aye, and that father of yers, a beautiful man he was. I remember him very well from the wedding. A beautiful laugh he had as well. I'm sorry to hear he died. Odd, but I hadn't expected that. It jest doesn't feel right."

"He had a very bad heart."

Mrs. Needle just frowned at her, then turned to frown into the fire.

Evangeline's eyes fixed on Mrs. Needle's face. "How could you know about my mother? Indeed, what can you possibly know of my character? You never met me until yesterday."

"I've lived for a very long time. I see things, ye must have guessed that already, and I know people, lassie. And of course her grace spoke of yer family. It's true of many people that their character shines in their eyes. You are one of those, Madame."

Evangeline moistened her lips. "You said I had heat in my eyes. What did you mean?"

The old lady's nearly empty mouth smiled wide. "Ye're all interested in that, are ye? I don't blame ye. It's a fine thing, having heat in yer eyes. Ye'll find out soon enough. Yer life is just beginning. I only wish ye'd tell me what bothers ye. Ye feel fear and the oddest thing—ye also feel tremendous guilt."

Evangeline jumped to her feet. "I shouldn't be here, that's why," she said, and banged the cup and saucer beside Mrs. Needle's on the small table. "I should never have come to Chesleigh. Please, you mustn't speak of this to anyone. There's nothing to it. Just forget, Mrs. Needle. I beg of you, just forget what you feel, what you think you see in me."

"I won't tell anyone anything. Except for the duke. I tell his grace everything. He's my proud boy, my beautiful boy."

"He is much more than that. He is utterly without inhibition. He is outrageous. He's also very amusing." She dashed her fingers through her hair. "I didn't expect him to be anything like the way he is."

Mrs. Needle cocked her head, her eyes intent on Evangeline's face. "His grace has tempered his wild ways, moderated his appetites. He's become a good man. He awaits the mate of his heart to become happy as his father was."

"You speak of love as though it was fate."

"For some it is."

"I don't believe there is a single special person on this earth made just for the duke, made just for me. The chances are too great of that female or that male ever coming anywhere near the duke or me."

"Aye, ye'd think that. It only makes sense. The world is a grand place, more people than one can imagine." The old woman smiled at her and nodded. Her eyelids drooped. Evangeline just stood there, staring at the old woman, who looked to be on the verge of falling asleep under her nose.

"I will leave you, Mrs. Needle. Don't get up. Thank you for the tea."

"Think about what I've told ye. Come back."

"I'll come back."

"I'd like to hear tales of this husband ye said ye had. Nay, don't tell me tales now." Mrs. Needle's eyes were very open now, sharp, filled with knowledge. "Ye know, little lassie, loyalties are sometimes dreadful burdens. They tear and rend us, even blind us if we let them."

"That's true, but it hasn't anything to do with me. Good-bye, Mrs. Needle."

As she let herself out of the North Tower room, she heard the old woman's soft snoring. Was she so very obvious that one could just look at her and tell that all was not well? No, surely not. The old woman was a witch, although Evangeline had never before believed in witches.

Dorrie arranged Evangeline's hair in two thick braids, plaiting them together atop her head. She pulled free loose tendrils around her face, several falling down her neck. It was an attractive style on her. She looked at herself in the long mirror, aware that Dorrie was standing behind her, awaiting her reaction. She smiled at her image. The yellow silk gown, high-waisted and cut low over her breasts, fell in soft folds to the floor. Dorrie had removed the adorning flounce, indeed made the gown over, and it now fit her as if it had been made for her.

Both of them knew it was a success. And she needed a success. Mrs. Raleigh had told her just an hour before that the duke was entertaining, and he desired her presence. Evidently, he'd already sent word to Dorrie since the beautiful gown had been ready and waiting for her.

She drew up short as Bassick moved to open the

door to the vast salon. The sound of a girl's sparkling laugh reached her ears nearly at the same moment as she saw the elegant young lady, laughing still, her white hand on the duke's black sleeve. She saw a much older lady, a huge diamond tiara balancing precariously on her iron gray hair, rouge spotting her cheeks red, seated near the fireplace, a gentleman standing on each side of her.

"Madame de la Valette," Bassick said in his deep voice.

Everyone in the room turned toward her. What the devil had she gotten herself into now? Who were these people? All she'd wanted was to be left alone so she could betray the duke and keep her father safe. She closed her eyes a moment, then opened them wide, smiled, and walked into the drawing room.

The young lady, whose hand was still resting possessively on the duke's arm, looked up and smiled at her. She was a blonde, so fair her hair looked nearly silver in the candlelight. Her eyes were a pale blue, laughing eyes, and Evangeline imagined that a smile was her constant companion.

"Do come in, Madame," the duke said easily, walking toward her. His dark eyes started on her hair, and she saw him nod in approval. She wanted to tell him that she'd even pinched her cheeks to bring color to her face, something she'd never done before in her life, and didn't understand why she'd done it now. He should look at her face, yes, and nod in approval. No, he was looking intently at her breasts, she knew it, and he knew that she knew it. He gave her a wicked grin as he took her hand, raised it to his mouth, and lightly kissed her wrist. "You look beautiful, but of course, you know it."

"Stop looking at my bosom. I have other parts that are just as nice."

"I'm not at all certain that you meant to say that. What parts are just as nice? Are these parts that would enchant me further south? Or perhaps these parts are tucked behind your ears? Later, you will tell me all about these parts. Perhaps I will concur with you, perhaps not. As for your breasts, it gives me great pleasure. Actually, they give me great pleasure. I wish my grammar to be correct, particularly in a situation as important as this one.

"Ah, Dorrie did a fine job on this gown. Now, before you forbid me to do other equally innocent things, let me introduce you to my great aunt, Lady Eudora Pemberly, and her goddaughter, Miss Felicia Storleigh. The gentleman with the wild-tossed hair who looks like he's just come in from a high wind, although his aim is to look dashing and romantic, is Lord Pettigrew, Drew Halsey by name. And this is Sir John Edgerton, a dapper gentleman who fancies himself as great an arbitrator of fashion as the departed Brummel. Both gentlemen just arrived from London not above an hour ago. Ladies, gentleman, my cousin, Madame Evangeline de la Valette, recently arrived from Paris."

Evangeline nodded politely to everyone, but it was difficult. She couldn't believe he was here. It was too soon, much too soon. Her heart began to pound, loud slow deep strokes. She felt faintly ill. She stared, frozen in place, at John Edgerton.

Chapter 13

He looked just the same. Perhaps there was a dash more of gray threaded in the light brown hair at his temples. Naturally, it hadn't been all that long since she'd seen him last. His face was lean, an aesthete's face, her father had once said, the face of a man with too much on his mind and not enough time. And now he was here.

Because she was.

She'd hoped she would have more time. She felt fear flood her, and for a moment she could think of nothing to say. No, she wished she had a gun. She'd shoot the bastard. The damnable, traitorous bastard.

She'd known he would contact her, oh yes, she'd known, but there'd been no time to prepare herself. She'd been a fool. She'd spent just a few hours with the duke, and she'd forgotten for minutes at a time why she was really here. Now everything was real again, far too real, and she hated it and she hated herself.

"You don't need to introduce me to Evangeline," John Edgerton said in his easy, deep voice, stepping toward her. "I have known Madame de la Valette since she was a little girl with stubby braids, dirt on her nose, and scuffed boots."

He bowed deeply, took her stiff hand in his, and lightly kissed her palm. His lips were dry and cold. But his eyes, when he looked at her, were strangely soft and warm, as if none of this were real, as if he'd been only a man who'd liked the girl, remembered her fondly, as would a kind uncle, nothing more. He said, "It's a pleasure to see old friends, don't you agree, Evangeline? I hope you are well. May I say that you are looking beautiful? You're the image of your dear father, except you have your mother's eyes."

"What is this?" the duke said, frowning from one to the other. Edgerton was still holding her hand. She looked odd, as if she were afraid to move, which was ridiculous. "You know her, John?"

Evangeline pulled her hand from John Edgerton's grip, and her voice, when she finally got the words out, was smooth and calm. "Yes, I know him. It's been a very long time. This is quite a surprise, Sir John. I hadn't expected to see you, particularly this quickly." They were nearly the same height. Her eyes met his, but she saw nothing in his eyes or in his expression except pleasure at seeing her. He was a master of lies, as well he should be, since his entire life was a lie and no one had appeared to have ever noticed. Well, what had she expected? To see the word *evil* written across his forehead?

"I hope all surprises aren't bad, Evangeline," Sir John said, only this time his eyes, warm and now caressing, strayed to her chest. The duke saw it. He also saw red. He drew back, surprised at himself. Good God, what was the matter with him? This woman was nothing to him, nothing at all, a relative who wasn't really all that much of a relative at all. Ah, he was feeling protective since he'd recognized her as a relative, since she was now, after all, under his protection. Yes, that was it. It was in his *seigneur's* blood to feel like he wanted to smash John Edgerton, who'd had the gall to stare at her breasts.

Sir John said easily, just a touch of humor in his voice, "Ah, I see your cousin hovering, Evangeline. He obviously believes I'm monopolizing you far too early in the evening. Yes, you must make your curtsy to Lady Pemberly. She's a dragon, but her fire won't burn you, just scorch a bit. You and I will speak at greater length after dinner. There is so much you and I have to discuss. So much time has past since we last saw each other, hmm?" He turned to the duke. "I haven't seen Evangeline for nearly two years. I knew her parents."

And Edgerton was seeing too much of her, the duke thought, wanting to strangle his friend, but knowing at the same time that it was absurd. He watched Evangeline turn to make her curtsy to his aunt Eudora. He heard her speaking, her voice too soft, indistinct for him to make out the words. What the devil was the matter with her? He looked back at John Edgerton, but he was now speaking to Drew Halsey, gesticulating with those long, thin hands of his.

"So you are Marissa's first cousin," Lady Pemberly said, looking her up and down. "There's no remarkable resemblance. Your hair is a rather muddy blond whereas Marisa had golden hair. Marissa was too short and you're too tall. There are other differences, naturally."

"Yes, my lady. I'm a big girl, it's been remarked upon before."

"I did the remarking, Aunt Eudora," the duke said, and she jumped, not expecting him to be so close.

"I doubt not that you've remarked on too many

things, my boy. Now, Madame, your English is more than passable. You speak nearly as well as a native. You are to be congratulated on your tutors. With more lessons, a lot of study, you just might become perfectly fluent."

"My mother was English. Actually, I was raised in England, my lady. If you don't mind, I would claim fluency."

"I think she is scorched enough," the duke said. "Come, Aunt Eudora, don't try to run her off when she's only just arrived. Edmund now believes the sun rises on her. Think of my boy's happiness, if you please. Edmund now prefers her to either Rohan Carrington or Phillip Mercerault."

"I had no idea he would shoot the peacock, Rex," Evangeline said to Lady Pemberly, and the duke laughed, then told his great aunt all about the gift Evangeline had given to his small son. "Edmund also shot the rope tying his boat to the dock. As you can imagine, he didn't do a great deal of damage." To Evangeline's surprise, Lady Pemberly's painted face was in danger of cracking when she smiled widely, those witch green eyes of hers clearly willing to be amused now. "Well, my girl, if you bring a gun to a child, you must be more English than French. Gentlemen and their guns. One would think they sleep with them beneath their pillows. My father shot more tree stumps than my mother had bouts of the vapors. Yes, you did well. My boy here will teach his boy not to shoot anyone except highwaymen or perhaps the prime minister or the prince regent, both ineffectual boobs who undoubtedly deserve it.

"Now, Felicia, come and say pretty things to Madame. The good Lord knows your papa spent a goodly number of groats so that you'd learn how to be a proper lady. You've had more than enough time to practice your seduction skills on the duke. I saw that he wanted to laugh, but he's fond of you and so he didn't. It would seem to me that you enjoyed more success with Drew. He, at least, is still smiling. Come along before one of the gentlemen sends you back to the schoolroom or gives you a kiss behind the potted palm, which they would do only to encourage you in your efforts."

Felicia batted her fair lashes up at Drew Halsey, then toward the duke. "Is it true, your grace? You haven't fallen in love with me? You've just been putting up with me? Oh, goodness, I've tried and tried." Felicia dipped a credible curtsy to Evangeline. "A pleasure, Madame. I hope you will forgive our intrusion, but Godmama insisted that we come to dinner and she insisted that three hours' warning was certainly more than ample. The duke has a splendid cook, so she knew we wouldn't starve. And as Lord Pettigrew and Sir John had just arrived to pay us a visit, she volunteered their escort for the evening. His grace, of course, is in an agony of delight at our presence. He's assured us that he adores surprises."

Lady Pemberly rolled her eyes. The duke said only, "Just seeing you, Felicia, makes me feel old."

"I was thinking the same thing," Lord Pettigrew said, but the smile he sent Felicia's way wasn't at all that of a disinterested elder.

"Bah," Felicia said. "Both you and the duke are only twenty-seven, an ancient age for a lady—something I've never understood—but for you, gentlemen both, you're considered barely ripened, barely grown out of your greenness, barely ready to please a lady with your newly matured logic and affection and sincerity. At least that's what my mama says."

"Your poor mama could never string that many words together in her life, at least once you were born," Lady Pemberly said.

"Old," the duke said again. "Perhaps a cane is the next step in our decline, Drew. Sherry, John? Evangeline? Anyone?"

After the sherry was poured, Lord Pettigrew said in his deep voice, "John, you scoundrel, you gave no hint that you and Madame were already acquainted."

"As Felicia said, the duke likes surprises," said Lady Pemberly. "You said you knew her parents, John?"

"Yes, my lady. Her father was an excellent scholar and one of the most handsome men I've ever seen in my life. Evangeline is the very image of him. I'm sorry, Evangeline. I heard of his death earlier this year."

Evangeline said nothing, merely nodded toward him. Of course he would know everything to say, know how to keep all of his facts straight.

"When did you last see Evangeline?" the duke asked Edgerton.

"She was all of seventeen years old. And then she married and lost her husband. So much happening in such a short time. Life burdens us, doesn't it?"

She said absolutely nothing at all. She didn't want Edmund's make-believe gun; she wanted one of the duke's. She wanted it loaded, aimed at John Edgerton's head.

John said, "I remember it wasn't the happiest of times. Her mother had died the year before, all the ladies in the neighborhood were after her father, and Evangeline spent most of her time hiding out in the maple forest. I remember that I had to search you out several times when I visited. What did you do there?"

"Nothing much," Evangeline said, really wanting to say that she'd been avoiding him.

"A maple forest sounds vastly romantic," Felicia said, took a sip of her sherry, and looked as if she'd like to spit it up.

"Only you would think so," the duke said.

Felicia said to Evangeline, "As you've possibly noticed, the duke enjoys looking at me, but he doesn't like me to talk. It drives him to the brandy bottle, at least that's what Godmama tells me."

"Flutter your eyelashes and keep your tongue behind your teeth," the duke said easily. "That, my dear, will get you a husband quickly enough." He shook his head. "Poor fellow, I can just see him the morning after his wedding night. You'll doubtless be talking a mile a minute, telling him what he did right, going into great detail over what he did wrong, informing him what you want to have fetched up for breakfast."

"Oh, I don't know about that," Felicia said. "I always thought I'd be sound asleep the morning after my wedding night."

That brought instant and thick silence, until the duke said, "I don't suppose you also talk in your sleep?"

"I will have my husband tell you after I am married," she said, and grinned demurely at him, like a wicked little girl, knowing she'd bested him.

"I'm in charge here," Lady Pemberly said, "and look where things have headed, straight toward the nether regions and other sinful places. Madame, if you're close enough, box Felicia's ears. My child, if you say another so impertinent a thing, I will call off your come-out ball."

"I saw nothing wrong with what she said," the duke

said. "One hopes, after all, that she doesn't marry a clod."

"Then it must be you, your grace," Felicia said, clasped her hands to her bosom, and heaved. "I've heard Mama say you were so expert with the ladies that you were thus a rake, but since you were a duke no one could call you that, except to your back."

"I'm going to be ill," the duke said. "I'm not a rake, Felicia. I'm a sober fellow, a solicitous papa, a gracious host. Look at the lot of you. You're still here, aren't you?"

"Yes, yes, my boy," Lady Pemberly said, "you are all those things. But you will refrain from encouraging her. It's all well and good that you're an outrageous, outspoken gentleman who just happens to be very invigorating to look it. Yes, my boy, even I, a mature lady, notice how very nicely you present yourself to the world, whether you're trying or not. Also, you've a bit more of a brain than this impertinent eighteen-year-old baggage whom I got stuck with as a goddaughter."

"Godmama, I thought you worshiped me from the moment I appeared in the world. I was told that you begged and begged to be my godmother. That isn't true?"

Lady Pemberly rolled her green witch's eyes.

Lord Pettigrew said to Evangeline, "Don't mind them, Madame. It's been like that since I met the duke when we were boys, more years ago than I care to contemplate. Actually, they're all very fond of each other."

"Yes," she said slowly, taking a sip of her sherry, "I can see that."

Lord Pettigrew laughed. "Actually, I've known Felicia since she was born. I realized soon enough that she was indestructible. She enjoys being chewed upon. It keeps her sharp, she tells me. It also makes her the center of attention, you know, and that's a spot she likes to be in."

"You don't like her, Lord Pettigrew?"

"Oh, no, you misunderstand me," he said, giving her a dazzling smile. "I actually plan to marry the little twit. I want her to have her Season first. Every girl deserves a Season before she becomes a wife. I'm thinking she will do quite well as a June bride." He frowned toward the fireplace. "I do wonder what she will say after our wedding night. I wonder if perhaps I should worry."

"I won't comment on that. Does Felicia yet know of the happiness that awaits her?"

"A bit of irony there? No, but she will soon enough. Now, I hope you're not overly fond of conversing over dinner. If you are, I fear that you are in for an exhausting evening." He paused a moment, then called out, "Felicia, I was just telling Madame here that John and I find ourselves reduced to sign language when we are in your company, for we can't get a word in edgewise."

"I don't believe you, Drew," Felicia said, and walked quickly back to him. She looked up at him, blue eyes intent and shining, like she knew him better than she knew anyone else in the world, and perhaps she did, Evangeline thought. She poked him in the chest. "I've never seen any of this before. What is this sign language? Show me?"

The duke was watching his longtime friend John Edgerton watching Evangeline. Like a hawk looking at a helpless field mouse. What was going on here? What had he been to her when she was only seventeen years old, just a young girl, barely a girl, many years away from being a woman? Or maybe it was a hawk looking at a female hawk. The duke didn't understand the look John Edgerton was giving her. But he knew enough to be riled.

"What the devil is wrong with you, my boy?" Lady Pemberly called out. "You look all down in the mouth, a bit of anger mixed with frustration. Ah, I know. You lost a wager. Hah! I'll just bet it was a wager, over a filly—the two-legged variety."

The duke laughed, there was no hope for it. He'd find out quickly enough what a role John Edgerton had played in Evangeline's life. He said to Lady Pemberly, "My dear ma'am, I sincerely doubt there is a man in the kingdom who would wager against me on such an occurrence." He sent a look toward Evangeline, who was standing by the fireplace looking down into the flames, shut away from the rest of them for a moment. "Or a woman."

Lord Pettigrew laughed at that. "He's bested you, ma'am. I wouldn't bet on that, would you, John?"

"I did hear a bit of talk a while back that the duke lost a lady he wanted to one of his friends—Phillip Mercerault. Is that right, Richard?"

"Yes," the duke said, "I did. No one likes to be deprived of something he believes he wants, but it was for the best."

Evangeline was aware of what he'd just said. She realized that she hadn't heard anyone else; just when he'd spoken, every word was clear to her. A lady turned him down? "No," she said aloud, her brow thoughtful, all her attention focused on him. "That's quite impossible. I don't believe that." She realized then what she'd said, laughed a bit shrilly, and added, "I fear you're beginning to sound quite conceited, your grace."

She believed that? He was inordinately pleased. "No, Evangeline. I said I did indeed lose her. It was you who insisted that was impossible."

She flapped her hands in the air, spilling her sherry, which she forgot she was holding, and said, "I'm very hungry. I wonder where dinner is?"

"Come, Richard," Lady Pemberly said, "you make yourself sound like your heart was dashed into the rocks. Nothing could be further from the truth. Only your pride was hurt, my boy. You know as well as I do that Sabrina Eversleigh did exactly as she was supposed to do. Phillip as well."

"I would think so," the duke said. He added to Evangeline. "The lady is an acquaintance who wedded a good friend of mine. Nothing more." He turned back to his great aunt. "As for you, my lady, your informants would serve Napoleon well. Thank God there's no more need since the bastard's incarcerated on his island. Just look at your sources of information. Madame de la Valette arrived only yesterday evening, and here you are, not twenty-four hours later, at Chesleigh for dinner."

Evangeline wasn't at all surprised. It was more than likely that John Edgerton was responsible for their being here, not Lady Pemberly. She looked toward the duke, wishing she could apologize to him. For what she'd done. For what she would do to him. For what she wasn't and would never be.

"I try to do my best," Lady Pemberly said, and smiled widely, showing several missing teeth in the back of her mouth. She rose, shaking out her stiff purple satin skirts; surely the purple was just what Mrs. Raleigh would appreciate. "I trust that Bassick has seen to laying four more settings. I, for one, am ready for my dinner."

She turned to bend an autocratic look at Evangeline. "The duke tells me that you wish to remain at Chesleigh as Edmund's nanny. I was expecting a faded, very bland girl with a tepid temperament and no pretense to beauty. You are not what I expected. At my age, the unexpected could result in my heart stopping, and that is something I wouldn't like at all."

"Never would we want that," the duke said. "Now, as to Evangeline, she did arrive a rather sickly-looking mouse sort of lady. Just look at her now. Not even twenty-four hours in my company and she is blossoming, like a, er, daffodil." He rubbed his fingers over his jaw, clearly a pose. "Isn't that the yellow, rather stringy flower?"

"I wouldn't say that Madame is at all stringy," said Felicia. "On the contrary."

"I look to you for continued support, Felicia," Evangeline said.

Lady Pemberly actually snorted. "Support, you say? That's an uncertain commodity from Miss Loose Lips. I'll probably be ready for my grave before I find a husband for her, one, preferably, who is deaf. I only brought her, and not one of the available other charming young ladies with me this evening, so the duke wouldn't accuse me of sticking my nose into his business. However, my nose is already stuck. You are still unwed, Richard. Only one heir won't do. Pay attention now, my boy. Not another word will pass my lips about your black behavior over the past weeks. Your poor mama is at her wit's end trying to jolly you out of your mood."

The duke pulled the bell cord rather viciously, Evangeline thought. What black mood? She remembered then he hadn't been all that was charming when he'd come upon her in his library the night before. Had something happened?

She found out quickly enough when Lord Pettigrew said quietly, "I'm sorry, Richard. We still haven't caught the man who murdered Robbie Faraday. We know there is a spy in the ministry, but as to his identity, there's still no clue. Who am I trying to fool? There are probably many more than just one spy. It's driving everyone frantic."

Evangeline said slowly, "But I don't understand, Lord Pettigrew. Napoleon isn't there to torment us anymore. He's incarcerated on Elba. Why are there still spies?"

She knew that John Edgerton was looking at her, his eyes faintly puzzled. Why? Because she was fishing in waters that could easily drown her? He was afraid she'd turn on him?

Drew Halsey, Lord Pettigrew, smiled at the very beautiful woman who was nearly his height. "Whenever there is more than one man, Madame, there is more than one idea. Once there are two ideas, both fiercely held, then there will be great disagreement. There are still those who want Napoleon returned to the throne of France. There is still a comprehensive spy network working diligently for his return."

"And one of these spies murdered a man that the duke knows?"

"Yes, Robert Faraday was a good friend to us all."

"You, Lord Pettigrew, you work for the government?"

"Yes, I do. So does John and so does the duke upon occasion."

She simply couldn't believe it. How could Houchard expect her to accomplish anything when the duke was so involved, and not simply a disinterested aristocrat?

A friend of his had been murdered. Perhaps murdered by John Edgerton. Or even ordered by Houchard.

"Indeed," said John Edgerton. "We all do what we can, isn't that right, Evangeline?"

"Enough," the duke said. He hated thinking about Robbie, about his needless death. It gnarled his insides, made him so furious he wanted to yell.

"Let us hie ourselves to the dining room," the duke said.

Chapter 14

"Come with me to the library for a brandy."

It was late, after eleven o'clock. She'd heard the loud downstairs clock chime long ago. She didn't want to go with him. She wanted to crawl under the covers of her bed and never emerge. But she knew she couldn't let him see that anything was wrong. And so she nodded, smiling her acceptance as if she meant it. As she followed the duke, she remembered John Edgerton's words as they'd walked to the dining room for dinner: "I always knew you'd become only more beautiful. You know how much I wanted you."

"I was seventeen years old."

He'd shrugged. "Old enough. Women are always old enough. Then you turned away from me. You told your father that I was too old. I do believe the bastard agreed with you. I knew then that one day I would have him at my mercy." He paused a moment, running his knuckles lightly over her cheek. "And you as well, of course. Yes, and now it's happened. You will do exactly as I wish, Evangeline."

He was right. He'd gotten both of them, she thought. He'd had to stop when the duke had looked back at them, frowning. "Ah, I don't want to make him jealous. I'm pleased he already wants you. It should make things very simple if he does find out about you and your, ah, mission."

"Nothing would make anything simple. You murdered one of his friends, this Robert Faraday. Nothing would stop him, particularly a woman he wanted to bed, which isn't true in my case."

Once in the library, the duke walked to the sideboard. He poured each of them a glass of brandy. "It's rich and deep and sinful," he said, and clicked his glass to hers. He watched her over the rim of his glass.

"What do you think of my great-aunt Eudora and Felicia?"

"Lady Pemberly is very protective of you. Felicia, ah, one could never be bored in her company."

"And Lord Pettigrew?"

"He is charming. He plans to marry Felicia."

"The devil you say." A dark eyebrow shot up. "He told you that?"

"Oh, yes. I assumed you already knew. He told me he would let her know of her good fortune in due time. He wants her to have a Season before they marry."

"Good God." He swigged down the rest his brandy, turned, and stared into the fireplace. "Good God," he said again. "The ways of a man's heart are incomprehensible."

"I think they'll suit admirably."

"And do tell me what you think of John Edgerton."

This was the only person he really cared about. All the others were just a prelude. She knew it deep down. There was no reason not to tell him the truth about him, at least a good deal. She raised her chin. "I don't like him."

"Why?"

"He wanted to marry me. My father wouldn't consider it. I was only seventeen years old. Sir John was too old, much too old, and my father told him as much. I was surprised to see him this evening. However, since he is your friend, I will be civil to him if I ever have to be in his company again."

The duke shrugged, setting down his brandy glass. He felt better, much better, but that was ridiculous. Just because John had known her, just because he'd stared at her breasts—no, she didn't like him. That was excellent.

He said, "Both John and Drew work for the government, each following in his respective father's ponderous footsteps." He paused a moment. "I know that you dislike Napoleon. But you know, there are always villains skulking about. Please don't worry. You're safe here. I'll see to it."

She could only stare at him, and slowly, slowly, she nodded.

"I'm tired," she said when the silence stretched too long. "It's been a very long day. Full of surprises."

"Yes," he said "My great-aunt coming with very little warning. She frets about me. She wanted to make certain you wouldn't murder Edmund in his bed. Trust me, if she hadn't been sure of you, she would have moved in without a by your leave, and probably slept at the foot of your bed to keep a better eye on you."

"Yes, she is very fond of you."

He walked slowly to her, stopped in front of her, and looked down on her face. "I'm glad you're here," he said quietly. Like Edgerton, he lightly caressed his knuckles along the line of her jaw. She didn't want to pull away from his fingers as she had from Edgerton's.

"I'll take very good care of Edmund."

"I know you will. If I'd felt otherwise, I would have

tossed you into a ditch. Curious, isn't it? And you've been here only twenty-four hours."

"No, closer to thirty hours now. Actually I feel as though I've been here much longer. I'm very glad I came. I hope you don't mind."

That made him smile. "There are many things I mind. However, at this moment you're not one of them." Then his look became intent. She recognized the change in him immediately. To her surprise, she responded to it. Her hands came up to cover her breasts, she couldn't help it. "You're looking at me again."

"It's impossible not to."

"No, I meant that you're looking at parts again."

"Impossible not to."

"I'm going to bed now."

He stepped back. He didn't want to, but he did. He wanted to brush his knuckles over her breasts. He closed his eyes a moment, nearly feeling the softness of her white flesh. "Good night, Evangeline."

Evangeline opened her eyes and stared into the darkness. She rubbed her hand over her damp forehead, pushed her hair away from her face. Another nightmare, nothing more, nothing less. But it had been so real. She could still hear Houchard's voice, dark and cold. "You're too innocent for your nineteen years, Mademoiselle. You will be careful that the duke doesn't toss up your skirts and take you without your even realizing what he is doing. You will be careful that your innocence doesn't endanger your common sense. Your dear papa's life depends on your clear head and your commitment to us." He'd lightly rubbed her earlobe between his fingers. She'd jerked away, and he'd laughed.

She rose and pulled on her wool dressing down. She pulled on her old slippers and headed downstairs. She didn't want to go back to sleep anytime soon. She was afraid she'd see more of Houchard. She'd see if the duke had any books that looked interesting for reading in the middle of the night. She raised her single candle high in front of her as she walked down the carpeted corridor to the staircase.

The vast house was quiet for the most part. There were a few creaks and groans that gave her a moment's pause, but nothing to scare her into gray hair. Lying in her bed, bound to that terrible dream of thinking about why she was really here at Chesleigh, was far more frightening. The huge clock at the top of the central staircase began to chime. One short, loud stroke. She'd believed it much later. She was walking down the stairs, candle high, when suddenly the great front doors flew open. She froze where she stood.

It was the duke. A slice of moonlight cast him into relief in the doorway. She watched him kick the doors closed with the heel of his boot, stride into the entrance hall, his step none too steady. She stepped from the shadows, her lone candle held tightly in her hand.

"Your grace?"

His head whipped up, and for a long moment he simply stared at her. He ran his hand through his disheveled hair, muttered an oath under his breath. "Evangeline? What the devil are you doing out of bed? Why are you standing here in the entrance hall?"

"I couldn't sleep. I had a nightmare. I was going to your library to get a book. I'm sorry to have startled you."

"I'll join you in the library," he said. He strode to

her and took the candle from her hand. "You can tell me about this nightmare," he said over his shoulder.

She realized he was drunk, not staggering and clumsy, but still he'd drunk too much. She shook her head. Why had he left his own house to drink? Where had he gone? What bothered him so much? The death of his friend? "I'm coming," she called after him.

She followed him into the library and watched him jerk off his greatcoat and gloves and throw himself into a chair before the fireplace. There were only embers burning, deep and orange, not giving much heat. She came closer.

He was silent. She walked quietly to him and gently touched his shoulder.

He was a bit drunk, but he wasn't dead. He felt the heat of her hand. Slowly, he turned in his chair and closed his fingers over her wrist. "Why are you touching me?"

"You seem faraway, sad, perhaps. I don't want you to be unhappy."

"Ah." He pulled her wrist down and tightened her hand in his.

"Please don't break it, your grace. However will I control Edmund with just one hand?"

He looked at her hand held tightly in his. Then he dropped her hand. "Forgive me, Evangeline." He leaned his head back against the back of the chair and closed his eyes. "You know I'm drunk."

"Yes. I wonder why. What troubles you?"

He turned penetrating, dark eyes up to her face and said unexpectedly, "Do you often have nightmares?"

"No, not really. It's just that the recent weeks have been rather trying to me. Why are you coming home so very late? Why did you leave here to drink?"

"Mind your own affairs, Madame. I don't justify

myself to anyone, least of all to a young widow who is here alone with me in my library and it's after midnight and she's wearing only her nightclothes. And she touches me."

She couldn't explain why she did it, she just did. She eased down onto her knees beside his chair and looked up into his dark-shadowed face. "My nightclothes are more modest than a nun's. Don't try to embarrass me, although you do it very well. I'm sorry that you're unhappy. I'm just worried about you."

"I don't want or need another mother." His eyes narrowed. It wasn't just that she was wearing her nightclothes. Her hair was loose down her back, some of it falling over her shoulders.

He reached out and began to wrap hair around and around his hand. "I don't think it was very wise of you to come in here with me, Evangeline. You're not ignorant. You've been married. You know what men want with women."

"You took my candle."

He kept wrapping her hair around his hand, slowly, ever so slowly. "I'll let you keep to that little lie, at least for the time being. So the pleasure of my company had nothing to do with it?"

She'd never known a man like him could exist. She was completely aware of his hand wrapping around her hair, pulling her close now, and then he leaned toward her. His fingertips traced the line of her jaw. He tugged the mass of hair wrapped about his fingers to bring her face even closer.

Evangeline fell utterly still, as if she'd been set here with this man, his hand in her hair, his fingertips lightly caressing her. She wouldn't have moved if the house was on fire. She just closed her eyes, waiting to see what he would do.

"Did I tell you that your hair is exquisite?" She opened her eyes to see him gently rubbing a thick tress against his cheek. A fleeting look of anger or pain—she couldn't be certain which—darkened his eyes.

"Your grace?" She closed her fingers over his large hand. "I'm not your mother. I have no wish to be your mother. I just want you to be happy. Is it the lady who wed another man? This Phillip Mercerault?"

He pulled slowly away. She wished in that moment that she'd kept her mouth shut. She wanted him close, wanted him to touch her. She couldn't believe it, but it was true. Then she felt cold filling her. She was betraying him.

She watched him look into the fireplace. He was still holding her with his hand wrapped around her hair, but more loosely now. "Sabrina?" he said. "No, she didn't break me, Evangeline. There are other things at work here that make me crazed with helplessness." He sighed. "You're a romantic, like most ladies. No, I didn't love her. No, she didn't break my heart, whatever that means. I sometimes believe that such an emotion is quite beyond my ken. But I wanted her. I wanted to take her to bed, and that, Evangeline, is what most men want of women, nothing more, nothing less. Marriage is forced upon us so that we have an heir that springs from our loins and not from another man's."

"I can't believe you're saying that. Why would a woman do such a thing? There is love, at least I've heard that there is. I've read about it. So much has been written, so believably. Just because I've never felt it doesn't mean that it doesn't exist."

She realized in that instant what she'd said. She grew utterly still, her eyes locked on his face.

"Ah, we're back to the esteemed André, that superior man who was your husband. You didn't love him. What was it, a marriage of convenience? At least you have to know that I'm speaking the truth—a man weds a woman so that he can bed her whenever and wherever he likes."

"André wasn't like that. It wasn't a marriage of convenience."

"You didn't love him."

"Of course I did. I was speaking philosophically."

"I believe," he said, and there was something intent in his dark eyes, something that held her and frightened her and excited her all at the same time, "that you lie more fluently that you doubtless speak French. I will have to show you, remind you how things really are between a man and a woman."

He lowered his head, and she felt his warm breath at her temple. She felt his hand stroke her throat, and when his lips lightly touched hers, she felt something she'd never felt before. It was hot and deep in her belly and spreading throughout her body and she didn't want it to stop, ever. His mouth was open, his tongue against her lips, pressing lightly. She parted her lips to feel his tongue. Without realizing it, she arched toward him, clasped her hands about his shoulders, drawing him closer to her. He released her mouth and rained gentle, caressing kisses upon her eyes, her cheeks, the tip of her nose. He drew back a moment, and his eyes were on her breasts. He watched his fingers move downward. Then he watched them begin to mold her breasts through her cotton nightgown and wool dressing gown. It wasn't enough, and it was more than she could begin to imagine.

"Oh," she said, and leaned into his hands.

"So many clothes," he said. She didn't move,

scarcely breathed when he pulled her dressing gown open. She watched him as he unfastened the ribbons of her nightgown. She knew this wasn't right. She didn't know this man. He was going to see her breasts. She should stop him, but she wasn't about to. All she wanted was his hands on her bare skin.

She shuddered when his hands slipped into her opened nightgown and lifted her breasts. She breathed in sharply through her nose. Her back arched. What she was feeling, she couldn't have imagined such a thing. It was too much, and, at the same time, not nearly enough.

"Yes," he said, "give me more of yourself. I knew you'd be beautiful. You're very white, Evangeline, and your breasts fill my hands. You like me touching you, don't you? You like my hands moving over your flesh."

He leaned down and began kissing her again even as his hands played over her, stroked her.

She was betraying him. She felt awash with bitter knowledge. She pulled back slowly. His hands stilled on her breasts. She felt heavy and, oddly, very hungry. She looked at his mouth, at his dark eyes. "I'm sorry, your grace. I shouldn't be here. I'm sorry."

"No, I'm the one to be sorry," he said on a sigh, but still he didn't release her breasts. "You're so beautiful. I hadn't ever thought this could be so difficult." Again, he was looking down at his hands holding her breasts, feeling them, stroking them. "I must release you, I must." Slowly his forehead furrowing in near pain, he eased his hands away from her. He put his hands in his lap, folding them. He leaned his head back against the back of the chair and closed his eyes. "I wouldn't dishonor you. You're under my protection. You're safe from everyone. In particular, you're safe from me. You have to be. Please, close your clothing, Evangeline. Please. I can't touch you again. It was hard enough for me to stop this time."

She stared up at him, mute, not moving. He wasn't looking at her, but she felt him, felt him throughout all of her.

He opened his eyes again and looked down at her. "You're a very responsive woman, Evangeline. The sainted André was a very lucky man to have you."

"No," she said, without thinking. "Really, this is the first time—oh, no. I'm sorry."

She still made no move to cover herself. The duke stared down at her bowed head. She was passionate. What if she hadn't stopped him? He would have stopped himself, then. He wasn't an animal. Her words struck the wrong chord in his mind. He shook his head. He was drunk. Everything was strange, off key when he was drunk, which he was too often these days. He had to bring it all to a halt. It was time to return to his life the way it had been, before Sabrina, before Robbie's violent murder.

He would prove to himself that he was again in full control. "Close your nightgown."

Still she didn't move. It seemed that she couldn't move. He laced her nightgown together over her breasts. He pulled her wool dressing down closed. Then he sat back, his chin resting on his fist. His flesh tingled from touching her.

"Was your husband a selfish man who didn't care for your pleasure?"

Why had he thought that? She shook her head, trying to drag her wits back into her brain. "I don't know what you mean."

He stood up quickly, pulling Evangeline to her feet with him. "I mean that you wanted me touching you, pleasuring you. You were yielding and giving, and you enjoyed everything I did to you. Didn't you enjoy your husband touching you? Caressing you?"

She stared up at him, saying nothing. After all, what could she say?

He looked like he wanted to strangle her. He stepped away, his voice brisk, cold. "Such a thing will not occur again, as long as you are living under my roof. I wouldn't ever want you to fear me or take me into dislike."

She felt torn apart by guilt. How could she do this? She merely nodded, her head down.

He felt hot lust twist in his groin. "You must go to bed, Evangeline. It's very late."

She stared at him silently for a long moment, then said in a curiously sad voice, "I could never fear or dislike you. That would have to fall to you. But you're right, it mustn't happen again. Good night, your grace." She picked up her candle with a trembling hand and walked quickly from the library, quietly closing the door behind her.

When the duke lay in his own bed some time later, he decided that this young woman who was dependent upon him, who would see to the care of his young son, had to be safe from him. He thought of tasting her breasts and shuddered. He would leave for London as planned, at the end of the week. She tempted him more than any other woman he'd ever known. She wasn't the most beautiful woman he'd ever known, far from it. He had no idea what drew him to her, but something did. He would put distance and time between them to clear his mind of her. It was what he wanted.

Chapter 15

Evangeline stood in the long picture gallery, the morning sun spilling down on her through the high, diamond-shaped window panes. It was just after eight o'clock in the morning. Already it was promising to be the second very warm day in the middle of February, a phenomenon that surely couldn't last after today. She looked up at a seventeenth-century Duke of Portsmouth, who looked out onto the world with a particularly stringent expression on his long, handsome face. She said to that long-ago duke, "Your grace, my father told me that all the young men I'd met were just that—young. In addition, they were woefully inexperienced. I pointed out to him that they were also possessive, like Henri. Goodness, Henri didn't want me out of his sight. He wanted me with him, always with him, as if he was afraid that I'd go haring off with one of his friends. My father laughed when I told him that and just shook his head. I remember he said that I was to be patient, that boys became men, just as girls become women." She paused and looked down at her slippers, not Marissa's. Marissa's were much too small. But the skirt that lightly touched those slippers was one of Marissa's, a rich forest green muslin with beautiful gold braid twisted beneath her breasts and braided trim for the circular neckline. She looked up at the painting again. The duke still looked stringent and not one bit interested in what she was saying. After the previous night in the duke's library, after he'd had his hands on her bare breasts, well, there was a lot to think about. She said, her voice quieter, a frowning voice to match her thoughts, "But Papa wasn't right. I've met older men, men he'd call sophisticated, but there was nothing there, nothing at all, except perhaps boredom." She drew in a deep breath. "I must be going mad to stand here talking to you. I know it, but at least I know you won't give away any confidences. Oh, dear. What I did last night, what I allowed the duke to do, it was wondrous. It was beyond anything I could have imagined. But I shouldn't have ever followed him. I guess I wanted to go with him, to see what he would do, to hear what he would say—I can't lie to myself about that. You still don't answer, and I'm beginning to expect you to. Ah, I'm well and truly mad."

The duke drew back behind one of his mother's favorite antiquities, a white marble bust of some ancient playwright in Greece. He was smiling. He wondered how much of her one-sided conversation with a ducal ancestor he'd missed out on. What he'd heard made him halt in his tracks. Wondrous, was it? It made him sweat. He'd wanted to lay her out on the carpet in front of the fireplace. He wouldn't have cared if she was on top of him or vice versa, truth be told. He'd wanted to kiss her until she was whimpering, and then he'd wanted to come into that beautiful body of hers and—

"Your grace. You are standing here seemingly without any particular purpose. A gentleman of your stature should always have a purpose. Is there some sort of problem?"

He turned to see Bassick, not a foot from him, looking for all the world like one of the dons at Oxford. Bassick was just standing there as well, also seemingly without purpose, looking as aloof and determined as that damned former duke who was being confided in by Evangeline. A lovely name, that. It was soft on the tongue. He liked the feel of it in his mouth, sounding in his mind. How long had Bassick been there? "You walk more quietly than a bloody shadow, Bassick."

"One endeavors, your grace."

"Is that sweat I see on your forehead?"

"It is too early to sweat, your grace, but perhaps later I will have to dab my handkerchief to my brow. I believe we may regard this as very strange weather for February in England. It is weather that properly belongs to August. Now, may I assist your grace?"

"I don't need anything. I merely heard Madame speaking and wondered who was the recipient. It turns out to be one of my ancestors. I doubt he's much for conversation now. Go away, Bassick. I'll fetch Madame down to breakfast."

"Yes, your grace," Bassick said, turned on his heel and began his stately march down the long corridor.

The duke called out, a smile on his face, "Evangeline, are you here? I thought I heard you speaking to someone."

There was silence for two heartbeats, then she said, her voice deep and guilty-sounding, "Yes, I'm right here. I was just admiring the gold frames on the portraits. There is a lot of gold."

She was walking toward him, wearing one of Marissa's gowns that he remembered, and he wondered where Dorrie had found all the additional material to accommodate Evangeline's marvelous breasts. She looked splendid. He saw those breasts of hers clearly in his mind, bare and beautifully glowing in the firelight the night before. He drew in his breath. This would never do.

"If I ever lose all my money, why, I'll just sell some of those gold frames. Surely they'll support me for a good long time." He added, looking down, unable not to, "You know, they are rather fine."

"What's fine?" she said, knowing very well what he was doing, and staring at him until she realized what she was doing. She jerked her head away.

"The frames, naturally. Now, would you like to come with me to breakfast?"

"Yes, I'm quite hungry. Shall we get Edmund to breakfast with us?"

A thick black eyebrow went up. "I don't fancy Bedlam with my coffee and porridge. No, we will leave Edmund to Ellen. After breakfast he's mine for the entire morning. You have nothing more to do than resume your doubtless fascinating monologue to my ancestors. Don't worry about him."

Had he really overheard her speaking to his oblivious relative? The thought that he had made her nearly trip over her slippers. "Your head doesn't hurt this morning?"

"Oh, no. I'm one of those lucky men who rarely feel more than just a bit drowsy if they've imbibed too much. Ah, and just how do you feel this morning, Evangeline?"

She was silent as a stone, walking beside him, her eyes straight ahead. He added, his voice lower, "I can tell you how you felt last night, but I suppose you wouldn't take that in the spirit in which I would present it to you. There goes your chin, up a good two inches. No, I won't tease you, but it's tempting, very tempting. I will be a gentleman." He sighed deeply.

She was trying desperately to remember if she'd said anything to the portrait about betraying him. No, surely not, but she'd been about to. The guilt had been near to spilling out of her. She tamped down on it. Not now. She'd have to stew alive in the guilt, for there was simply nothing she could do about it. Yes, there was. She could make herself stop slavering over him with every other thought in her head.

He ushered her into a small breakfast room that gave onto the east lawn. Sunlight flooded into this charming, airy room.

"I see that Mrs. Dent did as instructed," he said, and pulled back her chair for her. The footman moved back to stand by the door.

"Oh, goodness," she said and stared with delight at the plate of croissants in front of her plate.

"Good morning, your grace, Madame," Mrs. Raleigh said, sweeping into the small room. This morning she was wearing a gown of the palest pink with beautiful Valencienne lace at the collar and the cuffs, banded with a darker pink satin beneath the bodice. She looked slight and beautiful, and a bit strange with the huge ring of keys dangling from a narrow leather belt tight at her waist, particularly since there wasn't a waist. "I see you've noticed the croissants. His grace ordered them especially for you, you being half French and all. Mrs. Dent hopes they're to your liking."

"It's wonderful, Mrs. Raleigh. Thank you, your grace. It is very thoughtful of you." She had a mouthful even before he was seated. He smiled down the table at her. "No, you don't have to say anything, just eat." He served himself toast, eggs, and kidneys.

Mrs. Raleigh seemed loath to leave. She said to Evangeline, "His grace said you don't care for hearty English breakfasts, and as he didn't want you to fade away, he believed the croissants to be just the thing."

When Mrs. Raleigh said that, Evangeline looked at the duke. He wasn't looking at her face. "Yes," he said, taking a bite of eggs, "I wouldn't want to lose your, er, upper self."

Mrs. Raleigh was counting her keys, Evangeline saw, and didn't hear what he'd said. Evangeline tried to slump down, just a bit.

"Oh, dear," Mrs. Raleigh said, and lightly patted her on the back. "Dorrie did magnificently with the gown. She told me she removed panels from the skirt to add to other places. Now, I will leave you to your breakfast. There is always so much to be done, you know. I can't spend the time talking to you, even though I should like it immensely."

"She's remarkable," Evangeline said.

"Yes. She and my mother have been friends for years. She also told me all about girls when I was about twelve. She's very knowledgeable. Eat, that's not enough."

She laughed. "You're disgraceful. You were only twelve?"

"Perhaps twelve and a half. I don't precisely remember. But Mrs. Raleigh told me what was what, at least in very basic terms, like don't ever touch anything above a girl's wrist, don't ever let a girl whisper in my ear, nervy things like that."

"Goodness, why ever not? What's nervy about whispering in the ear?"

"Evidently having a female so very close to a male, even a very young one, could lead to uncontrollable urges on the male's part. The girl's breath in his ear would shove him right over the edge." He rose, tossing his napkin down beside his plate. "You will have to excuse me now. I promised Edmund we would ride. We will see you later. Don't rush, Evangeline. I'll see you later, at luncheon."

He'd left half of his breakfast untouched on his plate. She slowly spread jam on another croissant. She closed her eyes as she bit into it. What had he heard her saying to his ancestor?

She felt John Edgerton's cool, dry fingers on her wrist. She shuddered, then realized that she'd crumbled the croissant into a ball. She put it on her plate and wiped her hands on her napkin. She was to meet him tonight at the cove for instructions. At the thought the croissant she'd been chewing turned to paste in her mouth. She swallowed with difficulty. She'd forgotten for just a couple of moments, not long, but remembering nearly brought her to her knees. What to do?

She waited at the table until she heard the duke and Edmund leave the house. Then she walked quickly up to her bedchamber. Although Houchard had described the private beach and the hidden cave, she hadn't seen the cave before, which meant that it wasn't at all obvious. She'd find it now. She had no choice. There was too much at stake to risk being late for her meeting. How would she manage to make her escape from the duke this evening?

She didn't know. She'd worry about that later.

She changed quickly into one of her old gowns and an old pair of walking boots. The morning was very warm indeed. It was very strange to have summer in the midst of winter. By noon it would be quite hot. She breathed in the tangy salt air. A light breeze ruffled her hair. By the time she reached the protected cove and walked carefully down the long zigzagging path, she felt sweat on her forehead and at the small of her back.

When she reached the beach, she shaded her eyes with her hand and looked to the south. The cliff jutted out nearly into the water, its nearly barren, craggy face shadowed from the morning sun. She made her way quickly toward it through the coarse sand. She found the cave only when she nearly stumbled into it, overhung with scraggly bushes. It was immediately on the water's edge. Not more than a foot of sand between the cave entrance and the lapping waves. No one who wasn't looking specifically for the cave would ever see it.

The entrance was low, and she crouched down. Then it soared upward. Six more steps into the cave and she shivered. It was damp and the air was chill. Slowly her eyes adjusted to the gloom. She saw that the cave was long and narrow, extending some twenty-five feet into the cliff. She pulled up short, realizing that the ground was wet beneath her feet. She reached up and ran her fingers along the stone walls, slimy with sea moss, to a level well above her head. At high tide the sea filled the cave. It wouldn't be a good thing at all to be trapped in here.

She retraced her steps to the mouth of the cave and stood quietly for a moment, lifting her face upward to the hot sun, breathing in the sharp salt air.

She stepped out of the cave, looked over the water, and stopped cold. Her breath whooshed out. She saw the duke, waist high in the water, carrying Edmund upon his shoulders, some thirty feet up the beach. She jerked back into the cave. Oh, goodness, what was he doing here? He was supposed to be riding. Yet he was swimming with Edmund. It was certainly warm enough, but she imagined that the sea water was still very cold. Yes, he'd spoken of swimming with his son the day before. But here? Now? With her staring at him?

What to do? She considered staying tucked away in the cave until the duke and Edmund had left the beach, but she saw that the tide was rising quickly. She didn't want to get wet. She didn't want to drown.

She couldn't walk south because the cliff jutted out into the water. Very well, north it was. Back from whence she'd come. She walked out of the cave, head up, whistling into the warm breeze. If she just kept whistling, she'd be all right. She didn't mean to look at him, truly she didn't. But she did. Evangeline hadn't ever seen a naked man. He was only twenty yards away. She could see him very clearly, more clearly than she deserved, really. She watched him lift Edmund above his head and toss him forward into the water. She'd never really been all that aware of men, until last night, in the duke's library, when he'd touched her and kissed her. And now he was here, all naked and unknowing, and she looked at him and nearly swallowed her tongue. She hadn't imagined that a man could look like him. Surely her father was very beautiful, but he was slight, no muscle to speak of, not like the duke, who was hard and long and hairy, hairy from his thick, wet black hair on his head to the wet black hair on his chest, to the wet black hair on his groin. Goodness, she could see all of him from his knees up. She knew she should look away. She shouldn't be here, looking her fill at him, wanting desperately to race to him and fling him onto his back on the sand, and flatten herself against him.

She knew that man had a phallus and that it stuck out from his groin. She hadn't known what to expect, but this wasn't at all frightening or strange. His sex was against him, not sticking out or anything else to alarm her. No, he didn't look at all frightening, just different. She heard Edmund's shriek of delight and saw a tangle of arms and legs. When the duke stood again, Edmund was clinging to his back, his arms wrapped about his neck. She heard him say, "All right, Edmund, that's quite enough. Ten minutes, no longer, else we'll turn into blocks of ice."

She should leave. He hadn't seen her. Now, she should leave now. She walked quickly to a thick overhanging bush and stepped beneath it. And she continued to look. She watched the duke, Edmund still shrieking with laughter. Edmund said something, pointing toward a gull, and he laughed. She saw that both of them were shivering. Imagine even ten minutes in that water. She shivered just thinking about it.

She watched the muscles tighten and expand with his laughter, with his striding in the water, with his holding Edmund on his shoulders. She should leave. She still had time.

She had no shame.

Chapter 16

"Papa, Papa," Edmund shouted. "Look, there's Eve." He was waving his arms wildly toward her. "She's here to watch us swim. I'm glad she came. I didn't think she believed that I was a good swimmer."

The die was cast. She was trapped. She knew he was looking at her, but he didn't pause, didn't hesitate, just kept walking toward shore through the waves, some of them nearly knocking him down.

There was no hope for it. She ran past the cave to the south, only to draw up short. She'd forgotten that the land lunged out into the water, cutting any escape off in that direction. Slowly she walked back. She heard the duke shout, "I see her, Edmund. Yes, there she is, not more than twenty yards away from us. And just look, I believe she's now walking this way since she realizes she can't decamp the other way. Let's wait for her, Edmund. I'm sure she's going to tell us how much she's enjoyed our swimming exhibition. Yes, we've provided her quite a show, albeit a short one, since the water was so bloody cold."

Evangeline stopped in her tracks. How long had he known she was there, watching him, slavering as she watched him? He now stood ankle-deep in the water, the waves gently lapping around him, and he was changing. He hadn't looked at all frightening or alien before, but now he was changing, rapidly. He wasn't moving, just standing there looking at her, and changing and growing and sticking out more and more. If she had been the duke and she was changing like that, surely she would have done something, like run or turn around, but he didn't. He just stood there, Edmund still on his shoulders, smiling at her, and still changing before her eyes. Oh, goodness.

He laughed. He plucked Edmund off his shoulders and set his feet on the sand. "Fetch us towels, Edmund, and cover yourself well. I don't want you to catch a chill. Perhaps your cousin Eve would care to join us."

She didn't move an inch until he finally took a large towel his son brought to him and began to dry himself. "Eve," Edmund called, running to her even as he wiped himself down. "Did you see us? Papa threw me in the water, and I swam like a sea bass. Papa said I'd have to be careful because a fisherman might try to catch me because I swam so well. Then he'd fry me in a pan and eat me. Come and say hello to Papa."

What was a stunned and fascinated woman to do? She walked beside Edmund to where the duke was standing. Finally, he'd knotted the towel around his waist, and draped another over his shoulder. She studied that knot at great length. It looked well tied, but she knew she could have it unknotted in a second, two at the most.

"Papa said that ladies can't swim," Edmund said. He dropped to his knees and began scooping up sand, piling it up, patting it down, shaping it into conelike shapes. Castle towers? Then he began digging a trench.

"Your papa is quite wrong. Here, Edmund, put on your clothes, then I'll know you're warm enough. What are you building?"

"Papa's never wrong, cousin Eve. I'm going to build Chesleigh Castle."

"Perhaps," the duke said, "I can teach you how to swim even better."

"I don't need lessons. I'm a fish, just like Edmund. I'm more a lizard fish than a sea bass."

"Get dressed, Edmund," the duke called over his shoulder. "Tell me why you're here, Evangeline."

"It's February and it's very warm. I was out walking. Nothing more than walking until I happened to come down here and there you were and you didn't have any clothes on. At least now you have on a towel, and there's one about your shoulders as well, but that really isn't the same thing at all as breeches and a shirt and other things that men wear."

"I see. You enjoy seeing the scenery, then?"

"Certainly. I was raised in the country. There is always beautiful scenery in the country, particularly down on the beach, coming out of the water."

He knew he was very well made indeed, like his father before him. He also boxed at Gentleman Jackson's, as his father had before him. He was fit and lean and hard, as his father had been before him. He grinned at her like a thief with an eye on the silver. "I would certainly have enjoyed the scenery if I'd been the one out walking and come across you coming out of the sea."

Her tongue stuck in her mouth. Never would she have imagined such a thing, never. She, a young lady, raised properly, she was certain of that, and yet all she could think of since she'd met him was that she wanted to leap on him and kiss him until she expired.

She thought he'd continue to tease her, because he was so good at it, baiting her and reeling her in more times than not, but oddly, after a moment his dark eyes searched her face, his expression thoughtful.

"You must go back to the castle, Evangeline," he said very gently. "I'll try to see that Edmund doesn't shout to the world that his cousin Eve watched both him and his father swimming."

She looked out over the water, then back at him. "I can't believe that I'm doing this."

"Doing what?"

"You know very well what. I was standing here just staring at you. You know that. And what I did last night. I'm not like that. I don't know what's wrong with me. I am sorry. I'm just not myself. I guess, truth be told, I don't know who I am. And then there is what I must be, and that is very bad indeed. It's all very difficult." She turned on her heel and began her walk back up the cliff path without a backward glance.

Evangeline overheard Mrs. Raleigh say to Bassick as she came around the corner at the top of the grand staircase on her way to luncheon, "I'll miss him, Mr. Bassick. He wasn't here long enough this time. I wonder why he must return to London? And on Friday? Why, that's only three days from now."

She heard Bassick say something, but she couldn't make out his words. Then Mrs. Raleigh said, as clear as the church bell on Sunday morning, "I was rather hoping that since Madame arrived, his grace would be content to remain longer."

"Well, his grace never does the expected," Bassick said, and this time she heard him. When she reached the bottom of the stairs, the two of them were standing there, smiling at her. There was a bit of assessment in Mrs. Raleigh's eyes. Evangeline knew that the duke would be leaving. But Friday was too soon. She didn't want him to leave so soon. Appalled at herself, she knew he was making it much easier for her by leaving. Why was he going?

"Madame, good afternoon," Bassick said.

"No unexpected guests as yet?" she asked.

"I wouldn't have been surprised," said Mrs. Raleigh. "Lady Pemberly is a good lady, truly; it's just that she rather likes to tread upon everyone in her vicinity. So unlike Lady Charlotte, Rohan Carrington's dear mama, a lady who is so charming that everyone is in a rush to assist her or simply stand there staring at her, she's so beautiful."

"I understand," Bassick said, all upright and stately, "that Lady Charlotte is also very much involved in the cat races."

"That, Mr. Bassick, is surely a great sport. But even there, I fear, there is some scandal and corruption."

"There is corruption in the cat races?" Evangeline said, eyebrows raised.

"Oh, yes," Bassick said, nodding his head. "Wherever there is an exchange of money, there are those who will be up to no good. There have been investigations, and most of the excesses and abuses have been eliminated."

"It is a shame that the cats can't race for the sheer fun of it," Mrs. Raleigh said as she shook out the skirt of her lovely pink gown. Was it the same pink gown she'd worn just this morning at breakfast? Evangeline wasn't at all certain that it was.

Evangeline said, "I head you saying that the duke is leaving."

"Ah, yes, we're disappointed," Mrs. Raleigh said. "We'd hoped he'd remain longer on this visit." She paused, then smiled. "Of course, when all is said and done, one simply never knows, does one? Ah, the forest green muslin is indeed a treat on you, Madame. I see that Dorrie removed all the flounces that used to drape off the hem. Most disconcerting, those flounces. Her former grace loved this dress, flounces and all. She refused to accept that they were a bit on the overdone side."

Evangeline nodded, thinking about Houchard, who'd known all about Marissa and her clothing. He'd said, "You won't have to wear your rags long, Mademoiselle, you will see. Ah, yes, his grace will drape you with lovely clothes from his dead wife's closet." He'd given her a very cold smile then. "And, of course, he will want payment from you; men of his class always do. You will do what you must to keep him in ignorance of your activities." He'd paused again, rubbing his chin with one long, thin finger. "I worry that you will lose your head over him, Mademoiselle. Foolish of me to be worried about that given the fact that I have your dear father, and he is but a heartbeat from death, but still, I understand the duke is a man that women want, wildly. I don't understand it since he is English and all know that the English are clods and boors. However, if it is true, you will keep your head, Mademoiselle. And if you do part your legs for him, and if you do whisper to him after he's given you pleasure, you won't ever forget that I have a gun at your father's head."

She wished now that the duke had already left. Houchard had even been right about that. The duke was a man like none other she'd ever met. He was a man she'd never imagined could exist. And he hated Napoleon. Soon, she would be no better than Edgerton. The thought made her want to vomit.

When she met the duke in the dining room, she was still thinking of the pit yawning at her feet, her brain squirreling about for a solution, for anything that could keep her from betraying him, from betraying her country. He was standing by his chair at the head of the table, smiling slightly. She tried to smile back at him, but the guilt was eating at her innards and she knew the pain of it showed on her face.

The devilment in his dark eyes immediately disappeared. "What's wrong?"

Her head snapped up. "Wrong?" Oh, God, was she so transparent? If she was, it boded ill for her success, for her father's life. "Why, nothing, your grace."

"You looked like you've lost your favorite pet."

That brought a wan smile. "No, although I loved my pug Bonnie very much. It was a very long time before I wanted another dog."

"You have disarmed me, flushed me out of the bushes. I was going to tease you, perhaps try to make you blush for your quite refreshing and quite improper behavior on the beach. You are always surprising me, Evangeline. Come, sit down. You can see Edmund after your lunch."

It was not until after the duke had dismissed the footman that he said, "What were you thinking about?"

"Nothing, really," she said, and fell silent. She must become a liar. It would be the only way she had a chance to survive. She raised her chin as she watched him fork several slices of very thinly sliced ham onto his place. She should say something utterly boring, something that would nauseate him with its blandness, but what came out of her mouth was "I was afraid you and Edmund would freeze in that water."

"I was too, but Edmund was determined. We were

only in the water for ten minutes, no more. We swim when I'm in residence here and if the weather is mild enough. It's invigorating, to say the least. It will freeze the hide off your bones to say the best. That doesn't sound like it makes sense, but it does. Do you understand?"

"Yes."

"Edmund and I are usually down at the cove at about the same time every morning. Oh, yes, I saw you coming out of the cave. Do have a care if you visit it again, especially when the tide is coming in. When I was a boy, I was foolish enough to hide there from my tutor, and got a good soaking. My father did too since he had to save me. I remember it was one of the very few times that he gave me a good hiding."

She smiled, trying to picture him as Edmund's size. It wasn't possible. "I'll be careful. I noticed that the cave walls were damp and covered with slime. When the tide is high, it fills the cave completely?"

"Very nearly."

"It's a pity that one can't continue walking to the south of the cave, but the cliff juts right out into the sea."

"Yes. But still the remaining scenery must have pleased you." Why couldn't he leave it alone? He was losing what little was left of his brain.

"Indeed. I never try to miss an educational opportunity."

One of his black eyebrows shot up. "Surely I didn't provide you with an excess of new knowledge. I'm just a man like your husband, the saintly André."

She nearly choked on the bite of peas. She'd blundered. Lie, she thought, lie very well or you'll sink. Her chin went up. "No, don't be silly. Naturally you were nothing at all new to me. You were something quite old, in fact. I believe, however, that the towel you were wearing knotted around your waist was new, very new, I would say, given my examination of it. Behold. I am a woman of the world, your grace."

"I was just thinking that," he said and she knew he was mocking her and enjoying himself. "I knew just how worldly you were after I— No, I won't say any more. It isn't well done of me. Finish your lunch, Evangeline."

She was shaking her head. "I've come to realize that I'm the perfect foil for you. You can sharpen your wit endlessly on me."

"Fair is fair. It's what my mother does to me. Now, don't get me wrong. You're quick, you've a ready tongue— No, I won't continue along those lines. Those lines would surely bring me lower than I am right now."

"Perhaps it's time I left you," she said, and prepared to rise.

"No, don't go. I would consider it running away. Come, Evangeline, admit it. You enjoy trying to outdo me verbally."

She settled back into her seat. She folded her hands and propped up her chin. "I try never to run away, even when it would be in my best interest. As to outdoing you, well, I have to admit that you're not a nitwit, as I have found most Englishmen to be."

The duke nodded agreeably. "Since you grew up in the country, in Somerset, I'm not at all surprised at your prejudice. Red-faced squires abound. Provincial locals swagger about. Little lordlings have their noses in the air and their brains beneath their boots. All in all, I would agree that the lot of them wouldn't provide an impressionable girl exquisite examples of wit and grace and elegance."

"As in the qualities you exemplify?"

"Certainly. I trust you say that without irony. Now, was your husband such a man like those in Somerset? Tongue-tied around you? Only dealt well with his horses? A crashing bore at dinner? Dozed in the parlor after drinking too much port?"

"Certainly not. He was French."

"Shall I describe him, then? Let me see. He was short, quite dark, was thin through the chest, swaggered about on skinny legs, and undoubtedly possessed of an oily kind of charm, and didn't bathe every day."

Evangeline saw the hole she'd dug at her feet. She'd described her mythical dead husband, André, with Henri in mind, the young man who'd wanted her in France. The duke's description fit him quite nicely.

"He bathed often," she said. Then remembered that Henri was addicted to the cologne bottle. She'd hated that musky, slightly sour smell on him. She frowned. "At least I think he did."

"You *think* he bathed often? Really, Evangeline, if you had half the curiosity in your husband that you have shown for me in the past two days, I can't imagine that you would have any doubts at all on the subject."

For a long moment she simply stared at him, knowing she was near to slipping into that hole at her feet, deeper now than it had been just a minute before. "Er, actually, André, well, I'm not really certain. You see, he was a very modest gentleman."

"He sounds like an idiot, a—" The duke stopped, seeing that Evangeline was quite red in the face. "Forgive me," he said, rising slowly. "He was your husband. Now, I'm off to see a new hunter. Enjoy your afternoon. My heartfelt best wishes in your time with

Edmund." He paused by her chair, looking down at her. "Is there anything I may bring you?"

Yes, she thought, he could bring her a very different life. He could bring her father freedom. He could not then look at her with hatred and contempt. She shook her head, mute.

"Very well. When I return, would you like to go riding with me? I have some business with several tenants. I can show you some of my favorite spots."

One more time, she thought. Surely it wouldn't be horrible to have one more time alone with him. She nodded. "I should like that very much."

"Excellent. I will see you later."

Chapter 17

"There are too many letters. I never know when one should go behind another or in front of it. And nothing that sounds right has the same letters in it. Surely I don't need to know all those letters? Just the ones that the words sound like?"

Evangeline said as she patted Edmund's small hand, "I know there are lots and lots of letters. I hadn't realized that there were perhaps too many of them. You're probably right. And there are endless combinations, Edmund. I believe you must simply forgive all the long-dead folk who came up with them, and accept that all the letters, all the strange combinations, are here to stay. You've no choice in the matter You must simply gird your loins. I learned them. Surely you, as a very bright boy, can also learn them."

He looked convinced for only a moment. Not good headway. She said then, "I thought, Edmund, that you wished to be like your father." His whole face changed. He straightened and said in a very creditable lordly voice, "I am like my father. Grandmama has told me countless times I'm like my father and like my grandfather, and I remember him very well. He was a wonderful grandfather, but then he died, like my mama, and I didn't see him anymore."

"Your father knows how to read and write, as did his father before him. Your father girded his loins, stiffened his spine, and learned every letter and every combination."

"You're right," Edmund said slowly. "I've seen him read. You don't think he's pretending to read just to draw me in so I'll do it too?"

"I'd guess he enjoys reading."

He eyed her suspiciously. She examined her thumbnail. "If you learn your letters, Edmund, I promise you that after your father returns to London, I'll swim with you mornings that are warm enough." She frankly couldn't imagine even sticking her toe in the cold sea, but if it remained warm, she'd do so. And she'd teach Edmund how to swim better than his father had.

He looked her up and down. "You are big enough," he said, then leaned over to feel her arm muscle. She flexed it. "Yes," he said, "and you're strong, for a girl." But still he fidgeted, looking everywhere but at the blocks of letters strewn out over the desktop.

She sighed deeply and folded her hands over her heart. "All right, if you learn your letters, then I'll play the highwayman and you can chase me down."

"Can I shoot you once I catch you?"

"Yes," she said, her head drooping. "You can shoot me."

Edmund smiled. He squared his shoulders. "All right, I'll do it."

"A is for an apple that's big and red and tastes tart and wonderful." She placed her hand over Edmund's fingers, tracing the letter. "Can you think of another word that begins with A?"

Edmund said almost immediately, "A is for ass. Papa's always calling Phillip Mercerault an ass. I can't tell you what Phillip calls him. It's not a good word, my papa told me, for a lady's sensitive ears. He said I was never to say it unless I was alone or with my pony."

"Very well, then don't say it. A is for ass. Yes, ass is an excellent word."

And on they went. She didn't crack a smile when Edmund announced that P was for proud, just like his papa. Evangeline was surprised, when she chanced to look up at the clock, at how quickly the time had passed. She gave Edmund a quick hug, for he had proudly written out his name. She glanced up to see the nursery door open and a very tall man, so thin he was gaunt, step into the room. She'd seen him several times in the past two days, but hadn't yet met him. He was dressed in unrelieved black.

Edmund jumped to his feet and ran to the man, clasping his hands around his leg. "Bunyon," he yelled. "You're here to save me."

"I'm not precisely certain just whom I am here to save," Bunyon said. There was only a hint of a smile on that thin mouth. "Forgive my intrusion, ma'am," he said as he disengaged Edmund from his leg and walked to the study table. "His grace suggested that I relieve you of your duties at just the point before Lord Edmund made you into a stuttering bedlamite. I am Bunyon, you know, his grace's valet."

"I can write now, Bunyon, just look. See, that's my name and I printed it all by myself."

Unlike Ellen, Edmund's principal worshiper, Bunyon did not appear to be overly gratified by the Heir's attention. Indeed, he paid Edmund no heed, his dark eyes on Evangeline's face.

She smiled and rose from her chair. "I'm not even to the brink of stuttering. Edmund has agreed to learn his letters, and he's doing quite well. And here is his name." She watched as Bunyon examined the large block letters.

"His grace," Bunyon said, "will be pleased. You have done well." He shook Edmund's hand. "Now, it's time for you to find your bed and close your eyes. Not for long, just an hour."

Edmund said, "Eve said she'd let me shoot her if I learned my letters. Will you help me come up with a strategy so I may catch her before I shoot her?"

"It will gratify me to be used in such a fashion," Bunyon said. "Does Madame know what's in store for her?"

"Tell him, Eve. Tell him that you promised to be a highwayman. I'll catch you, then shoot you."

"A bribe," Evangeline said. "Purely and simply a bribe. Devise an excellent stratagem, if you please, Bunyon. I would not want to be shot after only a paltry chase. Shall I call Ellen, Bunyon?"

"Oh, no, ma'am. I shall tuck him in. He has Ellen wrapped around all his fingers. It's shameful."

The duke rode at a leisurely pace back to Chesleigh, quite pleased with himself. He'd purchased the hunter he wanted, and at a price that suited him. Indeed, he thought, he'd been tight-fisted, as was his father's occasional habit. When he turned Emperor into the stable yard, he saw Evangeline standing next to McComber, in serious conversation. His eyes crinkled in amusement, for she spoke very expressively, her hands leaving no doubt of her meaning.

"I really didn't test Dorcas's mettle much this morning, McComber. Just look at the duke on Emperor. He looks magnificent."

This is interesting, McComber thought as he watched the duke ride into the stable yard. He cleared his throat and said, "I exercised her myself this early afternoon, Madame. She won't give you a moment's worry."

The duke called out as he reined in Emperor, "Hello, Evangeline. You're ready, I see." He leaned forward to pat his neck. "My fellow's tired, so you can forget any racing. You won't rub my nose in the dirt today."

"Perhaps Trevlin can have Biscuit fetched for you, your grace."

He looked at her white throat just above the lace of her blouse. "I suppose I wouldn't get away with it," he said, and flexed his fingers.

"I know what you're thinking, and no, you wouldn't. I'm very strong. Edmund agrees."

Not many minutes later, the duke led them southward along a narrow road overlooking the sea. He was in the midst of telling her of the hunter he'd purchased when a loud horn blast sounded from an oncoming mail coach. "Pull over, Evangeline," the duke said, guiding Emperor down a slight incline off the road.

Evangeline tugged Dorcas's reins just as the rumbling coach pulled around a bend in the road. The driver sounded the horn once again, and Dorcas, startled, reared up and twisted, ripping the reins from Evangeline's hands.

She looked blankly at the duke as she went flying off her mare's back. She landed on her bottom by the side of the road. For a moment she simply sat there.

The duke was at her side in but a moment. "Are you all right? Where did you hit yourself?"

She rubbed her hip. "I'll be all right. At least that's where I have the most padding."

"I wouldn't say that, but it should be enough."

"I don't think anything is ever enough for you."

"Quite possibly," he said, and pulled her to her feet. His hands were out to rub her hips, perhaps pull her close against him whilst he was rubbing her hips, when he realized what he was about to do. He cursed and dropped his arms to his sides.

"How sad," she said, ignoring him, staring at the dust that still was flying about in the warm air. "A silly mail horn and I go flying."

"If you landed on your bottom, then why is the feather on your hat broken?"

"I don't have any idea." She pulled off the hat, pulling her hair loose with it. He stared as that hair of hers tumbled past her shoulders down her back, fell over her forehead, a long strand even dangling close to her mouth. He raised his hands to smooth her hair back off her face, perhaps hold her close while he smoothed her hair back off her face. He cursed and lowered his arms to his sides.

"The mail coach flung dirt all over you. Perhaps you should have ridden Biscuit. I doubt she would have thrown you. She's far too lazy."

"I daresay even you, your grace, would have been tossed off. Dorcas was merely startled. She's high-strung. She's got long, strong legs. She can kick very well."

"Hopefully she'll be docile enough now," the duke said. "Come, let's go home."

Chapter 18

"Bunyon has a very special way of showing his displeasure," the duke said over his haunch of rare roast beef at dinner that evening.

"I can't imagine anyone showing you displeasure."

"You believe me such a tyrant, then?"

"Not a tyrant, rather a man who is the undisputed master here."

"Of course I'm undisputed. Who else would be in charge?"

"No one. I was just remembering how you treated me when you found me in your library. You were very much the lord of the castle, and I was nothing more than an irritation to you."

"You still are," he said, then frowned over his forkful of potatoes. He looked at her down that too-long expanse of table, at the vastly becoming dark blue gown of Marissa's that Dorrie had altered to fit her. Dorrie had fashioned her hair into thick intertwined braids atop her head. Two lazily curling tendrils caressed those ears of hers. "You know exactly what I mean."

She did, but she wasn't about to admit it.

He frowned into his glass of wine. It wasn't wise to

look at her. "I was in a black mood that day. You surprised me." He shrugged. "How a man treats a woman in his own library—perhaps I shouldn't pursue that thought. But you know, even seeing you for the first time, I realized that you had to be taught your role."

"My role?" Her voice was very sweet. He grinned down at his plate.

"Your role is no different from any other lady's," he said, and raised his glass, toasting it toward her, enjoying himself immensely, preparing to see her turn red, perhaps hurl her wine glass at him, perhaps stutter a curse and then laugh. "And that role, naturally, is to serve her husband, bow sweetly to his every wish, bear his children, and naturally, keep her opinions to herself if they are contrary to his." He didn't have long to wait for her reaction. She took the bait almost instantly.

Evangeline didn't hurl her wine glass. She flung her napkin onto the table and jumped to her feet, nearly overturning her chair. She exploded into wonderful speech. "You pompous, arrogant ass. I have excellent opinions on many subjects, for I have studied and read and learned. You, I wager, have spent all your hours as a frivolous libertine, concerned only with your own pleasures."

"Pompous ass," he said mildly, grinning at her. "Now if you were teaching Edmund, then you would say P as in pompous ass?"

"How do you know about that?"

"I speak to my son, Evangeline. I was just thinking that it's not at all proper for you to admit knowledge about libertines. As to my pleasures, perhaps you should meet the ladies of my acquaintances. I have never been concerned with my own pleasure more than with theirs." He leaned forward. "Don't you remember last night in my library? Surely I wasn't at all selfish."

"No, I refuse to remember because I'm rather angry with you at the moment. If I admit to remembering, then you'll tease me endlessly. You'll remind me over and over that I enjoyed you touching me, kissing me, oh, dear. My tongue is moving again. I will change my tongue's direction. I can do it. Now, I don't wish to hear about all your mistresses."

He arched a dark eyebrow at that. "But you brought it up, Evangeline. I was just trying to explain matters to you." She was red in the face. He wanted very much to catch her up against him, perhaps whirl her about, then slowly bring her down the front of him, then kiss her until she was silly with it. He drew a deep breath. It was enough. It was too much. After a few moments he managed to remember something to say that wouldn't draw her, that wouldn't have her calling him an ass, that should, in fact, please her. "Now as I recall, we began dinner with me telling you about how Bunyon shows me his displeasure."

"Very well. You wish to change the topic. It is probably wise of you. I am calm now. What did Bunyon do?"

"He threatened to strangle me with my cravat."

"Goodness. Why did he do that?"

The duke swirled the deep red Burgundy wine about in the crystal wine glass. "He doesn't think I should leave you here. In charge of Edmund. Quite alone, in charge of Edmund."

She didn't like where this could be heading. "I don't understand." Surely he wouldn't particularly care what his valet had to say, would he?

"Bunyon believes that Edmund is old enough to

accompany me to London. He also believes he's old enough to have a male tutor. He doesn't believe that you should allow Edmund to shoot you in order to have him learn his letters. In short, he believes you're far too kind and far too young to have my strong-willed son in your charge."

She felt panic well up inside her. Oh, no, this couldn't be. She sat forward. "But if you take Edmund with you to London, there would be no reason for me to stay at Chesleigh."

"That's true enough. Therefore, Evangeline, both you and Edmund will come with me to London tomorrow. There's no need to wait until Friday."

"No!"

He blinked. She was both pale and flushed at the same time, half standing, her palms flat on the table. He arched a black eyebrow. "I beg your pardon?"

"It was but one word. Surely you can understand one word. I yelled it, after all." This couldn't be happening. She couldn't leave Chesleigh, she couldn't. Bunyon had done her in and all for the most noble of motives. What was she to do now? She was to meet John Edgerton in just under two hours. She'd been told in no uncertain terms that she was to remain at Chesleigh. Houchard would kill her father.

"Perhaps," he said slowly, "you'd best explain that simple one word to me, Evangeline. That simple one word that you yelled so loudly you nearly brought the chandelier down."

She was desperate, but she couldn't let him see that. It wouldn't make sense to him. "I didn't mean to scream it at you. It's just that I don't want to go to London. Please, your grace, let me stay here. I can deal well with Edmund. I won't fail you. He doesn't need a male tutor. I don't care if he tries to shoot me.

I shan't allow him to shoot me unless and until he manages to catch me. I'm not slow. It will be difficult for him. I must make it difficult for him so that he will have a challenge. I know how to deal with little boys. Please, I must stay, I must."

"You have said quite a lot there, Evangeline."

"I know and I'm sorry. But what I really want is to remain here at Chesleigh, with Edmund. I won't fail you, your grace. He will be reading the family Bible within a month. I will have him write you a letter every day, and each letter will be at least one sentence longer than the last one. Please, your grace."

This was all very strange. Why should she care about remaining here or going to London? Surely anyone would prefer London. He didn't understand her at all. Her reaction was extreme. Not natural. He'd honestly believed her initial refusal to go to London the result of her embarrassment at thrusting herself, a poor relation, upon his mother. He had actually felt pleased at his decision, for he realized that despite his thinking of the night before, he did want to take her to London, to show her the sights and introduce her to his mother. He wasn't at all certain of his intentions toward her. For God's sake, he'd only known her for two days. But he did know that he'd never met a woman like her before, that she fascinated him, that he wanted her more than any female who'd ever come into his orbit. She appealed to his senses, all of them. And the lust, dear God, the lust she evoked so effortlessly in him.

To put a better face on it, he reminded himself that he didn't want her to stay by herself at Chesleigh, her only companion his young son. And, he admitted to himself, although it was difficult to do, he didn't like having anyone go against his wishes, particularly when they were benign, well thought out, and really quite nice.

"I would worry about you," he said finally. "No, I won't allow it. Both you and Edmund will come with me to London tomorrow."

She was desperate. She'd pleaded with him, and it hadn't worked. She drew a deep breath and said in a cold voice, "I see. The lord's orders. Well, your grace, if you won't allow me to remain at Chesleigh, with Edmund, then I must leave. I won't go to London."

"You don't have anyplace else to go. Of course you will do as I tell you."

"You've become a blockhead, your grace. It no longer will concern you where I go or what I do."

He rose, facing her down the long expanse of table. "I've had quite enough of this, Evangeline. I don't know why you're being so stubborn about this. Tell me why, right now."

"I hate London. I refuse to go there."

"You've never been to London."

"It doesn't matter. I won't go."

"Sit down and eat your dinner. You're distraught. You're becoming hysterical. It isn't appealing. I will speak to you of this later."

Evangeline didn't move a hair. "No, you will not. Listen to me, you cannot give me orders. I'm not one of your servants. However, like Bunyon, perhaps I would like to strangle you with your cravat." He was seated again, his arms folded over his chest, unmoving. "Very well," she said. "I can see from that cold, set look on your face that you won't change your mind." She tossed her napkin onto the plate.

"I bid you good-bye, your grace. It has been something of an experience, albeit a very short one."

He bounded from his chair, toppling it to the carpet.

"Damnation, Evangeline. You're not going anywhere. You take one step and I'll take a birch rod to you."

She laughed at him. "Go to the devil," she said, turned on her heel, and walked toward the door. She wondered if Bassick, all the footmen and all the maids, were waiting outside the door, wondering what was going to happen. She said over her shoulder, her voice cold and contemptuous, "If I had Edmund's gun, I'd shoot you."

She didn't make it. He caught her, grabbed her by the arm, and whirled her about to face him. She didn't struggle. She wasn't about to waste her strength. He was furious. She could see the pulse pounding in his throat.

He shook her, leaned close to her, and said right in her face, "You won't go anywhere. Do you understand me?"

His eyes were on her mouth. Then his eyes were on her breasts. He forgot instantly every dollop of anger at her. He couldn't bear it. He pulled her roughly against him, and cupped her chin in his hand, forcing her to look up at him.

Evangeline felt suspended in time. She stared up at him, all that she felt in her eyes. He kissed her, his tongue probing against her closed lips.

"Open your mouth, damn you."

She tasted his anger, then she tasted only him and his mad desire.

It was as if he didn't know what to do first. He kissed her, kissed her again and again. Then he pressed her back over his arm and his mouth was on her throat, her shoulders. He moaned, then jerked her beautiful altered blue gown down to her waist. He stared at her breasts, then was on her, his mouth and tongue hot on her flesh.

She was overwhelmed.

This was passion, she thought. It was nearly painful, this need in her that she recognized but didn't understand.

Abruptly he let her go. He stared down at her blindly, trying to control himself. He buried his face in her hair. "Oh God," he said, "I'm sorry."

She forced herself to straighten, to move away from him. She stood there in front of him, detached, naked to the waist. It was her only chance. She had to remain at Chesleigh. She had no choice.

She looked at him as if he were nothing more than a minor annoyance to her. She looked to be utterly indifferent. She said in a light, amused voice, "I begin to think, your grace, that you have gone too long without a woman. Perhaps that is why you wish me to go to London—because there is no lady currently seeing to your pleasure? Is it that you see me as only a defenseless woman, without protection, a woman who is therefore yours for the taking?"

He drew back from her as if she'd struck him. His lust was dead; she saw only slowly building rage. She felt ill, but knew that she couldn't back down, no matter what the outcome. She wondered, stiffening, if he would strike her.

He said finally, in a voice so soft and deadly calm that she strained to hear him, "Some women are teasing bitches. Is that what you are?" He added, his voice going lower, deeper. "You surprised me, I admit it.

"You may stay at Chesleigh if you wish. I will expect reports from you on Edmund's progress. I bid you good night and good-bye."

He left her standing there, her gown bunched at her waist. He didn't look back, just quietly closed the door behind him.

She stared at that closed door. She knew in that moment, simply knew that she couldn't betray him. She would tell him the truth. He would believe her. He and Lord Pettigrew would arrest John Edgerton. They would help free her father from Houchard. Surely it could be done.

It took her some time to get her gown back into place. She had to hurry. She had to tell him that she was meeting Edgerton in but an hour. They had to make plans. She ran out of the dining room, down the long corridor to the entrance hall, only to see Bassick standing at the great front doors, shaking his head.

She stopped, drawing a deep breath. "Is something wrong, Bassick?"

He looked at her standing there, shaking his head slowly, back and forth. "No, Madame, there is nothing wrong that either you or I can fix."

"I don't know what you mean."

"His grace," Bassick said. "He's gone. Just gone, not three minutes ago."

Chapter 19

She nearly ran out of the castle but stopped herself. Perhaps it was better this way. She would see first-hand how the operation worked. She would have proof that Edgerton was a traitor. Then she would send a messenger to the duke.

Yes, that would work. She just had to keep her nerve with Edgerton. She couldn't allow him to suspect what she was going to do. It was difficult to wait to go to the cove, and she did sneak out of the castle early, pulling her cloak more closely about her. The summery weather had disappeared. It was cold now, not bitterly cold, but soon it would be. She walked carefully down the long path to the cove, a half-moon guiding her. When she reached the cave, she turned for a moment to look out at the sea. The waves built slowly, then tumbled gently forward, rolling over and over, like a huge bolt of cloth unfolding, until they reached the shore, there to lap softly over the sand, just a whisper of sound.

She didn't want to step into the frightening, dark cave. She walked to a rock near the entrance and sat down, waiting. Perhaps Edgerton wouldn't come. Perhaps he had been discovered and her father would be safe. Of course he hadn't been discovered. It was just a futile prayer. She knew she wasn't a good actress, but she had to be tonight with John Edgerton. He mustn't suspect that she was anything but obedient to him.

Tomorrow, she thought, tomorrow she would send a message to the duke. He would come back. He would help her.

She wanted to see John Edgerton in hell.

She also felt the huge weight of guilt lifted off her.

It was getting colder. She shivered. Where was Edgerton? Perhaps she'd misunderstood his instructions, perhaps—

"Good evening, Evangeline. Unlike most women, you are punctual. That pleases me and relieves me."

She whirled about, nearly falling off the rock. There was John Edgerton, silhouetted in the moonlight, standing quietly in the mouth of the cave. How long had he been there, waiting in the darkness, watching her?

She rose slowly, holding her cloak tightly fisted to her throat. "I have found that men, more often than women, are the ones who aren't punctual. Perhaps it is their desire to swagger into a room after all others are already present."

"You are very young, your experience limited, and thus your opinions are not very important. You are here. Had you been late, I might have wondered about your intentions. I didn't have a chance to tell you the other evening how delighted I am to see you again. Naturally, I would have preferred a different context for our reunion, but alas, it was not meant to be. But I digress. The next time you have occasion to visit the cave, bring a lantern. Come along now."

She watched as he set his lantern upon the cave

floor and knelt to light it. He straightened toward her, his face shadowed in its dim yellowish light. "In twenty minutes you will give a signal, using the lantern." He paused, looking at her closely. "You're afraid. That's not a bad thing. It will keep you from making mistakes, mistakes that could be fatal to your dear father."

She said nothing.

"Listen to me now. You will be meeting some men at the dock. I will wait here to see that all goes well. Come now, and learn, for we haven't much time. You hesitate. This is a very big step for you. Tonight you will perform a treasonous act against England. A single act, but one that will serve our purpose. Then the die will be cast. There will be no turning back for you."

If she'd had a gun, she would have shot him with no hesitation. No regrets. Oh, yes, she would turn back. "You're a fool, Sir John. You believe this some sort of game in which you dominate me. Don't lie to yourself. You're nothing but a miserable old man.

"Houchard holds my father. You know I have no choice. All the rest of this—it's nothing more than stage settings and bad melodrama. Get on with it, damn you."

She thought he would strike her. He raised his hand, then slowly, very slowly, he lowered his arm. "You push me, Evangeline. You believe I shall remember the girl I once wanted, the girl your miserable father refused me?"

"My father refused you nothing. I was the one who refused you."

He smiled, a terrifying smile in the gloom of the cave. "You are in my power now, Evangeline, make no mistake about that. I find your bravado somewhat amusing. I should even like to pursue this with you, but not tonight. We have more important things to do, and we must hurry."

"You're English. Why are you betraying your country?"

He shrugged, frowning down at the glowing lamp. Then he said, looking straight at her, "All of us make choices, Evangeline. I choose to assist a great man to fulfill his destiny. It is a destiny that will extend far into the future, and I will have been a part of it. But enough. I wouldn't expect you to understand. No, don't try to argue with me. We haven't much time. What we do here tonight is very serious business. Your duties will be varied, but none of them will place you in any particular danger. Your primary function will be to serve as a checkpoint. No one will be sent to me unless you have first verified that they are who they purport to be."

He drew a folded piece of paper from his cloak pocket and handed it to her. "All messages that you receive will be in this code. Only you, I, and Houchard know it. You will meet whomever you are instructed to, Evangeline, and you will examine their papers carefully. You will never clear a man until you have ensured that his instructions are authentic. Then you will write your initials at the bottom of each page to prove that you have verified the message. It is for my protection as well as for Houchard's. You and I have further protection. No one will know either your name or mine. You will be known as the eagle, *L'Aigle,* and I, the Lynx, *le loupcervier.* You are smart—study the code."

Evangeline moved close to the lantern and sank to her knees. The code was a formula substituting numbers for letters in various combinations.

"The vowels have a separate code. You will practice the code in a few moments."

She looked up at him. "What if a man carries a message that isn't authentic?"

"If you prove this to be true, you won't do anything. You will simply direct the man to this address in London." He handed her a small visiting card. "I don't expect anyone to successfully penetrate our network, but one can't be too careful. We try to foresee all contingencies. I trust you will be quite certain that you are sending along a Bonapartist, for if you make an error, purposefully or not, I assure you it will be your last. Of course, then your father will die also, not that you'll be alive to know of it."

She held up the card. "You mean that anyone I send to this address will be murdered?"

"Naturally. Now, here is my card. The men you clear, you will send here."

"Where is the letter from my father? Houchard promised to send one to me."

"You will have your letter when the boat arrives. Along with instructions for your next assignment. You will remain at Chesleigh. If there are any changes, I will send you a message. Has the duke already tried to bed you?"

"No. I don't think he cares for me at all. Indeed, he has already returned to London."

"No matter. Incidentally, you gave a fine performance the other evening. I was impressed with your abilities."

"I had no choice. The duke and Lord Pettigrew both regard you as a friend, someone they can trust."

"Yes," he said, nodding. "I have worked hard for many years to earn their trust. Now, as I said, the young lady you presented was perfect in her role."

"You are quite wrong," she said, rising to face him. "I'm not a good actress. If the duke hadn't already left Chesleigh, he would probably already suspect that something is wrong. Indeed, I've been here only a short time, and already there is someone who suspects me. Mrs. Needle is a harmless old woman, but she guesses that something's not right with me. Who will be next to guess? If I am so very transparent, surely I can't be much use to you or to Houchard."

"Who did you say this old woman was?"

Evangeline shook her head impatiently. "It doesn't matter. It's just that she seemed to see me, to really see me. Others might do the same."

"I trust for your sake, for your dear father's sake, that you will quickly learn your trade. Women seem to have a talent for it. Not such a surprise since generally women tend to excel in deception. Surely you're no different."

"Your opinion of my sex isn't very high."

"Oh, I adore your sex. All men do when it comes to seeing to their needs. It's just that I understand you. Not one of you can be trusted."

"Then why did you want to marry a seventeen-year-old girl if you wouldn't ever trust her?"

"For that very reason. You were very young. You hadn't had the time to perfect your woman's skills. I would have taught you, molded you to my liking." He pulled his watch from his waistcoat pocket. "It's time. Attend me carefully."

He pulled out a handkerchief, covered the lantern, and carried it to the mouth of the cave. Just then, in the distance, Evangeline saw a brief flicker of light, followed shortly by another.

He whipped off the handkerchief and raised the lantern high for some seconds. "You'll always receive a double signal. You have only to return it with a single, steady light, long enough for the men to get their bearings. They will row in and debark at the dock. You will meet them there." John Edgerton again lowered the lantern and covered it with his handkerchief and set it inside the cave.

"At the high tide the cave is flooded."

"The men know to approach only at low tide. They will never draw near in any case unless you yourself give the signal." He raised his hand. "Listen."

Within moments she heard the soft, rhythmic sound of oars dipping through the water.

"You'll go to the dock. Remember, my dear Eagle, that you are now one of us. You will greet the men and bring their packet of instructions back to me. We will read the code together tonight."

Evangeline nodded, and hurried from the cave to the end of the long wooden dock. She saw Edmund's small sloop bobbing up and down at its anchor, and beyond it, through the soft night mist, a longboat. Two men, muffled to their ears in black greatcoats, climbed up onto the dock, and one of them stepped forward. To Evangeline's surprise, he spoke fluent English. "All goes well. You are the Eagle?"

Evangeline merely nodded, not trusting herself to speak.

The man looked her up and down, then said, his voice low, "I was told that a woman was to be our contact. I hadn't expected anyone so young and so beautiful."

She wanted to vomit on his boots. She said, her voice as cold as the night had become, "Give me your instructions."

She made her way back to the cave, leaving the two men on the dock, waiting for her. Evangeline opened the packet and withdrew the papers. There were two envelopes, one of which, John Edgerton told her, contained a letter from her father and her next instructions. The other contained papers and a message in Houchard's code. Her hands shook; her mind squirreled about. She stumbled again and again over the letters.

"Keep calm. The men will wait until you are done, Evangeline. You have reversed the letters. Try again."

It took her another fifteen minutes to verify that the message was indeed from Houchard. The papers were letters of reference and letters vouching for the character of Allan Dannard for the post of secretary to a Lord George Barrington in London. Evangeline had never heard his name before, but she'd wager he was somehow involved in the war ministry. She memorized both names. She would tell the duke.

"They were legitimate," Evangeline said she folded them back into the packet.

John Edgerton withdrew a slender piece of charcoal from his dark waistcoat pocket. "Write your initials in the bottom corner. Without them the men couldn't continue to London."

When she handed one of the men the packet, and told them the address of the Lynx, they nodded and gave a quick salute to Evangeline. *"A bientôt, Mademoiselle L'Aigle."* One of the men kissed his fingertips to his lips. "Perhaps I will see you again, in different circumstances."

"I don't think so," she said, his new name stark in her mind. "Be assured that I will never forget you."

When they had disappeared behind the rise of the cliff and the longboat was no longer in sight, John Edgerton emerged from the cave. "You did well, Evangeline. You will find your next instructions in the envelope, as I told you." He paused a moment and touched his fingers to her cheek. She drew back.

"I regret that I'm the villain in this drama, but then again, it brought you to me and that was ultimately what I wanted. You will see me again, Evangeline. Perhaps soon you'll be more submissive, more willing to hear of other matters."

"No," she said. "No."

"Ah, we will see, won't we? Now, I saw it on your face, Evangeline. Saw it clearly. You are still wavering, wondering if perhaps you can't free yourself of us. You can't.

"Listen carefully and believe this. If anything happens to me, there are orders that Lord Edmund is to be killed. Killed quickly and cleanly, his small body buried where it will never be found. He will be dead and it will have been your fault. Then, there is of course your dear father. Two deaths, Evangeline, if you betray me to your duke or to anyone else. Do you understand me?"

He'd won and she knew it. He probably saw it in her face as well. Not Edmund, not her boy, who was becoming more dear to her by the day. She couldn't bear it.

"Do you understand me?"

Finally, she said so low he had to lean close to hear her, "Yes, I understand."

"Excellent. Perhaps you can keep in your mind a picture of your father holding little Edmund against his chest, the two of them buried deeply in the same grave."

Yes, she could see that clearly. She said nothing more, and her expression remained fixed. She felt cold and sick. Edgerton had won.

Eventually—she didn't know how much time had

passed—she made her way slowly up the cliff path, clutching her father's letter close. It was over for her, everything was over for her. She was now a traitor to England.

She had betrayed the duke.

There was no going back now.

Chapter 20

Trevlin sat back on the cushioned wooden bench in the White Goose Inn, his thirst slaked by a mug of porter. If he had thought it odd that Madame de la Valette wished to travel some five miles from Chesleigh simply to explore the tiny Norman church set atop the chalk cliffs, it wasn't his place to ask questions. He supposed that the young lady was restless, what with only Lord Edmund and the servants to keep her company at the huge castle, and had thus taken to exploring the countryside. In the past several weeks he had accompanied her to Landsdown, a picturesque village in the rolling hills near Southsea, and to Southampton, to visit an abbey that had survived despite centuries of political and religious upheavals, or so she had told him.

When she first arrived at Chesleigh, he had thought her a lively lady, whose laughter had more than once brought a smile to his lips. But lately, she seemed more withdrawn, even during their jaunts about the countryside. Trevlin crooked his finger at the barmaid, a pretty wench with an impertinent tongue, to bring him another mug. The wink she gave him removed further thoughts of Madame from his mind.

* * *

Evangeline's nose wrinkled at the overpowering smell of fish as she turned off the narrow cobbled road that served as the thoroughfare in the small village of Chitterly onto a winding path that led to its ancient stone church. Although there was no one in sight, she sensed that she was being watched. She heard a sudden rustling of leaves behind her and whirled about. There was no one.

She'd stayed close to Edmund since that night with Edgerton down in the protected cove. Of course, Edmund had tired of that quickly enough. She tried to act naturally around him, to laugh and jest with him, but it was difficult for her. Every shadow she saw, every unexpected noise she heard, could be a threat to him.

She'd begun a journal of everyone she'd met, where they were bound, their descriptions, everything she thought could be helpful. She supposed, deep down, that she wanted so badly for something to happen which would resolve the situation that she wanted to have all the proof she could gather.

When she lay in bed at night, alone, frightened, still she wondered if she shouldn't write to the duke, beg his help. Then she saw Edmund in her father's arms, and both of them were pale in death, silent, gone from her. She wondered how long she could go on like this. She even considered sneaking to London and killing John Edgerton herself, but there was Edmund, always her boy, for he was hers now, his laughter, his continuing attempts to chase her down in her highwayman role and shoot her with the gun given to him by an evil man who wouldn't hesitate to kill him. Who had Edgerton told to kill Edmund if she betrayed him?

Oh, Edmund. The threat to him defeated her as the

threat to her father hadn't. He was here, with her, in her care. She was responsible for him, and he was so very vulnerable. He was only five years old.

By the time she reached the top of the rise and the arched oak doors of the church, she was outwardly calm again. She grasped the heavy bronze ring and pushed inward, and the door opened with a loud creak. It was cold and damp inside, for little warmth could penetrate the thick stone walls.

The church was empty. She walked slowly up the narrow aisle, past the bare wooden benches, toward the vestry. She heard a soft scraping sound and froze.

"You are the Eagle?"

A slight man, dressed in the coarse woolens of a fisherman, stepped out of the shadows. He was a young man without a sign of a beard on his smooth cheeks.

"Yes," she said just above a whisper. "Were you following me?"

"Nay, it was my partner. He doesn't trust women. He would have sliced your lovely throat had you not come alone."

He was trying to frighten her, but oddly enough, his words didn't touch her. She'd gone beyond fear for herself. She held out her hand. "Give me your packet now. I have little time to waste with you."

He frowned at her, for she'd surprised him. Then he slowly drew a dirty envelope from the waistband of his trousers and handed it to her. Evangeline paid him no more attention. She sat down on one of the wooden benches and spread the single sheet of paper on her lap. She raised her eyes. "You're this man Conan DeWitt?"

The man shook his head. "He's my partner. He's the gentleman, not I."

"Bring him to me. I must see him."

He looked undecided. "Conan told me to meet with you."

"Nevertheless, he must come in. If he refuses, I cannot do anything further." Buried in the coded message from Houchard was the description of Conan DeWitt, a man tall and fair, with a mole on his left cheek near his eye.

"Very well," he said finally, "but there better be good reason."

She shrugged. "I care not what you decide to do."

"I'll see if he'll come."

He slipped out of the church and returned some minutes later accompanied by a tall man dressed in country buckskins, swinging a cane negligently in his right hand.

Conan DeWitt stared down at the girl. She had an uncommonly lovely face, despite its pallor. Jamie had called her a cold bitch, but his voice had held grudging respect. "What is it you want with me, Eagle?"

"Houchard provided your description. I have to be certain that you are the man he speaks of."

He touched his fingertip to the large mole. "Are you satisfied?"

Evangeline nodded, and quickly wrote her initials on the lower corner of the paper. She handed it to DeWitt. "Have you a packet for me?"

DeWitt handed her a thin envelope. Evangeline stuffed it into her cloak pocket and rose.

"Jamie was right. You are a cold bitch. I told Houchard that women aren't to be trusted, but he insisted that you were different, that he had such a hold over you that you would never dare to betray us. He believed Edgerton more than me." He shrugged. "We will see. I've always found that women's consciences are fragile. I will ask Edgerton what this hold is. He wants you, you know. And he will have you, eventually."

She found a laugh, one that was filled with all the contempt she felt for that traitorous bastard. "Your opinions are doubtless a result of your character, Mr. DeWitt. I believe our business is concluded. I'm away."

"Yes, a bitch," he said quietly, gave her one more long look, a fair brow arched. She quickly gave him John Edgerton's London address and turned to leave the church, but DeWitt's voice stopped her. "That man, Trevlin. Be certain that he doesn't suspect anything. If he does, he's dead."

She felt a leap of panic, but didn't show anything except her impatience with him. "Don't be a fool. The man suspects nothing. See to your own affairs and leave mine to me."

Evangeline turned on her heel and walked deliberately away from him, out of the church and into the bright sunlight. He was a handsome man, one who would undoubtedly gain entrance anywhere he wished to go in London. The mole, though, that gave one pause. She had a lot to write in her journal about Conan DeWitt.

The duke of Portsmouth stood at the wide, bowed windows in the drawing room of his town house on York Square, staring at the rivulets of rain that streaked down the glass. He held a letter from Evangeline in his hand, one of her governess's bloodless progress reports. It was written in the most formal of styles, impersonal, lifeless, and he wished he had her white neck between his hands, damn her. It was the fifth one he'd received from her. She could have been an utter stranger. Certainly she wasn't the woman he'd caressed, whose breasts he'd stroked with his hands, whose mouth he'd kissed until he'd believed he'd spill his seed if he didn't have her.

Now she was a stranger. She'd removed herself as far as she could from him. He was surprised that the pain of her final words to him still lingered, still pulsed deeply in him, making him wonder what had pushed her to say those things to him, what he had done to provoke them. And her insistence on not coming to London. None of it made any more sense to him today than it had the day before when he'd yet again chewed over it endlessly.

"Dearest, you might as well tell me what troubles you."

He turned at the sound of his mother's voice, and automatically shook his head. He hadn't meant to be so obvious. It was distressing, but then again, his mother knew him nearly as well as his father had. He wouldn't ever cause her distress. Thus he smiled and said, "There isn't anything, Mother. It's a dismal day, enough to drag a man's soul to his feet. Dreary and dismal, nothing more. Don't fret."

The dowager duchess of Portsmouth, Marianne Clothilde by name, regarded her beautiful son. Like his father, he protected her, even when it was foolish to try. But she said only, returning his smile, "How goes Edmund?"

"Madame de la Valette reports that he will soon be penning his first novel, he is that precocious. She sends me the opening paragraph to his budding opus." He handed his mother a single sheet of paper. Edmund's printing was well executed. There were four sentences. She read aloud: "It was a dark and stormy night.

There wasn't a moon. There were stars. There is more to come, but patience is required."

She began laughing. "It's wonderful. I believe Madame de la Valette is a genius."

"She probably told him what to write. It's nothing at all."

"Don't be such a pessimist, Richard. I'll wager that Edmund's thoughts are behind it, and Madame simply provided a few suggestions. I must write him this very day and praise him. I will ask for the next part of the story. I will tell him that patience is difficult with such a splendid beginning as this."

"It is good, is it?" the duke said, his voice gruff and filled with such pride that she wanted to cry.

"Yes, very good, and it's been just three weeks. It appears that Madame de la Valette is making excellent progress. I miss the boy, you know." She looked down at what she saw was hunger in her son's beautiful eyes. Hunger? For his son? Yes, that must be it. But then, why didn't he simply return to Chesleigh? That or bring Edmund here? She tested the water, saying, "I've been thinking, dearest. Edmund is no longer a baby. Soon he will need his father's guiding hand. Could he not come up to London with Marissa's cousin? I am curious to meet her as well."

The duke eyed his mother suspiciously. Her dark eyes, so like his own, were guileless, which made him all the more wary. Like his father, his mother never missed anything. As a boy, he'd always failed whenever he'd tried to lie to either of them. "I think," he said acidly, "that you have been talking to Bunyon. Damn the fellow for his infernal meddling."

The dowager duchess merely smiled at her son's show of temper. Naturally she'd spoken to Bunyon, but oddly enough, he'd said very little, which, she supposed, she admired. Loyalty was important, after all. But her son had acted differently, more aloof, more thoughtful perhaps since his return from Chesleigh. She'd thought that he was still grieving for his friend Robbie Faraday, but no, she'd decided that wasn't it. Nor had it anything to do with Sabrina Eversleigh, now Phillip Mercerault's wife. Ah, but he was touchy. And alone, terribly alone, she thought. She didn't know what to do, and that depressed her profoundly.

Marianne Clothilde lapsed into silence. Perhaps he wanted a new mistress, she thought, always a realist, something she refused not to be. Her son was every bit as lusty as his father before him—ah, but then his father had found her, Marianne Clothilde, daughter of an impoverished earl, and that had been when all his lust had stayed at home, with her, in their bed or wherever they happened to find themselves. She smiled at that wondrous memory. However, her son was very much his own man, despite the likeness to his father. She'd believed when he'd done as his father had wished and married Marissa that he would settle down, but he hadn't. He'd never said a single word against his young wife. He'd never said a word against his father-in-law, who was a despicable man. And then Marissa had died.

Marianne Clothilde sighed. She was beginning to wonder if the duke would ever find a woman to suit him, a woman to complete him. What was Marissa's cousin like?

She said to his back, for he'd turned to look out onto the rainy park opposite the house, "You know that Bunyon never tells me anything. I wish he would because you're as closed as a clam."

"Even now you could be lying for him. No," he continued over his shoulder, "I'll take the bastard, no, not that precise word exactly, at least not to my mother. I'll take Bunyon to Gentleman Jackson's boxing saloon and cave in his stomach."

It was then that she realized he'd never answered her question. She smiled at his very stiff back. "You know, dearest, I'm growing bored with inactivity. Perhaps you would consider bringing Madame de la Valette and Edmund to London." She added, with just a whiff of a whine, "I miss my only, dearest grandson. I would like to see him before I doubtless become very ill and unable to, and then die. Can't you bring him and Madame de la Valette here? For your only, dear mother?"

The duke turned to face her, and she momentarily forgot her acting at the haggard look in his eyes. He slashed his hand in the air, saying in a harsh voice, "Madame has no desire to come to London. When I informed her that I wished it, she threatened to leave Chesleigh. When I told her she had nowhere else to go, she said it was none of my affair what she did. Then she sent me straight to hell, if I recall correctly."

Marianne Clothilde blinked. She attached herself to what was really important. "You *informed* her, my son? From what Bunyon has told me, she is a pleasant young woman, but also possesses great pride. Also, she is a poor relation, dependent upon you. Perhaps you were too high-handed in your treatment of her."

As his only answer was an uncompromising stare, she continued, "What is her name, dearest? I cannot keep referring to her as Madame de la Valette."

"Evangeline," he said, his voice low and deep. His mother, suddenly enlightened, nearly lost her bearings. But she didn't. She wanted to know so much, but she wasn't stupid. The duke had stepped behind a barrier even she couldn't breach.

She said merely, "What a lovely name." Then she rose from her chair and shook out her skirts. She was a tall woman, still possessed of a graceful, willowy figure despite her fifty years. She walked to her son, lightly kissed his cheek, and said, "I have thought so many times that you are quite the most handsome gentleman of my acquaintance."

"I look like you, Mother, so you're merely showing your own conceit."

"Oh, not entirely. Your father was also a splendid-looking gentleman." She knew that her son, just as his father had been before him, was continually plagued by hopeful young ladies, as well as by married ladies, and ladies who were not ladies at all. She wondered if he hadn't fallen in love because women had so eagerly thrown themselves into his arms and into his bed since he'd reached the age of sixteen. Perhaps even younger, she thought. Her husband had been inordinately proud of his son's sexual prowess. He'd loved his son more than he loved his wife, she suspected. He would curse his son's wildness one moment, and preen like the proud papa he was the next. Ah, and then the son had bowed to his father's wishes, married, presented the world with an heir, lost his wife, and now conducted his life in a more discreet fashion. And he was bitterly unhappy.

She said in the most indifferent voice in her repertoire, "You've told me that Evangeline is half English."

"Yes," he said, and that was all. He couldn't begin to imagine what his mother would say if he added that he felt more lust for her than any woman he'd ever met in his life and he also wanted to strangle her, and perhaps hold her tightly against him when they slept together.

"I believe," Marianne Clothilde said, smoothing down her lovely pale blue muslin skirts, "it's time for Monsieur Possette to arrive. He arranges my hair most charmingly." With that, she walked from the drawing room. She paused at the door and said in an airy voice, "Who knows? Perhaps Evangeline will come to London soon. Perhaps I will invite her myself. What do you think of that?"

He looked hunted. What was she to make of that? "Don't, Mother," he said. "Don't."

In that moment, as he stood alone as the devil staring out into the rain, he saw her arching her back against his arm as he caressed her with his mouth. "Damn you, Evangeline," he said to no one at all.

He thought of his mistress, Morgana, but oddly, although he missed her cutting wit, her awesome skills, he didn't want her. He only wanted one woman, curse her.

He felt violent. He thought of Bunyon and rubbed his hands together. This afternoon they'd go to Gentleman Jackson's boxing saloon. Every punch would make him feel better, despite which one of them was hit.

Chapter 21

Evangeline was surprised to see Mrs. Raleigh very nearly running down the long corridor toward the north wing, her household keys jangling madly at her waist.

"What's wrong, Mrs. Raleigh?" she called out as she closed her bedchamber door behind her. "May I help?"

"Oh, Madame. Good morning." She stopped and turned to face Evangeline, her face pink from her exertion. "I'll tell you, Madame, I'm worried about Mrs. Needle. She always eats her porridge in the servants' hall precisely at seven o'clock in the morning. No one has seen her. It's after eight. Something's wrong, I know it. She is so very old, you know. I must go see."

"I'll come with you," Evangeline said, falling into step beside the housekeeper. "She probably lost track of the time while making up some new potion."

When they reached the turret room, Evangeline rapped on the door and called, "Mrs. Needle, it's Madame de la Valette and Mrs. Raleigh. Are you all right?"

There was no answer. Evangeline called out again. Still nothing.

"I knew it," Mrs. Raleigh said, "something is wrong. She's ill, I know it."

"Perhaps she's in the home wood gathering mushrooms," Evangeline said even as she turned the large brass doorknob. She didn't believe that, though. She didn't want to go into the tower room.

The smell of drying roses was strong in the air. "Mrs. Needle?"

Evangeline walked slowly about the room, Mrs. Raleigh close on her heels. She drew in her breath sharply. "Oh, dear," she said. "Oh, dear."

Evangeline ran to the other side of the screen, into the small alcove that was Mrs. Needle's sleeping area. The old woman lay crumpled on her side. Evangeline knew that she was dead even before she knelt down beside her and closed her fingers over her veined wrist. There was no pulse, and her body was stiff. Mrs. Needle had been dead for many hours.

"She was an old woman," Mrs. Raleigh said. "But still it is distressing. It must have been her heart. I pray it was quick. She never allowed any of us to remain long with her. Oh, goodness, I'm so very sorry that her time came when she was alone."

Evangeline sat back on her heels and closed her eyes. Unbidden, the peaceful face of her mother rose in her mind, her pale lips quirked in a smile, her sightless blue eyes staring until the doctor gently lowered her lids. She had felt only shock at first at her mother's death; the stiff figure that had been her mother had seemed alien to her. Grief had come later. "Yes," Evangeline said finally, looking up at Mrs. Raleigh. "She was an old woman, a very old woman. Fetch Bassick. He will know what is to be done."

Mrs. Raleigh nodded and hurried from the room,

the keys at her waist making light clanging noises as she ran down the stone steps.

Evangeline looked down into Mrs. Needle's face. All the ancient lines seemed to have been smoothed out. She didn't look as old in death. She reached down and rested her palm for a brief moment against Mrs. Needle's cold cheek. The poor old woman. She'd died alone, with no one to share her passing. Her eyes fell to the open neck of Mrs. Needle's old wool gown, and she saw in the hollow of her wrinkled throat two violet bruises, each the size of a man's thumb. She sat back on her heels, closing her eyes. Oh no, oh God no. She forced herself to look again, more closely. No, those horrible thumb marks were still there, deep, deadly. Mrs. Needle hadn't died alone—someone had strangled her.

She covered her face with her hands. It was all her fault. She'd told John Edgerton about Mrs. Needle. She'd probably even mentioned her name, but she didn't remember if she had or not. She'd told him that the old woman suspected that something wasn't right with her. She'd mentioned her only because—a sob tore from her throat, and she covered her face in her hands. The truth was that she'd told Edgerton hoping to use the poor old woman to frighten him into calling a halt to his madness. But instead he'd simply removed her, as if she'd been nothing more than a flick of lint from a jacket sleeve. He'd ordered her murder. And she was the one responsible. Mrs. Needle was dead because Evangeline had come to Chesleigh castle. There was no excuse for her, none at all.

Bassick found Evangeline rocking back and forth over Mrs. Needle's body, her face streaked with tears, her eyes blind, her body bowed with awful pain.

"Madame," he said quietly, dropping his hand to

her shoulder. "You must come away now. I'm sorry her passing has caused you such grief. The shock of finding someone who has died can be very distressing."

Evangeline looked up at him. "She's dead, Bassick. Don't you understand? She's dead."

He knelt beside her and carefully pressed the flat of his hand over Mrs. Needle's heart. "Yes, I understand. Leave now and I will see to things. It was her heart. She was old, very old. It just stopped, yes, doubtless it simply stopped. It was an easy passing, Madame. I have sent for the doctor. He will arrive shortly. Go, Madame."

"No, Bassick, it wasn't her heart. She didn't have an easy passing." She touched her fingers to the bruises. "Someone came in here and strangled her."

Bassick felt the circular room reel around him. He shook his head back and forth. "No, that's not possible. Not here, not at Chesleigh."

She said nothing.

Bassick studied the bruises on Mrs. Needle's throat. He knew what he was looking at, but still it shocked him to his toes. He couldn't accept it. "But why?" He felt helpless, beyond his ken, but he knew he had to act, do something to fix this dreadful situation. "Why?" he said again.

And Evangeline said, her voice dull and lifeless as the old woman crumpled on the floor beside her, "I don't know, Bassick. I don't know."

Bassick pulled himself together. He rose. He offered Evangeline his hand and helped her to stand. "Listen to me, Madame. It's best that we don't touch her. I must call the magistrate. It is Baron Lindley, an old fool, but we really have no choice in the matter. Come with me. We will both drink a brandy to steady us for what will come."

"Mrs. Needle didn't hurt anyone," Evangeline said as she let Bassick lead her from the room.

Baron Lindley, blessed with a thick head of white hair and stoop shouldered, whose gout was the only topic allowed in his household, arrived in the next hour. He found the young cousin of the duke, Madame de la Valette, unnaturally withdrawn. He thought it a shame that such a sensitive young lady should have been the one to find the old woman. After duly questioning all the Chesleigh servants, he returned to the drawing room and Madame de la Valette, for there was no one else to receive him. He wished heartily that the duke was in residence. He felt uncomfortable with his young cousin. His right foot hurt. He wanted to ask for a warm towel to wrap around it, but seeing the blank-faced young lady who looked so very alone, he didn't ask. He doubted she'd even understand him. He wondered if she was half-witted. He cleared his throat. Bassick continued to stand beside the closed door. He cleared his throat two more times before the young lady finally looked up at him.

"I have determined that the man who strangled the old woman was someone to whom she gave a healing potion and it harmed either him or a loved one. I have determined that it was revenge. The man was in a rage and strangled her."

"Revenge," she said, the word flitting through her mind, giving no meaning, not really. Had the baron really determined that?

"Yes, revenge," Baron Lindley continued. "She owned nothing of value. Indeed, nothing in her rooms was even disturbed. There was the strong smell of roses. I fancy the man who strangled her intensified the heat under the roses. Perhaps it was the favorite scent of the woman who Mrs. Needle harmed with her potion. It was probably a love potion. Yes, the fellow was maddened by his grief and killed her. I doubt we will be able to find out who he is. However, I will see that all local folk who have been given medicine by the old woman will be questioned. Now, I must return home. My foot pains me. I must elevate it while I drink a brandy. It is too much. Good-bye, Madame."

Evangeline knew that no one would be found. She doubted that local folk would even be questioned. In any case, it would be a waste of time. She managed to rise when Baron Lindley left the drawing room, Bassick at his heels. Mrs. Needle's death would remain a mystery, and soon everyone would forget. She wasn't of sufficient importance for anyone to remember.

After Baron Lindley left, Evangeline said to Bassick, "You were quite right about the baron. Even if he weren't a fool, little would be done. I must write to the duke and inform him of what has occurred." She paused a moment. "Please, Bassick, check all the locks."

Bassick saw the fear in her eyes. He didn't blame her. He felt fear himself. Someone had come into the castle and murdered one of its occupants. "Of course, Madame. I will also post footmen at various entrances. Perhaps the man who did this thing will return. Yes, you must write to his grace. He will be much shocked. He has always been quite fond of Mrs. Needle. He's known her all of his life, you know. He was always bringing her slips of plants he came across."

"Yes, I know he was fond of her. He really brought her plants and such?"

"Oh, yes. Just last month a ship captain brought a variety of plants from India to give to the duke. He gave them to Mrs. Needle. His grace told her he wanted her to mix a potion to make him the best horseman in the land. As I recall, Mrs. Needle told his grace that since he was already the best lover in the land, it would spoil his character to give him more. She laughed greatly when she said that, his grace too."

Evangeline sat at the duke's desk in the library, spread out a single piece of foolscap before her, and dipped her quill into the inkwell. How they had parted three weeks before was of no importance now. She needed to see him. But to say what? I killed your old nurse. No, I didn't strangle her myself, but I told John Edgerton about her and he had it done. Oh, God, what was she to do, to write to him? She knew she had to see him, or she'd quite simply go mad with guilt.

"Your grace," she wrote finally, "I'm sorry to have to tell you such tragic news. Mrs. Needle has died. The cause of her death was not natural." Her quill remained poised above the paper before she forced out the words. "Someone came into the castle, went to the north tower, and killed her. Someone unknown. I beg you to come to Chesleigh. Your cousin—"

She scratched her name and folded the sheet.

She quite simply wanted to die.

Chapter 22

The duke arrived late the following morning, having driven from London in under six hours. He was tired, dirty, stunned at the manner of his old nurse's death, and wild with worry for Evangeline.

"Thank God you're home, your grace. Welcome, welcome." Bassick was so relieved to see his master that he nearly hurled himself against the duke's chest. As it was, he did trip over a chair in his rush to assist him out of his greatcoat.

"I came as quickly as I could, Bassick. Where is Madame?"

"She is with Lord Edmund, your grace. I fear she is very much affected by Mrs. Needle's death. She has insisted on making the arrangements for Mrs. Needle's funeral. I have the footmen keeping watch at strategic points around the castle. All the locks have either been changed or fortified. Oh, yes, we are so glad you have come so quickly."

"She will do no more," the duke said, and strode away, Bassick looking after him.

He opened the nursery door quietly and stepped inside. The large room was very warm, a fire blazing in the fireplace against the far wall. She was on a rug, leaning back against a settee, Edmund close to her. He was holding an English wooden soldier in his hand. He was saying, "I don't know, Eve. You say you are just fine, but Bassick said I wasn't to try to chase you down and shoot you today. He said you wouldn't be enough sport for me."

"No, probably not," she said. "Forgive me, Edmund, but I truly wouldn't be any sport at all. I wonder, does Bassick know everything?"

"He said that I wasn't to say anything in a loud voice to you. He said I was to treat you the way I'd like to be treated if I had a bad tummy pain. He said a truce was in order."

A truce, she thought. She turned, smiling, and gave him her hand. "A truce it is, Edmund. We will recommence the fox and the goose tomorrow."

Edmund looked up to see his father standing in the doorway.

"Papa!" He flew to his father, laughing, shrieking, and the duke caught him up in his arms and kissed him soundly. "Are you here to see Eve, Papa? She's not at all herself. She's sad. Mrs. Needle died, you know. I heard Mrs. Raleigh talking to all the servants about it. Bassick said I wasn't to torment her."

"I know, Edmund. Now, here is Bunyon standing right behind me. So quietly he walks. He's going to take you for a ride, Edmund. I will see to your cousin Eve."

"You won't chase her and shoot her, will you, Papa?"

"Not at all."

"That's good. Only I get to do that. Make her smile, Papa. I like to see her smile."

Evangeline heard Bunyon's voice but didn't see him. In an instant Edmund was gone, and she was alone with the duke. He didn't move toward her, just stood there, looking at her. He closed the nursery door.

"I came as quickly as I could," he said. Then he held out his arms to her. "Come here."

And she did. She didn't run to him as quickly as his son had, but she was in his arms in but an instant. "It's all right now," he said against her hair as he stroked her back. "I'm here now. It will be all right."

All the pain and guilt broke inside her. She sobbed against his neck, uncaring, out of control, but he said nothing, merely held her, stroked his large hands up and down her back, slowly, steadily, and she cried and cried. She clung to him like a limpet, her arms tightly hugging him to her.

When her sobs became hiccups, he lightly kissed the top of her head. "It's all over now, Evangeline. I promise you it will be all right."

"No," she said, pulling back, "no, nothing is all right, nothing at all." Had it not been for her, Mrs. Needle would be alive, but she couldn't tell him that. Then Edmund would die. She struck his chest, wishing that she herself would be hurt. He ignored her blows and continued to hold her. When the Chesleigh servant had brought him her letter, the anger he was still trying to clutch to himself against her was lost in the shock of his old nurse's death and Evangeline's plea to him. He locked away his grief and set himself to comfort her.

Finally, there was nothing left in her, no more tears, no more violence, just an emptiness that was destroying her. He loosened his hold and pressed a handkerchief to her hand. When she did nothing with it, he took it from her and wiped her face—a beloved face, he realized, and it shook him to his very core. But he knew that it was true. Her eyes were swollen, and she was so pale it frightened him. Odd that she had grown very fond of Mrs. Needle in such a short time. It didn't matter. She was distraught.

Evangeline whispered into his handkerchief, "I'm so sorry, your grace. I'm glad you have come. I haven't known what to do."

"You've done more than you should. It is I who am sorry that you've borne all the burden." For an instant he saw such suffering in her eyes and so many other emotions that he didn't understand. He didn't let her go. He wasn't about to let her go. He pulled her closer. "We don't have to speak about it now. I don't wish to hurt you more."

She shook her head and got a hold on herself. She'd let her guard down, and it was dangerous. She had to keep her secrets to herself. "No," she said finally, slowly pulling back from him. "No, you must know what happened so that you may act. Baron Lindley is as effective a magistrate as Edmund is a dragon slayer."

"Dragon slayer? I thought he only wanted to hunt down highwaymen."

"When I read him a story about a dragon slayer, he was excited. He's just not certain that I'll be able to breathe fire at him when he's chasing me." She laughed, then choked on that laughter, wanting to die.

"It's all right. Laughter makes you forget for a moment. It's good." He held a chair for her, and she sat down, smoothing her gown with long, pale fingers. He remained standing, his shoulders against the mantelpiece. He knew in that moment that he was seeing her with new eyes.

She looked back up at him, the man who'd become the center of her thoughts, whose son was so dear to her now that she knew she'd simply lie down and die if something happened to him. What was she to do? The truth hovered, damning words that would forever make her his enemy, words that would earn his condemnation, his contempt. But the words remained unspoken, not because she was a coward. What held her again was the threat to Edmund. Now she had no doubt that John Edgerton would carry out his threat to kill the boy if she betrayed him. She had already brought death to his home. And lies, but lies were better than more death. "Baron Lindley believes the murderer was a man to whom Mrs. Needle gave a love potion. This potion evidently killed his sweetheart. It makes not a whit of sense to me, but the baron is quite pleased with himself. He has the gout. He came quickly upon this solution and quickly left to go home to a brandy and a cushion for his foot."

"Nothing was missing? Nothing stolen?"

She shook her head.

"I'm surprised he didn't immediately latch onto some poor tinker, the bane of Lindley's existence. Thank you for dealing with him. I'll see him again, for I must. Damn, I should be the magistrate, could easily have been some two years ago, but there were too many other things to occupy my time." He shook his head, frowning, she thought, at what he thought was a failure in himself. "There's no motive for this. Who would possibly want to kill Mrs. Needle?"

Of course she knew. She knew everything. She looked away from him. There was pain at his loss in his dark eyes, and it killed her to see it and know that she could avenge the harmless old woman.

"You've made all the arrangements. I thank you." He eyed her, seeing her pallor, the strange hardness in her eyes that he didn't understand. "You're tired.

Bunyon and I will take care of Edmund. I'll see to whatever else has to be done."

She leaped to her feet. "No, please, I don't want to be alone—that is, I don't want to rest. Please let me stay with you."

He didn't understand this either. "You don't want to be alone?"

She'd made a mistake. He seemed so attuned to her. It was disconcerting. "Perhaps," she said, rising slowly, not looking at him.

He laid his hand upon her shoulder. "You can stay with me if you wish it." He added after a short pause, "Death is always a shock. I remember when I found out about Robbie's death. I was bowed to my knees. It took a long time for me to even see the preciousness of my son, to enjoy laughter once again, to see the beauty of a woman and not feel the deadening rage and helplessness. It will pass, Evangeline, the shock, the grief. But you won't forget, no, you'll never forget and that is perhaps for the best."

But not the guilt, she thought, not the guilt. She merely bowed her head, saying nothing.

The following afternoon Mrs. Needle was buried in the Chesleigh graveyard, the resting place of both family and servants for more than two centuries. Evangeline stared at the mound of fresh earth while the vicar lamented the cruelty of Mrs. Needle's death, the duke's gloved hand holding her steady. She raised her eyes to the castle, to the north wing where Mrs. Needle had lived. The thought of the duke returning to London and leaving her again at Chesleigh seemed too much to bear. She shivered. It was very cold today, as a February day should be.

Over a quiet dinner after the funeral, as Evangeline

wondered what she was going to do, he said slowly, "You need a change, Evangeline. This hasn't been pleasant for you. Would you care to visit London for a while?"

She looked at him, unspeaking, disbelieving that he would offer her this chance. She didn't deserve it. She realized then that he expected her to deny him once again, but before she could speak, he said, "You and I haven't always dealt well together. Perhaps we can remedy that away from Chesleigh. You have told me that you don't want to go to London, that if I forced you, you would leave me. I don't want that. But I want to take you away from Chesleigh for a short while. Edmund too, naturally."

She saw that this strong man, this man who knew his own worth, was afraid she would turn him down again. She wanted to throw herself into his arms and shout her gratitude to him, but she didn't. She said simply, "Thank you, your grace. I would much appreciate going with you to London. It is very kind of you."

He hadn't realized how much her acceptance would mean to him. He slowly let out his breath. He slowly raised his glass of port and said as he saluted her, "My mother will be very pleased. She wants to meet you as well as see her grandson." He saw the relief in her expressive eyes and knew he would protect her with his life.

He said, "I too am glad you have changed your mind." He set down his wineglass and rose. "You're exhausted, Evangeline. I would like to leave early in the morning. I suggest that you seek your bed. Do you wish some laudanum to make you sleep?"

She stood to face him. There was such caring in him. She felt her guilt writhe and twist inside her.

His kindness, his strength, his acceptance of her, only worsened it. She shook her head.

He walked over to her and touched a finger to her pale cheek. Her skin was soft, so very soft. He wanted to bring her against him, just hold her, at least until she eased against him. He wanted to tell her that he would do his damnedest to lessen her pain at his old nurse's death, just as having her with him would lessen his pain. He said nothing. He couldn't find the words. He gently forced her head up. He saw tears in her eyes. He leaned down and lightly kissed her cheeks, and then her closed eyes, tasting her tears.

He said, still kissing her eyelids. "I won't leave you again." And then he kissed her mouth and was shattered.

And late that night, in a cold rain, Evangeline met another man down in a protected cove.

Chapter 23

"Grandmama, I'm here at last. I wanted John Coachman to go faster, but Papa wouldn't allow it. Look, I even brought Eve with me."

Marianne Clothilde heard that beloved little voice, all the words tumbling over each other as they burst out of his mouth, dropped her embroidery, and was on her feet to catch Edmund in her arms when he leaped upward. She smiled as she hugged him. "It's been too long, Edmund, far too long. I'm beginning to believe that London isn't such a horrible place for little boys. Perhaps your grandfather was wrong, your papa as well. Perhaps it's best for all of us if you stay right where we are so we can all be together. Goodness, let me put you down. You've grown into a young giant."

"Eve says I'm better than a giant. I'm an ox, all muscle and stubborn, and I can shoot anything at twenty paces."

"Ah, your cousin Eve. Why don't you introduce me to her, Edmund?"

"She's strong as an ox too. She's going to teach me to swim better than Papa." He frowned. "If it ever gets warm again."

"I can vouch that she's strong as an ox, Mother. After all, she's spent close to eight hours in the same coach with Edmund. I, alas, was unable to stay the course. As to her swimming, I have yet to judge her abilities in that direction."

Marianne Clothilde couldn't look away from her beautiful son. His voice was deep, amused. He sounded quite pleased. He stood just inside the drawing room, a striking young woman dressed in a dark blue silk gown at his side.

"You are Edmund's cousin Eve?" Marianne Clothilde looked at a young woman who was nearly as tall as she was.

Evangeline curtsied. "Yes, your grace. I'm Marissa's cousin."

"Madame de la Valette," the duke said.

Marianne Clothilde couldn't have been more shocked if someone had milked a cow in the drawing room. Her son, her arrogant, quite sophisticated son. He'd merely said her name, but the tone of his voice—it was filled with a mixture of pride and possessiveness. It appeared that her son had finally found the woman who'd been fashioned just for him. She realized then that he was standing very close to Evangeline, as if to protect her. From me? she wondered, blinking. Does he think I'll not be kind to the girl?

She gave the half-French cousin a beautiful smile, her son's smile, truth be told, and clasped her hand. She was lovely enough for her son, Marianne Clothilde thought, but what was wrong? There was something very surprising in the young woman's eyes. Was it fear? Of her? No, that was nonsense.

"I'm delighted to finally meet you, Madame," she said, and took that slender hand in hers.

The hand quivered, then subsided. "Thank you, your grace," Evangeline said, and wanted to sink into the floor. Here his mother was, welcoming a traitor into her home. "I'm very sorry about our unplanned visit, but Mrs. Needle, she died, and it was dreadful and there was nothing, and I didn't know what to do and his grace—"

"Yes, I know, and I'm very sorry for it."

"His grace was kind enough to include me with Edmund."

"Now, there's a piece of information that's news to both Edmund and me." He looked over at his son, who was carefully studying a very old globe. "Don't touch that, Edmund."

"No, Papa, I was just wondering why it is round when Mrs. Raleigh has told me many times that the world is flat. This is the world, isn't it?"

Marianne Clothilde laughed. She said to Eve, "Mrs. Raleigh has belonged to this club called the Flat Earth for the longest time. You will have a good deal of convincing before you change his mind, Madame."

"Edmund," the duke called out.

"Yes, Papa?"

"You will listen to me and you will believe me, and that will be the end to it, all right?"

Lord Edmund walked slowly back to his father and stood staring up at him.

"The world is round. Repeat that."

"The world is round, Papa. Are you certain?"

"Have I ever lied to you?"

"No, Papa. I've never even known you to be wrong."

Evangeline groaned.

Marianne Clothilde laughed until tears were swimming in her eyes.

"Good. The next time Mrs. Raleigh tells you that the world is flat, you will smile and nod, but you will know that the world is really round."

"Yes, Papa."

The duke smiled at his son, picked him up, and tucked him against his side.

"Goodness, your grace, that was well done," Evangeline said, and Marianne Clothilde heard nothing but humor in that rich voice, no flirtatious sighs or giggles that her son was treated to so very often.

"Yes, I'm very impressed. Now, do not think that you're intruding, Madame. I quite wanted to meet you. My son has told me a good bit about you."

"Oh, dear," Evangeline said.

"I told her that you were stubborn as a pig, a passing good rider, and you very much enjoyed the scenery at Chesleigh. Oh, yes, I did tell her that you also had a bit of charm."

"I suppose I must be relieved that you didn't go into a good deal of detail."

"Why don't you think I did? She's my mother, after all. She admires me, tells me that I can do no wrong at all."

"That is quite true," Marianne Clothilde said. "But he's my son. What's a mother to do with such a splendid son?"

Evangeline groaned, the duke tossed Edmund once into the air, and Marianne Clothilde said, "Do come and sit down, Madame. I will ring for tea. May I call you Evangeline? Madame surely doesn't fit on an earth that is round."

"I don't know, Grandmama," Edmund said, frowning. "Mrs. Raleigh is always so certain when she tells me."

"Round, Edmund," the duke said. "Round."

"Yes, Papa. Grandmama, did Papa tell you that I'm the finest shot in the country?"

"He did say that you had cleanly shot Rex the peacock at least a dozen times."

"Yes," Edmund said, then gave a big yawn. Evangeline leaned down and pushed his face up with her fingers. "Now, I want no arguments. You're as tired as your papa. Because you're young, you'll get to go with Ellen to the nursery and rest for just a little while."

The duke lifted his son back into his arms. "No, I'll take him to Ellen. Yes, I'll come back. I won't leave you to the dragon here. Mother, don't frighten her to her toes while I'm gone."

"But, Papa, what about my story? I'm ready to tell Grandmama more of my story."

"You will, after you've reposed yourself." He said from the doorway, "I'll tell Grayson to bring tea."

He left the young lady with her, quite alone. Marianne Clothilde prayed that this was the right woman for her son, prayed with all her heart. She gave her a charming smile that was quite natural. "Do sit down, Evangeline. Did you ride the entire time with Edmund?"

"All but one hour when I had the headache. His grace insisted that I ride with him."

"Ride with him?" Marianne Clothilde said.

To her delight, Evangeline flushed. "You see, the duke was riding his beautiful stallion, and he said—in any case, I rode seated in front of him. That was all, your grace, truly."

But it wasn't all, Marianne Clothilde saw, and was immensely pleased. She said, "It's nearly impossible to say no to my son. He's very forceful upon occasion."

"Yes," Evangeline said. "I have found that to be true." Actually, he hadn't forced her to do anything. Indeed, nothing at all had happened. Evangeline had leaned back against him, in the circle of his arms, and slept soundly. She hadn't felt so safe in a very long time.

Marianne Clothilde patted the seat beside her, and Evangeline unfastened her cloak, laying it over the back of a chair, then sat down. Now, this was a very nice thing, Marianne Clothilde thought. The young lady had an elegant slim figure that, truth be told, was very much like her own—even to her very full bosom. She supposed that the gown had been Marissa's, poor foolish girl.

"Actually, Evangeline," Marianne Clothilde said after a moment, "my son finally admitted to me that he'd given you orders, quite in his best lord-of-the castle manner. As I recall, he came very close to snarling."

"Oh, no," Evangeline said. "He didn't mean to do that precisely. He's so very used to having everyone obey him instantly. It's just that I couldn't allow him to at that particular moment. That is—"

"I know. My son has been kind to you, all sweetness."

"I've not ever known him to be sweet. That's not in his character. He's more often jesting to get his way, that, or he frowns at you, knowing that only a fool would dare to go against him and— Oh, dear, I don't mean to insult your son, your grace. Truly, the duke has been very solicitous toward me. Yes, that's the right word. He wouldn't resent being called solicitous. Would he?"

Marianne Clothilde patted Evangeline's clasped hands. "We will ask him. You don't yet know me well enough, but I will tell you the truth. My son and I are very much alike, for better or for worse. You, my dear Evangeline," she continued without pause, "are feeling very guilty, aren't you?"

How could she possibly know?

When she said, "Yes, I suppose that I am," she sounded terrified.

"You're part of the family. You belong here for as long as it pleases you. Incidentally, Marissa's gown becomes you. It's an excellent color for you. I fancy Dorrie altered it for you?"

"Yes, she's quite good."

"I know. I realized that a very long time ago. I was the one who assigned her to Marissa. Marissa liked her very much."

A tall, plump man with a headful of thick reddish-white hair came into the drawing room, carrying a heavy silver tea service in his black-clad arms. He had very thick dark red eyebrows that looked perpetually arched, making him look mildly surprised.

"Ah, Grayson, you've brought sustenance."

"Yes, the kind of sustenance that pleases you, your grace." He set the tray down on the table in front of them.

"Grayson and I grew up together," Marianne Clothilde said as, to Evangeline's surprise, the butler himself poured tea.

"Madame?"

"I like it plain, Grayson."

"He's so very good at it," Marianne Clothilde said. "You see, I have arthritis. It has made me clumsy the past few years, so Grayson does many things for me.

That is another reason I cannot stay at Chesleigh. The damp chill makes the condition worse." She smiled at the butler as she took her cup of tea from him. "I think we make an impressive pair, particularly now that our bones are brittle, our hair is graying, and our consequence is at its peak."

"Just so, your grace," Grayson said, "but I am of the opinion that the redder the hair, the more naturally consequence sits upon the shoulders."

"You would," Marianne Clothilde said as she gracefully bit into an apple tart. "Ah, this is excellent. Not as good as the Dinwitty cook of Phillip Mercerault's, not as good as Mrs. Dent's, but acceptable. Now, Grayson, this is Madame de la Valette. She is one of the family and is at present also Lord Edmund's nanny."

Grayson eyed Evangeline, then slowly nodded. "I believe this will do just fine," he said, and left the drawing room.

Marianne Clothilde laughed. "Now, you're staring at the scones. Do have one, Evangeline."

"However do he and Bassick get along?" Evangeline said between bites of an apple-flavored scone.

Marianne Clothilde laughed. "Very astute of you, Evangeline. Actually, they've never met. The duke agrees with me that we should keep the households apart. Now, Tsar Ivan—that is what I have taken to calling our butler at St. John Court, Richard's estate in the north—I have always thought him to be cut from far starchier cloth than either Grayson or Bassick. He unbent himself sufficiently upon one occasion to inform me that if the Conqueror had enjoyed the services of a butler, he would doubtless have been one of his ancestors."

Evangeline was laughing when the duke entered the drawing room. He paused a moment on the threshold, a smile lighting his eyes. And such a smile, his mother thought, staring at him.

Chapter 24

Marianne Clothilde said, "Do come in and sit down, dearest, and pour yourself a cup of tea. Evangeline quite likes Cook's scones. I've been telling her about Tsar Ivan."

"Tsar Ivan is a terror," the duke said. He added with a smile, "I gather from your laughter, Evangeline, that my mother hasn't tried to interrogate you about the grandeur of your ancestors, accuse you of trying to steal my son's affections, or threatened to pull out your toenails if you dare to provide a single criticism of either me or my son?"

"We have only discussed Tsar Ivan's ancestors, your grace. Mine, as you know, are noble enough, but not at all as grand as his."

"He's an old Methodist. He quite terrified me when I was a boy. He still does." He poured himself a cup of tea, refreshing his mother's cup as well, something he did with his customary grace.

Evangeline laughed again, a lovely, free sound that seemed to expand in his chest, making him want to grab her in his arms and kiss her until he could manage to pull her gown down to her waist and caress her breasts and taste her and . . . dear God, he was in his mother's drawing room, drinking tea, and he was thinking about making love to her, kissing her until she was screaming his name. He shook himself and choked on the damned tea.

Marianne Clothilde banged him on his back. When he'd recovered, she thought he looked rather flushed, but said, "We have not yet discussed Mrs. Needle's murder. Yes, I use that very stark word because it is the truth. Now, what do you know about all this?"

"Baron Lindley treated Evangeline to a dose of his idiocy, namely, that one of Mrs. Needle's potions must have killed a man's lover or wife and he strangled Mrs. Needle in his rage and in revenge. Nonsense, of course, but the old bugger, er, excuse me, the old idiot wanted nothing more than to go home and put his head back in his brandy bottle and his gouty foot up on a cushion." He paused a moment. "We owe our thanks to Evangeline. She had dealt with just about everything before I came." He paused for a moment, his dark eyes resting on the heavy emerald signet ring on his left hand. "I've taken steps to see that Chesleigh is more carefully guarded. Her murder makes no sense at all. She was harmless. And that scares me to my toes. Why was she killed? Why Mrs. Needle in particular? We will see. I don't plan to simply forget it and go on. No, I will find out who did this and why."

Evangeline wondered what he'd done, what he planned to do. Perhaps he would discover that traitors were using his private beach for entry into England. Perhaps he would discover that she'd betrayed him. She kept her eyes upon the Dresden china cup in her lap.

"I received a letter from Mrs. Raleigh," Marianne Clothilde said after a moment. "Everyone is very distressed. I'm glad you won't simply let life go on as usual, my dear. Mrs. Needle was a dear old woman, and she *saw* so very much. Did I ever tell you that she foresaw your birth, down to the month and the very day? She told me that you would be more handsome than your father, smarter than I—which I scarce believed possible—and a grand lover, something a mother really didn't care to hear." She smiled and patted his shoulder. "Now, no more of this for now. We will speak later."

Suddenly the duke stood up. "Evangeline is tired. I will take her to the Rose Chamber, and she can rest until dinner. We will dine here this evening, just the three of us. Come, Evangeline." And he held his hand out to her. She looked up at him, and very slowly she nodded and gave him her hand.

"Oh, dear," Marianne Clothilde said. "We have guests coming. I would be shot if I canceled this late. What shall we do?"

Evangeline heard the duke curse. "By any chance will Lady Pemberly be here? And Miss Storleigh?"

Marianne Clothilde gave her an engaging grin that was the very copy of the duke's. "So you've met Eudora? She could be one of Wellington's generals. Yes, she'll be coming."

"She and Tsar Ivan are two of a kind," the duke said. "She was camping on my doorstep on Evangeline's second evening at Chesleigh. She wanted to make certain that some fortune-hunting hussy wasn't there to take advantage of me. She dragged Drew and John Edgerton with her. She was in excellent spirits when she left. She approved of Evangeline."

"Will Lord Pettigrew and John Edgerton also be coming, your grace?"

"I will invite them," Marianne Clothilde said. "Two

more gentlemen at the table is just what I had in mind. Hopefully they will come."

And Evangeline knew that John Edgerton would certainly come, damn him to hell.

Marianne Clothilde turned to the duke. "It is very strange. Drew is constantly with Felicia. He's seen everywhere with her." She shook her head. "It never ceases to amaze me which girl will make a man fall to his knees."

"It's repellent, Mother. No man should ever fall to his knees."

"I was speaking only metaphorically."

"It is still repellent. No man worth his salt would ever be brought that low. My God, I doubt Felicia could stop chattering even when they are—well, never mind that, but it's nonetheless true." He brought himself to a halt as his mother's teacup rattled in its saucer.

Evangeline wasn't listening. She wondered how she was going to get a message to John Edgerton, and the duke's mother had solved the problem for her. She ran her tongue over her lips. "I thank you for allowing me to come, your grace."

"What do you think, Richard? Should I instead have a tray sent to Evangeline's room?"

"I should prefer that both of us could eat in my library, alone, in front of a nice warm fire."

"That isn't an alternative," Marianne Clothilde said. "You will gird your loins, dearest."

"At least you will rest now," the duke said, pulling Evangeline closer to his side. His mother's beautifully arched dark brows went up a good inch. This was fascinating. His tone was peremptory.

Evangeline merely nodded. At least now she would have some time alone, to think, to decide what she would tell Edgerton. She wanted nothing more than to kill him.

"Why are you trembling?"

She raised startled eyes to his face. "No, I'm not, not really, your grace."

"I will see you later, Evangeline," Marianne Clothilde said. "You know, you do look a bit weak in the knees. The Rose Room? Yes, that's a very nice bedchamber."

As they walked side by side up the wide circular staircase, she said, "Your town house is very elegant."

"Yes," he said. "Most of it is done in my mother's style. She quite disliked her mother-in-law's taste. I like it myself. My mother many times gets things exactly right. Not just about style but about people."

"She is also very kind."

He said, his voice low, "You don't have to come to this dinner my mother has planned."

"Do you think your mother doesn't want me there? She is so very kind that I'm not certain of her feelings. Unlike you," she added, smiling up at him. "I always know exactly what you're thinking."

"Actually, you don't." If she did, he thought, she wouldn't be standing here, not an inch away, smiling up at him. "Now, as for my dear mother's feelings, they're of no consequence. They have nothing to do with what I meant. You see? You don't understand at all."

"Very well. Tell me. What is it you wish, your grace?"

Naturally, he couldn't just spit out all the things that were flooding through his brain. It would scare her witless, or it wouldn't, and then what would he do? His belly tightened. "I just don't want you to be tired, nothing more."

He stopped and said, "This is the Rose Room. I do believe that Queen Charlotte just might have slept here, for what reason I have no idea. Maybe it was Queen Bess. On the other hand, the house isn't old enough for that particular female monarch."

He raised her hand to his mouth. She felt the heat of him through her glove. Unconsciously she leaned into him.

"No," he said. "No."

She drew back. "I'm very strong," she said finally. What had she done? She'd thrown herself at him, that's what she'd done. "Really, you don't have to ever worry about me. I am strong."

He raised his hand and touched his fingertips to her pale cheek. "Are you really so invincible?"

She raised her eyes to his dark face. He was looking at her mouth. She wanted more than anything to bring him close, to hear his strong heartbeat, to feel his flesh against hers.

No, no. She straightened and gave him a meaningless smile. "No, of course not. I'll see you this evening, your grace."

When the duke returned some minutes later to the drawing room, his mother said, "She is lovely, beautiful actually, not that that matters at all. Does it?"

"No, of course it doesn't. Be quiet, Mother. I have no intention of indulging you in speculation."

"I doubt there's much speculation to be had at this late date. You treat her quite masterfully."

"That's ridiculous. I simply treat her appropriately, quite properly."

"She's a grown woman, and a widow. She's probably used to making her own decisions. Do you think her father or her husband ordered her about?"

"No, I don't think that's possible. It's just that I don't understand her."

"You haven't known her long."

He turned to her and smiled. "No, I haven't. On the other hand, I have no doubt whatsoever that I'll know her forever. What she needs is a strong hand, that's all. My strong hand."

"You've decided very quickly."

He shrugged. "Yes, it appears that I have. What will happen? I have no idea."

She adored her son, but even she had to admit that she'd never before seen him so very caring. His behavior toward this young woman was fascinating. He realized exactly what he was feeling, but it hadn't sunk all the way in yet. He had no doubt he'd know her forever? Well, that was certainly sinking very far in. She raised her half-filled cup of tepid tea and sipped it slowly. She knew his reputation well, and she knew quite well that the beautiful women that had come and gone in his life hadn't touched him. It appeared that her proud, cynical son had finally found a woman who would hold him.

A widow who was half French.

A young woman who also appeared to adore both her son and her grandson, if Marianne Clothilde was any judge, which she was most certainly.

Chapter 25

Evangeline stopped cold at the bottom of the wide circular staircase. Standing at full attention were six footmen, all dressed in the duke's livery of crimson and gold. Grayson, a stark contrast in somber black, his reddish-white hair glistening beneath the huge chandelier, appeared to be inspecting the pristine white of the footmen's gloves. He turned to say to Evangeline, "Madame, the duke and her grace are in the drawing room. They are expecting you. You are punctual, something her grace appreciates."

Since a very sour-faced maid had awakened her, Evangeline couldn't take any of the credit. "When will the guests arrive, Grayson?"

"In five minutes, Madame. No one, I might add, even the prince regent, is often late to an affair at Clarendon House."

"No, I can't imagine that he would," she said, and meant it.

Grayson opened the double oak doors, and Evangeline preceded him into the drawing room. The duke was standing negligently against the mantelpiece, his arms crossed over his chest, his legs crossed at the ankles, smiling at something his mother was saying.

He looked magnificent in his black and white evening wear. She wondered if he or Bunyon had tied his cravat, which was so snowy white it looked to be cold to the touch. He gestured as he spoke with those long-fingers of his. She could almost feel those fingers of his lightly stroking her cheek, her jaw, her throat. And then down to her breasts. She heaved out a breath. She couldn't think of him in that way, in that very sexual way that must have shone in her eyes because she knew, simply knew that when she was thinking of him in that way, touching her, kissing her, that he knew it as well.

She was young, she thought, to have life become such a wasteland.

The duke stopped in mid-sentence when he saw Evangeline come into the room. He'd never seen a more beautiful woman in all his life. She looked exquisite in Marissa's cream satin and lace gown that banded snugly beneath her breasts and pushed them up. Pushed them up too high. They were too much on display. Her cleavage didn't seem to stop. He frowned. He supposed he would have to speak to her about that. He didn't want her insulted. That made him shake his head at himself. If he had but a moment alone with her, he would walk right up to her, and very gently ease the bodice of her gown to her waist, and then he would look at her and feel her and taste her. He couldn't seem to look away from her. Then he saw her eyes. She looked desolate, yes, that was it. But why? It made no sense unless she was unhappy here, in London, with him. He was aware that his mother was looking at him. He had to get hold of himself.

He had to say something, something that had nothing to do with jerking down her gown and taking her right here in front of the fire. He cleared his throat and took two steps toward her, stopped because he quite frankly couldn't trust himself, and said, "You're late, Evangeline, but I won't remark upon it because you were tired. At least you're here now."

"I am not at all late, your grace. Grayson even remarked that I was quite punctual, just as is her grace."

"Well, you were almost late," he said, and knew he was being a fool.

"Your grace," she said, ignoring him, and curtsied deeply to the dowager duchess.

"Oh, goodness," Marianne Clothilde said. "My dear, you will have to protect Evangeline. She looks utterly ravishing. I fear the gentlemen will lose their heads."

"They will have every right to. Just look at her neckline, Mother. It's nearly to her waist. There is too much flesh on display. Since we're all gentlemen here tonight, they should endeavor, at least, not to ogle her openly. However, if any one of them goes beyond the line, I will smash him into the ground, back by your rose bushes."

"I assure you, your grace, that no gentleman will even give me a second glance. I'm a widow, I have no money, and surely I'm not beyond ordinary." But her hands were covering her breasts. She'd argued with Dorrie and lost. But it was true, no gentleman would be interested in her.

The duke was standing not a foot away from her in but an instant. He said low, just for her ears, "If you say anything more like that, I will thrash you. Do you understand me?"

Evangeline forced a smile, forced her hands back down to her sides. "I understand your words, but I don't understand you."

"You won't ever denigrate yourself again. Surely you can understand that. You will believe me that your gown is cut too low. Have Dorrie pull it up at least two inches. I don't want men looking at your breasts."

"Why?"

"Because they're mine," he said.

She nearly leaped on him, and he saw it and grinned down at her.

"Dearest, are you teasing Evangeline?"

"Oh, no, Mother. I was just telling her what I expect of her this evening."

Marianne Clothilde frowned at the sound of laughter and voices coming from the entrance hall. What had her son said to Evangeline? It must have been something quite wicked, for Evangeline was red from her bosom to her forehead. Oh, damn, she wished she could just ask, and turn red herself. She regretted on this particular occasion that the guests were being so punctual, curse them.

This was the duchess's idea of a small dinner party? Evangeline stared around the vast dining room table at the twenty-five beautifully garbed, laughing guests. Lady Pemberly had greeted her affably, and promptly told her that she had too much flesh showing, which made the duke, who'd overheard her, frown ferociously. And Felicia, who had been tapping Lord Pettigrew's arm with her delicate ivory fan to gain his attention, turned to tell her laughingly that the duke had been sorely remiss in keeping Evangeline hidden at Chesleigh for so long.

"I needed to remain in the country," Evangeline had said, then shrugged.

"But no more, I see, Madame."

Evangeline knew he'd be here, but she hadn't realized he'd arrived, that he was standing right behind her. Slowly she turned to face the man she'd willingly kill. She raised her chin. "As you see, Sir John."

Sir John bowed. "Allow me to lead you into dinner, Madame. Naturally, it is our pleasure that you have chosen to leave the country. I'm certain you will find much to do here in London to provide you entertainment. Perhaps we can discuss the city and all its amusements later this evening."

She was aware that the duke was looking at her, then at Sir John. She kept her eyes down and walked beside him to the formal Clarendon dining room.

To Evangeline's surprise, the duke waited beside the chair at his right hand. He himself held it for her, the footman staring at him blankly until he got hold of himself and stepped back. John Edgerton left her there, his brow slightly arched, and took his place some distance from her, thank God. The place to her right was reserved for Lord George Wallis, a whiskered gentleman, a retired military man who, she soon learned, had the disconcerting habit of inserting odd remarks into any conversation he chanced to hear. And he hated Napoleon with a passion. His two brothers had both been killed fighting the tyrant.

Opposite her sat Lady Jane Bellerman, the eldest daughter of an earl, a lovely girl dressed in pink satin and gauze, who studied her closely and gave her a very cold look indeed. There was nothing she could do about it. She kept her head down and pushed a small bit of salmon around her plate.

Course after course appeared. The footmen were attentive. Her head began to ache. She spoke to Lord George Wallis, listening to his interminable accounts of every battle on the Peninsula. "The bastards are still among us," he said, and drank a very large amount of his wine. "It won't be over until he's dead and underground."

"I would like to see him underground as well," Evangeline said.

"Doubtless you know that a very good friend of the duke's was murdered—Robert Faraday. Poor Robbie. If the duke finds the man who murdered his friend, the fellow will be dead before he can even begin to beg for his miserable life."

"That's true enough," the duke said.

Lady Jane Bellerman said in a low, quite enticing voice, "What's true, your grace? That you much enjoy the waltz? I vow you're very dashing when you dance. Perhaps you will indulge me later?"

"There won't be dancing tonight," the duke said, his eyes on Evangeline, who looked so pale he was afraid she'd faint in the veal tureen. It was all the talk about Napoleon, the death of his friend. Naturally it would be upsetting to a lady. Then he frowned.

Evangeline looked at him in that moment, and he saw the cold anger in her eyes, cold and quite hard. No, she wasn't about to faint. What was going on here?

Evangeline knew he too easily saw through her. She wiped the rage from her face, but it was difficult to hear about all that Napoleon had done. She was looking at Grayson, who was standing like a guard behind the duke's massive high-backed chair, when she heard Lady Jane laugh and saw that the young lady was looking at her. She raised her eyebrows. "I beg your pardon?" she said, smiling.

"Lady Jane is speaking to you, my dear," Lord George informed her as he took a large bite of Cook's specialty, Melton Mowbray pork pie. He'd told her that when it was served, sighing deeply with pleasure. "All come here," he'd said, "when Cook is bringing out her pork pie."

Lady Jane said when Evangeline looked across the table at her, "I was just telling the duke that you don't appear to be enjoying yourself. It must be depressing when a guest appears so completely bored, do you not agree, Madame de la Valette?"

Evangeline said easily, "I must admit that my thoughts were otherwise occupied, Lady Jane, but my mind is back now, at attention and ready to be charmed and hopefully to respond by replying in a suitably charming manner."

The duke grinned over his fork at her.

"His grace said you are recently arrived from France, Madame."

"Oh, no," Lord George said, staring at her as he were seeing her for the first time and didn't like what he was seeing. "But you sound so very English. I don't understand."

"I'm half English, Lord George," she said. "I was raised in Somerset. It's true that I was married to a Frenchman, but he was a loyalist. He hated Napoleon, as do I."

"I was just telling his grace," Lady Jane said, "that such a topic is scarcely appropriate for the dinner table. His grace doubtless feels that you're depressing his guests."

The poor twit, Evangeline thought. Lord George was very red in the face at her insult, and the duke had his head down. She knew he wanted to laugh and was, with difficulty, holding it in.

"I'm a bad guest," she said, and smiled over her wineglass.

"That's true," said Lady Jane, then added in a very

low voicc, "Perhaps you should leave. Perhaps you should return to France where doubtless you'll be more at home."

Evangeline shrugged. She carefully laid down her fork. She smiled again at the lady, showing all her white teeth. "If the duke wishes it, all he has to do is turn to others who will more readily amuse him."

"He will soon enough," said Lady Jane, and patted his black sleeve with her white fingers. The duke gave her a lazy look, his dark eyes promising immensely wicked pleasures.

But wicked pleasures weren't in his mind at that moment. Why the devil had his mother placed Lady Janc at his left hand? Of coursc she'd had no idea that he hadn't wanted to amuse himself with Lady Jane. He looked toward Evangeline, who sat silently, her eyes on her Melton Mowbray pork pie that sat cold in the middle of her plate.

"I suppose it's because of your English blood," Lady Jane said, her voice as sweet as an angel's.

Evangeline cocked her head to one side. "Very possibly," she said, not knowing what the ax was, but knowing it would fall.

"You're not small and dark like most of your countrymen or countrywomen."

Evangeline looked down at the remnants of her pork pie. She had only one bite. It didn't look at all pleasant now. She shook her head when a footman softly asked her if she wished for an apple tart. That was her ax? It didn't seem all that sharp to Evangeline. She said merely, "Whatever you say, Lady Jane."

"Yes, indeed," Lady Jane said. "It appears that mixing blood in you came to a bad end. The ladies here feel positively tiny standing next to you."

Evangeline wondered why this particular lady, at

this particular time, had to reduce herself to very lame insults in order to gain the duke's attention. Her voice was warm with laughter as she said, "It's quite remarkable that you should say that, Lady Jane. I'd noticed the same thing myself; only I was thinking along squat lines, not tiny."

Lady Jane sucked in her breath, her eyes narrowing with spite. "It's unfortunate that you're a widow. Unlike Frenchmen, Englishmen rarely seem to be drawn to ladies who have already known the married state, except, of course, for the obvious reasons."

The duke said clearly, "Jane, did you know that my mother is taller than Evangeline?"

Lady Jane looked at him helplessly.

Oh, no, Evangeline thought, don't make me feel sorry for you. She said, "Ah, your grace, but your mother is unusual in all ways. To be your mother she would have to be."

What the hell did that mean? the duke wondered.

As for Lady Jane, she subsided. Now she felt pure hatred for the woman, not simple jealousy.

As if she knew she'd been too kind, too generous to Lady Jane, Evangeline said, "You know, I don't feel the least need to secure an English gentleman's attention. I'm merely a visitor to England. I'm not in search of another husband. You know, I can imagine no more repellent an idea than that a gentleman would find me unacceptable because I am widowed. If English gentlemen are such blockheads, then you may keep them."

Lady Jane was obviously pleased. She smiled toward the duke.

He said, "I see that my mother is ready to escort the ladies from the dining room."

Marianne Clothilde said clearly in a very charming

voice, "Ladies? Shall we leave the gentlemen to their port?"

How did they have their timing so perfect? Evangeline wondered as she allowed a footman to pull back her chair. She said to Lord George, "The pork pie was delicious."

Evangeline did not have to concern herself with any more attacks from Lady Jane Bellerman, for Lady Pemberly and the chattering Felicia claimed her attention once the ladies had seated themselves in comfortable groups in the drawing room.

Felicia spoke of the food, how much she'd eaten, detailing every dish she'd tasted. Lady Pemberly told her that if she continued to eat like a stoat, Lord Pettigrew would soon look elsewhere.

Evangeline, who had eaten very little, perjured her soul. "It was a delicious dinner, and I must agree with Miss Storleigh, ma'am. I'm truly grateful that ladies must no longer wear those dreadful stays."

Evangeline was speaking to Pauline, Viscountess Demster, when she heard the duke's voice. "Excuse me, my lady. Some dear friends of mine have just arrived and I must introduce Madame de la Valette to them."

Chapter 26

As the duke led her across the drawing room, tossing a smile here, a compliment there, he said to her at last, "I judge you the winner of that joust."

For a moment Evangeline didn't understand what he was talking about, and he saw that she didn't. "Lady Jane," he said, and shook his head.

"Oh, her. That poor jealous little twit. You wouldn't want her for a wife, your grace. Trust me on this. She would bore you silly very quickly. Can you imagine that she was threatened by me?"

He gazed at her, mesmerized. "Surprising, isn't it? Threatened by you, a veritable witch with no beauty, no wit, not a hint or promise of charm, no figure to distract a man's thoughts."

"You don't have to go that far," she said. "Now, who are these friends you want me to meet?" She was thinking about John Edgerton. She had to speak to him before he left. They walked into the immense entrance hall.

"Forgive us, Richard," a handsome gentleman said, stepping forward. He looked at Evangeline. "I'm Phillip Mercerault, you know, Viscount Derencourt. This is my wife, Sabrina. Our babe still isn't showing itself yet. My wife assures me that our daughter is just fine."

The young lady, who had masses of beautiful auburn hair piled up on her head, poked her husband on the arm and laughed. "Forgive him, ma'am. I'm Sabrina, and it's true that I'm breeding and that Phillip wants a little girl, but I'm determined that it will be a boy. Oh, goodness, I'm sorry we're late, but Rohan and Susannah Carrington called. They didn't have time to come with us, and they sent their regrets. We're late, but we're here now."

"Yes, all two and a third of you," the duke said. "This is Evangeline de la Valette."

"How do you do?" Phillip said, taking her hand and raising it to his lips. "I understand that you are presently taking care of Edmund. If Sabrina insists upon birthing me a boy, I should like another Edmund."

"He's the very best of little boys. Do you know, I understand that I have beat you out, my lord," Evangeline continued. "I gave Edmund a gun, you see, a toy gun, and he's shot all the peacocks. He composes strategies with Bunyon so that I, the highwayman, can be chased down and summarily shot when he catches me. He said your gifts were nothing compared to his gun."

"That little ingrate," Phillip said, his eyes narrowing. "I have given him many gifts over the years, and yet he abandons me with just one offering from you. Richard, speak to your son. Assure him that loyalty to his own sex is the only thing that saves men from sinking under the ladies' slippers."

Evangeline was laughing when she looked at Sabrina, who was giving strange and wondering looks at her husband.

"Goodness," Evangeline said. "What are you doing?"

"Oh," Sabrina said. "You mean the way I'm devouring him with my eyes?"

"Exactly. How do you manage to do that exactly?"

"That's a secret. You see, Rohan Carrington's mother, Lady Charlotte, is the most beautiful woman in all the world, and she's been giving me eye lessons so that I can seduce my husband whenever I feel so inclined."

"Fascinating," the duke said. "The last I heard, Lady Charlotte was off to Russia with some dashing specimen of manhood."

"No, Russia was last summer, or was it Venice?" Phillip said. "She's off somewhere, just left last week." He looked down into his wife's eyes, and his own eyes nearly crossed. "She's learned how to seduce me quite efficiently. I don't know exactly what Charlotte taught her, but it works. In an instant."

"On the other hand," the duke said, "you've been married less than a year. I've never heard of a man needing any encouragement that early on."

Phillip leaned close to whisper to the duke, only the women heard it as well, "Don't discourage her, Richard. She quite believes herself to be the Bathsheba of seduction. I enjoy it."

"As well you should," Sabrina said.

Evangeline saw John Edgerton from the corner of her eye, standing quietly in the doorway of the drawing room, looking toward her. She smiled at the duke's friends, whom she would probably never see again, and said, "I have torn my gown and must see to mending it. Also, I must speak a moment to Sir John. A pleasure to meet you both, my lord, my lady. Excuse me." And she was away before Sabrina could say a word about helping her. The duke stared after her. He saw her speak with John Edgerton, saw the two of them go back into the drawing room. What the hell was going on? He felt his belly harden with fury. Sir John Edgerton?

"You seem to be quite one of the family, my dear," Edgerton said as he led her onto a small balcony off the library. It was very cold, the moon hard and full overhead. There were myriad stars, but Evangeline wasn't interested in any of them.

He said, "Just imagine you leaving the esteemed Viscount and Viscountess Derencourt to come with me. The duke wants you. You must know that, all women do."

"I imagine that the duke would just as soon throw me through a window," she said.

"Dare I ask you for an explanation? No, I don't think so, there's so little time. I don't want the dear duke to become suspicious. You're here in London. I did not give you permission to leave Chesleigh. Tell me why you disobeyed me. It had better satisfy me, Evangeline, or I will see that little Edmund is planted in a grave with his toy gun placed on his chest." He laughed at the hatred in her eyes. He snapped his fingers. "The boy will die just that easily. Don't ever think of betraying me."

Her voice trembled, she was so enraged, so very afraid. "Listen to me, you bastard. You had Mrs. Needle strangled. That poor old woman never did anything to anyone. Don't you see? I'm responsible for her death because I just happened to mention her to you that first night. Damn you, you killed her!"

"You're the one responsible, my dear. If you hadn't said anything, why, the old hag would still be brewing her noxious potions, but you did say something. I acted. I always act when it is necessary. I will act just as swiftly if you even dream of betraying me. Why did you come to London?"

"I came to London because I couldn't bear to stay at Chesleigh."

John Edmund slowly pulled a snuffbox from his waistcoat pocket and, with an expert flick of his thumb and forefinger, snapped up the lacquer lid. With exquisite precision he pinched a small quantity of the scented snuff and inhaled it. He sneezed delicately, then slowly replaced the lid.

"Such a tender conscience you have, Evangeline. It pleases me. Now I won't have to worry quite so much about you spilling all your secrets to the duke, hoping he can save you, save your father. He can't, no one can. Never forget Edmund, Evangeline. Now, I will let you remain here."

"I cannot bear it," she said, trembling, so afraid, so miserable that she wanted to cry and scream both at the same time. "Please, no more. I've done enough. Let me go."

"Shut up, Evangeline. We're alone, but there are bound to be servants near who could overhear. I want no questions. Now, if you will calm yourself, I will tell you that I shan't punish you for disobeying me." He paused a moment, his eyes upon his snuffbox. "As it happens, there is a small service you can perform for me while you're here in London."

"I can't," she whispered. "I can't. Please, no. Don't you understand? How can I continue doing all this in the name of protecting my father and Edmund, when you are killing innocent people?"

"You are becoming dramatic and hysterical. Calm yourself. Listen to me, now. As you have probably heard from Lord Pettigrew and others, Napoleon will arrive in Paris any day now. All will be resolved soon, very soon. Then you will be free, I promise you."

She hadn't heard a thing. Napoleon was free? Oh, God, it couldn't be true.

"Just how would things be resolved? That monster is free again to butcher and maim and steal?"

Sir John shrugged negligently, but there was mad excitement in his eyes. He said, "We shall see, shall we not? Napoleon will win this time. The allies will be crushed. It will be done. Then we will see."

"Do you swear that my father will be freed? Do you swear that Edmund will be safe? Do you swear that you will have no more innocent people killed?"

He lied quickly and cleanly and she knew he lied, but she felt as if a coffin lid were closing inexorably over her. She felt utterly helpless. She watched as Sir John threw his head back and laughed heartily. "You're such a child. Yes, my dear, I swear it all to you as the Lynx, and he, believe me, is a very trustworthy fellow."

She said, her voice as lifeless as she felt, "What is it you wish me to do?"

John Edgerton smiled gently, patted her arm, and told her. "No," he said finally, "don't say anything. You will figure out how to accomplish what I ask. Now," he added, "now." He grabbed her upper arms and jerked her against him. "You're cold. Why didn't you say anything? Let me warm you. Yes, let me." He kissed her cold mouth, pressing hard, his tongue probing against her. He said over and over against her mouth, "I've wanted you for so very long. Let me have you now, Evangeline. Yes, give yourself to me, and I'll free your father myself. Come to me, tonight.

Yes, tonight, come to me. I want to bed you, I must—"

She brought up her knee and struck him hard in his groin. He gasped, dropped his hands from her arms, and stared at her. "You will regret that. You will indeed."

"You filthy bastard." She jumped away from him. "I will do as you ask, but you will never touch me again."

She was through the doors to the library in an instant, so cold she wondered why she didn't crack into a thousand pieces. She couldn't bear it. She ran upstairs to the beautiful Rose Room and locked the door. She wrapped herself in all the blankets she could find. She sat there, staring at nothing at all for a very long time.

"The war ministry? Why the devil do you wish to visit the ministry?"

Evangeline merely smiled and shrugged. "I thought it would be interesting. It is the heart of the English government. Napoleon is free, he's nearly in Paris, I hear. Yes, I want to visit the ministry, feel the excitement, the anticipation."

"This is the strangest thing I've ever heard you say."

"Is it? Well, there's no reason for you to accompany me. I can take a hackney. It's no trouble."

He looked as if he wanted to smack her. "When do you want to go on this exciting outing?"

"This afternoon. You don't have to worry that they won't allow you to enter, your grace. I asked Lord Pettigrew last night and he said he would be pleased to see me. Ah, and you as well."

"Drew is excessively polite, damn his eyes. The last thing he really wants is to have a lady poking about.

I had intended to drive you to Richmond. I doubt you could ever find your way to the center of the maze, but I was willing to let you try."

Evangeline rose from the breakfast table and looked down at him. "If you're going to be in such a foul temper, I would prefer a footman's company." She tossed her napkin onto her plate.

He roared out of his chair. "You will hold your damned tongue, my girl. You must know that as your host, as the man who protects you, I have no choice at all. Of course I will accompany you. Now where are you off to? We're talking."

"I'm off to see Edmund. I have nothing more to say to you, your grace."

He toyed with his napkin for a moment. "I have already been to see him. Ellen was stuffing him full of toast. Bunyon was lecturing him on how a young gentleman behaved when he went to Astley's, and my mother was offering to let him shoot her with his gun. When he saw me, another slave for him, he offered to let me teach him how to play chess."

"That little fraud," Evangeline said, and laughed, her entire face lighting up. "I was teaching him, you see. Now he believes himself a master."

"What he needs," the duke said slowly, looking from her mouth to her breasts, completely covered this morning by a pale yellow morning gown, "is brothers and sisters."

She gulped. "Perhaps," she said finally, "Lady Jane could be trained to be more human. What do you think?"

"Well," he said, his eyes alight with wickedness, "she did assure all of us that she was a virgin. That must weigh something in the scales."

That got her goat but good. She leaped to grab the

bait he'd so easily tossed. "You pompous, arrogant English bastard. You—" She drew herself up, her hands fisted at her sides, to see that he was laughing at her.

"I will go with you to see Edmund. We will both give him a chess lesson."

"Go to the devil," she said, turned on her heel, routed, and stomped out of the breakfast room. His laughter, deep and sweet, swept over her, and she collided with a footman.

Chapter 27

Evangeline held her reticule close to her chest. Inside was the envelope John Edgerton had had a messenger deliver to her that morning. She didn't want to know what was inside. But she was afraid, dreadfully afraid.

The day was so cold she could see her breath in the carriage.

The duke leaned over and patted the blanket more closely around her legs. "Can you believe that just weeks ago we were basking under a summer sun?"

The carriage came to a halt. Juniper appeared at the window, all sharp and smiling. He very much enjoyed being in the thick of things, the duke thought. But he imagined that Juniper also wondered why the devil he was bringing a young lady to the war ministry. Why indeed?

"No," she said. "I can't believe it." She was standing in front of a soot-darkened gray stone building, stark and uninviting. It appeared to be in need of a good cleaning. It was surrounded by a high black iron fence. It seemed unnaturally quiet on the street, for there were no scrambling hawkers here to disturb the important men behind its walls. Two of his majesty's uniformed guards stood in silent scrutiny.

"You can see Westminster from here," the duke said, pointing a gloved finger.

"How utterly delightful," Evangeline said briskly and, ignoring the duke's look of incredulity, walked with a determined step to the tall black gate in front of the ministry.

The duke had no need to identify himself to the guards. Immediately the great iron gates swung open.

"Your grace," said one guard.

"Stay with the horses, Juniper," the duke called out. "Just as you normally do."

They walked up a dozen deeply worn stone steps to the huge double doors. The guard pulled at a heavy iron-ringed knob and bowed low to the duke. "Your grace," he said. "Lord Pettigrew's secretary will now assist you."

"You have every right to be the most conceited man in all of England."

"Oh, no. The prince regent leaves me in the dirt. Besides, I pay no attention." He gave her a bewildered look. "Would you rather we were treated in a paltry manner and ignored?"

"Certainly not. It's just that everyone treats you as though you were the prince regent."

"Oh, no, they don't. Everyone in the know is much more polite to me, I assure you."

Evangeline drew up, startled. The duke's softly spoken words reverberated off the walls like a mighty echo. She glanced about. The main hall rose upward some four stories, wrought iron railings enclosing each of the floors. Uniformed guards stood quietly at each landing. Gentlemen of all ages, dressed in somber colors, walked purposefully through the main entrance hall, slowing only briefly when they saw Evangeline pass. The duke was greeted by every man and bowed to. It was disconcerting. She was roundly ignored.

"It must be obvious to you by now that ladies don't normally grace this place," the duke said smoothly after a young man, with less aplomb than the others, nearly tripped over his feet at the sight of her.

"Richard, Evangeline. You are exactly on time. Welcome to my second home." Lord Pettigrew appeared from the far side of the entrance hall. Unlike the secretaries and clerks, he was attired in a buff coat and dark brown breeches. Despite his warm welcome, Evangeline sensed that he was harried. Doubtless he thought her request to visit the ministry a frivolous one, and was not overjoyed that she was taking his valuable time. She didn't blame him at all. She looked at him, knew what she was doing, and wanted to die. Instead, she gave him a charming smile and said, "Thank you for letting me come."

He nodded, then said to the duke, "We have more information from Paris. If you are free this evening, there are those of us who would like to meet with you."

"Certainly," the duke said. "Now, let's have a tour for Madame Curiosity here. Do we have you for a guide or one of your many minions?"

"The great Duke of Portsmouth escorted about by a clerk? Hardly."

Lord Pettigrew led them through stark and somber conference rooms that reeked of stale tobacco smoke. "I have so longed to see the Lord Deputy's Chamber," Evangeline said as Lord Pettigrew led them into that ancient, oak-timbered room that had known endless discussions about England's future.

She was near to shrieking at Lord Pettigrew when

finally he said, "All that remains is my office. It's not all that impressive."

She gave him her best charming smile. "Oh, how I should like to see exactly where it is you work, Drew."

For the first time he seemed to hesitate.

"I promise you that I will then be content and leave you alone." Still he hesitated. She added, "I daresay ladies can't be blamed for wanting to see where gentlemen like you spend their days."

"Very well, Evangeline," Lord Pettigrew said finally, good-natured once again. "The good Lord knows that both the duke and I have spent hours in here. To the best of my knowledge, my Felicia has never even considered stepping one of her dainty feet into this mausoleum."

As Lord Pettigrew escorted them to the second floor, he and the duke discussed the triumphant return of Napoleon. "He will be in Paris by tomorrow, I have it on the best authority. It's difficult to accept that the French are welcoming him back with open arms. It will soon be all over England. It's time that Englishmen everywhere realize the danger this man poses to all free countries."

She stumbled.

Napoleon will soon be in the Tuileries, where he belongs. It was happening, just as Houchard and Edgerton had predicted. Somehow, she had nourished hope that the French would have nothing to do with Napoleon, that the French army would hastily escort him back to Elba. Houchard would have had no further use for her or her father then.

"Evangeline?"

"It's the heat, your grace," she said, her voice dull as the light that tried to shine in through the dirty windows overhead. "I'm all right."

"Excuse me? The heat, you say?" He was staring down at her, his eyes narrowed, seeing too much.

"I will excuse you," she said only.

She became aware that Lord Pettigrew was apologizing for the clutter that filled his large office. There were maps everywhere and piles of papers stacked atop every surface. At the back of the office stood a huge mahogany desk, and two men were leaning over it, looking at some maps.

"Gentlemen," Lord Pettigrew said, "be so kind as to await me in the antechamber. I will be but another minute or two."

They both eyed Evangeline with a mixture of admiration, impatience, and condescension, gathered up several papers, and left the inner office.

She ignored them and walked nonchalantly toward the windows at the back of the office. She made a point of remarking on the view of the Thames through the uncurtained glass. She supposed that Lord Pettigrew replied in a suitable phrase, but she wasn't attending either him or the duke. She was looking from beneath her lashes at the second shelf of the bookcase on the far side of the room. It looked little used. It was there, between the third and fourth bound volumes, that John Edgerton had instructed her to leave the envelope. She stood at the window, responding to Lord Pettigrew when it was appropriate, all the while wondering how she would ever get the wretched envelope into the bookcase.

"Have you seen your fill?" the duke asked at last.

She turned and smiled brightly, and extended her hand to Lord Pettigrew. "Yes, indeed. Thank you so much, Drew, for your kindness. I know that you are quite busy. I don't wish to take any more of your valuable time."

Evangeline walked slowly to the wide doorway, and let her glove slip unnoticed to the wooden floor. When they reached the outer office, she said, shaking her head at herself, "Oh, dear, I dropped my glove. Just a moment, I shall fetch it."

Before Lord Pettigrew could assign one of his clerks to the task, Evangeline had whisked back into his office. With trembling fingers she quickly pulled the small envelope from her reticule and slipped it between the thick books. She returned in not above three seconds, waving the glove in her hand.

"I'm so sorry. It was so forgetful of me, so stupid really. But all is well now. And I've seen where all you masterful gentlemen spend your days to protect England." She would have continued her nonsensical speech had not the duke looked at her as if ready to clap his hand over her mouth.

Back inside the carriage, Evangeline spent many minutes settling herself, folding the blanket over her legs, settling her gloved hands in her lap, staring out the window.

"That was truly a remarkable experience," he said, staring hard at her, but she didn't look at him.

"Goodness, yes. So very exciting. I fulfilled a childhood dream, seeing—"

"Be quiet, Evangeline." He continued studying her profile, wondering, always wondering what was in her mind. He said, "I look forward to the day when I will finally come to understand you."

She said nothing at all.

"I suppose you would like to visit the Commons?"

She looked at him, controlled again. "No," she said, sounding like a twit, "what I would prefer is a drive to Richmond. I want to see this famous maze of yours."

Chapter 28

Evangeline sat in the cushioned window seat in Edmund's nursery, looking at the fog-laden park across the square. She'd been in London for nearly a week now, perhaps the longest week of her life. Whenever a visitor was announced, she knew it would be Edgerton with more orders for her. He hadn't come yet, but she knew he wouldn't let her go now. What had been in the envelope she'd left in Lord Pettigrew's bookshelf?

Edgerton and Houchard had been right. The papers were full of Bonaparte's triumphant return to Paris, the French army at his side. Wellington and Napoleon were on everyone's lips, as was the talk of war, another bloody war. She studied the paper every morning in her bedchamber when the duke had finished with it, given to her by Grayson, looking for any information at all about conditions in Paris. She felt suspended in time, waiting anxiously for something to happen, yet fearing what was likely to come to pass.

At least she had Edmund. He was kneeling by the fireplace, rearranging his toy soldiers, half of them French, the other half English. He was exhorting one of the majors to mind his troops. She smiled. She appreciated Edmund more than she could ever tell him. She could imagine the look on his face if she did say something of the sort to him, perhaps hug him for longer than a little boy deemed necessary. She spent all her time with him. At first he'd been wary, but then, when he realized that she wouldn't stuff too much learning down his throat, he laughed and hooted and claimed he wouldn't try to capture her and shoot her for at least another week. She'd been profoundly grateful, clasping her hands over her chest and thanking him endlessly. He'd snorted, then to her surprise, he'd hugged her before running off to do something else that amused him. He had become her boy, and she never wanted to give him up. No, she wouldn't think about it. She couldn't bear to think about what would happen in the future, in a future where she was branded a traitor—that or dead.

But Edmund would have a future. She'd do anything at all to ensure that future for him. He was growing more like his father with each passing day. When he wasn't with her, he was with the duke, who took him riding, took him to Tattersall's to look at horses, even took him once to Gentleman Jackson's boxing salon. She knew about everything they did because Edmund gave her a thorough recital every night when she tucked him in.

He was like his father in another important way. He never bored her. Edmund didn't realize it, would probably have been appalled if he did, but the truth was, he was her only comfort. Just yesterday he'd confided that he liked her better than Phillip Mercerault, a singular honor. Maybe he liked her even better than Rohan Carrington, something, he'd assured her, that he didn't say lightly.

Edmund said now, "It won't be long, Eve. Just you

wait. Wellington will kill him dead. He'll ride his horse right up to him and stick his sword in Napoleon's gullet. Then you can be happy again."

Oh, dear.

Evangeline rose unsteadily from the window seat and came down to her knees beside Edmund on the thick carpet. She couldn't let him come to such conclusions, despite the fact that they were alarmingly accurate. "What do you mean, Edmund?"

But Edmund's attention, for the moment, was back on his English battalion. He straightened a good dozen bayonets. He turned a major to face all his men, now in a perfectly straight line. He finally raised his eyes to her face.

"Papa said I wasn't to tease you."

Oh, dear. Was she so obvious? But she hadn't even seen Edmund's papa. At least she'd seen him only rarely.

She said, "But I like it when you tease me. Where is your gun? I believe I'm ready to execute a grand escape, and surely some brave boy will have to come after me, a ruthless highwayman, and shoot me right off my horse. Oh, no, you didn't use all your ammunition on the peacocks, did you, Edmund?"

He gave her a look too wise for his years. "You're trying to make me forget things, make me think of stories instead of what's really here now. Papa said—"

"What is it your papa said, Edmund?"

The duke stood in the open doorway, his arms crossed over his chest. He must have just stepped into the room. Hopefully, he'd been there only a moment.

Evangeline started to scramble to her feet, but the duke stayed both of them with a wave of his hand. "No, Evangeline, don't move. You look very comfortable. Now, Edmund, what did I tell you?" As he spoke, he strode over to them and dropped to his knees.

Edmund rubbed a cannon between his hands. "I'm heating up the gunpowder," he said at his father's raised eyebrow, then added, "You said she was unhappy. You said the last thing she needed was for me to plague her, like all those locusts did to the Egyptians. I told Eve that Wellington would grind Napoleon's bones for good. I wanted to make her smile. She did smile for just a little bit, Papa."

The duke looked at her over his son's head. "Did you succeed? Ask her, Edmund."

Edmund aimed a general's horse more to the left, then said, "I make you very happy, don't I, Eve?"

"Happier than a cat who's just lapped up a bowl of cream. Don't you remember? Last night you told me more of your story and I laughed and laughed?"

"She did, Papa. I made my story funny, and she liked it very much. So did Grandmama. I thought she would fall over, she laughed so much. She told me I was the best grandson she'd ever had."

"You're her only grandson. She was indulging in irony."

"Irony," Edmund repeated. "I shall have to work irony into my story. Perhaps you'll tell me exactly what it means when I'm ready to use it. Do you want to hear the story, Papa?"

"Yes, this evening I'll tuck you in. You will tell me and make me laugh as well."

"He is very clever, your grace. Now, Edmund, show your father what strategies you would use to defeat Napoleon."

She eased away from Edmund's battleground, as father and son realigned the soldiers' positions and shifted the artillery about, all to the sound of Edmund's excited chatter.

"Not a bad shot at all, Edmund. Yes, aim the cannon on the flank more toward the front line. Yes, like this. That's just excellent. Now, fire."

"I got you," Edmund shrieked. "I hit you right in your underbelly."

"Damn, you did. I'll have to take care or you'll wipe out my entire battalion. Where did you hear that word, underbelly?"

"Bunyon calls my tummy my underbelly. He said I had to be careful of my middle parts because they're softer than any other part of me. Look, Papa, Eve's laughing."

"Yes, even her eyes are shining, just a bit. Now, how would you like to take your grandmama to the Pantheon Bazaar today?"

Edmund was nearly speechless with excitement. "I haven't been there just yet. Oh, yes, Papa, yes."

"Very well. Bunyon is outside with your coat and gloves. Your grandmama is doubtless awaiting you with ill-concealed joy."

Edmund grabbed Evangeline about her neck, kissed her cheek, bowed low to his father, then bounded out of the nursery. She heard Bunyon's voice in the corridor, but couldn't make out his words. However, Edmund gave another shout. She said to the duke, who looked large and lazy and immensely beautiful sprawled out on the floor, toy soldiers and guns surrounding him, "Does her grace know of the treat you arranged for her?"

"You think I forced her into it because I wanted to have you to myself?" He rose, gave his hand to her, and pulled her to her feet. She looked up at him, impossible not to because, quite simply, he was there, and it gave her immense pleasure just to look at him. She swallowed, tried to take a step back, but he was holding her hands in his. "It's quite true that I wanted you here alone, very close to me, but to be honest, it was her idea. If I'd had it first, I would doubtless have used it ruthlessly to get to you."

He ran his large hands lightly up her arms, until his fingers circled her throat. His thumbs pushed up her chin. "I believe I must kiss you now or go quite mad," he said, leaned down, and very gently touched his mouth to hers. Her breath whooshed out in a soft sigh.

She wanted to pull away from him, truly she did, but she didn't have the strength to deny him or herself. She leaned into him, and felt him quicken. He pulled her tightly against him, bringing her to her toes so that she fit perfectly against him. She felt him against her belly, knew what it meant, this man's desire, and felt herself pushing more against him because the intense pleasure it gave her nearly knocked her off her feet. He kissed her more deeply, his tongue lightly touching hers, not ravaging her. Careful, oh, yes, he was being careful not to frighten her.

Frighten her? Now, that was surely nonsense. There was no fear in her, not a bit. She wanted him naked, she wanted him flat on his back, and her on top of him. She wanted to kiss him until he was panting with the pleasure of it. She desperately wanted to touch him, caress him, know all of him, touch him and kiss him all the way to his big feet. But more than anything she wanted to tell him the truth, to tell him all of it, and—

She managed to heave herself away from him. It was the hardest thing she'd ever done. He let her go. He was panting, his eyes so dark and filled with shadows that she couldn't bear to look at him because, she imagined, that was the way she was looking back at him. Filled with hunger, near desperation. She turned away, looking into the fireplace.

What to say to him? What to do? "I can't imagine any lady avoiding you, your grace."

He said easily, "I have a given name, you know. I would say that any lady who responds to me as you do deserves to call me by it. You may call me St. John if Richard displeases you. My father called me St. John when he wanted to hide me, which was very rare indeed.

"When you're not avoiding me, Evangeline, you try to distract me. You've an agile tongue. But as you just saw, it can't make me keep my distance. I want you. I want you more than I did even yesterday, even this morning. We must do something about this."

She closed her eyes against his words. He wanted her. Well, she wanted him, and that was a vast understatement. She more than wanted him, she—no, she couldn't think that. She had to be logical about this. The duke was a highly sexual man, had probably enjoyed dozens of women, so naturally he would want her, a reasonably comely woman. She said, "It is you who have the agile tongue."

"It pleases me that you think so, particularly if you mean when my tongue is in your mouth."

She saw him naked, coming out of the sea. She was mad. She was beginning to understand lust very well. It was a highly frustrating commodity. She wanted to scream. "Don't you have an engagement?" she said, trying to keep her voice cool and disinterested, a social voice that held no meaning. "Surely there must be a mistress or two hanging about in the wings waiting for you to come to them."

"Perhaps," he said, and thought of Morgana. He

was paying the rent on her lovely apartment through the end of the quarter. "It doesn't matter." He raised his hands and gently closed them about her throat, his fingers lightly caressing her pulse. She didn't move, just stared straight into the fire, but the heat she felt was from him, standing close behind her. His voice was a warm whisper against the back of her head. "What's wrong, Evangeline? Are you afraid of me for some reason? Afraid that I will seduce you and leave you?" His strong fingers continued to caress her throat. Slowly he turned her to face him. "Are you afraid of me?"

"No," she said. "I'm afraid for you."

A black brow shot upward. "What does that mean?"

She shook her head.

"Won't you tell me what you meant?"

She shook her head again, remaining mute. She felt his mouth, feather-light, touch her lips, and instantly she wanted him, although she wasn't quite certain about everything that was involved. She did know that he would come inside her body, an odd thing, surely, but it had to be wonderful because he was. She wanted to pull him tightly against her this very instant; she wanted no space at all between them. She wanted his heart to pound against hers. She wanted him to do anything he wanted to do, and she knew that anything he wanted to do surely would make her feel wonderful. He was so close now, and hard, and his scent, she loved his scent, the heat of his body, the gentleness of those long fingers. She closed her eyes, letting his mouth make her dizzy.

"Your saintly departed husband was an absolute clod," he said into her mouth.

She tried to draw back, but he held her firmly. "No, André was a wonderful man, I've told you that."

"I'm teaching you how to kiss me, Evangeline. If I didn't know better, I'd think I was the first man to touch you, to kiss you."

"André," she said. "He was my husband."

He kissed her again, this time his tongue going more deeply into her mouth, startling her, and she gasped, just a bit, just a light in-drawn breath, but he pulled back and looked down at her. "You are a mystery, Evangeline."

He didn't begin to realize what she was. Her mouth was open to tell him, despite—oh no, Edgerton would have Edmund killed. No, she couldn't bear that.

"Your grace, forgive the intrusion, but your tailor is here."

It was Grayson, standing outside in the corridor, speaking through the closed door.

The duke touched his forehead to hers, drew a slow breath, and dropped his hands. He didn't raise his head as he called out, "Thank you, Grayson. Tell the fellow I'll be with him shortly."

He straightened finally. He raised his hands and lightly patted her hair here and there, then tugged her gown, straightening it. "There, now, no one would guess that you were quite ready to fall to the carpet and let me have my way with you." He turned, saying over his shoulder, "We must decide what to do, Evangeline. I hope that your dear departed André still isn't holding your heart and your affections."

He gave her no chance to answer him. He was gone, closing the nursery door behind him.

Chapter 29

Marianne Clothilde said to her son, "Edmund wanted examples of irony, dearest. 'Irony', I repeated after him, one of my eyebrows at half-mast. Do you know I couldn't think of a single example to give him? He said he needed irony for his story, for you."

"This entire situation is a fine example of irony," the duke said, wondering where the devil his life was headed.

"Perhaps this is an interesting thing for you to say. I suppose you realize that Edmund is going very well with Evangeline. She loves him dearly, and he appears to adore her. Yes, it is a fine arrangement. It's very odd, though, dearest," she added after taking a sip of her tea, "but she outright refused to attend Sanderson's masquerade ball this evening, because she claimed she didn't own an appropriate costume. When I offered to procure her a mask and domino, she refused to hear of it. Naturally, it wasn't my intention to make her feel like a poor relation. Her pride in this instance is misplaced. Will you speak to her? She's so quiet, scarcely ever leaves the house, and she's lost flesh. I don't know what's wrong, my dear, but you must fix it. I know she'd enjoy a ball, anyone would. You'll see to it, won't you? Even Grayson has ruminated about it, and that is unusual. He's fond of her as well."

The duke frowned at the glowing embers in the fireplace. She'd kept her distance since he'd very nearly taken her in his son's nursery the day before. He wondered what would have happened if Grayson hadn't arrived announcing his tailor. He knew very well what would have happened, and nearly groaned with the thought of coming into her.

She wanted him very much. It seemed he had only to touch her, and she very nearly hurled herself at him. He loved it and knew very well at the same time that he shouldn't touch her, ever. But it seemed he simply couldn't keep his hands to himself when he was alone with her. He'd told her they had to resolve this, and he'd meant it. He just wasn't sure what to do, since he simply didn't understand her. He said more to the softly hissing fire than to anyone else, "I'm nearly ready to be shown the door into Bedlam."

"No," Marianne Clothilde said very quietly. "I've never seen you in this condition before, dearest, but it's quite obvious, at least to your mother who loves you and knows you really quite well."

He shot her a harassed look. "Spare me your motherly advice or your damned motherly observations."

"Very well. I shall simply sit back and watch you flounder, a very new experience for you."

"I've experienced everything a man possibly can," the duke said and kicked one of the glowing embers with the toe of his boot.

"Actually, you truly have as of now, but you don't know it as yet, you just think you do."

"Very well, you will have your way, you will think

your motherly thoughts, you will make no sense at all. I will speak to Evangeline. I want her to go to that damned ball. I will tell her she is to come with us. I will tell her to accept a domino and a mask from you. She won't refuse."

Marianne Clothilde looked down at her white hands, the long, slender fingers, just like her son's. "You know, you might consider using just a bit of guile, just a hint of deception, instead of this rather forceful approach that seems to come so naturally to you when it involves Evangeline."

The duke frowned at her ferociously. "She will do what I tell her to do. If she doesn't, then I'll—"

"As I was saying, perhaps in this particular instance your lord-of-the-manor attitude wouldn't work to your best advantage."

He banged his fist down on the mantel and promptly winced at the pain he'd brought himself. "You might consider a bit of guile yourself, Madame. Talk about holding the reins too tightly, you threaten to choke me. Your own subtlety is less than stunning."

Marianne Clothilde said, her voice filled with laughter that made the duke want to fling one of her prized chairs out the bow windows, namely, the one she was currently sitting on, "Yes, dearest, I won't say anything more. Never would I want you to consider me an interfering mama."

"Ha," the duke said. "I'll send Edmund to you, since he presently is doubtless with her, and I'll need to handle this without my son present." With that announcement he strode out of the drawing room.

As the duke expected, he found Evangeline with Edmund in the nursery. They were both seated cross-legged in front of the fireplace, their heads together, poring over drawings of Paris. "And that, Edmund," she was saying, "is the Bastille. When the French people had no more food to eat, when they saw there was no hope at all, they stormed the Bastille, this giant, grim prison, and they tore it down, stone by stone. And that is what started the French revolution in 1789."

Edmund was looking very thoughtful. Evangeline said, "Do you think that perhaps calls for a special story?"

"Yes," Edmund said. "Perhaps there could be a little girl locked up in this Bastille because she refused to eat her dinner horribly made for her by her stepmother, and a little boy comes to rescue her."

The duke cleared his throat. "And who would this little boy be, Edmund?"

"Me, Papa, me."

"I thought as much. I trust you would then have her eating only excellent meals."

"Yes. I'd ask Mrs. Dent to make her food. Then she wouldn't have to go back to the Bastille. She is a very sweet little girl, and I don't want any harm to come to her."

The duke wanted to grab up his son and squeeze him until he squeaked. It sometimes astonished him that this splendid child had come from his loins. He was a lucky man to be blessed with such a child. He felt a sudden tightening in his throat. He could clearly hear his father telling him that there was no better a son than he was. He closed his eyes a moment. He cleared his throat again. "Excuse me, Evangeline, but Edmund's grandmama is expecting him downstairs. Instead of a bad stepmother making him vile biscuits, I believe Cook's made him lemon tarts, his favorite."

"Really sour lemon tarts, Papa, that make your mouth all curled up?"

"Those are the ones," the duke said.

"May I, Eve?"

"Since you've contrived to look like a starving child, I have no choice but to send you on your way. Perhaps this evening you can tell me more about the little girl the boy rescues from the Bastille."

"I will think about that," Edmund said, gave her a kiss as natural as could be, and ran out of the nursery.

She smiled up at the duke. "It's late. I let the time get away from me. Thank you for rescuing him."

"Actually, I'm quite pleased and relieved that you didn't bound after him."

"I'm not particularly fond of lemon tarts."

"No, you would have bounded with him to avoid being alone with his papa."

That chin of hers went up. "I told you I wasn't afraid of you."

"No, you're afraid of yourself, and you're afraid for me, which makes no sense at all, and you're afraid of what you want to do when I'm close to you."

That was more than true enough, she thought, and said, a bucketful of scorn in her voice, "Your conceit is showing, your grace."

"Don't look so wary. I'm keeping my distance. I'm going to be strong about this. It would be the height of foolishness for me to touch you as I did yesterday. This time we just might end up naked in front of the fire. Any of a good dozen people could walk in on us."

Her eyes dilated. She looked both wary and excited. It was an aphrodisiac, the way she was looking at him, heady and nearly impossible to resist. He took two steps back from her. Then he saw the dark smudges beneath her eyes. She had lost flesh, as his mother had said. She looked thin, tightly drawn. His worry for her made his voice unnaturally harsh. "I've come to settle things, Evangeline."

"I don't know what you mean," she said, but she did and she had no idea what she would say. Did he want her to become his mistress? After all, she'd been married before and—

"How long have you been Edmund's governess?"

Her head snapped back on her neck, she was so surprised. "Ah, give me a moment, your grace." She blinked down at her fingernails. She had to remember that he was a man of vast charm and equally vast experience. He wanted her, but it didn't mean much more than that to him. She sighed, then forced a smile. "That's not what I am. I'm much more a nanny than a governess. That makes me sound very well educated. Perhaps I'm more a companion to Edmund, one who knows a bit about this and that, but little else. In short, a nanny, simply a nanny."

"You're making me angry, Evangeline. You will stop belittling yourself. Now, I see that you will continue to quibble. In any case, according to my calculations, you've been responsible for Edmund nearly two months now. You haven't yet been paid for your services."

Her services? "I don't understand, your grace. Not only have you given me all of Marissa's gowns, but you've also treated me like an honored guest. It's far more than I deserve."

He ignored her. "I wish to recompense you for all your labors." He pulled a note from his waistcoat pocket. "I hope you will consider fifty pounds a fair amount for your services to date."

Evangeline rose slowly to her feet, so stunned by what he'd said to think of a single word to say back to him. Pay her for her services? She said, her voice raw and deep, "How could you offer to pay me as you would one of your servants? Damn you, I don't want any of your money."

His fingers were itching to close around her white throat, and so for the next few moments he made a project of shaking out the ruffles over his wrists. She was flushed scarlet to her hairline. Why? It made no sense to him. "Of course you aren't one of my damned servants." He looked at her white throat, then lower to her heaving breasts, and said coolly, "The fifty pounds, as I have told you, is for your services to date, for your instruction and companionship to my son. You will accept it, graciously, if possible, in the spirit in which it's offered."

She gazed at him bleakly, beyond anger at him. He didn't even realize what he was doing to her. She said, "I don't want your money." She rose slowly to her feet, the mantel at her back. "Why are you doing this? To make me come to understand what it is that you want of me? Dammit, is that what you pay your bloody mistresses?"

She surely sent his boat right over the waterfall with that insult. That's what she thought of him? He was just a womanizer, all he wanted was her body? Yes, he wanted her, particularly her white throat between his hands. "Hardly, Madame. I pay my mistresses for their beauty, charm, and skill. In my company you have shown only the first of my three requirements, and perhaps just a dollop of the second. Let me make myself even clearer, Madame, for I can see that you're itching to yell at me for some further supposed slight. You will take the fifty pounds, or I swear to you, Evangeline, I will bare your bottom and thrash you."

She took a step toward him, waving her fist at him.

"So I have beauty and just a bit of charm, do I? I notice you don't require a brain in your mistresses. Isn't that just like a man. Your mistresses swoon and coo over you, and you're pleased well enough, is that right?"

He watched her, fascinated. "Perhaps," he said. "There's something else, though. You forgot any mention of skill. That comes after the swooning and the cooing. Even with your marriage to the divine departed André, you didn't seem to glean a great deal of anything from that experience. André was a dolt, Madame, and you were obviously just too stupid to realize it. In short, I'm dealing with a blockhead."

She was looking around wildly for anything to throw at him. The book of engravings. She bent down, grabbed up the book, and hurled it at him. He caught it handily. "This belonged to my grandmother. I would ask that you take care with my belongings."

"I'm not one of your servants. You aren't my lord and master. You can't give me orders. I'm sorry about your grandmother's book. I shan't do that again."

"I can try to give you orders, not that it appears to gain me much at all."

"You make me feel like I'm banging my head against the wall. Listen to me, your grace. You will take your insults and your precious money, and go to the devil."

He was on her in an instant, hauling her up to an inch from his face. "Now you will shut your damned mouth and listen to me, Madame. You're behaving like a rag-mannered witch. You must always think the worst of anything I have to say to you. If I sometimes speak to you in an overbearing way, it's doubtless because you've dug in your heels and refuse to heed me, and thus you deserve it. If this is a question of pride, then your intelligence is very much in question."

She realized he hadn't meant any insult. He believed her too proud. He simply didn't understand. She surprised him to his toes by burrowing her face into his shoulder, saying, her voice all muffled in the wool, "I'm sorry. Say what you will say and I won't try to hit you again."

He was caressing her back, holding her close, kissing her hair. "I want you to have your own money, don't you see that? I don't want you to feel you can't do something that would be pleasant because your pockets are empty. It's nothing more than that. I just want you to be happy." He felt her shoulder muscles, taut and knotted beneath his hands. He said quietly between kisses, "There's something else that bothers you, isn't there? It's just not that you feel wary of me, of yourself. What's wrong? Let me help you. I would, you know." He waited, knowing he was right, waiting for her to speak to him. Then, after several moments, he knew she wouldn't say anything to him. It hurt, surprising how it hurt so badly. "It concerns your being afraid for me, isn't it? What does that mean?"

She said, "There's nothing that troubles me, your grace. I once told you that I didn't like London. It seems that I'm not getting along too well here. That's all, nothing more."

"You may leave London whenever it pleases you to do so. You have but to tell me the date you wish to return to Chesleigh."

She was a fool, a thousand times a fool, and she knew he saw the utter dismay on her face. She'd had no further instructions from John Edgerton, nothing to tell her when she could leave. She had to see him, she had to know. She shook her head and said in a voice that sounded like it was fading into nothingness, "Yes, I'll tell you, your grace."

"I wish you would trust me," he said. She remained silent. "Very well, perhaps soon you will change your mind. Now, I would like you to attend the Sandersons' masquerade ball with me this evening."

"But I don't have—" She started shaking her head; there was even a smile on her face. "I see now. The blessed fifty pounds. Your mother. My pride." She sighed. "You tried nicely to trick me, your grace. Actually, if I hadn't wanted to strangle you, your deception would have worked marvelously well. Now I have money of my own. I want no more from you. Do you agree to that?"

"You forced me to go to great lengths. I believe I should like to see you in a crimson domino and a matching crimson mask. What do you think?"

"Crimson will look wicked. I should like it very much."

"So shall I."

Chapter 30

"A masquerade ball, unfortunately, gives license to certain behavior that isn't always pleasing or circumspect. In short, it makes both men and women forget that they have a well-bred bone in their bodies and behave as if it were their last night on earth. Now, what you will do is remain close to either me or my mother."

The carriage rocked gently back and forth on the cobbled streets. The moon shone brightly overhead, sending enough light into the carriage windows for its three occupants to see each other quite clearly enough.

Marianne Clothilde wished there was no moon. She was very close to laughter at her son's unprecedented sermon. She merely turned her head more to the side and waited for Evangeline's answer, which was quick to come.

"I believe, your grace, that any such harangue from you on how I should conduct myself stretches credulity. I'm not a young girl. I'm young, that's true, but I've been married. I know what to do and what not to do. I'm a grown woman, widow of the saintly departed André. I have a brain and breeding, breeding down into my bones. Now, leave me alone. Apply all that sanctimonious advice to yourself."

A snicker escaped Marianne Clothilde. Neither of them noticed, thank heaven.

"My conduct isn't at issue here," the duke said, his ire rising predictably. "You've never been to London. This is my jungle. I am the king here. I understand all the rules, I know all the other animals' killing habits and eating habits. You don't understand anything at all. You will do as I bid you. I don't want any of our friends to remark upon you with disfavor. You will behave as is becoming, and that means that you will stick close as a tick to me. You won't leave my side. I will protect you, I will see that you don't do anything stupid. I will prevent you from being placed in any situation that you wouldn't understand. Such a situation might include an overeager young man, or an older man, or any age a man might attain, a possibly drunken man of any age at all, who would want to fondle you or even try to do more."

"I should slap this overeager young man or man of any age, your grace, if he tried such a thing. Or would that embarrass you? Have you ever been an overeager young man, your grace?"

"No. I was born with finesse and grace. I was born with breeding already knit into my bones. I've never fondled a woman who didn't want me to fondle her." He looked at her, and she drew back, flushing, caught in her own tangle.

"All right," she said, and turned her head to look out the window. "I will act a shy virgin."

"You will perhaps try," he said, then closed his own mouth. A shy virgin. Good God, that sounded close to horrifying.

He thought he heard a noise from his mother and said, "Are you all right?"

Marianne Clothilde cleared her throat and said, "Naturally, dearest, I'm very happy that we are nearly to Sanderson House. This has been quite one of the longest rides of my life. In truth, Evangeline, my son has experience in all manner of things. He surely meant his advice to be helpful to you, not draw your fire."

"If you mean by that, your grace, that the duke is experienced in every wickedness known in this jungle of London, then I can see your point. Oh, dear, forgive me. I shouldn't have said that. It's just that he makes me want to throw him out the carriage window."

"I wouldn't fit," the duke said. "You wouldn't either, given your, er, well, you wouldn't."

"I know. His father made me want to hurl him about as well. Such a lovely man he was." She sighed and closed her eyes.

"This is the longest ride of my life," the duke said. The remainder of the trip was horse-hoof clopping and no conversation. When the carriage finally turned onto the long gravel drive that led to Sanderson House, Marianne Clothilde said brightly, "Here we all are. Ready to enjoy ourselves. You children will enjoy yourselves won't you, and not argue any more? Now that you've relieved yourselves of all your mutual bile. You won't seek to replenish it?"

"I have no bile," the duke said. "I never had any bile at all until she came."

"Yes, dearest. I'm always struck by the beauty of all the lights here. Isn't it lovely, Evangeline?"

She said, "Yes," but she was looking at his shadowed face.

"Do you like to waltz, your grace?"

"Yes," he said.

"He's one of the best dancers in all of London," Marianne Clothilde said.

"You're his mother. You must say all manner of things because it is your duty to do so."

"Do you really think so, Evangeline? I'm not so certain. Were I younger, why, I believe I should fall in love with him just as all the other ladies do."

"I hope there will be enough sober gentlemen who can waltz well," Evangeline said.

They heard the strains of the German waltz. It made her tap her foot in the carriage. She wondered if John Edgerton would be present. She knew she had to see him, but she didn't want to, not tonight. Tonight she wanted a bit of enjoyment for herself, a few hours to forget what she'd done and what she was.

At the top of massive stone steps, a butler, looking dashing in a bright red velvet doublet, stiff white ruff, and the hose of the sixteenth century, said, "Your grace, welcome." The duke slipped on his mask, as did Marianne Clothilde. Evangeline's was already firmly in place. No one knew her here. She could do as she pleased. She gave the duke a wicked smile as she placed her hand on his other arm. The butler led them up a wide staircase, past dozens of laughing guests dressed in outlandish fashions. There were footmen everywhere, dressed as courtiers from Queen Bess's court. They should have looked ridiculous, but in the sparkling, outrageously garbed company they looked dashing.

"I want you to enjoy yourself tonight," Marianne Clothilde said to Evangeline when the duke turned to speak to one of his friends. "My son is being proprietary, which I find quite charming. Normally he is anything but. Yes, do have fun, Evangeline."

"It is kind of you to invite me, your grace. Thank you. I don't think it would be possible not to enjoy oneself here," she added, looking about her. "How can one possibly dance? There are so many people."

"You will need an experienced partner," the duke said as he again took her arm. "I daresay that I will manage quite nicely."

"Not just yet, dearest," said Marianne Clothilde. "Here's Lady Sanderson, dressed as a Roman matron. I suppose it is clever. Lucille, how are you? Such a delightful evening. And so very many guests."

"Yes," said Lady Sanderson. "It's so very nice, isn't it? Now, who is this person with her hand on our dear duke's arm?"

"This is Madame de la Valette, Lucille. She is a cousin."

"A cousin? I do wish I could see your face, my dear. I hope you're lovely enough for our duke. He's so very amiable, yet it is difficult to present young ladies who will please him. You are relatively young, aren't you? He has very high standards, doesn't he? So fickle. How are Sabrina and Phillip, your grace? Did you feel any more of the tender emotions toward her when you saw her married to one of your oldest friends? She is breeding, you know."

The duke, who was quite used to Lucille's heavy hand, her relentless monologues meant to distress, amuse, and outrage, merely smiled and said, "Everything is in its proper place. Madame de la Valette is quite young, and tolerably toothsome. Bring me no chattering debutantes, Lucille. Now, if you ladies will excuse us, Madame and I will waltz. Do you think you're spry enough, Evangeline?" he added in a low voice.

"I'm wavering, your grace, but I shall try. Goodness, that woman is amazing."

"Yes, and Lady Sanderson knows well what she's about."

"There are always so many cousins," they heard Lady Sanderson saying to Marianne Clothilde. "I hope this one isn't destitute as most of them are."

"Ignore her," the duke said. "If you don't, you will make me think you're a fool. The crimson domino looks well on you, quite wicked, just as you wished. I would like to see you in Lady Sanderson's Roman gown. It would doubtless drape magnificently over your breasts." There, he thought, that should get her mind off what Lady Sanderson had said. "Waltz with me, Evangeline."

"Oh, yes," she said and raised her arms.

Marianne Clothilde was looking at her son and the cousin. She said thoughtfully, "They waltz well together. In fact, they look quite perfect."

"She is very tall."

"The duke is also very tall. He detests getting cricks in his neck. Now, Lucille, do you think you could conjure up a suitable partner for me?"

The duke's hand tightened about Evangeline's waist as he guided her expertly through a crowded knot of dancers.

"To be fair," Evangeline said, panting slightly from being whirled about at least a dozen times, "you do dance well."

"Dancing well, like good manners, was bred deep into my bones."

"You won't let me forget that, will you?"

"Probably, if you distract me." He smiled down at

her and saw that her eyes were glowing behind her mask. He saw a portion of the dance floor that was relatively free and whirled her around in wide circles. She laughed aloud, nearly humming in her pleasure.

When he was forced to rein in his steps, she said, "Is there anything that you don't do well?"

"Do I sniff a compliment? Surely not."

"Forgive me. I believe it was a compliment. Do you want me to take it back?"

He lowered his head and touched his chin for an instant against her hair. Her hair smelled faintly of roses. "There are a goodly number of things I'd like to do better."

"For instance?"

"Ah, an example? Very well. When you enrage me, I would like to be able to hold to my anger just a bit longer. But the fact is, if you come close enough, then I grab you and I forget I want to strangle you. I want to strip off your clothes and pull you beneath me and kiss you until you're quite red in the face and then—"

"That example was too detailed. It isn't designed to maintain any sort of equilibrium."

"Well, yes. It did something to you. You've stepped on my foot at least three times now since I started with the details. Do you know that I'd even like to just lie beside you and look at you for a very long time, not even kiss you or examine every last inch of you, no, just look at you because you please me. Oh, yes, you're an excellent dancer. Not quite at my level, but with practice you will match me perfectly."

All she had in her mind was a very clear picture of herself, lying quite naked, with him over her, looking at her, but interspersed with those looks were kisses. She gulped, then smiled. "You know, your grace, after you've looked your fill at me, I should like to look at you, at great length, indeed, until I am perhaps on the old and withered side."

It was like a fist to the belly. He could only stare at her, this woman who'd just knocked him down and made him so hard he thought he'd spill his seed in the very next instant. The orchestra ended the waltz; because they were both breathing hard, they stood there, staring at each other, until the duke became aware of laughter, aimed at them. Good God, he'd lost himself completely. As for Evangeline, she was breathing as hard as he was. It pleased him so much he still thought he'd lose his seed. He didn't move from her side, nor did he say anything.

"There's Lady Jane Bellerman," Evangeline said, "and she's coming this way. I knew it was too good to last. She's even taken off her mask."

The duke eyed the young lady, who was bearing down on him with alarming purpose, and said, "A shepherdess's costume. Thank God she isn't carrying a staff. She'd probably hit you with it."

"I think she looks lovely, more's the pity," Evangeline said, wishing the lady to Hades. "I suppose you're going to dance with her?"

"Would you tear out her hair if I did?"

"Your conceit is showing again, your grace. I can see that there are a long line of ladies already forming a queue to grab you. Yes, I would say by the look on Lady Jane's face that she should like to throw me off the balcony."

"Quite possibly, but you may trust me to protect you. Now, where is this line of ladies? No, don't hit me. It isn't done in the middle of a ballroom with more people watching our every action than you can imagine. Yes, I'll do my duty by Lady Jane. As for you, don't dance with any gentleman more than once."

"Why ever not? I was going to dance with you again."

"You're being a blockhead again, Evangeline. It would provide unnecessary gossip, that's why."

"You mean you won't dance with me again?"

"That's quite different. You're my cousin. I must see to you, it's my duty. Ah, Lady Jane, that lovely virgin shepherdess, is very nearly upon us."

"I didn't know that all shepherdesses were virgins."

"Only the most valuable ones. Now I must be off, Evangeline. Stay close. Ah, dare I believe that for just this once I've had the last word?"

She said in a very sweet voice, "Since you're my employer, since you pay me so very well for my services, why then, I should fear losing my recompense."

"Perhaps," he said finally, stroking his chin with his long fingers, fingers that itched to stroke her, any part of her, "I will rectify your father's failings. He never thrashed you, did he? I didn't think so. Perhaps soon you'll be over my knee, that quite nice bottom of yours all white and soft beneath my hand. Now, I must see to Lady Jane." He strode off, not looking back, damn him.

At least he drew the young lady's fire by catching her a good six feet from Evangeline. She was grateful for that. And yet again, she pictured everything he'd said clearly in her mind.

The orchestra struck up another waltz, and she was at once pulled into the knot of dancers by an Arthurian knight who was a good four inches shorter than she was. She saw the dowager duchess waltzing with an aging Greek philosopher, Lord Harvey, her Arthurian knight told her, between hiccups, for which he apologized continuously. She saw the duke dancing with Lady Jane. He was laughing down at her, at something she said. She didn't remember a single clever thing out of Lady Jane's mouth at the duchess's dinner party.

A Puritan partnered her next, only this one wasn't at all ready to deny the flesh. She had to give him a little kick in the shin. Next there was a knight with armor that looked very heavy and uncomfortable. He was amusing, she'd give him that.

Between dances she had only enough time to catch her breath and an occasional glimpse of a nodding smile of approval from the duchess. And she watched the duke. He never approached her again. He danced each dance with a different young lady, and he danced every dance.

Hadn't he spoken about his duty to her? Why didn't he come to her? But no, the righteous clod was much too occupied with English shepherdesses, giddy nymphs, even a goddess with stout gold ribbons crossing and separating the soft white material covering her breasts.

When a French chevalier of the last century said it was near midnight, she was frankly surprised. When he wanted to remove her mask for her, she said quickly, "Oh, no. I see the duchess waving to me. Good-bye, sir," and made her escape. She slipped out of one of the long French doors that gave onto the balcony. The night was cold, the moon bright overhead, splashing light onto the beautiful gardens beneath her. She walked to the iron railing, still feeling warm from all her dancing.

"Hello, Madame de la Valette. Fancy that finally you're free of all the gentlemen and out here all alone."

She whirled about at the softly spoken words to face a tall, slender man costumed in a gray domino and mask. There was something familiar about his voice, but she couldn't grasp it.

She remembered the duke's warning and took a final step back, her side against the iron railing. "You know my name," she said, eyeing him closely. He didn't appear at all drunk. Perhaps he'd just wanted a moment of cool air and quiet. No, she didn't believe that for an instant.

"It's midnight," he said, raised his gloved fingers to his mask, and pulled loose the ribbons.

Evangeline stared at him, at the mole on his cheek, at his eyes. It was Conan DeWitt, the man she had met at the old Norman church in Chitterly.

Chapter 31

He was wearing a gray domino, the gray mask held in his long, gloved fingers. "Don't look so shocked, Madame Eagle. I'm quite accepted in society. Naturally, since you're connected to the duke, you are as well. I nearly gave up speaking to you. You've been quite popular."

"What do you want, DeWitt?"

"You remember my name, do you?"

"I remember the name of every traitor I've seen. What do you want?"

He took a step toward her. "Don't anger me, Madame. I believe you dangerous to us, no matter what Edgerton says. He's told me he's got a hold over you that will never be broken, no matter your pathetic attempts to escape us, no matter your tender virtue. Now, let's get this over with. The Lynx asked me to come here. He was unable to come, though I know he wanted to see you very much. This is his message to you." He handed an envelope to her. Evangeline quickly stuffed it in her reticule. "My letter from my father?"

"It's in the envelope."

He looked at her more closely. "I still doubt you

no matter what Edgerton has over you. He killed that foolish old woman whom nobody cared about, and yet you allowed your delicate woman's conscience to collapse."

"I cared about her, Mr. DeWitt. Tell Edgerton to release me from this."

"You'd like that, wouldn't you? No, you won't be released from anything as yet. Our emperor is in Paris. Soon, Madame, he will destroy the allied armies and will rule once again. This time his name and dynasty will stretch far into the future. When that happens, then you will be free, but not before."

"Napoleon will never hold power again as he did before. All he has is one country filled with madmen, and if it comes to another battle, he will lose."

She saw that his hand was trembling when he withdrew an enamel snuffbox from his waistcoat pocket and flicked it open. As he inhaled a pinch of snuff, he said, his voice low and controlled, "I don't like you, Eagle. I do consider woman occasionally useful, but my uses for them are somewhat different than Houchard's. I believe that Edgerton has allowed his lust for you to blind him. You're dangerous. Edgerton told me that if you balked at all, I was to remind you of two deaths, not just one. I see from your face that the warning makes sense."

Without warning he grabbed her arms and jerked her to him. She felt the fury in him, and was so afraid she nearly bit her tongue. "Let me go."

"Oh, no, not just yet. I'd like to fling you up against the railing and take you right here. I'd like to find out what keeps Edgerton enthralled with you, for you've surely let him bed you, haven't you? What do you say? The duke's probably had you as well, why not I?"

"You fool. It's very cold out here." And then she spat in his face.

He held her left wrist and released her right. He pulled a handkerchief from his waistcoat pocket and wiped his face. He said very softly, "You'll pay for that. I'm accounted a handsome man, a good lover. Is it that damned duke? Yes, it is, isn't it? He's rich and titled, and that's what little whores like you want. That would make me more acceptable, wouldn't it? No, don't try to kick me or I'll throw you over this railing. I care not that you won't see to your next mission. They'll find that letter in your reticule, and all will know you're a traitor."

"The only thing that would make you acceptable to me is if you were flailing at the end of a hangman's noose."

"You little bitch, I'll—"

"Evangeline."

Conan DeWitt dropped his hands and took a lazy step back. Evangeline looked up to see the duke stepping onto the balcony. She clasped her reticule tightly against her and quickly stepped around DeWitt. "Your grace," she said.

The duke looked at Conan DeWitt, at Evangeline, whose face was pale as the white moon shining overhead, and wanted to commit murder. He said, his voice calm and dry, "DeWitt, may I ask what you're doing here with my cousin? It's very cold."

He knew DeWitt, she thought, and took another step toward the duke.

"Yes, we were just discussing how very changeable the weather is in England. I was just telling Madame that she would catch a chill if she remained out here. I saw her coming out and wanted to meet her. She's kindly been giving me her opinions of England and

Englishmen. But now even I feel the cold to my bones. Your grace. Madame." He nodded to both of them and walked away. The duke wanted to grab him, but he held himself back. Evangeline looked ready to collapse, she was so pale.

The duke had seen her leave the dance floor and go onto the balcony. He'd seen a man in a gray domino and mask follow her. He'd been on her heels as soon as he'd been able to get away from Lady Winthrop, who had wanted him in her bed since her best friend had wagered that she wouldn't win him.

That damned pallor of hers. She looked as if she'd just been destroyed, flattened. He pulled her against him, just as Conan DeWitt had done. He said, his voice warm against her forehead, "Did he insult you? What did he say to you?"

She felt his anger pulsing over her. His large body was shaking. He was angry? She shook her head against his shoulder. "He said nothing. He just wanted to seduce me. I dealt with him, your grace," she added, terrified that he'd go after DeWitt.

She felt him stiffen taut as a bow string pulled tight. "No, please, you were right about such an occasion as this. At least half a dozen gentlemen have tried to seduce me. There's really nothing to it after the first three. DeWitt is a horrible man, but I would have shoved him over the railing if he'd tried anything. Who is he? How do you know him?"

"He hasn't been in London very long. I met him through Drew. He's Lord Hampton's secretary, from the Lake District, I believe. He's involved in all his lordship's political maneuvering. Now tell me, why did you come out here alone?"

He tried to pull away from her, but she wouldn't let him go. She stayed close, holding his lapels with her fists. "I wanted to be alone for a moment. There was nothing else. I saw that you were dancing. You were dancing with every lady here. You only danced with me once. Please, may we leave now?"

What the devil was going on here? He wanted to yell at her, but knew it wouldn't gain anything. He said, "Very well. But you will have to release me."

"I don't want to, but I will." She did release him but left her hands flattened against his chest. "Thank you," she said, looking up at him. "Thank you for coming after me."

She'd disarmed him. He had to shake his head. "Damn you, I came after you to beat you for being such a fool as to come out here alone. When I saw DeWitt follow you, I nearly threw my dancing partner into the punch bowl." He gave her a smile that held still a bit of anger, and she saw it plainly since she knew him so well. But he hadn't yelled or ranted or run after DeWitt and pounded him, thank God.

"Thank you," she said again. She stepped away from him, her reticule held tightly to her chest.

He said from behind her, "DeWitt has a reputation that isn't at all nice. I've heard it said that he likes to hurt women. He likes them at his mercy, both in bed and out of it. He was certainly wrong to follow you, wasn't he?"

"I did spit on him," she said, still so frightened and guilty that she wanted to fold up and let the cold freeze her to her soul.

"What would you have done if that hadn't worked?"

"I would have kicked him in the groin. My father told me to do that, as an extreme measure to stop a man."

"That would be the result, certainly. Now, if you

would excuse me, I want to speak to DeWitt, teach him a very small lesson that would perhaps better his manners and his judgment."

She grabbed his arm with strength she didn't know she had. "No!"

A black eyebrow arched upward.

"No," she said again. "Please don't go near that man. He isn't honorable like you are. I know it. He's the kind of man who would laugh and smile to your face and slip a stiletto in your back the moment you turned away. No, don't go after him. Please, forget him. Please."

She looked distraught, even terrified. Because she was afraid for him? Evidently so. He was again disarmed, and annoyed.

"Please," she said again. "I want to go home. Please don't go after him. He's not honest and good like you are. He's an animal."

The duke flung back his domino and took her arm. "Let's fetch my mother, then, and we'll leave."

She laughed. "If you had a cutlass right now, the image would be perfect. Oh, dear, I'm actually laughing instead of shaking in my slippers."

"What damned image?"

"You looked like a pirate when you flung back the domino, the moonlight behind you."

He groaned. "Listen to me. If I were a pirate, I'd be wise to have you flogged. No other woman has ever made me see myself as you have. Let's go."

An hour later, when he stopped at her bedchamber door, she said, "Do you remember your promise to me?"

"Which one would that be?"

"I could return to Chesleigh whenever I wished to."

"Yes," he said.

"I want to return to Chesleigh tomorrow."

He was silent overlong. Finally he said, "Would you like to tell me what's going on?"

"I want to go back to Chesleigh."

"Why?" he said, his voice very low, very gentle. "Tell me why you want to leave."

He blinked in surprise when she said suddenly, "Now that Napoleon is back in power, what will happen?"

He shook his head. "Napoleon is a man who must rule, not just one city or one country. He must have everything. He will never stop, never. There will be war, nothing else will stop him. Didn't you know? Wellington is now with the Prince of Orange in Brussels. Perhaps a month from now? Two months? It will be bloody, but you know, I'm not a doomsayer like many of our countrymen. The fact is that Napoleon decimated his army on his ill-advised invasion of Russia some two years ago. He has inexperienced boys now swelling his ranks. Wellington will win, he must."

"I know he will as well. Thank you," she said, not looking at him. "I will leave in the morning, Edmund with me, if that pleases you. There is no need for you to escort us back to Chesleigh."

"Don't be a twit. You're under my protection. Naturally, I'll take you and my son back to Chesleigh."

She looked as though she'd argue, then shook her head. "Thank you," she said again, turned on her heel, and went into her bedchamber. She closed the door quietly behind her.

He stood there, staring at that damned door. She was on the other side. All he had to do was open that door and go to her. He knew if he did, he would make love to her, probably make love with her until they were both unconscious. His hand was on the doorknob. Then he drew it back.

He would see her in the morning. He planned to see her every day for the rest of their lives. But first, he knew, he had to find out what was holding her back from him. What was wrong? He shrugged. He would find out everything he wanted to know about her. The problem was probably something niggling and insignificant, and he would fix it. Even if it was something more than insignificant, he would fix it. Wasn't his son always telling him that he was the strongest papa in the world, and the smartest?

He was whistling at he walked to his bedchamber.

"You don't have to return with us, your grace. Surely there are so many more interesting things for you to do here."

He gave her a lazy grin. "No, not this time. I've decided you need my guilding hand, Evangeline. I've decided that whenever I let you out of my sight, you flounder, nearly get yourself seduced, and then when I come to save you, you don't want to let me go."

She hadn't slept well, had dreamed of Edgerton slipping into Edmund's bedchamber, a length of rope in his hands, or a stiletto, or just his hands, his fingers, that could squeeze the life out of a child. She wanted only to leave London.

"I won't rise to your bait," she said. He let her be. She didn't look at all well.

Marianne Clothilde said as she held Edmund against her side, "My son will take care of you two, Evangeline. Leave everything to him. You look tired, my dear. Just beg Edmund to let you sleep. Perhaps he'll be good enough to allow it."

"If she promises to make the weather warm again, Grandmama, then I'll let her nap with me."

"You are a sainted child," Marianne Clothilde said, kissing her grandson. "I imagine Evangeline will be able to deal with something as easy as England's weather."

"That's what I thought," Edmund said.

Marianne Clothilde kissed him again.

"Thank you for your kindness, your grace," Evangeline said. "I hope I will see you again."

"Oh, you shall. I fancy you and I will be seeing quite a lot of each other in the future. Now, dearest, may I speak to you for a few moments?"

When Evangeline had taken Edmund from the drawing room, Marianne Clothilde said, "I wish you luck. There is something wrong here. Leaving with no warning, it makes no sense. I haven't a clue to what it may be. Do you?"

"Not as yet. If there is something bothering her, I shall wring it out of her."

"I'm glad that Edmund is so very fond of her. I don't suppose you'd ever use your son as a lever, would you?"

Her handsome, very confident, sometimes arrogant son raised an eyebrow and said, "Damnation, Mother, do you think I will have to stoop to such a level as that?"

"It's possible. Evangeline is a strong-willed young woman."

He started to say that she would do what he told her to when he realized that if he said those words, his fond mother would likely laugh at him. Actually, he'd probably laugh at himself. "I'd even use Bunyon if it would gain me," he said.

Marianne Clothilde said as she turned to look up

at the portrait of the late duke, "It's a shame that she was just a child when your father wanted you to marry. I fancy that things would have turned quite differently had she been Marissa's age."

"Father liked to tell me that if I always looked to the future and didn't whine about the past, only corrected my past mistakes, then all would work out and I would be a better man." The duke swept up his mother in his arms and hugged her tightly. "I miss Father as do you. Do you know that he was right? Do you know I fancy that a widower and a widow are well matched?"

"I believe," Marianne Clothilde said, "that you and your father are two of the best men who have ever graced the earth. I loved him with all my heart. I don't expect Evangeline to feel any less about you."

Chaper 32

The duke's face was perfectly straight, his voice perfectly even as he said, ". . . And then Bunyon swore to my father that the bully did indeed fall off the bridge. He also swore that I'd been standing at least ten feet away, that I couldn't have been responsible. To which my father said, 'I already know that my son's a devil, Bunyon. That he's also a magician comes as no surprise.' "

Evangeline laughed. "Did the bully know how to swim?"

"As I recall, Teddy Lawson was torturing other children the very next day."

"Whatever happened to him?"

"The last I heard, he was a vicar somewhere in the Cotswolds. Life is interesting, is it not?"

Her head went down. She drew stillness over her as if it were a shield to protect her. He frowned at her bent head. "You didn't answer me," he said. "Don't you agree that life is interesting? That life prepares sometimes very unusual dishes to put on your plate?"

"Yes," she said, raising her head again, still not looking at him. "Life is so unexpected that I sometimes want to die. No, I didn't mean that. How silly of me to say such a ridiculous thing."

It was a start, the duke thought. They'd been back to Chesleigh for only two days. He already knew that she'd suffered pain in her short life; the sainted André had departed this life, and her father and mother had also died. But there was something else, and it was different. He felt immense frustration. Why had she wanted to come back to Chesleigh, and with so little warning?

He leaned his shoulder against the mantelpiece, a glass of brandy in his hand, and looked thoughtful a moment. He said abruptly, "Perhaps you would like to come with me to Southampton. We could sail to the Isle of Wight. If it pleased you, we could remain at my house in Ventnor for several days. Edmund loves it there, as I already told you. It would be a rare treat for him."

She felt fear, panic, and a terrible regret well up inside her. The instruction given to her by Conan De-Witt was that she meet one of Houchard's men the following evening at the cove and he would have further orders for her. "No," she said quickly. She saw the puzzlement on his face and added quickly. "That is, I'm a dreadful sailor. I have a fear of boats, even big ones. I know it makes no sense, that it's stupid, really"—she fanned her hands in front of her—"I just can't help it."

He'd finally caught her in what seemed to him to be an utterly meaningless lie. He said, "Ah, a good swimmer, but afraid of the water."

"No, just boats."

"You know, Evangeline, you don't have to lie in order to remain here at Chesleigh. Or is it Chesleigh itself that holds you? No, that isn't it. As I recall, you couldn't wait to leave here just a very short time ago. And now you're back again. It doesn't make sense, does it? Perhaps you just don't want to be in my company. Are you thinking I'll try to seduce you? Rid yourself of such a notion. That is something altogether different; our coming together is something that is between you and me. I truly believe you'd enjoy Ventnor."

A headache was building ferociously over her left eyebrow. "I'm not worried about seduction. I'm not worried about anything. I want to stay at Chesleigh. I love it here. I don't want to leave."

"Until you beg me to take you to London again?"

"I don't fancy I will want to go to London again."

"Why the devil not?" She just shook her head, not looking at him, not saying anything at all. He pushed away from the mantelpiece, snapped down his glass, and strode over to her. He grabbed her arms and pulled her to her feet. He shook her. "Damn you, we've been home now two days. You've done your best to avoid me. I wanted to go riding with you, and you pleaded the headache. You're skulking around like a damned shadow, that or a convict hiding from the magistrate. What the devil is wrong?" He eyed her with growing frustration.

"There's nothing at all wrong."

He let her go and began pacing. He said over his shoulder, "I hate games, Evangeline. If you find my company distasteful to you, then all you have to do is say so. I won't order you to leave Chesleigh. I won't kick you into a ditch. If you don't want me, damn you, just tell me. I assure you that I've never forced a woman in my life. By God, every time I've touched you, you've gone wild for me. We've gone wild for each other. Now, tell me, what's going on?" In the next instant he pulled her up tightly against him, his arms wrapped around her, so close to her that he could smell her scent, feel the steady beat of her heart against his.

"Ah, Evangeline," he said. She looked up at him and saw all that he felt for her in his eyes, dark, dark eyes, the most beautiful eyes she'd ever seen in her life. Oh, no, she thought, oh, no. She became aware that he was studying her, a curious expression in his eyes.

"Evangeline?"

She hated the tenderness in his voice, hated what it meant because she wasn't worthy. She wasn't anything that was good or wholesome or honest.

"Will you do me the honor of becoming my wife?"

She stared at him, bereft of words. She couldn't move. He wanted to marry her? That meant he cared for her, truly cared for her; it wasn't just that he wanted her body. No. She licked her tongue over her bottom lip. She felt him tighten. "No," she said very quietly, so unhappy, so despairing, that she wondered how she'd go on. "I cannot. You don't mean that, surely you don't. You've just been thrown in my company too much. You like my breasts, that's all. That's it, isn't it?"

He brought his thumbs under her chin and pushed up her face. "I worship your breasts. They are divine breasts. Also, I just happen to adore your company. I don't want to spend time with any other woman, just you. I don't want to make love to any other woman, just you. I want you to marry me. I will be so faithful, you'll occasionally want to kick me off your hearth. And if you didn't hear me the first time, yes, I revere your breasts."

She pulled away from him, and he let her go. It was

her turn to pace. She wanted to run but knew she couldn't. He'd catch her. He already knew something was terribly wrong. She had to convince him that she wasn't anything he could possibly want. His wife? Oh, God, no.

"You're mocking me. You are amusing yourself at my expense," she said at last. "It isn't well done of you."

"I suppose I did rush my fences a bit," he said. "And here I've always considered myself a bit of an expert on handling women. I wouldn't ever amuse myself to hurt you, Evangeline. Marriage is a serious business. I don't think I could jest about how I wish to spend my life."

She felt a nearly overwhelming burst of utter joy, but almost immediately she saw Edmund, dead, his lifeless eyes staring up at her. She saw her father, and he was dead as well, his white hands folded over his chest, his eyes closed, two copper pennies covering them, just as her mother's eyes had been closed with copper pennies in her death. She couldn't bear it, she just couldn't. She wanted to shriek. Instead, she felt tears sting the back of her eyes, tears of rage at her helplessness.

There was no choice for her. She forced herself to turn away from him. She forced herself to say in a faraway voice, "I thank you, your grace, but my answer to your gracious offer must be no. I don't wish to marry again. I don't wish to be at the whim of another man for the rest of my life. I'm sorry, truly, if I've distressed you—"

He laughed. "I've never before heard that phrase, but I know it's one that's supposedly popular with young ladies who want to be polite as they turn down a suitor. Is this the first time you've had to use it?"

She had to find something else, anything. "It's an English lady you must wed, your grace, not some half-French nobody without a dowry who has already been once married."

He laughed again, shaking his head at her. "No, Evangeline. I don't want an English lady. It's a lady who is half French, who is a thorn in my side, who is more stubborn than a stoat, who loves my son as much as he loves her. Ah, and don't let me overlook her tongue that flays me when she isn't kissing me or looking at me like she wants to leap on me.

"You must know that the last thing I need is a dowry. As to your having already been married, it makes no difference. How could you ever think that it would? Believe me, I've no interest at all in some young twit who's as ignorant as the winter is long. As to being at another man's whims, I promise you that if I ever become an autocrat, you can pound me in the head. Isn't that fair?"

"I don't want to," she said, and she knew that it wasn't enough, but her brain was blank, only emptiness remained. "Please, don't speak of it further."

"This is the most unusual experience of my life. Here is a woman I wish to marry. I know she wants me. I fancy that she cares for me. I'm not a blind man. You also care mightily for my son. I believe there is some sort of problem that is apart from the two of us. If you would but tell me, I'll do my best to fix it." Then his dark eyes widened. "No," he said, "oh, no. Your husband, the sainted André. He isn't still alive, is he?"

She was shaking her head even as she realized he'd given her a perfect reason.

He held up his hand as he saw her mouth open.

"Don't do it," he said. "Don't even try. Why won't you marry me, Evangeline?"

"I won't deny that I want you," she said. "But I don't love you. I don't want to marry you. I don't want you for a husband. And I simply don't understand why you, a man who told me he didn't even believe in love, should want to tie himself to one woman? Why?"

"Ask me again in three or four decades, and then we can discuss my obvious weakness for you."

She was drowning and he was offering her life, only she couldn't take it. One day he would discover what she was. On that day he would revile her. He would curse her. She was his enemy; he just didn't yet realize it.

"You've mistaken my feelings. I don't love you."

He didn't believe her. She'd been silent for too long. He'd told her he wasn't a blind man. He'd seen the myriad expressions on her face, one leaving, another shadowing her eyes, and he'd seen more anguish than he could begin to understand. He wanted to shake her, yell at her, but something held him back. He said quite mildly, "Then what are your feelings for me that I have so misunderstood?"

She raised her eyes to his face, knowing that she must hurt him, and herself. She remembered Lady Jane Bellerman's insults, so childish, really, but she had no choice but to try them. She hated herself even as she said, her voice cold, "You don't have to offer me marriage, your grace. You asked me what my feelings for you are. I find you a very desirable man, as I suspect most women do. I would like to bed you, not wed you." She forced herself to shrug her shoulders indifferently. "As Lady Jane said, Englishmen don't wed ladies who have already known another man. You may admit it to me, your grace, it's my body you want, not interminable years in my company. Believe me, I'm honored that you would push for marriage just to get me in your bed. You may stop your marriage talk now. I'll come to your bed, willingly."

It was odd. He'd known her for less then two months, but he knew she was lying. Actually, she didn't lie all that well. What to do? To buy himself time, he said only, "I don't understand you, Evangeline."

She gave what he assumed was her rendition of a Gallic shrug, not a very good one. "If I were entirely English—one of you—and a virgin, no doubt I should view such an offer with far different eyes. But I've been married. I don't wish to do that again. Perhaps you were right that André was a clod with lovemaking. I know that you're not. I know that you'd be perfect about all of it."

What would he say? What would he do? Would she shortly see contempt for her in his eyes?

"So," he said, and there was simple amusement in his dark eyes. "So, now you appear to have found a use for me. At least now you admit that the dearly departed Saint André wasn't a magnificent, godlike specimen." He paused, and his voice lowered. "Did he abuse you? Did the bastard hit you?"

"No, of course not. Listen, I simply prefer my widowed life. I enjoy doing what I wish." No, that couldn't be right. "While it's true that I haven't much money, I do enjoy Edmund, I enjoy living at Chesleigh." Good God, she was digging a hole that would shortly land her in faraway China.

"And what you wish," he said slowly, "is that I become your lover and not your husband?"

"I enjoy kissing you."

"Ah, that's nice to hear." What was going on here?

He walked to her slowly, his eyes never leaving her face. She didn't back away from him. This was getting more interesting. He closed his hands about her shoulders and pulled her slowly against him. She tried to free herself, but he tightened his hold and brought her closer. Her breasts touched his chest, and he knew he was hard as a stone. Then he felt all of her and wanted to howl with the overwhelming lust and tenderness and urgency that were flooding over him. Would she always have this effect on him? He imagined so. He smiled at her as he forced her face upward. "You're mine," he said, his voice warm and light against her forehead. Then he lowered his head, slowly and deliberately, and kissed her. "You're mine. Now and forever, you're only mine."

"No," she said, and knew she wanted him so much she would shatter if she couldn't kiss him now, this very instant.

"Oh, yes. No more playacting, Evangeline."

"Please," she said, and he kissed her once, again, not forcing her mouth to open, but she did open her mouth, eagerly. His hands were in her hair, pulling out all the pins, freeing her hair, stroking his fingers through it, then down her back, cupping her buttocks in his big hands. Then his hands were back in her hair, tangling it around his fingers, and he didn't stop kissing her. He said into her mouth, his voice not at all steady, "Do you remember when I told you your hair is exquisite?"

"Yes," she said, just the sound of her voice nearly bringing him to his knees. His hands were on her hips again, lifting her against him, pressing her tighter and tighter. He wanted more than anything to have her naked, pressed this tightly against him.

She felt his lips against her temples, her cheeks, the

hollow of her throat. He drew back, his hands still cupping her hips, and looked down into her face.

"What are you feeling, Evangeline?"

She didn't think it an odd question, for she had no experience with men. She opened her eyes, and for a long moment she found herself unable to say anything.

"I would give my life for you," she said.

He stared at her, even as he felt a surge of lust so powerful that he nearly pulled her to the carpet beneath their feet. No, no, he thought. Not yet. He got a grip on himself. "Will you always surprise me with the unexpected? Would you tell me why a woman who merely has a wish for a lover would feel so strongly about her lover's well-being?"

He heard her breath catch, felt her go rigid in his arms, felt that resistance in her, and said, "I love you, Evangeline. It's far beyond lust, if lust it ever truly was. I imagine that I will love you until I cock up my toes and pass to the hereafter. My father found his mate in my mother. I have found my mate in you. Come, are the words so very hard for you to say?"

She pressed her face inward against his shoulder and shook her head.

He kissed her temple, her cheek, smoothed a fingertip over her eyebrows, kissed the hollow of her throat. Then he closed his hands over her breasts. She was trembling, her breasts heaving. She arched her back, pushing her breasts against his palms. "Do you want me, Evangeline?"

"Yes. Yes." She threw herself against him, her fingers tangling in his hair, pulling his head down so she could kiss him. He laughed. "I see that you do. Will you come with me now? Will you make love with me?"

She should stop this, now. But she couldn't bear the

thought that soon she would have to leave him, that she would probably have to sneak away during a dark night very soon. She would live and die without ever knowing passion with him. Surely it wasn't so wrong to show him she loved him, to give herself to him just this one night? Tomorrow night, when she met the man who was coming from Houchard, she would tell him that she was of no more use, and she would ready herself to leave. Perhaps she would go to London with him, never see the duke again after tomorrow night. She didn't want to deny him herself. And her body was all she could share with him. No, she thought, tell the truth. She didn't want to deny herself. She had to know him, she had to have this one night with him. She said, "Yes, I want to make love with you."

Chapter 33

"After you, Evangeline."

She surprised them both by hesitating, her eyes wide and wary upon his face. He smiled at her, gently shoved her inside his bedchamber, and closed the door.

Her lips were dry. Suddenly she was very afraid. She was a fool. She would shame herself. She would disgust him. She backed away from him. "I don't think this is a good idea, your grace."

"That's a fact," he said, and he laughed. "But it doesn't matter now, it's far too late." He pulled her into his arms. "Open your mouth to me, Evangeline. You know it will heighten your pleasure."

She started to speak, but his mouth closed over hers, and he pressed himself hard against her belly. The knowledge that he would enter her, just as his tongue was possessing her mouth, frightened her and excited her so much she was shaking. She kissed him, so excited that she was clumsy in her awakened passion. She clutched him, wanting more but having no idea what to do.

"What do you feel now?" His breath was hot in her mouth, and his tongue touched her bottom lip.

"Wild, but I don't know what it's all about. I don't know, just that I feel like there's so much for you to give me and so much for me to give you. Help me."

The image of her faceless husband rose in his mind. How could any man have cheated himself of her passion? It was a good thing that the saintly André had made his way out of this world; else the duke would have been eager to assist him out.

He took over. He pulled her hard against him and unfastened all the tiny buttons that marched up her back. They parted easily under his practiced fingers, and her gown slipped free from her shoulders. It fell softly to the carpet, billowing at her feet.

Soon she'd be naked. "I don't know about this," she said. "You must believe me, for I mean it. Oh, dear, what are you doing?" He untied her single petticoat and watched it fall atop her gown. He was on his knees in front of her, his hands on her leg. "I'm pulling down your stockings. Nothing alarming." What had that damned departed André done to her?

"I won't marry you, I won't." She was panting, her words tripping over each other. "You'll see, once you've had me, you won't want me anymore. I promise you."

He appeared to consider her words quite dispassionately for a moment, though he had difficulty suppressing a grin. So insistent she was even now. Well, they would both know soon what was to be. He pulled down her other stocking, then removed her slippers. She was wearing only a shift that came mid-thigh. He rose, looked down at her a moment, then gently eased away the lace straps and watched the soft muslin fall away from her full breasts to her belly. He tugged it again, and it fell from her hips, floating to the floor. She was naked, finally utterly naked, and she was his.

He looked at her belly, wanting desperately to touch her deeply, to caress her with his fingers and his mouth, but something stopped him. He saw panic in her eyes.

She tried to cover herself. He gently pulled her arms away and stepped close. "Close your arms around me. Yes, that's it. I like that."

His hands were on her bare back, stroking up and down. When he cupped her hips in his hands, she realized that the feelings that were building deep in her belly were something she'd never before even considered could exist. It was remarkable. Then his fingers pushed slightly inward, and she felt his warm fingers touching her woman's flesh, flesh only she herself had ever seen or touched. She started to shake her head, started to pull away, then realized that the last thing she wanted was to pull away from him, pull away from his fingers.

She raised her face. "Please. Give me more."

He felt poleaxed. "Oh, yes. But there's no need to rush. Feel what you've done to me. Put your hand over my heart, because I'm not about to let your beautiful bottom out of my hands."

"Your heart's beating very fast," she said.

"As is yours." His fingers went inward again, and one of them was eased inside her. "Oh, goodness," she whispered. "I never imagined, oh, goodness."

She was very small and very tight around his finger. He kissed her, his eyes closed against the power of it, against a need that would surely consume him if he didn't have her very soon. He felt her become moist as his fingers touched her, lightly stroked her. She was loosening, opening to him, wanting him. It was heady, it was almost too much. He had to pull away from her or spill his seed, and that wouldn't be at all good for either of them.

She blinked at him, pressing close, wanting him to touch her again, feel her, come inside her with his fingers. He touched his forehead to hers, his breathing so heavy he wondered what would happen if she was to suddenly touch him.

"What do you want me to do?"

"Stop squirming against me."

"Was I doing that? Yes, I suppose that I am. I don't know what to do. Please."

"Even if the sainted departed André was a pig, surely you know what to do to please a man. I'm just a man, Evangeline. Nothing at all different about me." He kissed her lightly, still fighting for control.

"Well, if you're certain that you're no different, then of course I understand." But he'd heard the discordant note in her voice and she saw that he had. She pulled his head down to hers and began kissing him with urgency and passion and not a single whit of skill.

He thought, quite simply, that it would be all over for him. He jerked away from her, panting so hard, he wondered if he'd survive it. "No," he said. "This is worse. Now I can see you instead of feel you against me. All right, enough of this or I'll go quite mad." But he couldn't help himself. He was on her, kissing her until they were both trembling. His hands were frantic on her hips, caressing her until she threw back her head and keened with the power of it. Then, to his immense pleasure, she was pulling and jerking at his clothes. She was trying to kiss him and at the same time unbutton his waistcoat. Then she realized she couldn't manage it. She howled a curse. He laughed, but it wasn't the least bit funny, not when he knew he was hovering on the edge of sanity. He shoved her away and pulled off his clothes more quickly than he'd ever done in his life. He swept her up into his arms and nearly ran to the huge bed set high on its dais. He dropped her in the middle of the bed, managed to light a half dozen candles on the branch beside his bed, and stood, staring down at her.

"I've never seen a woman I've wanted more than I want you," he said, and the truth of his words filled him to his very soul. Then he stood over her. "Evangeline, what's the matter? Why are you staring at me, your mouth open?"

"You're naked," she said, never looking away from his groin. "You're very naked." She licked her lips, nearly sending his body into spasms. "Like you were coming out of the sea, but not really just like that."

He stood there, pulsing with life and urgency.

"Now you're so different from me I know this won't work. It won't. I take it all back. I don't want a lover. I want to go to my own bed and pull my nightgown over my head."

"Oh, Lord," he said, and began to laugh. He started to say something about the departed André's male endowments, but he wanted to get between her legs, right now.

"I'm not about to hurt you. I would hurt myself before I'd ever hurt you. Come now, love. No, don't close your eyes. A man wants his lover to look at him, perhaps even admire him." He leaned over and lightly laid his palm on her belly. He said nothing more, did nothing more, just stood there, his palm warm and large, just lying on her stomach. Then, very slowly, his fingers moved downward, and soon she was holding her breath, looking at his face, her eyes open very wide, knowing he was studying her, looking at her, looking at his fingers that were touching her. She opened her mouth, heaved upward against his fingers, and yelled. He lifted his fingers from her warm flesh, and she sucked in her breath. She looked utterly disappointed. Her breasts were heaving, and he didn't know what to do first. He wanted everything at once.

"What you did," she whispered, her eyes on his face, "what you did. That is something I never imagined. Is that normally done? Would you do it again?"

"Damnation," he said, and came down beside her. He leaned his head to her breast and took her in his mouth. She was filled with passion, but oddly, she didn't seem to know what to do to heighten her pleasure, how to guide him to please her more. He suckled her breasts, and again he let his hand skim over her ribs to her belly. She was squirming against him, her breath coming in short gasps, and her fingers were squeezing his shoulders. "Please," she said, and he said against her breast, "All right." His fingers were over her, then one eased up inside her. She cried out even as her hips jerked upward.

"Easy," he said into her mouth. He would give her pleasure first. She was very close. "I want you to look at me now, Evangeline."

Her head was twisting back and forth on the pillow.

"Look at me now."

She did. He looked at her when he found her with his fingers, when his fingers slicked over her soft woman's flesh, and in but a moment of time, her eyes turned wild and vague, and she was breathing so hard she was nearly choking. And she never looked away from him.

"Now come to me," he said, and kissed her as his fingers caressed her and loved her until he felt a tightening in her, a tensing of her legs, felt the wonderful tremors that started deep inside her. He raised his head and watched her release wash over her and through her.

She wondered if she was dying; then she didn't care, just let herself be thrown from one height to another. She was crying and tossing, then shouting when her body seemed to lock in an arc of pleasure so intense it felled her. She went limp then, feeling small pulsing waves of pleasure feeding through her, and wondering when she could do this again. She looked up into his face, dark and harshly beautiful. She smiled up at him and said, her voice low and scratchy, "Thank you. I never imagined that anything could be quite so wonderful." She closed her eyes a moment at the delicious warmth that was stealing through her, softening her, easing her mind, and she knew that she wanted more than anything to belong to him. But that couldn't happen. No, all she could have was this one night with him. She felt tears trail down her cheeks; a sob burst out of her mouth. She reared up, burying her face against his chest.

Although he didn't understand her, something he was growing rather used to, he set himself to soothe her, his fierce passion temporarily in check. But sweeping his hands down her back, pressing her breasts against him, kissing her ears, her throat, all soon had quite another effect on her. Evangeline didn't question any of it. Her tears dried quickly as her hands stroked down his back. It was she who sought out his mouth, saying between kisses, "Yes, please. Just tell me what to do."

He studied her face, drawn to the vague, smoky sheen in her eyes. His hand caressed her belly, and he felt the taut muscles tense beneath his fingers. Her flesh was smooth, like slick silk.

She tried to move upward against him, but he pressed her back. "No, lie still. My mouth this time, not my fingers."

And he moved between her legs, kissing her belly, his fingers probing her, finding her and sliding into her. When his mouth touched her, she lurched upward, panting so hard she wondered if her heart would burst.

She yelled his name. He raised his head a moment, and grinned up at her, a very male grin, filled with pleasure and satisfaction. "Hold still. No, twist and turn about as much as you want. Yell, Evangeline. Yes, that's it. Now, come to me again." Any embarrassment disappeared in an instant. She bit his shoulder, her fingers tangling in his hair, and she cried, her pleasure was so intense and binding. As she flew out of control, he jerked away from her, pulled her thighs wide, and came into her hard.

She was hot and so tight he gritted his teeth not to tear through her. He slowed himself, but it was the hardest thing he'd ever done. He was stretching her. He looked down at her face and saw that she was still now, no longer squirming beneath him. Now she was staring at him.

She was afraid. He saw it clearly on her face, but he didn't understand. God, he wanted her so badly. He went into her more deeply. She moaned, her hands grabbing his arms to hold him still.

"Hold still, Evangeline, it will be all right. Just hold still for me. You'll become used to me. I'm going as slowly as I can." And he eased deeper, and her fingers dug deeper into his arms.

"No, please stop, please. It hurts. I didn't think it would hurt. You told me you wouldn't hurt me. I believed you."

He made himself stop. He held himself perfectly still as he balanced himself over her on his hands. "Get used to me. Yes, you can do it."

She eased, just a bit, and he went deeper. Then he froze. He stared down at her, disbelieving.

He was butting against her maidenhead.

Her damned maidenhead. Dearly departed saintly André had never existed. Her eyes were wide upon his face as he stared at her. And he thought the words very clearly: *You didn't even realize I would know you were a virgin.* Just thinking those words made him go mad.

Before either of them could breathe another breath, he drove forward. "I know it hurts. Just hang onto me."

She screamed, but this time it was pain, not pleasure, that tightened her body, that made her muscles lock. "No, hold on. Don't fight me. There, I'll hold still. I'm inside you now, all the way inside you, and you won't have any more pain. Hold still for me. That's right." He ducked his head down and kissed her, hard and deep as he was in her body.

She moved, and it nearly drove him over the edge. "Lie still. You must or I'll be gone from you."

"No, I want you to stay with me," she said, kissing and biting his throat, his shoulders. "Why did it hurt?"

He laughed, then moaned as once again she shifted beneath him. "It won't ever hurt again."

She was trembling beneath him. He didn't know whether it was still pain or if his weight was too much for her. In another moment, though, it didn't matter. She moved once again, and it was over for him. He gritted his teeth against the power of his need, his voice deep and hoarse. "I've tried, I've truly tried to distract myself, and you, but it's just no good."

He tried to calm himself, to move just a bit inside her, but it was no good, just no damned good. He heaved over her like a savage, groaned into her mouth like a madman, and then he flew apart, reveling in every moment, knowing more pleasure than he'd ever imagined possible.

As he calmed, as he kissed her ear, he heard her say, "I love you. I've loved you probably from that first evening in your library when you thought I was a former mistress. I'll love you forever."

He managed to pull himself up on his elbows. He smiled down at her. "Good," he said. "I know." He collapsed over her, his head on the pillow beside hers. "Never," he said, close to her ear, "never will I let you out of my sight again."

Chapter 34

He waited for her to say more, but she didn't.

He came up over her again, balancing himself on his elbows.

He saw her bite her lower lip, and close her eyes before he could look at her, but still, she wasn't fast enough. He saw a wrenching pain. He felt instant, blinding fury. "What the hell is going on, Evangeline?"

She looked at him, felt him still deep inside her, felt the tensing and easing of her muscles around him, and said, "I didn't mean to say that. It was very nice, but it's over now, even though you're still inside me and I've never felt anything like this in my life, and I don't want it to stop, ever."

"Now there's a bit of news."

She refused to rise to the bait, which was probably a good thing, since she didn't understand. She said nothing because there was nothing more to say.

"I'm crushing you," he said, and pulled out of her. He rolled onto his back, grabbing her as he moved, and pulled her against him. He felt her sigh deeply as she pressed her face against his shoulder. Her hand was palm down on his belly. He kissed her forehead and said, "You make me nearly blind with rage when you refuse to trust me. I believe you have a lot to tell me now."

She tried to rear up, but he held her down. "Talk to me," he said. "Now. Trust me."

She bit his shoulder, then raised her head and yelled right in his face, "Why can't you leave me alone? Why must you push and shove and prod? You're worse than a nanny I had for a very short time when I was six years old. She picked, picked, picked. Just stop it. I have nothing at all to say to you, nothing. Leave me alone, your grace."

"Your grace? For God's sake, woman, we have just made love—can't you bring yourself to call me by my name?"

"You're 'The Duke' to me. That's your name."

"Very well," he said. "I can bear that for the moment. I'm a title to you. Dear God, you will age me before my time." He squeezed her very hard against him. He waited a few moments. "All right. Talk to me, now."

Another lie, Evangeline. You must lie to him again. No, redo the lie, make him believe you this time. It's over. Her voice was muddled, for she could not bring herself to look at him. "I don't love you. It's merely that you pushed me to feel such things that just forced the words out of me. I believe that's how men make women succumb to them. They make them feel these wild feelings, make them drop their wits to the floor, and it's all over for the women. Indeed, you're unquestionably the most exciting man I've yet met. Thank you for the pleasure. It's all I wanted from you, nothing more. I already told you that. Believe it." She tried to pull away from him, but he held her firmly against him. What was he thinking? Would he yell at her? To her bewilderment, he burst out laughing. He laughed and laughed. She wanted to kill him.

Finally he said, "I'm glad you didn't spit all that out when I was inside you. It would have shriveled me fast." And he laughed some more.

"It's the truth. Let me go. Leave me alone."

"So I'm the most skilled of all your lovers to date?"

"Even though it will puff you up all the more, I told you the truth. Yes, damn you."

"Even though I hurt you?"

"I felt immense pleasure first. I suppose it's a fair enough trade."

"Normally it doesn't hurt the woman at all. Didn't you know that?"

"Certainly. You're large."

"Then you say I'm also the best-endowed of all your lovers to date?"

She felt the rumbling laughter deep in his chest. She arched back against his arms and hit him on the shoulder with her fist. "Damn you, stop this. I don't understand you. Why are you doing this? I've told you the truth. Leave me alone."

He grabbed her hands and easily rolled her onto her back, jerking her arms above her head. She struggled briefly, then lay rigid beneath him.

"I should beat you," he said, his voice soft and thoughtful.

"You try it and I'll hurt you badly." He wasn't moving, was just lying flat on top of her, their bellies pressed together. She had to leave him now. She had to escape.

She took him by surprise, but he managed to keep her down with his weight. He looked down at her pale face, her tangled hair, her mouth, beautiful, so very beautiful, and those eyes of hers that were so deep and held secrets he wanted to know.

"Let me go," she said. "Just let me go."

"I'd take myself to Bedlam if I let you up. Oh, no, as your most skilled lover to date, even more skilled than that clod, the saintly departed André, I want to leave an impression that will always be with you, until you're an old woman and your memories are faded and blurred. You'll still remember me, Evangeline. I'll still be with you," and he lowered his face and kissed her.

She fought him, willing herself not to let him make her wild again, even when she felt those urgent feelings welling up inside her.

He kissed her chin, her throat, licking the wildly beating pulse. Then he came up between her legs, pushing them even wider, and he smiled down at her, his eyes black and gleaming in the candlelight. He told her what he was going to do to her, and then he began kissing her breasts, every few breaths repeating what he was doing to her, what he was going to do to her next. By the time his mouth was hot and urgent against her belly, she was heaving and mewling, her hands in his hair, squeezing his shoulders, reaching any part of him she could. When his hands lifted her to his mouth, she was tense and ready. She heard herself begging him not to leave her. And he didn't. When she bucked and yelled, he felt as if the world was his. And he was king of this world.

He came into her hard and fast and deep, and though she was very small, her flesh quivering around him, he knew he wasn't hurting her. He wanted it to last, he wanted to bring her to pleasure again, but his body wouldn't allow it. He'd wanted her for so very long. He roared his pleasure to the rafters in his bedchamber.

Finally, he raised himself on his elbows over her. "Tell me again that you don't love me."

She raised wild eyes to his face. She stared at him, just stared, not speaking. Then she started crying.

He rolled onto his side, leaned over her, and began to smooth the hair from her face. He lightly kissed her forehead, her temples, and the salty tears on her cheeks. "What is this? My Evangeline breaking into tears like just any weak woman? I wouldn't have believed it possible. Not you, not my strong, stubborn girl."

She turned her face away from him. He heard her sniffing, heard her begin to hiccup.

"Don't move. I'll take care of this ailment of yours." He started to get up, but to his delirious pleasure, she held him, trying to bring him back to her. He grinned at her, and she hiccuped. "Let me go," he said, and finally she did. "No," he said over his shoulder, "I'm not leaving you. I'm just getting you a glass of water."

When she drank the water and sniffled into the handkerchief he'd brought her, she looked away. He stared at her tousled head, wondering why he must always be forced back further than where he'd originally begun.

He frowned when he saw her thighs streaked with her virgin's blood and his seed.

This time when he left her, she said nothing. He imagined her brain was squirreling about madly to find more excuses, more lies to throw at him. He didn't say anything, just returned with a basin of water and a washcloth.

That roused her. "What's that for?" she said, struggling up on her elbows.

"Be quiet and lie back down."

"Oh, no. I won't do anything until you tell me what you're doing."

He raised an eyebrow. "Of course you know what I'm doing. I'm going to bathe you, naturally."

"Oh, no, you won't. Are you mad? That is certainly something I shall do for myself. Oh, goodness, I'm covered with blood."

He ignored that and said easily, his voice as matter-of-fact as a magistrate's, "It's always the lover who performs this task." He added with infuriating calm, "I assume that Frenchmen are no different from Englishmen in that regard."

That confused her, and he would have laughed openly if only things weren't so damned serious, if only his life weren't on the line here.

"Of course not," she said finally, and he could feel her struggling with herself to accept what he was doing to her, not wanting to, but knowing she had to accept it because it was the done thing.

"Sometimes one wonders," he said, "if there are differences amongst men of different countries." She lay on her back, her eyes tightly closed, while he stroked the wet washcloth over her flesh. She'd bled a lot. But it seemed to have stopped. He leaned closer. Her woman's flesh was chafed. He'd not been rough with her, but still it had been a lot for her.

It was time to end it, but he said only, "Evangeline."

She opened her eyes to see him looking intently at her face. "It seems to me that you're only expressive when I'm kissing you or caressing you or making you yell. It's all going to stop now, all of it. All the secrets, they're going to come out now. I can see that you're already trying to think up more ridiculous lies. Let's begin with an easy one. I know that you are—were—a virgin."

She was a doe facing a hunter. "That's a stupid thing to say, your grace."

"I suppose I didn't give you much time to make up something with more wit, with more punch, something with even a twinge of believability. You're so bloody innocent that it still shocks me to my toes. I was blind. All the clues were there for me to see, to hear in your bravado. But I was blind and deaf to what you were. I saw only what you wanted me to see and hear."

She remained as still as a post.

He sighed. "All right. Suffice it to say that at least I know a good bit about you. You were a virgin, and that's why I hurt you. It hurts the woman the first time because the man has to get through her maidenhead. Then it doesn't hurt, that is, if the man isn't a clod, like the dearly departed saintly André who never graced this earth, did he?"

"No," she said, nothing more. "No, I've never been married." It was over, she thought, because she'd been too stupid, too ignorant to realize that a man knew when a woman was a virgin. What would he do now? She didn't have but an instant to wait.

His long fingers began to stroke her shoulders. "Then why don't you tell me what brought you to Chesleigh as Madame de la Valette, a poor widowed cousin to my dead wife?"

A kaleidoscope of faces whirled through her mind. Houchard, grim and unwavering in his mission. John Edgerton—the Lynx—a murderer, the man who swore he'd murder Edmund as well as her father, and she believed him to her soul, for hadn't he strangled Mrs.

Needle as if she'd been of no account at all? Evangeline saw her clearly, cold and pale and dead in the dull morning light. She ran her tongue over her dry lips. There was nothing for her now, nothing except more lies. She said nothing, because her brain held nothing but unspeakable pain. She just shook her head.

He rose and tossed the washcloth into the basin. It was a simple physical movement that calmed his immense frustration, his growing anger. "As odd as it may seem," he said in a flat, emotionless voice, "I know that you love me. Your offering of yourself to me tonight was proof of that. No, don't interrupt me yet with more lies, Evangeline. You will never have the wherewithal to play the harlot; it was foolish of you to attempt it, particularly with me. What I cannot understand—and believe me, I have tried—is why you came here in the first place. You must believe that I would provide you any assistance in my power. You have but to tell me what it is that troubles you." He paused a moment, staring down at her. "My God, you're terrified. Damn you, tell me!"

She was more than terrified, she was desperate. She was caught and there was no escape. She was shaking her head even as she said, her breath harsh and ugly, "It's true that I love you. I didn't want to. I never even considered such a thing when I came here. But I couldn't help myself. You're right, of course. Since I couldn't have you for my husband, I wanted what I could have from you. I wanted to give to you what I could as well. As for the rest—I know I can't expect you to trust me. I've treated you too poorly to expect that. You have to believe me, though. I don't want to hurt you, you or any of your family."

"Then what do you want from me now?"

"I must—no, no, that is, I would like to remain at Chesleigh, just for a little while longer."

He just stood there, naked. And she saw that he didn't know what to do. She jumped up from the bed, ran past him to bend down and pick up her gown. She looked at him again over her shoulder, shaking her head, then dashed toward the bedchamber door.

He took three steps toward her, his hand out.

"No," she yelled. "No." She pulled the gown over her head and thrust her arms through the sleeves. She grabbed the doorknob and was out of his bedchamber in but an instant, closing the door very quietly behind her.

He stood there, staring at the closed door, then at her slippers and stockings lying in a small pile in the middle of his bedchamber.

Chapter 35

It was the blackest of nights, the only light from the white caps cresting the waves that were rolling gently into the cove. It was cold, very cold, and she pulled her dark cloak more closely around her as she walked to the cove. She kept to the cover of trees and bushes, as was her habit.

Tonight, she thought, tonight she would give the man coming in a letter to Edgerton, telling him that she couldn't continue. It would stop. It had to stop.

She thought of that morning, when the duke had come upon her at the stable. She'd been so close to escape, and there he stood, just smiling at her. "You nearly made it," he said. "I thought you'd try to avoid me this morning, and thus decided a little subterfuge would possibly work. We must talk, Evangeline."

She'd nodded, for there'd been nothing else to do.

"You didn't sleep well?"

Of course she hadn't, but she hadn't realized it was so clear on her face. He said matter-of-factly, "Don't be alarmed. I have no intention of throwing you over my shoulder and hauling you off to my bed. In truth, I'd like very much to have you naked and my hands all over you, but I'm not going to touch you."

And what was there to say to that? That she'd give just about anything to have him naked and her hands all over him?

"I've decided that I don't want you in my bed until you've agreed to be my wife. Ah, I take it from your averted eyes that you still don't want me, that is, you don't want me for a husband? A lover, then. You'd prefer to be my mistress? From the scarlet flush that's creeping up your neck to your hairline, I take it that I now have Mademoiselle Evangeline de Beauchamps in front of me and not the widow of the saintly departed clod André?"

"I made André in the likeness of a young gentleman in France, the Comte de Pouilly. He wanted to marry me."

"I hope you refused the idiot?"

"I did."

"You're not going to try to deny that you don't love me again, are you?"

"No, I won't ever try to deny that. You might laugh at me or tease me until I stick you with one of your own ancestral swords. But listen to me, your grace, if you love me, you will grant me time—time to think about what it is I wish to do. Is it too much to ask?"

He rubbed his fingers over his jaw. "That is quite a concession coming from you," he said finally. "I do believe I'm making progress. It's not too much to ask, no. You see before you the most patient of men. Well, I'm really not at all patient. What I'd like to do right now is strip you naked and toss you into the hay and come over you. I've already told you I wanted my hands all over you. Well, I want my mouth all over you as well." He sighed deeply. "No, you have my word. Now you must promise you won't try to avoid me."

And she'd agreed.

Evangeline gathered the hood of her cloak about her face. It was getting colder from one minute to the next. She was nearly to the water—that was why it was becoming bone cold. She walked down the path quickly, for time was growing short.

After she lit the lantern and gave the signal, she walked to the dock to meet the longboat that was cutting through the waves toward her. She heard hushed whispers among the men as the boat scraped against the dock. Two of them sprang out and spoke quietly to the two men remaining in the boat; then one man pushed it with his boat away from the dock.

A man walked softly toward her, his boots noiseless on the wooden planks.

"You're the Eagle?" She was used to the incredulous surprise in the men's voices. None of them expected a woman. Her secret was being held close.

She nodded. "You're Paul Treyson?"

He smiled at her and took a step closer. "Yes." He handed her a thick envelope. "Here are my instructions. I was told that I am to give you time to read them."

Instead of returning to the cave, Evangeline knelt down on the beach, lighted a match, and quickly read through his letters of introduction. He was to become an assistant to the powerful Rothchild in London. Dear God, she couldn't begin to image the political access it would provide him.

She dropped the burned match, quickly wrote her initials on the bottom of the paper, and rose. "Very well, Monsieur. It grows late, you must make haste. Oh, please take this with you. You will see that it gets to the Lynx."

He frowned but then nodded. "Very well. Here are your next papers."

He handed her two envelopes. One she recognized as her next instructions from Houchard; the other was a letter from her father.

"It won't be long now," the man said, "before your position takes on new and special meaning. The emperor will engage the allies and their English Iron Duke within these next several months. You will be more valuable than ever to us."

Evangeline's hand fisted about the envelopes. She had assumed that it would be over for her and her father once Napoleon had taken the reins of power firmly in his hands. She'd been a fool. She'd believed Houchard. If he were here with her, she'd kill him with no hesitation, with no regret.

"Go," she said, and quickly retreated toward the cave. She pictured the duke, his dark eyes on her face, telling her that he would give her time to think. There had been nothing else she could have told him, and it had been a lie. Once she got word from Edgerton that she was free, she would join her father in Paris. She would never see him again. She was despicable, and there was simply nothing she could do about it. She knew her letter to Edgerton would bring him here or at least bring a message from him. She would have to wait, but not much longer, she just couldn't.

Suddenly two shots blasted loud in the night, up along the cliff. There was a man's cry of pain. Then another shot and a man's yell. Another cry of pain. She whirled about, looking upward. She heard shouts from the cliff. For an instant she froze, unable to move or to think. They'd been discovered. Oh, God, they'd been discovered.

She crouched low and dashed to the cave, her eyes

straining to see in the darkness. In the distance she heard the tramping of heavy boots and loud, excited voices. She turned and saw black-cloaked men rushing down the cliff path to the beach, cutting off her escape.

She heard a cultured gentleman's voice above the others. "Search the beach, every inch of it. The other man must be nearby. He's the English traitor. Don't let him escape." It was Lord Pettigrew.

Evangeline ran to the back of the cave, her mind clogged with fear. She would be killed, or worse, captured. She thought of her father. He would die with her because she'd failed. And the duke—surely no one would believe him guilty of being a traitor to England.

She sat huddled into a small ball at the back of the cave, waiting for them to discover her. She heard the muted splashing of water and men's voices drawing closer. She sat there watching the cave entrance. Then she pictured Edmund in her mind. Her boy was shrieking with laughter when he'd happened to say something that made her double over with laughter. Her boy could die if she was discovered. Edgerton would still be free. He would kill Edmund. No, she wouldn't let Edgerton hurt Edmund. She had to stop him. She ran toward the cave entrance, only to draw up short when she heard men talking.

"Damnation," she heard one man shout. "We can't get past this point. The tide's coming in. The man couldn't have come this way, else we'd have seen him."

"You're right. The cliff nearly meets the water and it's sheer. Let's go back the other way."

She heard them pause, then splash their way back up the beach.

The incoming tide. She had a chance now. Water

was already lapping at her ankles, so cold, yet she hadn't felt a thing until now. She dragged her feet slowly through the rising water to the entrance, listening for the English soldiers, but there was only the sound of the sea.

She forced herself to wait for what seemed an eternity, until the rushing water licked about her thighs. Her legs were at last nearly numb. It was time. She couldn't wait any longer, or else the tide would be too strong for her to swim against. She pushed with all her strength forward. Just a few more feet, she chanted to herself, and she would be able to swim outward.

A wave crashed unexpectedly upon her, throwing her off her feet, pulling her under the water, throwing her against the rocks at the mouth of the cave. She felt a sharp pain in her ribs, and for an instant she couldn't draw breath. Edmund, she thought, Edmund. She grabbed frantically at an outjutting rock, struggling against her heavy, sodden clothing, and pulled herself, rock by rock, toward the far side of the cave. When there were no more rocks to ground her, she swam until the water shoved her against the wall of the cliff. She pushed her hair out of her eyes and looked upward at the sheer cliff above her. There was no way to scale that cliff, no way at all. Then she thought of Edmund and knew she had no choice. She had to get to the top. But not here, it was impossible. She drew a deep breath and swam outward, fighting the waves with all her strength. When she simply couldn't fight any more, she stopped struggling and fell forward in the freezing water, and let the sea wash her back to shore. When she felt coarse sand and sharp stones, she felt no pain, but she knew they'd torn her. No, all she felt was tremendous relief. She wasn't dead yet.

She lay facedown on the beach and vomited salt water onto the wet sand. Finally she knew she had to move; she had to get to safety. She pulled herself to her feet and stumbled, hunched over, toward the cliff. She heard muted voices up the beach, beyond the outjutting land, beyond the cave, near the cliff path. She looked up. What had seemed utterly sheer really wasn't. There were rocks worn away more deeply than others. There were roots. She could do it, she had to. She grabbed a rock and pulled herself upward, reaching for the roots that were sticking out some feet above her head. She prayed they'd hold her weight. They did. She found another rock small enough for her to hold firmly and pulled herself up. She paused, then. Where could she climb now? She'd nearly given up when she saw a huge rock sticking out of the cliff, long and narrow. She knew she could use it to pull herself up, and yes, there was a deep indentation in the cliff, a bit beyond her reach, but she could make it, she had to. She was thirty feet above the beach when suddenly, with no warning, no shifting of rock or dirt beneath her feet, the ground gave way beneath her. She hung there, scrambling madly to find purchase. Finally, finally, she found a rock sticking out just enough to hold one of her feet. She lay against the cliff as loose rock and rubble fell over her. It sounded like an avalanche. Then there was silence. No more falling rocks, no sound of men's voices. Finally, she saw the edge of the cliff above her, and pulled herself up.

She rolled onto the even ground and lay flat on her stomach, not really believing that she'd managed to climb that damned cliff. But she had. Slowly she rose. She tried to stand upright and discovered she couldn't. Her ribs hurt too badly.

She saw Chesleigh in the distance, its few lighted windows pinpoints of white in the dark night. She ran toward it, crouched over, her wet clothes slapping her legs.

She heard a shout in the distance. A man yelled. "Wait, I see him. Stop!"

Evangeline fell to her knees and crawled forward. She heard a shot, then another, but they weren't close to her. Thank God, it wasn't her they'd seen. There were more shots, coming from an even greater distance away. She hauled herself to her feet and ran to the line of lime trees bordering the gravel drive that circled around to the north face of Chesleigh. She pulled herself up and slumped against a tree. She could barely breathe, there was a stitch in her side, and her ribs felt as though someone had caved them in with a cannon ball.

From a great distance she heard a man's shout, "No, it's this way, men. I saw the bloody bastard over there, near the road." Lord Pettigrew's shout was frantic. "Don't kill him. We've got to have him alive."

She closed her eyes tightly and pressed her cheek against the rough bark of the tree. She heard their heavy booted steps moving back toward the road. She forced herself to remain still, waiting as long as she dared.

She crawled through the thick hedges that bordered the drive, and rose to her feet only when she was facing the north wing. She drew the key from her pocket, sucked in a deep breath, and ran, bowed over, to the castle. The stone walls shadowed her as her numbed fingers fought to insert the key. "Come on, get in there, damn you." Then the key was in, and she twisted it frantically. It wouldn't move. She leaned against the castle wall, so exhausted both in mind and in body, she wondered if they'd just find her here in the morning, propped up, her eyes open, but quite dead. "Open," she said, cursing the key until finally it clicked into place. She pushed the door only wide enough for her to slither through. When she stood safely inside, she leaned heavily against the thick door, then quickly turned to lock it. Upstairs, she thought, she had to get to her bedchamber. She walked bent over, holding her ribs, her heavy breathing the only noise breaking the silence in the castle.

She lit a candle in her bedchamber and turned to stare at the torn and filthy shadow in the mirror. She was sodden, her hair plastered against her head, with cuts and scrapes everywhere. She couldn't seem to stop shaking. She stripped off her wet clothes, gritting her teeth against the pain in her ribs. She pulled her nightgown over her head, pulled on one of Marissa's thick velvet dressing gowns. Still she shivered and quaked, her teeth chattering. She burrowed beneath all the blankets on her bed. Although she gradually warmed, she couldn't stop shaking. At least she could think more clearly.

She'd won, she'd truly won.

She could still hear the shouts of Lord Pettigrew's men when they believed they'd seen her. Maybe they had. Maybe she'd just beaten them. Soon they could burst into her room. In a frenzy of anxiety, she bounded from her bed and stuffed her wet clothes under the armoire. She stumbled back into bed and forced herself to close her eyes. There was, quite simply, nothing more she could do.

Chapter 36

Shafts of bright early morning sunlight fell on her face. Slowly she opened her eyes. The night had finally passed. She'd slept fitfully, terrified at any moment that they would come for her. But no one had banged on her bedchamber door. Morning had come. She lay there, thankful that it was another day and that she was still safe, at least here in her room. She ignored the pain in her body, because she couldn't do anything about it, and forced herself to think.

Had Lord Pettigrew's men caught both Paul Treyson and the other man? Or just one? Which one? She thought of the letter she'd given to Paul Treyson. She'd not used either her name or John Edgerton's. She closed her eyes, feeling relief wash over all the pain.

They were scouring the area for an English traitor. They were searching for a man, unless one of the men had confessed to Lord Pettigrew that the English traitor was a woman. If they had confessed, then it was over. There was nothing she could do. She had to believe that they hadn't told Lord Pettigrew anything; surely they wouldn't.

Lord Pettigrew's men had probably already come

to Chesleigh. She couldn't stay in bed. She had to act naturally. Were she to plead illness, the duke might suspect or Lord Pettigrew might think it odd. She wasn't a good actress, but she would have to be today.

She thought of her father; she thought of Edmund. If she was to save them, she must first save herself. When she saw herself in the mirror, she nearly expired on the spot. Her hair was sticky and tangled around her face. Oh, and the rest of it. She couldn't bear to look at herself. Nor did it matter. She would simply cover herself very well indeed. At least she hadn't broken any bones.

Two hours passed before she finished drying and curling her hair. She chose a very feminine, frivolous gown, one that fit snugly over her breasts and flared out to a ruffled hem. If ever she needed to appear the epitome of helpless, fragile womanhood, today was the day. She looked down at her hands, winced at the sight, and pulled on a pair of white mittens.

She saw no one downstairs. She was on the point of going into the breakfast room when she heard carriage wheels on the gravel drive. She walked quickly into the drawing room and drew back the heavy curtain to see Lord Pettigrew climbing out of his carriage. He looked very tired.

She heard Bassick bidding him welcome. It was some minutes more before she heard the duke's voice.

"Drew, I'm glad you're here. We scoured every bush, visited every farmhouse between Chesleigh and three miles to the south. We didn't find the traitor, dammit. Did you find the man?"

Thank God. They were looking for a man.

"We did find something of interest," Drew said in a low voice. "Let's speak privately."

Evangeline pressed close to the wall until their footsteps receded down the corridor. She forced herself to wait some minutes longer before she followed them.

If Bassick thought it odd that she should suddenly appear, he gave no sign of it, merely bowed and bade her a good morning. She forced herself to greet him brightly before turning away to walk to the duke's library. She drew a deep breath before the closed doors, then drew them open and walked in, her smile as brilliant as the morning sun.

Drew Halsey had just begun speaking when Evangeline wafted into the library, looking so exquisitely beautiful and softly female that both men stared at her for a moment. Then Drew got hold of himself. He frowned, impatient to get this all out and discussed. Then he saw her eyes widen and forced himself to smile. He wasn't about to frighten this lovely young woman. He didn't think he'd ever before seen her looking so very lovely, her face alight with carefree laughter. He thought of Felicia and smiled more widely. "Good morning, Evangeline," he said, quickly rising and walking to her. He took her mittened hand and kissed her fingers. "You are looking remarkably fine this morning."

She pulled her hand away, laughed at his compliment, and said, "I hope I'm not disturbing you. Both of you look so very serious. I thought his grace and I could take Edmund for a drive to Rye. Oh, goodness. I hope nothing is wrong? It isn't anything to do with Felicia, is it, Drew?"

The duke was standing against his desk, his arms crossed over his chest. His eyes were upon her thick honey-colored hair, piled in careless curls atop her head with soft tendrils falling over her ears. She looked like an exquisite model of the fashionable lady, complete to her white mittens. But when she'd spoken, he'd stiffened. She sounded for the world like a young lady trying out her wiles on the first available gentlemen.

"No, no, don't worry, Evangeline," Drew said quickly, wanting to remove the fear from her lovely eyes. "Felicia is just fine. Actually, I've been here for the past two days. Felicia is in town."

"Good morning, Evangeline," the duke said. He walked to her, stood before her, silent for a moment, then nodded slowly. "A ride into Rye with Edmund, you say?"

"Yes, your grace," she said, then looked quickly away. He saw so much, always, perhaps too much.

The duke was silent for a moment longer, then stepped back to lean against the mantelpiece. "Attend us a moment, Evangeline. Then certainly you and I and Edmund will do something doubtless quite exciting, beginning with breakfast. In fact, I think you should join us. I believe it only fair that you hear what we have done."

"Richard, are you certain? She's a lady, I don't wish to alarm her."

Evangeline ignored Drew and said, "What do you mean, your grace?" She sounded to her own ears as guileless as a nun. Hopefully the duke had the same hearing. She fluttered her hands. "Goodness, how mysterious you sound. I believe I shall sit down in case I begin to feel weak."

The duke said nothing as Evangeline sat down. Drew Halsey looked from one to the other, shrugged, and walked over to the duke's desk.

The duke looked down at his thumbnail, frowned because it was on the jagged side. Had he hurt her with that jagged nail? He shook his head at himself. He said, "I didn't tell you sooner because I didn't wish you upset further. When I received your letter about Mrs. Needle's murder, I hired a Bow Street Runner to come back with me to Chesleigh to investigate while we were in London. He told me that before you and I went to London, he'd been by the cove and he'd seen strange goings-on down on the beach—a lantern light as a signal and bloody mysterious chaps rowing to the dock. He thought they were French. I spoke to Drew, and he believed it worthwhile to investigate the matter himself. How many evenings have your men spent hiding in the trees up on the cliff path, Drew?"

"It's been nearly two weeks. I was with them last night. As I was telling you, Richard, your Bow Street Runner was quite right."

Evangeline clapped a hand over her breast. She stared at him in absolute horror.

Drew shot the duke an harassed look, but the duke merely looked down at his thumbnail again. "Yes. Please continue, Drew."

"Late last night we spotted two cloaked figures on the dock, meeting with a third man. When two of the men gained the cliff path, we confronted them. Unfortunately, they lost their heads and ran, and we were forced to shoot. I don't know how the other man, the one who brought them in, escaped, but he did. I have no idea how he managed it. You know, Richard, how treacherous the cliffs are. By God, I've always believed them perfectly sheer. But somehow he must have scaled the rocks and gained the cliff top, all without our seeing him. It was very cold last night, with no moonlight. There were countless shadows the men saw, but none of them were the traitor."

"That's horrible," Evangeline said, her mittened

hands still covering her breast. "Do you have proof that the men you killed were French?"

"Yes, Evangeline," Drew said. "There was a packet on one of the dead men, some sort of coded instructions that we'll break—I have no doubt about that. The traitor had scrawled his initials on the bottom right corner. Also, before he died, the man who carried the instructions whispered something in French. All I could make out was the words *l'Aigle,* and *traitre.* It seems likely that he thought the man who'd met them had betrayed them, but of course he hadn't. There was also another letter in the man's pocket, addressed to the Lynx, evidently the traitor's contact in London. As I said, it's written in some sort of code that we'll break soon. It was signed *L'Aigle* or *Eagle.*" He continued toward the duke, "As you know, we went north of Chesleigh. Nothing, Richard. The man got away from us. It's frustrating. We've got to catch him. I can't imagine the damage he's already done. I've had three men working to break that code since last night. It shouldn't be long now."

"I've been thinking about it," the duke said. "The man has to be local. He must be. And the damned bastard has been using my property to bring in spies. I'll kill the fellow when I get my hands on him."

"If you find him before I do, please don't kill him. We need information from him. Then we'll hang him and save you the trouble of dirtying your hands. I know it angers you that the French have been using Chesleigh as an entry point into England. As we thought, Richard, Mrs. Needle's murder must somehow be connected. She must have discovered something. You know that she still moved about the county at will, despite her advanced years, so the chances of her overhearing something or seeing something makes sense. I would like your permission to question your servants. I don't hold out much hope, but perhaps someone saw something last night."

The duke nodded, saying nothing. He looked at Evangeline.

"Is there anything you can tell Drew? Did you see anything last night? Perhaps you were awake and at your window around midnight?"

"It was very cold last night. I never left my bed. Goodness, this all seems so fantastic."

To Evangeline's immense relief, Drew Halsey finally prepared to leave. He said as he rose, "My men won't hold your servants long. I'll keep you informed. It is doubtful that the Eagle will again use your beach, but I will, of course, have several of my men continue to watch."

Evangeline rose as well. "I hope you find the man, my lord. I vow I won't sleep tonight. If you gentlemen don't mind, I shall see to Edmund now."

Evangeline gave both men a brilliant smile and left the library. The duke looked after her, saying nothing.

"I'll be at the Raven Inn today, Richard, but I must leave for London this evening. My latest intelligence is that Napoleon will start for Belgium within the next few days. Wellington is waiting for him. Hopefully, I'll take the decoded instruction with me to London to the ministry."

"I wonder if this group of spies had anything to do with Robbie's death?" the duke said. "After all, he was my friend, he spent time here at Chesleigh, and the men were using Chesleigh as their entry point."

"I'm certain as I can be now that it was. Imagine, the bastards used your private beach. That's an incredible show of gall, if nothing else."

And the duke said, his voice cool, "Actually, the idea is beginning to seem less fantastic."

The duke gave Bassick instructions, nodded briefly toward the two men Lord Pettigrew had left behind, and headed for the nursery. He didn't find her there. He entered her bedchamber, saw that the room was empty, and turned, only to stop at the door.

Ten minutes later he found her in a small, sunny parlor on the second floor. She was standing near the window, looking out over the Channel, her back to him. He closed the door firmly behind him and leaned against it. She didn't turn, but he knew she was fully aware of him.

"Your performance was exquisite," he said easily. "Drew was either admiring your beauty or cursing your frivolous woman's prattle. Naturally, you were there to avert suspicion if anyone could possibly suspect you and to learn what we knew and what was being done. As I said, you did very well indeed. The only thing, Evangeline, did you honestly believe you could fool me?"

She closed her eyes at those smoothly spoken words. She shook her head, not turning. "I don't know what you're talking about, your grace. Surely any lady would be horrified at what's been happening." She managed a shudder. "A traitor here, at Chesleigh."

He didn't move, just said in that same easy voice, only it was deeper now, the calm more deadly, "Yes, let's talk about traitors here at Chesleigh. Let me be quite specific. Shall I call you Evangeline or by your traitor's name—the Eagle?"

She turned slowly to face him. It was over, but she knew she had to try. She said with desperate calm, "You're weaving a fantasy, your grace. Look at me. How could I possibly be a man?"

"Yes, I believe I'll look at you even more closely." He walked to her, his eyes never leaving her face. "How odd it is that you're wearing mittens. I've never seen you wear mittens."

He grabbed her hands in his and jerked them off. "I hope you didn't suffer these unfeminine scratches from our lovemaking?" He shook his head. "No, don't bother to lie to me, Evangeline, unless you would also care to explain the damp and torn clothes I found stuffed beneath your armoire. Damn you, Evangeline, you will tell me the truth."

His face was taut with fury. She managed to wrench her hands away. He knew, and there was no hope for it. But what about her father? What about Edmund? "Very well," she said finally. "It's true."

"You're this damned Eagle?"

"Yes."

He didn't trust himself to touch her, because if he did, he didn't know what he'd do. "I've never thought of myself as being particularly blind to others' faults before. You certainly played me for a perfect fool, though. An indigent relation, a beautiful woman who needed my help. A beautiful woman who looked at me as if she wanted to tear my clothes off and seduce me. And you did seduce me, didn't you? You think that will make any difference at all now that I know what you are? God, you're a damned liar, a cheat, and a traitor."

She looked at his hands, fisted at his sides. "I did only what I had to do."

"And I played my role admirably, didn't I? Tell me, what decided you to come to my bed? Did you think I might find something out unless you distracted me further? Did you really believe that I'd be less likely to give you over to the hangman just because I took your damned virginity?"

"I had no choice," she said. "Enough, your grace. You must let me explain."

He laughed at her. "Why not? I'm certain you've worked on your explanations a good long while. After all, you've been playing a very dangerous game. Naturally, you'd have to come up with good excuses to lay out when you were finally caught."

It was then that he couldn't help himself. He grabbed her and began shaking her. She opened her mouth, then blinked at him. "No," she whispered. "Oh, no, this can't happen," and then she slumped, unconscious, against him.

Chapter 37

He caught her in his arms, feeling both frustrated and afraid. Damn her. He wouldn't yell at her now, couldn't confront her further, because she'd had the gall to faint. He carried her to his bedchamber, past a gaping maid and two frozen footmen, and laid her on his bed, jerking loose the high muslin collar about her throat. Several angry scratches slashed downward to her shoulder. He cursed as he quickly stripped off her clothing, furious with her, wishing he could strangle her, for she could be seriously hurt. He gazed down at the ugly, mottled bruising over her ribs, on her legs, and on her shoulders, at the many scratches and cuts, and drew a deep, steadying breath. It struck him with blinding force that she could easily have been killed. She'd managed to climb up that bloody cliff, by herself, in the dark, terrified. Oh, God, he didn't think he could bear it. He pulled the covers to her neck.

Evangeline slowly opened her eyes to see the duke staring down at her. "Damn you," he said.

"I fainted," she said, astonished. "I've never fainted in my life. You took off my clothes. I'm a mess, but it's nothing serious. My ribs aren't broken, but it was a close thing for a while last night."

He closed his eyes against her words because he himself had been out there searching. He knew the sheerness of that cliff, knew how she'd had to swim against that icy incoming tide even to gain the beach that gave onto the cliff. Then he looked down at her, murder in his eyes, and said, "I'm glad you didn't kill yourself last night. Now I can kill you."

"I will be punished, never fear. But you must let me escape. You must. You can't be the one to hang me."

"So you'd disappear from me just as suddenly as you arrived? No, Evangeline, I'm not about to let you out of my sight." He pulled back the covers and looked at her. "You are really quite good, do you know that? You have my compliments. And to have you a virgin, despite all your blatant interest in me—why, it wasn't at all necessary. I was expecting a woman with a bit of skill, but no, you'd saved your maidenhead for me. To think, I, the duke of Portsmouth, a man who wants to see Napoleon in a very deep grave, a man who hates all who want to bring down England, that proud fool was brought low by a woman, and it wasn't all that difficult for you to do. There's sure to be something edifying in all this, but I doubt I'll see it for a long time to come." He jerked the covers down to her ankles. She made no move to cover herself; she had no more fight. He laid his hand on her belly. "The only part of you that isn't scraped or cut or scratched."

She tried to jerk away from him, but he held her down.

"Cover me," she said. "I can't fight you."

"You would be a fool to fight me now. I'll cover you soon enough. First I'm going to make sure that you've done yourself no lasting injury."

He changed from the man who'd been her lover,

from the man who'd spewed his anger at her, to a man who simply didn't care. She turned her head away and closed her eyes. She felt his fingers lightly probing her ribs.

"You were right. Your ribs aren't broken. You should count yourself very lucky. No, don't move. Otherwise, you're a mess, but there isn't anything serious. Hold still. I'm going to put some of Mrs. Needle's healing ointment on you."

She lay there naked, wondering what would happen to her, to her father, to Edmund. When he came back to the bed, his face was set, his hands were steady. He said only, "Hold still."

She felt his fingers lightly massaging an ointment into the worst of the scratches. He realized that his hands were shaking. He stared down at her averted face.

As if she sensed that he was looking at her, she slowly turned her eyes to his face. There was a bitter, helpless smile on her mouth. "I never wanted to hurt you, never. Now it's too late. You must protect yourself, you must protect Edmund."

"You can spill your innards to me in a moment. Right now, just keep your pleas to yourself." He turned her onto her stomach. There were scratches and bruises on her back and hips, the backs of her legs. He cursed. She didn't move as he rubbed in ointment, lightly touched his fingers to the bruises. She heard his heavy breathing.

He was seeing her struggling back to Chesleigh, her life in the balance. Unwillingly, he found himself marveling at her force of will. If Drew had somehow come to suspect her, her performance would have convinced him of her innocence. Drew doubtless believed her a foolish, quite frivolous woman.

"There," he said finally, helping her onto her back again and pulling up the covers. "It's done."

He drew a chair to her bedside and sat down, formed his fingers in a steeple, and tapped them thoughtfully together.

He said in a very controlled voice, "Certain things are now quite clear to me, Mademoiselle. Your unexpected arrival at Chesleigh, your indigent status, and your unremitting insistence on remaining at Chesleigh. Even your claimed widowhood. Had you arrived as a supposed innocent young lady, the proprieties would have demanded that I provide at the very least a chaperone—that, or you couldn't have remained." He paused for a moment, recalling Evangeline's grief at the death of the old woman. He frowned. "I'm certain that you were innocent of Mrs. Needle's murder. Indeed, it very nearly destroyed you. But you know who killed her, don't you, Evangeline? If I hadn't taken matters into my own hands, if I hadn't brought a Bow Street Runner, why, you would still be bringing in spies."

"Yes," she said.

He suddenly remembered her insistence upon visiting Drew at the Ministry. "Ah, another little something. Your visit to the Ministry. That wasn't a lady's frivolous request, was it?"

"No, I was ordered to leave an envelope in Lord Pettigrew's office, in one of the books on the second shelf. I don't know what was in the envelope."

"I believe it's time for you to tell me everything, Evangeline." He saw such pain in her eyes that he nearly stopped. But he had to know. He had to know every damned thing she'd done and why. Still, she said nothing. He said, "I see. You would have me believe that you're nothing more than a devious traitor who has, in the most calculating manner, deceived me and my entire family."

"No," she said, her voice cold and dull. "It wasn't like that. Please, your grace, I had no choice at all about anything."

"Tell me. No more dancing around it. Trust me, Evangeline. Tell me why you did it."

"My father isn't dead. He's being held prisoner by a man named Houchard in Paris."

She told him in a halting voice of the night the two men had broken into their home, of the journey to Paris, her meeting with Houchard. "He knew all about my family and yours. You were to be my dupe, my cat's paw; else he would have my father killed as a traitor. Only the Lynx would know the truth."

"Who is the Lynx?"

"John Edgerton is the Lynx."

He started forward in his chair. "The devil, you say."

"That's what I think he is. He or one of his men murdered poor Mrs. Needle. That first night I met him, I knew I couldn't succeed at this. I told him there was already someone who thought something was wrong. I mentioned her name to him. Oh, God, he killed her. I think it was more a lesson to me than to silence anything that she might have said. He wanted me to know that if I told you, asked for your help, there would be consequences that I wouldn't be able to bear." She drew a breath, remembering. "I had made up my mind to tell you. Edgerton must have guessed I was wavering. He told me that if I ever let anything out to you, he personally would kill Edmund. I never said a word then. I never would, except now this has happened." She swung her legs out of bed, grabbing the covers to keep herself covered. "Listen to me, your grace. You must get Edgerton now or Edmund is in danger."

"You would have confessed all to me but for his threat against Edmund?"

"Yes. Believe me, Edgerton isn't mad. He's simply willing to do anything, even murder a child and an old woman, to gain what he wants, and that is Napoleon's success."

"I have known John Edgerton since I was eighteen years old, new to London, and he was a polished gentleman of thirty. He is well liked. He has access to so many decisions, to so many men. This is hard to believe. You're not a Bonapartist, are you?"

"If I were the only one involved, I would willingly have died before betraying my country or you."

The duke thought about the vagaries of fate that had brought her to him in the first place. "You would have told me but for Edgerton's threat toward Edmund?"

"He more than threatened. He painted a picture in words what he would do to Edmund. He said that my father and Edmund could be buried together. I knew then that he'd won. Edmund was my boy, you see. Nothing was worth Edmund's life."

He lowered his face to rest against her hand, held between his. "No one will hurt Edmund," he said finally. "But your father. What do you think will happen?"

She swallowed. "I don't know. Soon Edgerton will discover what happened. He will return to Paris, and then my father will die. Perhaps he will come here first to kill Edmund and me, naturally."

"I will see what I can do about your father. I will see that you and Edmund are both protected."

"I forgot to tell you. Drew was frantic about those

spies who are already here. I kept a journal with all their names and to whom they'd be assigned in London. It's in the bottom of the cushion of the window seat. Remember Conan DeWitt at the Sandersons' ball? He's one of them. He was threatening me that night. He's a very dangerous man, perhaps even more dangerous than John Edgerton."

"Jesus," he said, the enormity of it for a moment overwhelming him.

"One of the men last night, Paul Treyson, he was bound to London to become an assistant to Rothchild."

He began to laugh. "Here I believed that I led the most mundane of lives. I wish I could tell my mother about all of this. She would find it as incredible as I do, but we won't tell her." He sobered then, saying, "Now, there's something else I want to know. Why did you make love with me?"

For the first time she smiled. "I couldn't help myself," she said, and he saw that it was true.

"You came to me because you saw no future for us?"

"There was no future. There was just one night with you, and I wanted it very badly. I didn't know that a man could tell if a woman was or wasn't a virgin."

"I was surprised," he said. "Actually, I was very surprised, but that's not important now." He kissed her fingers. "If you ever try to keep even the flimsiest secret from me again, I'll beat you."

"There still is no future," she said, then closed her eyes. "I've failed, yet won, but Mrs. Needle died and now my father will die as well."

He lay next to her on the bed, pulling her into his arms. He stroked her hair, pulling the pins out as he whispered to her that everything would be all right, he promised, she would see. She cried quietly for a long time.

"Hush, you'll make yourself ill. Now that you've told me everything, I swear to you that I'll do my best to see that your father survives this. And you as well. I don't want you at the center of an appalling scandal. I want you to be my duchess. Now it's no longer just you. Now it's both of us. I fancy that the two of us can overcome just about anything or anyone."

Every chance word, every detail, was recalled and discussed to the duke's satisfaction. They pored over Evangeline's journal. The duke sent a message to Drew to come immediately to Chesleigh. The Bow Street Runner, a small man Evangeline had occasionally seen in the kitchen, was assigned to stick to Lord Edmund closer than his skin.

The duke said, "John Edgerton will learn quickly enough that Paul Treyson hasn't yet arrived in London. How much time we have, I don't know, but we can't assume it will be very long. Perhaps a day, two at the most. Damn, where's Drew?"

Evangeline, now dressed, against the duke's wishes, said as she paced back and forth in front of him, "I must return to Paris, it's the only way. I will see Houchard myself, I must, to plead for my father's life. Surely now that Napoleon's in Paris, and everything is in motion, there's no reason for him to kill him. I'm not responsible for everything falling apart. Indeed, it was Edgerton who was responsible when he had Mrs. Needle killed. Houchard will see that, he must."

"Rubbish," the duke said.

When he saw that she would argue, he caught her in his arms, kissed her ear, and said, "Dear one, listen to me. I believe I have found a way that won't extricate just you from this mess but your father as well. I'm going to go find Drew. We must move quickly. Damn the fellow for not coming instantly when I called him." He lightly pressed his fingers against her lips. "Evangeline, do you remember our first night together—it was all of two nights ago? You trusted me then. Trust me now. Stay close. Don't think of leaving. Bassick knows that no stranger is to be allowed inside. I'll be back very quickly."

He kissed her hard and was gone.

Chapter 38

The duke returned to Chesleigh an hour later to find Evangeline ferociously pacing the library. As he tossed his driving cloak onto the back of a chair he said, "I'd hoped you'd be resting in bed or letting Edmund try to hunt you down, yet here you are instead wearing holes in my carpet."

She ran to him, ready, he thought, to embrace him, something that pleased him immensely, and he caught her against him and squeezed her tightly. She reared back in his arms. "You're back. Oh, goodness, what happened? Did you see Drew? What will he do?"

He pulled her against him again and kissed her hard.

"He believes I'm a traitor, doesn't he?"

He saw the burst of terror in her eyes, saw the color drain from her face. He was shaking his head even as he said, "Oh, no, Evangeline. There's been no talk of any of that, trust me."

She nearly fainted, she was so relieved. "You're smiling. Tell me, what have you done?"

"I told you I had an idea that needed both Drew's approval and some refinement. I made it clear to him that you, my dear, the unwilling Eagle, possess a good deal of information that would be his if he is amenable to forgetting your past transgressions. When I told him that the very beautiful, very feminine chattering female he'd just seen was indeed the notorious Eagle, I thought he'd expire on the spot. Indeed, he was so incredulous, it took me some time to convince him that it was true. As I recall, he said, 'Damn, Richard, that a woman could do this, it makes me afraid for the future of men everywhere.' Then he drank two snifters of brandy. He received an even greater shock when I told him that John Edgerton is the Lynx, a Bonapartist, and a traitor to England for as long as both Drew and I have known him.

"Once I had told him all the facts, he became like a man possessed. In short, dear one, one of Drew's men will pose as the dead spy, Paul Treyson, and seek out Edgerton in London. Once Edgerton makes it clear to his esteemed audience that he knows the code, we will have him."

Evangeline was shaking her head. "No, no, listen to me. He has no reason to see Edgerton, none at all. I cleared him through. He is supposed to go directly to Rothchild."

The duke smiled. He gently cupped her face in his hands. "Don't you remember the letter you gave Paul Treyson to be given to the Lynx? Yes, you remember now. Our man will be with Edgerton when he reads your letter. Once he shows that he can easily translate the code you used, we've got him. It's that simple.

"Then Drew and I, and of course Lord Melberry, one of the highest-ranking members of the Ministry, will be close by. When it's done, our man will give us a signal, and we will be on Edgerton immediately. Then it will be over. Why are you wringing your hands again? You don't like the plan?"

"Oh, yes, it's a good plan." She pulled away from him and began pacing. "It's just that I don't trust Edgerton to do the expected. He's very smart. He's always seemed to know more than he should. I'm scared that something will happen."

"I will tell Drew what you've said. Incidentally, he's in the carriage outside. When I asked him to come in, he couldn't bring himself to face you just yet. He said he was going to have to revise the way he regarded young females. He said he wasn't so certain that Felicia was as guileless as he believed her to be, to which I said that Felicia was smart, loved him, and would thus hide any guile she possessed from him. He was gnawing his thumbnail in the carriage when I left him.

"Now, you will remain here at Chesleigh, quite safe. No, you won't come to London with us. Once we have Edgerton, Drew is certain that the Ministry will agree to exchange him for your father, and for all the information you will freely provide them."

For several moments she was speechless. "This is too simple. You believe Napoleon will exchange my father for Edgerton? Drew is willing to allow Edgerton to go free? What if Napoleon will not accept the trade? What if the gentlemen in the Ministry refuse to allow it?"

"You have lived under an enormous strain far too long. Listen to me. Trust me on this. Napoleon, whatever else he may be, is loyal to his men. As to the gentlemen in the Ministry, ah, believe me, I do have some power. Now I must leave you. We must move very quickly before Edgerton realizes something is amiss. I should be back tomorrow or the next day at the latest. Stay close. Have you met Mr. Bullock, the Bow Street Runner?"

"Yes. Edmund thinks he's here to assist me with

his lessons. I heard Mr. Bullock telling him about a highwayman who was hung just ten years ago. This pleased Edmund enormously."

He pulled her against him, kissed her, and said into her mouth, "When this is over, you and I will marry, and I won't let you out of my bed until next winter, if then."

"Maybe," she said as he released her, "I won't let you out of my bed until the following spring."

"Good God," he said, grinning widely, "I have indeed found my mate." He said at the doorway, "All will go well, Evangeline. Don't fret." He added, his eyes clear and brilliant, "Guard my son."

He was gone. She walked to the wide bow windows and watched the carriage with its four horses until it disappeared from view. Nothing, she thought, nothing could ever be counted on to go well, could it?

It happened so quickly she barely had time to draw a breath, no time at all to yell. A man's hand was over her mouth, his body pressing her hard against her mattress.

"You're such a fool," he whispered against her cheek. "Such a fool for believing for even a moment you could beat me."

She stared up into John Edgerton's face, leached of color in the pale dawn light. She knew utter terror. They'd failed. He'd somehow gotten into Chesleigh Castle, somehow found her bedchamber. She didn't make a sound, just looked up at him, as if mesmerized, thinking, thinking.

"How lovely to have you speechless, my dear. Usually all I've seen in you is that helpless rage that quite enchants me. I've known you wanted to kill me to save yourself and your dear papa, but you knew just as well that you couldn't. Impotence in a woman is a wonderful thing. But now you're silent. You're afraid, to your very bones, and you deserve to be."

Still she remained silent.

He straightened up a bit, smiled down into her face, and lightly pressed his palm over her mouth. "In case you decide to scream. Yes, just the light pressure of my hand will remind you that silence is best. Do you know I watched you sleeping for a little while, wondering what I was going to do with you after I killed Lord Edmund?"

"No," she said against his hand. "No."

"Oh, yes, I promised you what would happen if you betrayed me. Yet you did it anyway. That was beyond stupid, my dear. I hadn't expected it of you, truth be told."

She felt his dry palm against her lips as she whispered, "I didn't, not really."

His hand was heavier now. He didn't want her to speak further. He ignored her words, saying, "You're quite beautiful, you know that? Naturally, you do. You took the duke for your lover, didn't you? How long ago? Did he make you scream? I've heard it said that he's had women begging him to bed them. Do you think that's true? Did you beg him?"

He lifted his hand just a bit then and she bit him as hard as she could. But she couldn't bite deeply enough to hurt him. He lifted his hand again and slapped her hard, then slammed his palm back over her mouth. He paused a moment, then said, "You're not a weak little girl, are you? No, I move an inch and you'll be fighting me, perhaps even yelling. Do you feel the pressure of the gun barrel against your ribs, Evangeline? Good, you do. Try to hurt me again and I'll simply pull the trigger and leave you here in your bed to bleed all over these lovely white sheets. Of course, you won't care. You'll be dead. I don't want to do that, but I will. No, what I want to do is have you watch me kill Lord Edmund."

"No," she said again. "Please no. I'll do anything you ask, just not Edmund."

He laughed. "Tell me about how the duke pleasured you until you told him all about your transgressions." He lifted his hand just a bit even as he pressed the gun barrel harder into her ribs.

"He believed me a traitor. I told him nothing until it was all over and there was no other choice. Don't you understand? It made no difference. Drew Halsey and his men were already there on the cliffs above the beach, waiting."

"Yes, I know all about that. Indeed, I managed to escape London just in time. That was a pathetic ruse they were attempting. Poor Drew, he does try so very hard, but he isn't as smart as I am. Now he will realize that and he will be broken. As for your duke, he will lose you and his son. It is sufficient punishment for a man, I believe."

She heaved up against him, jerking her arms free, and tried to smash her fists against his throat.

"Now you give me no choice. Well, there's no hope for it." He slammed his fist against her jaw.

When she opened her eyes, Evangeline didn't know where she was. A sharp pain went through her head. She tried to raise her hand to rub her jaw, then realized he'd tied her wrists together, but at least in front of her and not behind her back. She lightly rubbed her fingers over her face. He hadn't broken her jaw, the bastard. Her ankles were tied as well. There was a gag stuffed in her mouth, another cloth tied over the gag and tied behind her head.

"What a remarkable girl you are," she heard Edgerton say. She shook her head and looked up. He was sitting in a chair, facing her. She was still in her bed, still in her nightgown, only now the covers were at her feet. "I've never told you how much I admired your lovely hair. And now it's all tangled about your face and down your back. Does the duke enjoy that hair of yours? Ah, you aren't going to say much to me right now, are you? I've always believed that a woman silent is a blessed thing." He grinned at her. Then he rose. "Pray that we don't see any servants, Evangeline, or I'll just have to shoot them. Now, as much as I would like to remain alone with you, perhaps caress you and make love to you, I haven't the time. Yes, I must leave very soon now. At least I will be with my beloved emperor again, very soon now. You betrayed me. I mustn't ever forget that, else it makes me feel a certain amount of sorrow and regret. No, you're nothing but a perfidious bitch, nothing more, nothing less. You have to die now. But remember that once I'm in Paris again, your father will follow you shortly to death. Yes, once I make a promise, I keep it. I can't allow any weaker emotions to rule me, not like you let them rule you. Now, you and I are going to see Lord Edmund." She heaved and bucked, but he managed to pull her over his shoulder. "Hold still," he said finally, panting, "or I'll just slam this gun down over your right ear. When you awake from a blow like that, you'll wish you were dead."

She held completely still. "Good," he said.

She was hanging upside down, growing more dizzy by the moment. No, she had to keep her wits about her. She couldn't let the fear swamp her. But her father, her boy, Edmund. No, she couldn't let him kill them, she just couldn't.

Her brain squirreled about madly.

Thank God they saw no servants on the way to the nursery because she had no doubt whatsoever that Edgerton would shoot them with no hesitation.

Ah, but Ellen would be in the nursery. Evangeline closed her eyes and prayed. She remembered Mr. Bullock, short, bowlegged Mr. Bullock. Seeing him in her mind's eye didn't bring her a great deal of confidence, not now. He didn't stand a chance against Edgerton. She was a fool to have believed that he would be sufficient to guard Edmund.

But the duke had believed him ready and able. She had to believe that he knew how to protect Edmund. Surely Mr. Bullock slept in the same room with Edmund? If he did sleep in Edmund's room, then Edgerton would get them both. Who could be prepared for this? Poor Mr. Bullock, the chances were good that Edgerton would kill him as well.

One last chance. She reared up and brought her fists into Edgerton's back. He nearly fell forward with the weight of her blow. He cursed, low and viciously. Then he simply turned quickly and her head struck the wall. She fell instantly into blackness.

She regained her wits when Edgerton was easing open the nursery door. "Come now, Evangeline, I didn't hit you against the wall all that hard. You're awake again and chastened, I hope. Now, which way is Edmund's bedchamber? Ah, I keep forgetting you're blessedly mute. Perhaps behind that door on the left?"

He slowly eased the door open. He heard nothing. He stepped inside. He saw Edmund lying there, surrounded by piles of pillows. "Edmund," he called out softly. "Edmund, come, lad, it's time for you to wake up."

Edmund sat up, scratching his head, then rubbing his eyes. "Who is it? Where is Ellen? Oh, no, what's happened to Eve?"

"Come up, my little lordling. I've got your cousin Eve over my shoulder. She's all trussed up because I can't trust her to hold still and be quiet."

"Eve? Are you all right?"

She tried to rear back, but Edgerton twisted to the side, nearly slamming her head against the door.

"Come now, Edmund, the three of us are going to take a little trip."

Edmund looked at Eve, helpless, silent, slung over Sir John's shoulder. He raised his chin. "No, sir. I won't go anyplace with you. You will lower Eve now, very gently. If you don't, my papa will hurt you."

Edgerton laughed. He took two steps toward the little boy, who was standing by the side of his bed, his nightshirt long to his ankles and white, his small hands fisted at his sides.

Evangeline wanted, quite simply, to die. Once again, she reared up, knowing he just might end it and kill her now. She dug her fingers into the small of his back. He yelled, distracted.

Evangeline thought she'd heave with relief when she heard, "I believe that's plenty fur enuf, sir." It was Mr. Bullock. "Sorry, I didn't git ye right away, missus. I 'ad to wait fer ye to get beyond me and now, finally, the bighter 'as. Lay 'er down, sir, or I'll blow a 'ole right through yer ear."

Edgerton was cursing, but Mr. Bullock just shook his head. "No, sir, don't say such things in front of the little sprat. 'Is pa wouldn't like it attal. Lay down the gun, now."

"No!" Edgerton shouted. He whirled about, ran straight into Mr. Bullock, and threw Evangeline off his shoulder and against Mr. Bullock's chest, sending him crashing to the floor. Mr. Bullock's gun went off loud and raw in the small bedchamber.

Mr. Bullock cursed, pulled himself from under Evangeline and ran through the open door into the nursery. "Stay down!" he yelled back at Edmund and Evangeline. " 'Old up, yer blighter! Now, or else I'll shoot ye where ye stand, right in front of that nice globe what belongs to the little sprat."

Edgerton stopped in his tracks. Finally, his head bowed, he dropped the gun. Slowly he turned to face the little man who shouldn't have been more than an insect to crush underfoot. He'd been brought low by an illiterate, pathetic little man. No, he'd been brought low by a lying, betraying bitch. He saw Evangeline standing in the bedchamber doorway, Edmund held close to her side. The boy had untied all the knots and she was again free.

"Take a step back. That's right. Now sit down in that chair."

Edgerton sat.

Edmund tugged at Evangeline's hand. "You're all right, Eve? He didn't hurt you? Oh, goodness, look at your jaw. He hit you." Edmund suddenly got a look on his face that mirrored his father's. He rushed at Edgerton and slammed his fists into his chest. Edgerton tried to grab him and Mr. Bullock shouted, "Lord Edmund, get back now!"

Edmund jumped back before Edgerton could grab him.

"Edmund," Evangeline said very calmly, very quietly, "come here, love, and help me. I'm not feeling very well right now. I stood up too quickly. I'm not sure I can remain standing up without your assistance. Yes, come here. That's right. Now, let's have you help me stand here all straight and tall and face this awful man who would have hurt us."

Once Edmund was safely beside her again, Evangeline felt both immeasurably better, and immeasurably mean. She wanted to leap on Edgerton herself and strangle the life out of him. She felt Edmund take her hand.

"Mr. Bullock," she said, "thank you, sir, for being alert. Now, shall we tie this bastard up? Or perhaps can you give me your gun and I can shoot him?"

"Let's shoot him, Mr. Bullock," Edmund said, standing there with his nightshirt flapping around his ankles, his hair, black and thick as his father's, sticking up around his head. "He's a bad man. He hurt Eve. Yes, I want to shoot him like I would a highwayman. I'll get my gun." Edmund dashed back into his bedchamber, ran to his bed, reached under his pillow and pulled out his wooden gun. He was back into the nursery, aiming it directly at Edgerton.

Evangeline laughed, actually laughed. "You see his toy gun? It was a gift from me upon my arrival here at Chesleigh. You recall who procured it for him, do you not?"

Edgerton looked at her with such dull hatred in his eyes that she nearly yelled with the pleasure of it. "Nothing matters now except that you'll no longer be in our lives. You've lost, sir. Finally, you've lost."

"Conan DeWitt was right about you," he said.

"Oh, yes, indeed he was," Evangeline said. "But you know, truth be told, it was you yourself who brought the whole thing to an end."

"Impossible," Sir John Edgerton said.

She just smiled at him. "Oh, yes," she said. "Oh, yes."

"Now, missus," Mr. Bullock said to Evangeline, "it's time fer me to tie this feller up real tight."

"Allow me, Mr. Bullock." Evangeline said. "Edmund, keep your gun pointed at him while I tie him to that chair."

When the duke, Drew, and six soldiers arrived four hours later, the duked was so frantic, he nearly crashed through the front door. He was met by a smiling Evangeline, and his son holding his toy gun, his small face wreathed as well in smiles. The duke, so relieved that she and his son were safe, drew them both up against him and simply wouldn't let them go until Edmund said, "Papa, my ribs are bent inside out. Goodness, Eve and I are heroes. We let Mr. Bullock help us, too."

The duke released his son. "What happened here?"

"Papa, come with Eve and me. We've got a surprise for you. It's almost better than my gun. Come, Papa."

The duke and Drew Halsey followed Evangeline and Edmund into the library, where Mr. Bullock stood beside a seated John Edgerton, his gun pointed at Edgerton's head. "I didn't want to take a chance," Mr. Bullock said. "This fellow's a shifty worm." He grinned widely and stepped back. John Edgerton was all trussed up, his face pale with fury. Thankfully, he was blessedly gagged.

"It's over," Evangeline said and walked to the duke and wrapped her arms around his back. "It's over. We won."

"Tell me," the duke said, and she did, with Mr. Bullock and Edmund weaving in and out, some of their details, Edmund's primarily, not all that valuable or pertinent, but it didn't matter.

As for Drew and the duke, they'd gone to Edgerton's house to put their plan into action, only to find him gone. "I can't recall ever being quite so scared," the duke said. "Someone warned him in the nick of time. I died a thousand deaths between London and here." He shook his head and hugged Edmund so tightly that his son squeaked. "Dear God, at least we've got him and it's over now."

"Yes, all of it," Drew said. "I even found that envelope you put in my office, Evangeline. Jesus, it made me a perfectly placed traitor. As for the journal you kept, a lot of the damage can now be undone. My men are tracking down all the spies. We'll be clean of them before the end of the day."

She was afraid to ask, but she had to. "My father? Is there any chance at all that he'll survive this?"

"We will send a message shortly to Paris. We believe that Napoleon will trade your father for Edgerton. As the duke told you, Napoleon is loyal to those who are loyal to him. Ah, as for yourself, my dear ma'am, the duke assures me that once you're married to him, you won't have time for any more visits to the beach at midnight."

"I'm pleased you can now speak to her without swallowing your tongue, Drew," the duke said, and buffeted his friend in his arm. "She doesn't bite, usually."

"She's bitten you, Papa?" Edmund wanted to know, staring at Evangeline with undisguised awe.

"Only in situations where she's so mad at me she's lost all her words, Edmund."

Drew Halsey, Lord Pettigrew, stared at Evangeline, who was leaning into the duke, a vivid smile on her face, and just shook his head. "Life," he said after looking deeply into a snifter of brandy, "is sometimes stranger than a man's wildest nightmares."

"I'm not quite certain how to receive that proclamation," Evangeline said, and laughed, even as the duke leaned down to kiss her. "Forget Drew," he said into her mouth, "I never have wild nightmares."

"Is she going to bite you for nuzzling her, Papa?"

"I pray she'll do no biting at all until much later," the duke said.

Drew coughed behind his hand.

Edgerton had closed his eyes, Mr. Bullock hovering over him, his gun at the ready.

Two hours later, the duke, Drew Halsey, and their soldiers escorted Edgerton back to London.

"When will Papa come back, Eve?"

"Very soon, Edmund. Probably by tomorrow afternoon at the latest. Trust me that he didn't want to leave, but it seems there are more matters he had to attend to in London before he can come back to us."

"I saw him kissing you again, not just talking into your mouth," Edmund said, and he was frowning. "He wasn't patting your back like he sometimes does to me. No, he was rubbing your back, up and down and up again. He looked really interested in what he was doing."

"Well, yes," she said. "I suppose he was rather absorbed in what he was doing. Actually, I'm rather fond of both you and your papa as well."

"I didn't know you bit my papa, too. I never thought about anybody biting anybody else. Fancy that both you and Papa do it. Once I saw him bite your ear and you stretched your neck up so he could bite you better. Why he'd want to bite your ear?"

She came down on her knees in front of him. She looked into his beloved face, and lightly laid her hand on his shoulder. "Do you like to have me here, Edmund?"

"Yes," he said clearly. "I like to chase you."

So did his father, she wanted to tell him, but caught herself just in time. "I like you to chase me, too. Getting shot is sometimes disconcerting, but I'll manage it well enough."

"You're going to stay here with me? You'll teach me how to swim better than Papa?"

"Yes," she said, "I'm staying. When your papa gets back from London, we'll all talk about it."

"I'm going to go shoot a peacock and when he's lying there dead, I'll bite him."

"You'd get feathers in your mouth. That wouldn't be fun at all. Ellen would have to wash your mouth out. No, you wouldn't like that, Edmund."

"All right," Edmund said, nodding. He turned to run back up the stairs. "I'll go bite Ellen."

Lucky Ellen, Evangeline thought, watching Edmund run upstairs. Even after he was gone she continued to stand in the magnificent entrance hall, shaking her head, grinning like a loon, so relieved, so happy, she thought her heart would surely burst.

Chapter 39

It was the following morning. The sun was bright, the breeze off the sea tangy and light. It would be a mild day. Evangeline was whistling as she walked from the breakfast room to the drawing room.

"Madame," Bassick said. "There's a gentleman here. He says the duke sent him to you."

She nearly ran to the drawing room, a smile on her face. "Thank you, Bassick," she called over her shoulder.

"Close the door."

She stood frozen in the doorway, staring at Conan DeWitt. He was pointing a gun directly at her. "Close the door, or else I'll kill that old man standing out there. Do it now."

She closed the door. Slowly she turned to face him. "What are you doing here?"

"I'd like to tell you that I'm Edgerton's emissary here to inform you that the bloody duke is dead. Unfortunately, it isn't true. They've got Edgerton. I believe, thanks to you, Eagle, they've got all the men who have come into England through you as well. I got away. The same men who warned Edgerton that Lord Pettigrew and his men were here at Chesleigh also told me. If he'd waited even an hour longer, I would have been caught with all the rest."

"Why did you come here? Surely you know that they're looking for you?"

"Let them look to Scotland, they'll not find me. I told John not to trust you. I warned him repeatedly, but he wanted you, you see. What's more, he wanted you in his power, so that what you were, what you would become, would all be in his hands. He was a fool as well because he'd convinced himself that his hold on you was strong enough to keep you in line. But still, regardless of whatever it was he was holding over you, I still knew you would betray us."

"Actually, it was because of Edgerton's actions that everything fell apart for you. Because he strangled poor Mrs. Needle, he set events in motion for his downfall, yours as well. You see, the duke had a Bow Street Runner come with him to help find out who had murdered her. The night before the duke and I returned to London, I met a man on the beach at midnight. The Bow Street Runner saw everything and told the duke. Evidently, he didn't realize that I wasn't a man, what with the long cloak I always wore. I didn't betray you. Edgerton himself did you all in."

"No," DeWitt said. "No, you're twisting things." He walked to her. She could hear his furious breathing. "Oh, yes," he said, very close to her, "I'll go back to France, but I'm not going back alone. I know you've told them everything you know. I'm taking you back with me to Houchard himself. He will kill you, and I will smile when he does it.

"You're an excellent hostage. Don't do anything foolish. You're not worth much more to me alive than dead."

At least Edmund was safe. Thank God, only Edgerton had known of his threat to Edmund. She had no doubt at all that if DeWitt had known, he would try to kill Edmund. She'd won and she'd lost. But it wasn't over yet. As long as she was alive, it wasn't over.

The duke jumped down from his curricle, threw the reins to Juniper, and strode up the great stone steps. He shoved open the great front doors of Chesleigh castle and shouted her name.

"Your grace, what are you doing here? I don't understand this. The gentleman you sent is here now, telling Madame of your delay and—"

"Bassick, what man?" He grabbed the butler's arms and shook him. "Quickly, Bassick. What man? What delay? What's going on here? Where's Madame?"

"She's in the drawing room, your grace, with the gentleman you sent to see her. I'll inform her of your early arrival."

"God in heaven, I sent no man!" He didn't wait for Bassick to reply. He rushed through the entrance hall and flung the drawing room doors open. He saw a heavy brocade curtain lifting slightly in the breeze through an open window. The room was empty.

He strode back into the corridor, a knot of fear twisting in his belly, and nearly collided with Bassick. "Who was the man?"

Bassick, like every denizen of Chesleigh, knew that French spies had been caught doing their shady deeds in the Chesleigh cove. He as well as everyone else knew that Madame was somehow involved, but no one knew exactly what the facts were. But now something horrible was happening. "He said his name was Ferguson, your grace."

The duke cursed. "What did he look like? Quickly,

Bassick, can you remember anything at all about him?"

"He wasn't much older than you, your grace. A pleasant gentleman he seemed, and a large man. A mole, your grace, yes, there was a large mole on his cheek. Oh, dear, the man wasn't named Ferguson?"

"No," the duke said. "It's Conan DeWitt, a very bad man, Bassick. Get all the men together. He's taken Madame. Quickly, Bassick."

He was running to the library to get a brace of pistols, when he called over his shoulder, "Was he in a carriage, Bassick? A horse? What?"

"He was riding a horse, your grace. Yes, that's right, there was no carriage."

Once the duke had his two loaded guns, he headed toward the stables. DeWitt had come either to kill her or to take her with him to France as a hostage. He couldn't very well expect to get far if he held Evangeline before him on his horse. He'd have to have another horse. Then he'd have to get her to Eastbourne. It was the closest town to catch a ship to France.

Trevlin was sitting on his haunches at the stable entrance, mending a bridle.

"Trevlin, have you seen Madame?"

"Yes, your grace," Trevlin said, scratching his left ear. Then he sensed the urgency in the duke's voice and jumped to his feet. "I wondered. Yes, I wondered what she was doing with him. She's with a man, your grace. They were walking toward the cliff, right over the cove."

The duke heard a half dozen men running toward them. He shouted over his shoulder even as he sprinted away from Trevlin, who threw the bridle to the ground to join in the chase, "He's taken her to the cliffs." He rounded the rear of the stables, ran down the rutted path, men at his heels trying to keep up with him. DeWitt had a boat waiting.

The duke was some thirty yards distant from the cliffs when he heard Evangeline's terrified scream, and then a thin, wailing yell.

The duke didn't stop. Blood pounded at his temples, and his breath sounded like thunder in his ears. He was afraid to think of what that scream meant. The rocky terrain sloped upward to the cliff edge, and he saw her locked in Conan DeWitt's arms. He was pulling her toward the cliff. There was no horse in sight. Dear God, he was going to kill both of them.

"DeWitt, let her go!"

The man turned to face him, Evangeline held tightly against his side.

"Fight me, you puling coward. Let her go." Suddenly, in that instant when DeWitt was distracted, Evangeline brought her knee up and struck him in the groin. He yelled, and his hold loosened. She jerked away from him, stumbled on a rock, and went flying forward, flailing the air to keep her balance. DeWitt twisted around, saw her falling toward the cliff edge. He was on her then, his hands outstretched. Only she didn't stay standing. She fell to her hands and knees, and when he struck out at her, she fell flat on her stomach. Conan DeWitt went flying over her back, screaming.

When the duke reached her, she was standing, looking over the cliff to the beach below. He stood behind her, looking down. Slowly, all the men came forward, looking over the cliff down to the beach.

Conan DeWitt lay on his back, his black greatcoat spread out about his body like huge wings. It was then that the duke saw a boat being rowed frantically away from the dock.

He hadn't been going to kill her. He was going to take her to France.

He gathered her against him. "It's over now," he said against her hair. "It's over. DeWitt's dead." He was rubbing his hands over her shoulders, up and down her back. His hands were trembling. He was so filled with relief that for a moment he couldn't speak.

She slowly raised her face, and he saw that her pupils were nearly black. "You came," she said. "You came. I knew he was going to kill me. I saw the boat come in, you see, and I saw there was only enough room for one more. He didn't want me for a hostage. He just wanted to kill me. He kept pushing me closer and closer to the cliff edge, and the path wasn't even near here." Suddenly, her arms were around his back. She was panting, her eyes wild. "I didn't want to die. Oh, God, I just found you, I didn't want to leave you."

Still he had no words. He simply held her, feeling her heart beating against his.

"After I kicked him, I just wanted to run, but I tripped and fell. Then he fell over me."

"Yes, I know. We all saw it. It's over. All over now. He's quite dead."

Evangeline turned then to see a good dozen Chesleigh people, both men and women, each of them carrying a weapon—a branch off a lime tree, a pitchfork, a gun. Mrs. Raleigh carried an umbrella, Bassick a large candelabrum. Trevlin held a bridle wrapped around his fist.

Evangeline said, "Thank you all so very much for coming to my rescue."

The duke said, "I thank you as well. Evangeline de Beauchamps will soon become your mistress and my duchess."

Evangeline heard the cheering as she and the duke,

arm in arm, walked slowly back to Chesleigh castle. "Drew asked me if we were going to marry. I told him that I felt it my duty since you seemed so utterly helpless without me. At which he had the gall to laugh his head off. As I recall, he yowled, 'Helpless, by God, helpless!' before I smashed my fist into his shoulder and he wisely quieted his mirth. I then said that very well, you weren't all that helpless, but you certainly couldn't seem to tread the straight and narrow without me. He brought himself to agree with that and said, only giving an occasional hoot of laughter, that the Ministry would be relieved that things had solved themselves so neatly."

When they were in the drawing room, the door closed, the duke brought her against him, and for a long moment he simply held her, his face buried in her hair. "We'll leave for London tomorrow and marry as soon as your father arrives from Paris. Now, we must speak to my son."

"Yes," she said, "I will promise to let him chase me if he'll give us his blessing."

"I doubt he'll be overly surprised," the duke said.

At that moment Ellen came down the corridor, her hands raised above her head. They heard Edmund say from behind her, "Keep walking, Terrible Tom, or it will be the worst for you. Stop a moment, and I will take these travelers' money."

The duke laughed and called back, "Edmund, are you a Bow Street Runner or a highwayman?"

"I have this great calling," Edmund said. "I will be both."

"My father," Evangeline said, "will adore Edmund."

"Right now I'm just praying that he'll give us his blessing."

"Why would he not? Oh, the rift between the families. Won't you tell me what happened?"

"It all seems rather ridiculous now. It had to do with Marissa's dowry, a large part of which was supposedly jewels. They turned out to be paste. Your uncle refused to hear of it, accusing my father of stealing the jewels to wring more money out of him. I thought my father would expire from apoplexy. He severed the ties between the Clarendons and all the Beauchamps from that day onward. Of course, your father took his brother's side, which is why I never saw that terribly serious half-French girl for six years."

"Well, now you've got her for life." She shook her head. "I really don't think we have to worry about my father. I believe he'll be so relieved that both of us are once again safe that he'll kiss you. He'll even forgive you for being a boring Englishman."

"A boring Englishman is certainly preferable to the saintly, blessedly departed clod André."

"Hear, hear," she said, and reached down to catch Edmund up in her arms.

"Eve, Papa looks like he's going to bite your ear again."

Laughter, she thought, there was no greater pleasure than laughter.

SIGNET

New York Times Bestselling Author

Catherine Coulter

Evening Star

Giana Van Cleve, the heroine, has fallen in love with a vicious fortune hunter. Her mother, the renowned shipowner and builder Aurora Van Cleve, is desperate to save her daughter. She agrees to support Giana's wedding if Giana agrees first to spend an unusual three months in Rome with her uncle Daniele. But Giana's uncle takes his bargain far beyond what Aurora ever imagined.

Midnight Star

The story of Delaney Saxton, a man who struck it rich in the California gold rush of 1849 and stayed to build a great city, and Chauncey FitzHugh, an heiress from England who travels to San Francisco to avenge her father. She belives Delaney Saxton ruined him and plans to destroy Saxton in the same way he destroyed her father—leaving him betrayed and penniless. But her prey isn't what she expected. He is charming, too handsome for his own good, rich—and elusive as a wisp of smoke.

Available wherever books are sold or at penguin.com